*Ace Books by K. J. Taylor*

*The Fallen Moon*

**THE DARK GRIFFIN**
**THE GRIFFIN'S FLIGHT**
**THE GRIFFIN'S WAR**

*The Risen Sun*

**THE SHADOW'S HEIR**

# The Shadow's Heir

## THE RISEN SUN
## BOOK ONE

# K. J. TAYLOR

ACE BOOKS, NEW YORK

**THE BERKLEY PUBLISHING GROUP**
**Published by the Penguin Group**
**Penguin Group (USA) Inc.**
**375 Hudson Street, New York, New York 10014, USA**

Penguin Group (Canada), 90 Eglinton Avenue East, Suite 700, Toronto, Ontario M4P 2Y3, Canada
(a division of Pearson Penguin Canada Inc.) • Penguin Books Ltd., 80 Strand, London WC2R 0RL,
England • Penguin Ireland, 25 St. Stephen's Green, Dublin 2, Ireland (a division of Penguin
Books Ltd.) • Penguin Group (Australia), 707 Collins Street, Melbourne, Victoria 3008, Australia
(a division of Pearson Australia Group Pty. Ltd.) • Penguin Books India Pvt. Ltd., 11 Community
Centre, Panchsheel Park, New Delhi—110 017, India • Penguin Group (NZ), 67 Apollo Drive,
Rosedale, Auckland 0632, New Zealand (a division of Pearson New Zealand Ltd.) • Penguin Books,
Rosebank Office Park, 181 Jan Smuts Avenue, Parktown North 2193, South Africa • Penguin China,
B7 Jiaming Center, 27 East Third Ring Road North, Chaoyang District, Beijing 100020, China

Penguin Books Ltd., Registered Offices: 80 Strand, London WC2R 0RL, England

THE SHADOW'S HEIR

An Ace Book / published by arrangement with the author

PUBLISHING HISTORY
Ace mass-market edition / January 2013

Copyright © 2012 by K. J. Taylor.
Map by Allison Jones.
Cover illustration by Steve Stone; sword © Vertyr/Shutterstock.
Cover design by Judith Lagerman.

ISBN: 978-0-425-25823-1

ACE
Ace Books are published by The Berkley Publishing Group,
a division of Penguin Group (USA) Inc.,
375 Hudson Street, New York, New York 10014.
ACE and the "A" design are trademarks of Penguin Group (USA) Inc.

PRINTED IN THE UNITED STATES OF AMERICA

10  9  8  7  6  5  4  3  2  1

**ALWAYS LEARNING**　　　　　　　　　　　　　　　　**PEARSON**

For my father, who is definitely the real one

# Acknowledgments

Thanks to all the usual suspects who made this book possible: Russell, my agent; Anne, my editor; and Katherine Sherbo, my other editor. And once again, thanks to Janice Jones for her Welsh translations.

# Author's Note

Hello, everyone, and welcome to Cymria. If you're returning after reading The Fallen Moon, then welcome back, and if you're new, then just welcome, full stop! I hope you like what you find enough to want to stay a while.

For those who'd like to read my little creation aloud, here's a quick guide: The Northerners speak Welsh, and in Welsh "dd" is pronounced "th." Hence the name Arenadd is pronounced "Arrenath."

Meanwhile, "Taranisäii" is pronounced "TAH-ranis-eye." "Griffish," on the other hand, is pronounced exactly as it's spelled—griffins can't read anyway.

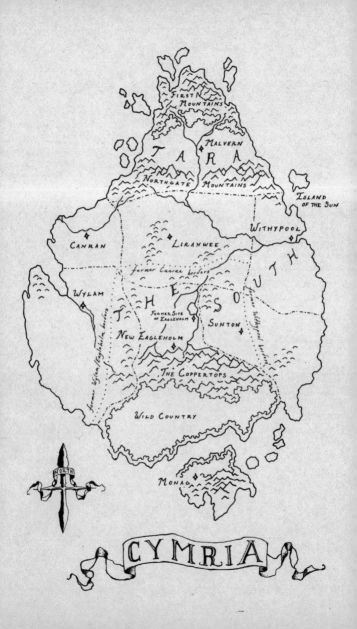

# 1

# Alone

She knew what it meant. She had *always* known what it would mean. In a way, she had been waiting for it her entire life. But nothing could have prepared her for it. And nothing could have dulled the shock. But what possibly could have?

She sat on her stool by the front door of their house, slowly whittling a piece of wood. It had been much larger when she had started, but by now it resembled a very thin carrot. Curled wood shavings were piled up between her feet. Some had caught on the rough wool of her dress, but she couldn't summon up the energy or interest to brush them off.

She couldn't keep her attention on her knife, either; she let it slide away toward the sky and stared vacantly at the white clouds drifting over it. It would be another fine day tomorrow.

The knife slipped, and she started at the sudden blossoming of pain in her hand. It woke her from her reverie, and she put the knife down and hastily covered the cut with the edge of her skirt.

As if the pain were a kind of release, she let go of her hand and started to cry.

The tears didn't last long. She fiercely wiped them away on her sleeve and bit back her sobs until they left her shuddering with them before they died away. The anger she felt toward herself gave her strength, and she stuffed her knife into her belt and strode over to the rain barrel.

The cold water made her feel a little better. She splashed it over her face until her fringe was dripping and took several deep breaths. As the water's surface stilled again, she looked down into it and saw her own faint reflection rippling there.

Pale skin, with a scatter of freckles over a pointed nose. Her eyes were blue, but above them her eyebrows were jet-black, and the long, curly hair she tried to keep tied back and covered was black as well.

She stared at it and shuddered again. *Gryphus help me, if only I could cut it all off. If I could only* hide *it!*

She had tried, many many times. She had tried dye, but there was no dye that could overpower pure black. Cutting it short only made her look like a freak . . . more of a freak. And covering it still didn't hide the other signs. The signs on the outside, or the inside.

She let out a sudden, wild scream, and punched the water, shattering her reflection. The anger bubbled inside her as she turned away, and she wanted to scream again, or hit something else, but she knew it wouldn't help anything.

*No point to anything,* said the cold, rational side of her mind. *Never was, never will be.*

But this was her fault. Always had been.

*Stop it. He needs you.*

The voice was right. She straightened up, forcing herself to breathe deeply, and went inside.

Her father was there, hunched in his favourite chair by the fire. For a moment she thought he was asleep, but then he stirred and coughed.

"Laela. C'mere."

She went to him. "Dad, how're yeh feelin'?"

He peered at her. "Like shit. Where've yeh been?"

"Just outside, Dad. Not far."

"Yeh know y'ain't s'posed t'go out there, girl," he reminded her. "Temptin' fate ain't what yeh need t'be doin' just now."

Laela looked away. "Well, I won't have much t'worry about there soon, will I? May as well get used to it, right?"

Her father sighed. "Laela, we ain't sure this is it. Yeh can't be sayin' that now."

Laela softened and touched his hand. "But yeh know it is, Dad. Even if yeh ain't ready t'say it out loud yet."

He coughed again, and shivered. "I never was much of an honest man, Laela. Yeh know that."

She managed a smile. "Yeah, I know. Yeh won't tell me my mother's name, will yeh? Or *his* name, either."

Her father looked away. "Yeh know my name, girl. Branton Redguard, that's yer dad's name."

Laela straightened up impatiently. "Oh for the gods' sakes, stop it! Yeh know I ain't buyin' that, Dad, I ain't bought it for years! I love yeh, but yeh ain't my father, an' yeh know it, an' I know it. My mother wasn't no Northerner, an' neither are you. So if she wasn't, my dad was, an' he ain't you."

Bran rose slightly in his chair. "An' who raised yeh, Laela?" he snapped. "Eh? Tell me that. Who raised yeh? Who loved yeh? Who kept yeh safe all this time?"

Laela backed off. "You did, Dad, but that ain't what we're talkin' about. I'm talkin' about my *other* father. The one who bedded my mother. The one whose blood's in me. I love yeh, Dad, an' I always have, but yeh ain't my father by blood."

He subsided again, suddenly exhausted. "An' so what if I ain't? What's it matter? Yeh mother's gone, Laela, an' so's yeh father."

Laela stepped closer, suddenly excited despite herself. This was the most he had ever said about her father. "So he's dead?"

Bran rubbed a hand over his face. "Bin dead nearly twenty years."

"Are yeh sure?"

He looked her in the eye. "I saw him die, understand?"

"How did he die?" Laela asked quietly.

"He fell to his death," said Bran. "Tryin' to escape from . . . us."

"Us? Who's us? Yeh mean . . . Dad, did *you* kill him?"

"I was a guard captain. Yer father escaped from prison, an' we were chasin' him. We had him cornered, an' I told him to surrender. It was right at the edge of a high platform, at the top of a mountain. He gave up, but he fell before I could pull him back. That's how he died. End of story."

"What was his name?" said Laela.

Bran squinted. "Can't remember any more."

"But how did he meet my mother?" Laela persisted. "Why would she bed a Northerner? He didn't . . . ? Did he . . . ? Was that why he was in prison, Dad?"

Bran sat back and closed his eyes. "I dunno that much about it either way, but yer father was a criminal."

Laela looked away. "So that's how it happened."

Bran kept his eyes shut. "That's how it happened, girl. Yer parents are gone, an' there's no point dwellin' on that. I'm yer family. Now . . . I'm tired, an' I want t'sleep. Could yeh help me t'bed?"

"Yeah, I'll do it. 'Course I'll do it."

Laela helped her adoptive father to his bed, supporting him with her arm around his waist while her mind reeled.

So that was it. That was all it was. The secret Bran had kept for so long was . . . nothing. No terrible secrets, no shocking heritage, no dramatic revelation. Her mother was a Southern girl who had been raped by a Northern criminal. And Bran had told her the story so matter-of-factly, so briefly. Just as if it wasn't anything very important at all.

L ater, when he was asleep, she sat in his chair by the fire and poked at the ashes.

In all her life, Bran was the only family she had ever known, and her only friend, too. Nobody else wanted to know her. When she was small, other children had been happy enough to play with her, but as they grew older, things changed. The opinions of parents moved on to their children, and suddenly play turned to bullying. Suddenly, she found herself learning new words. New meanings.

Blackrobe. Half-breed. Freak. Darkwoman.

That was when she truly began to understand.

Now her thoughts turned toward her father, as she looked at her lap and the long, thin fingers he had given her.

"Bastard," she muttered aloud. "Gods-damned evil bastard. Yeh raped my mother. Yeh turned me into this. Yeh made me a gods-damned half-breed. I swear by Gryphus' flames, if yeh weren't dead, I'd find yeh an' do it with me own hands."

Strangely enough, her anger helped to sustain her over the next few days.

She stayed close to home, as always, preparing food for her adoptive father and keeping the house tidy.

There was nothing she could do for him directly. Even if she had been a healer, he was beyond the help of any medicine.

Years of bad living and heavy drinking had destroyed his body from the inside out.

Neither of them mentioned their conversation again. Laela thought of bringing it up, but she felt guilty over it now, and she kept her silence. Her adoptive father didn't need to talk about painful things any more.

She did her best to keep him comfortable and happy, staying by his side whenever he was awake and talking to him as cheerfully as she could, or even singing. He'd always liked it when she sang. Bran didn't say much himself, but he'd never been very talkative. Sometimes she felt afraid that he resented her presence, but one evening when she was hesitating over whether she should leave him alone, he reached for her hand and gave it the gentlest of squeezes.

"Yer a good girl, Laela, yeh know?"

She looked down at her hand, almost lost in his big, rough fist, and bit back a sob. "I'm sorry what I said before, Dad. You was right; it din't matter who my *real* father was. He was a criminal what raped my mother. *You* was the good man what looked after me, an' that's what counts, ain't it?"

Bran's tired face crinkled in a smile. "I'd say so, Laela. I'd say so."

"I'd like t'know more about my mother, though," Laela added. "What was she like?"

"*Aaahh . . .*" Bran sighed. "I don't remember that much, girl. Yeh know that."

Laela didn't believe him. "I know, but if there's anythin' . . . anythin' at all. If yeh don't tell me soon, yeh never will."

"I know," said Bran. "Well . . . yer mother." He sighed again. "Ain't thought about her in years, yeh know. Well . . ." A long pause.

"What?" said Laela, eagerly. "What d'yeh remember, Dad?"

"Yeh mother was a merchant's daughter," Bran said slowly. "Had the most beautiful eyes, she did. Blue like a summer sky." He squeezed her hand. "Like yer own, Laela. Like yer own."

Laela smiled. "Always bin proud of 'em, Dad."

"She was a fierce one," Bran added in distant tones. "Beautiful as a rose, an' just as thorny, Arren used t'say."

"Who?" said Laela.

Bran started. "What?"

"Who's Arren?" said Laela.

"What? Oh. Friend of mine," said Bran. "Long dead. Knew yeh mother, same as me. We used t'go drinkin' together. By Gryphus but we couldn't've known what would happen to us . . ."

Laela leaned close to listen. "What happened?"

"We grew up," Bran said briefly. "Bad things happened t'all of us. That was just before the war started."

"What bad things?" said Laela.

Bran's brown eyes narrowed. "Bad things," he repeated. "Young Gern, he died in a fight. Yer mother . . . pregnant out of wedlock, to a Northerner. Arren, he . . . he died, too."

"How?" said Laela, mostly driven by morbid curiosity.

"Murdered," said Bran. He sighed. "My best friend, was Arren. Him an' me, always together."

*Great Gryphus,* thought Laela. *No wonder he took to drink.*

"So yeh took me after Mum died," she said. She paused. "But what happened t'her?"

Bran coughed. "Laela, there are some things . . ."

"Tell me!" Laela almost shouted. "Dad, I've got t'know! It's all I'll have of her, so give me that, at least!"

"She was murdered, too," said Bran. "When yeh were still in the cradle. Died defendin' yeh." His voice broke. "I came in right after it happened. The murderer . . . he'd slit yer mother's throat wide open with . . . she was dead right by the cradle, with you in it. I came in . . . the murderer ran away, an' I took yeh and left. Never went back there."

Laela withdrew, suddenly cold all over with shock. "Oh, Gryphus . . ."

"So that's it," Bran muttered, as if he were ashamed. "That's how she died, an' there's no reason t'look back. It's over, girl. Over."

"Who did it?" said Laela. "Who killed her? *Why?*"

Bran said nothing.

"Who?" said Laela.

"I'm tired," said Bran. "Let me rest now, girl . . . get t'bed and rest yer own head a while. Yeh've earnt it."

Laela stood up. "What was my mother's name, Dad? Please, can yeh tell me that?"

But Bran didn't reply, and she knew he wasn't going to tell her, whether he remembered it or not.

"Well," she muttered. "G'night, then."

Bran opened his eyes again and smiled sadly at her. "I'm sorry, Laela. For everythin'."

She touched his cheek. "Yeh ain't got nothin' t'say sorry for, Dad, so stop that. Now, get some sleep, an' I'll see yeh in the mornin'."

She left him and went to her own bed, which was actually nothing more than a straw pallet near the fire. They'd never had much money, especially recently, since Bran had been forced to leave his job because of his illness.

Laela snuggled under the blankets, thinking. She had never had anyone apart from Bran, and soon she was going to lose him, too. And when that happened . . . what then? She could stay in their house, but how would she support herself? And how long would it be before someone decided to take it away from her?

No . . . she couldn't stay. But if she left, where would she go?

*It doesn't matter where I go,* she thought bitterly. *Everyone knows I'm a half-breed the moment they see me. No-one here's gonna welcome someone like that; it's worse than bein' a bloody blackrobe. Oh, Gryphus, Dad, why did yeh have t'die now?*

She fell asleep with those painful thoughts circling each other in her head.

Uncomfortable dreams followed her.

She dreamt of her mother—an indistinct figure, but one whose blue eyes were kind. A dark shape reared over her, holding a dagger, and after that, blood splattered over Laela's face. Murder. But she felt no fear.

The dark figure turned toward her, dagger raised.

Laela backed away. *Leave me alone, curse yeh! I ain't done nothin'!*

The murderer only laughed. *Go. Go . . . go . . .*

*You can bloody go, yeh bastard!* Laela yelled back. *I ain't goin' nowhere, see?*

*Go,* the murderer repeated. *Go back. Go back.*

*I won't!*

*Go back . . .*

Laela ran at him, lashing out with her fists, and he faded for a moment but then returned, his darkness parting to reveal the mocking faces of the village children.

*Blackrobe! Blackrobe!*

*Darkwoman!*

*Blackrobe! Go back to the North, blackrobe!*

*Go back to the North!*

*Go . . . go . . .*

Laela woke up shivering in the grey light of dawn, the dream still lingering in her ears. It felt very cold in the room.

The fire had gone out.

Laela stood up, intending to rekindle it, but almost as soon as she had stood up and the cold air embraced her she felt—not a premonition—but hard, bitter certainty.

Walking as if her feet had turned to stone, she moved toward her father's bed to check on him.

Bran lay on his side, his face turned toward her. His skin looked grey in the dim light, and his eyes were half-open.

Laela reached out to touch him. He felt cold and rigid under her finger-tips.

He was dead.

# 2

# Choices

Laela buried her father in a makeshift grave in the wood out-side the house, where he had liked to spend time alone every day. Thinking of her mother, maybe—Laela had never asked.

It took most of the morning to dig the hole, but she was used to hard work and kept at it, using the strain to stop herself from thinking about what had happened.

When it was done, she lifted her father's body into the hole as gently as she could. She folded his arms over his chest and tried to smooth down his hair and beard.

"There yeh go," she said huskily. "I hope . . . hope yeh like it. I did me best. It ain't much, I know, but it's the best I could do. I'm sorry."

She found herself choking on a sob.

"I'm sorry, Dad," she said again. "Sorry . . ."

This time, there was no way to hold back the tears. She slumped beside the grave and cried—not beautifully, or ele-gantly, or dramatically like people in stories, but in a harsh and untidy way that made her chest hurt. The sobs sounded ugly, and she hated them, but they went on, and she felt as if some-thing had crumbled inside her.

"Oh, Gryphus," she moaned. "Oh, Gryphus, help me. What am I gonna do? What . . . ? Oh, Gryphus . . . Dad . . ."

And she sobbed harder.

A noise disturbed her mourning, and she looked up, tear-streaked, and froze.

Something huge was emerging from the trees, coming forward. It looked like . . .

Laela's mind raced, but she sat very still, remembering the advice her father had given her. *With a wild animal, sit very still. They go for movement . . .*

The thing came closer, moving slowly. Its huge head reared high above her—if she had been standing, she guessed she would barely come up to its shoulder.

At first, it looked like a bird—the head was beaked, and the neck and chest were covered in thick, rusty-red feathers. The legs were thick and muscular, scaled like a bird's, with long, grasping toes the size of her arm. The talons at their tips made them longer.

But as the creature came closer, Laela saw other things, beyond the wings folded on its back. The *other* legs—furred and shaped like those of a giant cat. The long, lashing tail, partly covered by a fan of red and yellow feathers.

Laela's heart had leapt into her mouth. She started to crawl away from the grave, backward, not taking her eyes away from the beast.

The animal ignored her. It stepped over to the grave and inspected it, huffing through its beak and sending up little puffs of dirt.

The word came to Laela through a haze of terror. *Griffin.*

The griffin paused by the grave, and then clumsily bent its forelegs and put its head down into the hole. Laela could have run then, but the horrible thought crossed her mind that it was going to eat her father's body, and that pushed her over the edge.

Like a lunatic, she wrapped her fingers around the handle of the shovel and stood up, holding it like a spear.

"Get away!" she shouted. "Leave him alone, damn yeh!"

The griffin pulled its head out of the hole and stared at her. Its eyes were yellow, and to her intense dismay, Laela saw the last thing she had been expecting to see in them: intelligence.

She hefted the shovel, trying to look braver than she felt. "Go on, clear off!" she said, and her voice came out weak and wavery.

The griffin only stared at her. Then, moving slowly and deliberately, it stepped over the grave and came straight for her.

Laela stood her ground for a few moments, and then backed away.

The griffin came closer.

Laela's mind screamed at her to run, but her legs felt weaker than a couple of twigs. She continued to back away, not knowing what to do, until she hit a tree. The griffin cornered her in an instant, its head outstretched toward her.

Laela pressed herself into the bark, sobbing in fear. The griffin brought its beak down to her face, and she closed her eyes tightly and braced herself, ready to die.

She felt the animal's hot, stale-smelling breath on her face. The beak rubbed against her skin—smooth and hard and rounded, almost like the top of a skull.

Laela dared to open her eyes again and found the griffin's big yellow ones looking back. It blinked, and then took a step back. For a moment it stood and stared at her, and then it turned and walked away with a swish of its tail.

The instant its back was turned, Laela pulled away from the tree and ran straight back to the house.

She ran, expecting to be struck from behind at any moment, but the blow never came, and she threw herself through the back door of the house and slammed it behind her before collapsing on her father's bed, shaking violently.

She was convinced the griffin would come looking for her and spent a good portion of that day hiding before she even had the courage to peer out of the window. But the griffin had gone, and it didn't return.

That afternoon, screwing up her courage, she left the house for the village marketplace. There, she sold everything the house had contained, down to the last stick of furniture. She didn't care if she was being given what they were worth; all she wanted to do was get it over with and empty the building, which had now become a mausoleum, full of memories of her foster father that she didn't want to stay.

By nightfall, the house was empty but for her old straw pallet, a couple of blankets, and some food. She had even sold the cook-pots and spoons.

She spent that night lying awake in front of the cold fireplace, staring at the ceiling.

From time to time she cried, but never for long. She felt . . . numb.


When morning came, she bundled her few remaining belongings together in a blanket—food, spare clothes, the leather bag that contained all the oblong she had earned in the marketplace, and . . .

She crouched at the spot where her father's bed had once stood and lifted up a few loose floor-boards. He'd thought she didn't know about them, but she had seen him move them one morning while she pretended to be asleep. By now she already knew what was in there.

She pulled out a wooden box. It was full of oblong, and she tipped them into her money-bag. There were also several bottles of strong barley wine—she hesitated for a long moment before stuffing two of them in her makeshift bag. And, hidden under that . . .

Laela brought out a long object wrapped in cloth.

She pulled away the wrappings, and uncovered a short sword. It was a well-made thing with an oiled-steel blade and a plain bronze hilt, and it had been stored with a red leather sheath.

Laela tied the sheath to her belt and replaced the boards before she stood up. The sword's weight felt reassuring at her hip.

Once that was done, she paused to take one last look around at her former home.

"I'd stay," she mumbled aloud, in answer to the feeling of longing that hung in the air. "I would, honest. But I can't. Not any more. But I hope whoever lives here next remembers I was here. An' Dad. Him, too."

She left the house via the back door and locked it before walking slowly and warily back toward Bran's grave.

There was no sign of the griffin. She hastily snatched up the shovel and filled in the grave without looking into it, muttering the ritual prayers as well as she remembered them.

When that was done, she walked away without a backward glance.

Out in the village streets, people openly stared at her as she passed. Some of them called out to her, but she ignored them—whether they were insults or friendly greetings, she didn't care.

She made straight for the centre of the village, for the modest building that was home to, not the governor of this piece of land, but one of his officials, who had been given the unrewarding job of living in the village and handling its official matters.

Laela nodded curtly to the guard by the door. "I want t'see Kendrick."

"That'd be *Lord* Kendrick to you, girl," the guard snapped.

Laela straightened up. "He ain't no lord an' everyone knows it, Gower, so let me through."

"You got a fine tongue on yer for a peasant," the guard muttered, but he knew better than to pick a fight, and went on more moderately. "What's it regardin'?"

"I'm here t'talk to him about the rent," said Laela. "Dad sent me."

Gower nodded. "Right then," he said. "May as well let yer in. How's yer dad, by the way?"

"Much better today," Laela mumbled, and went in.

She had been in this building before, when Bran went there on official business, and she found Kendrick's office easily enough. She knocked on the door.

"Come in."

Laela obeyed.

Kendrick, a pasty-faced middle-aged man, squinted at her. "Oh, it's you," he said. "What d'you want? Why are you carrying all that, may I ask?"

Laela dumped her possessions on the floor but kept the sword. "Just wanted a quick word with yeh, sir."

"If it's quick," he said, in rather ungracious tones. "What's the problem? How's your father, by the way?"

"He's dead, sir," said Laela.

He started at that. "Oh. I didn't . . . uh, I'm sorry to hear it."

Laela knew he wasn't. "I'm leavin', sir," she said. "Dad's dead, so I'm gettin' out of this bloody place while I can an' before people know about it."

"I see. So why are you telling me this?"

"I won't need my Dad's house no more," said Laela. "So I'm sellin' it back to yeh."

Kendrick gave her a look. "I'm afraid it's not as simple as—"

"I ain't interested in no arguin'," said Laela. "I know how much my dad paid yeh in rent, an' I know what the property's worth. So I want two hundred oblong."

"You want—" Kendrick controlled himself. "You don't seem to understand," he said in patronising tones, as if he were speaking to a small child. "Your father didn't *own* the house, he *rented* it from me. Therefore, you can't sell it."

"Fine," said Laela. "But my dad paid rent in advance for this whole month comin', an' this whole month just started today. So give me the money back, an' I'll get goin'."

"Well." He softened. "There's no need to be so hasty—"

"Yeah, there is," Laela snapped. "An' I don't need any of yer blather about paperwork an' all the rest of that nonsense. Yeh don't want no stinkin' half-breed hangin' about the place, so just give me the damn money, an' I'll be out of yer hair."

"I'll give you a hundred and fifty oblong," said Kendrick.

"Two hundred."

"Young lady, this is not marketplace bartering," said Kendrick. "I'm offering you a hundred and fifty oblong, and that's final."

"Two hundred," Laela repeated in a flat voice. "Two hundred, an' I'm gone."

He threw up his hands. "Why should I be giving you money at all? You weren't the one who paid the rent. It's not even your money to take."

"My dad didn't have no other family," said Laela. "Just me. An' I was *here* when he told yeh I'd get everythin' he owned after he died, see? I inherit everythin'. So hand it over."

He glared at her.

She glared back.

Finally, Kendrick threw up his hands. "All right, fine. It's not as if it's my money anyway. Show this piece of paper to the treasurer, and she'll give you what you're after. I suggest you take it and go."

Laela waited until he had finished scribbling down the order and calmly took it from him. "See yeh."

"Laela?"

She paused in the doorway and looked back. "What?"

Kendrick had stood up. "Where are you going to go?" he asked, almost gently.

Laela stared coldly at him. "I'm gonna take the advice people've bin yellin' at me in the street for years. I'm goin' North."

Kendrick stared at her. "What? Laela Redguard, you can't be serious! The North . . . ?"

"I *am* serious," she said. She sneered at him. "Where else is a half-breed gonna go?"

He paused briefly, and then sat down again. "You'll be killed," he said bluntly. "The instant you set foot in darkman territory . . ."

"What, they'll treat me worse than *you* would've?" said Laela. She spat. "I ain't known nothin' but prejudice from anyone here 'cept Dad. Maybe a *blackrobe* would understand that. It's a hope, an' I'm takin' it."

She walked out of the office.

At noon that day, she left the village, too, with a bag of gold oblong, her sword, supplies for a few days, and faint hope wavering in her chest.

L aela had never left the village before in her life, and she did so very nervously now. She followed the main road on foot until she managed to beg a ride on a vegetable cart heading for the next village. It arrived after nightfall, and once she had disembarked, she snuck into a barn and slept hidden behind a pile of hay.

She woke up at dawn and slipped out before anyone found her.

In the marketplace, she bought some food, careful to keep her hair covered by a hood as she had since leaving home, and went on her way.

And that was how she travelled: sometimes on foot, sometimes on a cart or with a group of other travellers, never exchanging more than a few words with anyone. She kept her money well hidden and her sword not so well hidden, and most of the time, people left her alone. It was a hard life, and lonely, but she held up well enough, and after a few days, she began to feel a sense of freedom, and even excitement, through the cloud of misery that had been hanging over her head ever since her father's death.

Toward the end of her second week on the road, she had fallen in with a group of traders who had let her ride on the back of a cart in exchange for a few oblong. One of them, walking behind it, had been watching her curiously, and now he took a few long strides to catch up with the cart.

"Hullo," he said.

Laela woke up from her daydream and looked at him. "Yeah?"

"Just wanted someone t'talk to," said the man.

Laela yawned. "All right."

"So, where are yer goin'? I got to say, it's not that often yer find a woman travelling alone."

"I ain't goin' anywhere in particular," said Laela.

"Well," said the man, "yer gonna have to pick a destination soon, 'cause we're gonna be enterin' the Northgates pretty soon."

Laela started at that. "How soon?"

He squinted ahead. "I'd say the next day or so by my reckonin'. But y'wanna be on yer way before that happens."

"Why would yeh be goin' into the Northgates?" said Laela. "Yeh ain't goin' into the North, are yeh?"

"'Course not," said the traveller. "Use yer brain, girl. There's not a Southerner in Cymria would go *there*, not for love or money."

Laela sat back and thought. It had been a long time since any Southerner had gone North, that was very true. Once upon a time, the North had been Cymrian territory—ruled over by griffiners. The lords of the land, given power by their partnership with griffins. They had conquered the North centuries ago, and its inhabitants had become either slaves or vassals.

But that was before what was now referred to as the Dark War, or the War of the Darkmen. That had been before Lord Arenadd Taranisäii, a renegade Northerner, had allied himself with an extremely powerful griffin and led a rebellion against the griffiners. Together, the man Southerners called the Dark Lord Arenadd and the griffin, simply called "the dark griffin," had ruthlessly slaughtered and burned their way through the griffiner cities in the North. Any Southerner living there had been killed or driven out, and in the end, the rebels had captured Malvern, the capital city, and massacred its inhabitants.

Today, the North was its own country, and Arenadd

Taranisäii was its King. And no Southerner would ever enter it unless he was stupid, or insane.

Still.

"So why are yeh goin' into the mountains if yeh ain't gonna go through 'em?" Laela asked. "What's the point?"

"We're goin' to Guard's Post," the traveller explained. "The men livin' there don't get much in the way of supplies, so they're happy to buy them off us."

Laela nodded to herself. In that case, she would stay with this cart until it got to Guard's Post, and when it arrived she would do whatever she had to to pass beyond it and into the North. And if the men living in it resisted, well . . .

She reached into her bundle of possessions and fingered the bag of oblong, which was still nearly full. Her father had taught her that a sword was the best persuasion, but Laela had always thought money worked far better.

With that in mind, she stayed with the cart for the next two days, ignoring her new acquaintance's suggestions for her to leave before they reached Guard's Post.

By midmorning of the second day, the Northgates loomed ahead. She had never seen mountains before, and these looked enormous to her. She watched them as the cart trundled on, marvelling at their sheer, rocky slopes and wondering why and how anyone would ever climb them.

Fortunately—of course—the cart and its owners weren't going to try. The road led them to a wide pass that led through the mountains, and they entered it at around midday and then trundled along it, walled in by cliffs on either side.

Laela shivered and pulled her dress over her legs. The cliffs were high, and it was cold and dark between them. For a moment she had the irrational feeling that they had gone underground, but after a while, the pass opened up a little, and the sun warmed her face.

She looked ahead, her heart thudding now in anticipation. They were nearly there.

They reached Guard's Post by evening. Laela, standing up on the back of the cart to look ahead, had seen it some time ago, and she watched it come closer.

Guard's Post had been partly carved out of the walls of the pass and consisted mostly of a huge archway. Below it was an enormous iron gate that had to be raised and lowered by chains. Above it there were towers, built on the cliff-tops. Laela thought they looked familiar, but it took a while for her to decide why.

She remembered a drawing she had seen once, in a book. A tower, tall but solid, its sides full of strange, arched openings, each one with a platform jutting out from it. A griffiner tower, her father had explained. The platforms were for the griffins to land on, and the openings led into nesting chambers.

The towers at Guard's Post had openings just like that.

Laela hugged her knees and shivered with excitement. Griffiner towers! She had always wanted to see one, and now she was seeing two.

There didn't seem to be any griffins around them, though. Privately, she was relieved. Griffins were notoriously dangerous and temperamental creatures—not even a griffiner could really control one, or so her father had told her. They had magic. They also had beaks and talons meant for tearing flesh, and they were carnivores. That last part bothered Laela far more than magic.

The cart reached the gate before the driver pulled the oxen to a halt and waved to a small figure standing on the crenulated wall above. The figure waved back.

The driver sat down.

"An' now we wait," one of his companions muttered.

Laela got off the back of the cart, suddenly nervous.

At first it seemed nothing was happening; she kept expecting the huge gate to open, but it never did. Were they going to have to turn back?

The driver tensed in his seat. "Here they come," he said. "Throw yer weapons down."

Laela pulled her sword around to the back of her belt and took her blanket-roll down off the cart and slung it over her shoulder, hoping it would hide the weapon. Nothing would make her part with the sword unless it was a matter of life and death.

A few tense moments passed, while the travellers laid their weapons down at their feet in plain sight, and the driver got down off the cart. Laela stood tall to look past them, and her heart beat fast as she saw a group of men come toward them.

"Who are ye an' what d'ye want, Southerner?" a harshly accented voice demanded of the driver.

He bowed nervously. "I'm here to trade, sir. I've brought plenty of goods."

Laela, keeping well back, clenched her fists with nervous impatience. She desperately wanted to see the Northerners, but the bulky forms of her fellow travellers were in her way, and she didn't want to draw attention to herself.

"Out of the way," the first voice said, and the travellers obligingly moved away from the cart.

The Northerners—six in all—surrounded the cart, while two of their number climbed up on it and began to search through its contents.

Laela, seeing them at last, felt her breath catch in her throat. *No.*

The Northerners were tall and long-limbed—lightly built, but sinewy. Their hair was black as coal, and they had pale skin, and when one of them turned toward her Laela saw his eyes—glittering black, impassive.

*Oh, Gryphus,* she thought, suddenly trembling.

One of the Northerners lifted up a box. "What's in this?"

"Melon seeds, sir," said the driver.

The Northerner grunted and prised the box open. Laela saw his fingers, long, elegant fingers . . . his face, sharp-featured and cunning . . .

Without thinking, she ran a hand over her own face. Was that what *she* looked like? Was she one of them? A *darkwoman*?

But she was. She knew she was. Everything about them matched her own looks, everything but the eyes . . .

"We'll take it," said the leader, his sharp voice breaking into her thoughts. "Ye can bring it in through the gate—*only* ye, mind. The rest can stay here. We don't need no bloody Southerners stinkin' up the place."

"Yes, sir," the driver nodded, and climbed back onto his seat.

The Northerners seemed to find something very amusing about this, and they sniggered among themselves as the cart moved forward again.

Laela darted forward. "Hey!"

One of the Northerners turned sharply. "What d'ye want, girl?"

Laela faced him. "I'm goin' through, too."

He planted a hand on her chest and shoved her backward so hard she nearly fell over. "Ye're goin' nowhere, Southerner. We're only lettin' this one through under sufferance. An' we don't buy whores."

Laela felt ice-cold rage burning in her chest. "Yeh'll let me through, Northerner," she said. "I've come 'ere because I want t'go into the North."

The Northerner laughed at that—a rough, cruel laugh. "Ye, go North? That's a nice 'un. Listen t'this, lads—we got a Southerner wantin' to come into the King's lands!"

"I can pay yeh—" Laela began.

The Northerner had had his fun. "Sod off, Southerner," he said.

Laela ran after him. "I ain't no bloody Southerner, understand?" she roared. "I'm one of *you*, damn it!"

The man turned. "Look—"

She reached up to the hood she had kept in place for weeks and tore it off. The long, jet-black hair she hated tumbled free in greasy curls around her face, and she glared defiantly at the Northerners.

Everyone there started in shock.

"There," Laela said loudly. "Yeh see that?" She held up a hand. "See *these*, yeh bastard? I'm a Northerner, an' I want t'go home."

The leader of the Northerners pushed past his comrades to look at her. His black eyes narrowed. "Ye ain't no Northerner. Look at them eyes. Ye're a Night-cursed half-breed, ain't ye?"

"Me father was a Northerner," Laela said steadily.

"But not yer mother," the man finished. "Go away, girl. We don't need yer Southern blood on our soil."

Laela took a deep breath—this was her last chance. "Fine, so I'm a half-breed. But I'm a half-breed what's carryin' five hundred gold oblong."

The commander stopped at that. "Five hundred—don't try an' play games, half-blood, or I'll carve yer throat out."

Laela swung her bundle down off her shoulders and pulled out the bag of money. She opened it and pulled out a single oblong, holding it so it flashed in the light. "I'll give it to yeh," she said. "If yeh let me through."

The man fingered the hilt of the wicked-looking sickle in his belt. "An' what's t'stop me takin' it anyway, girl?"

Laela reached behind her back and freed her sword. "This is," she snarled, and pointed it directly at his throat.

The man stared at her. Then he glanced at his companions, who were looking on, unreadable.

Then, suddenly, he burst out laughing. "Hahahah! Hark at that half-breed, would ye? Thinks she's gonna walk straight through here with her trusty sword an' her bag of oblong."

"I'll walk through with the sword," said Laela. "The oblong're yours."

The commander became serious. "What's yer name, girl?"

She lifted her chin. "Laela Redguard of Sturrick."

"An' why are ye tryin' t'go North, Laela Redguard of Sturrick?"

"'Cause . . ." Laela hesitated. "'Cause once all Northerners . . . once *darkmen* like you din't have no place to call home. Yeh were all slaves, in the North or anywhere else, an' nobody thought yeh were anythin' but worthless. Now yeh've shown the world yeh ain't that, an' yeh've got Southerners callin' *you* 'sir.' Well, I ain't no Southerner, an' I ain't no Northerner, an' I got no home an' no respect neither. But I thought if I went North an' found my father's people, then maybe I'd find somewhere, 'cause you people'd understand. Or maybe I'm wrong," she added more softly.

The commander watched her in silence while she spoke. When she had finished, he looked her up and down and then turned away.

"Right," he said to his companions, as if nothing had happened. "Let's get goin'. Ye, run back an' tell 'em t'open the gate. Ye there—Southerner—get them ox movin'. I want that cart inside before the Night God wakes. C'mon, hurry it up!"

The men sprang into action. Laela, for her part, stayed where she was, still holding the sword and the bag of money. Nobody went near her, and the commander, busy ordering his men around, paid her no more attention.

Slowly, laboriously, the gate rose on its chains. When it was high enough and the signal had been given, the cart moved forward again.

Laela followed it. Nobody tried to stop her.

They passed through the gateway and into a big open area with curving stone walls on two sides and another gate in front. There the cart came to a stop, and a group of Northerners—including some women—began to unload its contents while the commander argued with the driver over prices.

Laela stood to one side, expecting to be attacked at any moment. Nobody paid her any attention.

Finally, when the cart was all but empty and the driver had collected his money, the gate opened again, and the oxen did a clumsy turn and began to walk back out the way they had come. Laela watched, not knowing if she should stay or follow.

"Where d'ye think yer goin', girl?" said the commander's voice from behind her.

Laela turned and silently offered him the bag of money.

He ignored it and ushered her toward the other gate. It stayed closed, but there was another, far smaller door set into the stonework beside it. The commander opened it.

"Go," he said, gesturing to the landscape on the other side.

Laela tried to put the bag into his hands. "Here," she said. "Payment, like I promised."

He pushed it back toward her. "Keep it," he said. "I get paid plenty."

Laela looked suspiciously at him. "Why are yeh lettin' me through then, if yeh ain't takin' the money?"

He straightened up. "The North's a home for warriors, girl, not traders. I dunno if ye'll find a home there, but ye'll need that money. An' maybe ye've got Southern blood in ye, but ye've acted like a darkwoman, an' that's enough for me."

Very slowly, Laela refastened the string around the neck of the bag and stowed it away again. "Thanks."

The commander smiled very slightly at her. "Go on," he said. "An' good luck, Laela."

Laela glanced at him and stepped through the door. Into the North.

# 3

# Malvern

She travelled toward Malvern though she wasn't sure why. Perhaps because it was the nearest city, or perhaps because it was the seat of the King. She didn't have a plan, and Malvern seemed like the best place to go, so that was where she went.

Travelling in the North was far more difficult than it had been in the South. The road to Malvern was wide and well-marked, but there was virtually nobody else on it. Nobody, therefore, to beg or purchase a ride from. Nobody to trade with. Nobody to tell her if she was going in the right direction.

Under the circumstances, she did the only thing she could: She kept doggedly following the road, hoping to find someone or something that could help her.

Eventually, with her food running low, she came across what looked like abandoned farmland. Crops were growing wild, and she spent some time picking whatever looked edible before she moved on.

Finally, after nearly a solid week of walking, she came across her first village.

She wasn't sure what she had been expecting a Northern village to look like, but now she saw one, she felt vaguely disappointed to discover it was barely any different from any farming community in the South.

But the *people* were different.

Laela walked through the main street, heart pounding, waiting for someone to single her out.

Nobody did. She garnered a few curious stares, but nobody shouted at her, nobody came up to accost her. There were no jeers or insults.

Laela felt all her anxiety drain away. Thank Gryphus, she had been right. She could blend in with these people.

Her confidence soaring, she approached a farmer busy unloading a cart.

"What d'ye want?" he asked—impatient but not hostile.

"I'm tryin' t'get to Malvern," she said, careful not to look him in the eye. "Could yeh give me directions?"

The farmer looked curiously at her. "I ain't heard an accent like that before—where're ye from?"

"Nowhere yeh'd know," said Laela. "But I want t'get to Malvern. Just tell me if I'm goin' the right way."

"Well, the main road leadin' out of here goes straight there," said the farmer. "Just keep followin' it an' ye'll be at Malvern's gates in the end."

"How far is it?" said Laela. "I'm on foot."

"On foot!" the farmer repeated. "Ye gods. Ye'll be lucky to make it there in two months, girl."

Her heart sank. "D'yeh know how I could get there faster, then?"

The farmer scratched his nose. "If ye see anyone goin' in that direction, ye could try an' hitch a lift, or ye could buy a horse if ye had the money . . . it's playin' with fire, takin' horses into Malvern, mind."

"Why?" said Laela.

"The place is swarmin' with griffins, ain't it?" said the farmer. "An' we all know how much *they* like horses."

Laela hadn't heard of this. "Er . . ."

"Griffins *hate* horses," the farmer told her. "Mostly they kill the things on sight. Ye know, I heard this old story once how there was unicorns in Cymria once, but the griffins wiped 'em out."

"Oh," said Laela. "I never knew that. Can't ride, anyway."

"Well, I'll tell ye what," said the farmer. "Tomorrow I'm headin' off on a jaunt northward meself. I might be willin' to give ye a ride on the cart if ye can pay."

"I can," Laela said promptly. "An' I'll pay yeh extra t'let me sleep in yer barn."

"How much?" said the farmer.

"Ten oblong for the ride, an' ten more for the barn," she said.

"Done," said the farmer. "My name's Mawrth, by the way."

"Laela," she said.

She handed over the money—keeping ten oblong back in case he decided to change his mind the next day.

"Thankye kindly," said Mawrth. "I'll give ye some food, too."

Laela smiled. "Thanks."

"Well, it ain't every day I meet a lady as attractive as yer-self," said Mawrth. "No need t'look so surprised—I mean it! Ye don't need t'be so shy, girl."

Laela, keeping her eyes on the ground, blushed. "Thanks," she mumbled. "Can yeh show me where the barn is?"

Her new friend obliged, and she settled down into the straw very gratefully. It was good to have something close to a proper bed again.

She slept, and dreamt of her father. He was trying to tell her something, but there was a scream in the air that made his voice impossible to hear.

Mawrth was as good as his word. The next day, his cart rattled out of the village, and Laela found herself riding on the driver's seat rather than on the back, which was piled high with cabbages, while her host, apparently oblivious to her nervousness, made cheerful conversation.

". . . an' they say that in Malvern, the King himself comes t'celebrate the Wolf Moon every month. I heard once the priests tried t'conduct a funeral for a friend of his without tellin' him, an' he showed up halfway through, punched the High Priestess in the face, an' then finished the rites himself."

Laela wanted to look him in the face, but forced herself not to. "Have yeh ever seen the King?"

"Once," said Mawrth. "Not up close, mind. I was there when he announced that he was lettin' traders come in from Amoran."

"What was it like?" said Laela. "What was *he* like?"

Mawrth paused to wipe his nose on the back of his sleeve. "He looked ordinary, mostly. Young, but old. Wore a black robe, like a slave would. It's said he never wears anythin' else. An' he had the Mighty Skandar with him, of course."

"The Mighty . . . you mean the griffin?"

"Aye. The dark griffin. 'Darkheart,' some call him. By the moon, but that was a sight t'scare any man. I've seen griffins. Not up close, but I've seen 'em. But the Mighty Skandar is the biggest I ever saw in my life. They say he's killed more people than any griffin in the world, an' that his magic is so powerful, it could kill a whole army in one go. They say," he added darkly, "they say he eats people. Enemies of the King."

Laela shivered. "People're scared of him. The King, too."

"'Course they are," said Mawrth. "Ye'd have t'be an idiot not t'be. But they protect us, Laela. See? They might be scary t'some, but without them, we'd be lost. It's thanks t'them we're free, an' it's thanks t'them we *stay* free, too. The Southerners outnumber us, but they'd never dare invade again. They're too scared to, after what Skandar an' the King did to their friends here all them years ago. An' it's a damn good thing, too."

Laela frowned to herself. It was odd to hear the King, who in the South was always spoken of with fear and hatred, referred to as a heroic protector. But, she supposed, it only made sense, after all . . .

She travelled with Mawrth for nearly a week, and by the end of it she had come to like him. It was almost sad to say goodbye.

"Good luck, Laela," he said as he pocketed her money. "I hope ye find the new home ye're lookin' for."

She couldn't stop herself from looking him in the face at last. "Thanks for everythin', Mawrth. Yeh were a good friend."

Mawrth nodded and smiled. "It was my pleasure."

Laela walked away from his cart. He hadn't shown any sign of noticing her blue eyes. Maybe he just hadn't seen them. But then, who noticed the colour of someone's eyes?

That part of her journey didn't just bring her much closer to Malvern—it also gave her even more confidence.

And it showed her that her belief had been correct: Here in the North, she could blend in. Here, people treated her like an ordinary person—some of them were even friendly. Here she could make a new life—she knew it.

Her belief was confirmed over the next few weeks as a combination of money and the kindness of strangers made her journey quicker and easier. In one of the larger towns she passed through, she bought a new set of clothes—made in the thicker, warmer Northern manner. She even went so far as to enjoy a drink or two in a tavern, and aside from the usual drunken leering, no-one molested her.

By the time Malvern's walls came in sight, she had all but lost her fear. In fact, she had come to love the North. She had barely been there any time at all, but it already felt like home. Even her misery over her father had begun to leave her. He would be happy to know that she was safe, and that thought cheered her up.

And then, at last . . . Malvern.

She chose to go on foot for the last leg of the journey, wanting to see the famed city for the first time on her own. This was an experience she wanted all to herself.

It was bigger, far bigger, than she had expected. At first it looked like a black blob, squatting on the horizon, but as she drew nearer and nearer, she began to get an idea of how enormous it really was.

The city had walls around it, as she'd expected. They were enormous, built from stone, and she could see guards patrolling along its top—tiny from that height. But beyond the wall were the five towers of the royal Eyrie, rearing into the sky.

They looked like ordinary griffiner towers, but . . . huge. Laela could see the openings in their sides and the banners flying from the tops. The towers varied in size—the one in the centre was the thickest and tallest. She could see what looked like bridges connecting them to each other.

The city gates were open, and travellers were passing in and out of them apparently unimpeded. Laela strode through, unnoticed.

So this was the big city.

She wandered through the streets with no particular destination in mind, staring in wonder at everything she saw. In most ways it was no different from the smaller towns she had already seen . . . but so full, and so busy! The streets were simply packed—people were *everywhere*, walking in all directions. She had never seen so many people in one place. All of them, of course, were Northerners, and for the first time in her life, Laela felt like she was just a face in the crowd. Everywhere she looked were people with black hair. Wonderful, *ordinary* black hair.

Long fingers, angular features, a tall and long-limbed build . . . the features that had once singled her out, made her an outsider wherever she went . . . here they were normal.

Exultation filled her.

Like one in a dream, she wandered the streets, going wherever she pleased. She found the marketplace and spent a few oblong on trinkets before her empty stomach brought her back to the present. She bought an apple and a few pastries from a stall and ate them as she walked along. But the gathering darkness quickly reminded her of her original plan. Find a job, and somewhere to stay, and quickly.

The former could wait.

She left the market district and wandered further into the city, hoping to find an inn or a tavern where there could be a room to let. But she had no idea where to find one, and the city was enormous. Eventually, tired and foot-sore, she stopped a passing woman.

"'Scuse me . . ."

The woman looked at her. "What d'ye want?"

"I was hopin' t'find an inn or somethin' like it around here," said Laela. "I ain't been here long, an' I need somewhere t'stay."

A suspicious glare. "Where did ye get that accent?"

"Dunno. Found it lyin' around somewhere," said Laela, trying to sound nice and light-hearted though the woman's unfriendly tones weren't helping. "Look, can yeh help me? I'm in a hurry."

"Try the south end," the woman said briefly, and went on her way.

Laela glared at her back. "Hope that didn't cost yeh life savin's or nothin', yeh bitch."

Lacking anything but these brief directions, she headed in what she hoped was a southward direction. The streets darkened as the sun sank lower, and although the city guard were lighting the lamps, it had the effect of making the shadows that much deeper and gloomier.

Laela, beginning to feel nervous, sped up. Eventually, after much wandering around and with her belongings chafing painfully on her shoulders, she did come across a public building of some kind. She couldn't read the sign over the entrance, but light and loud, cheerful voices spilled out of the windows, drawing her toward it.

The door was open, so she peered through. Her heart leapt. A tavern!

She strode in, ignoring the curious stares from the almost exclusively male customers. At the bar, a young and not exactly overdressed Northern woman was serving drinks.

Laela walked up and leant on the bar. "Oi. You."

The barmaid shoved a mug of beer down the benchtop toward a customer. "What'll it be?"

"I'm lookin' to find a room," Laela said, raising her voice over the chatter. "D'yeh have one here?"

The barmaid looked slightly puzzled. "Ye're lookin' for a place t'stay, is that it?"

Laela opened her mouth to reply, and shut it again as a chorus of shouts and clinking mugs from behind her drowned her out. "Yeah, I'm lookin' t'spend the night somewhere," she said rather irritably. "Have yeh got anythin'?"

The barmaid only increased Laela's bad temper by taking a moment to sell several more drinks. Laela waited and growled under her breath until the woman's attention was on her again.

"Sorry, love, what was that?"

"I said—" Another uproar from behind her. "I *said*, do yeh have any rooms here where I could spend the night?" said Laela. "I can pay."

The barmaid gave her a look. "How old are ye, girl?"

"Nineteen," said Laela. "Can yeh just answer me?"

There was a long pause, while the woman gave her a long, slow look. Then she put down the mug she was trying to clean and leant down toward her. "What sort of place d'ye think this is?" she asked kindly. "Does this look like an inn?"

Laela glanced around. The place was full of tables, and there were men everywhere, drinking and laughing among themselves. The few women were dotted around the room, some of them sitting in laps or pausing to caress a face.

She looked back at the barmaid. "Well, there're men drinkin' here, ain't there?"

The barmaid laughed. "Well, yeah. We don't get that many women here. Most of the girls what come here are lookin' for a job, not a drink."

"What does that have t'do with anythin'?" Laela snapped. "D'yeh have a room or not?"

"We got a few, upstairs," said the barmaid, going back to her cleaning. "But I don't think ye'd want t'stay in any of 'em. Pretty noisy up there, if ye get my drift. Them rooms sees a lot of use."

Laela frowned. "What are yeh talkin' about?"

"Good gods." The barmaid wiped a grimy arm over her forehead. "Where've ye been livin' all this time—under a rock?"

"I ain't from around here," said Laela, still thoroughly mystified.

"This ain't an inn," said the barmaid.

Laela turned to look at the clientele, and the scantily dressed young women walking among them. Realisation finally dawned.

"Oh, holy . . ."

She almost ran out, her ears ringing with raucous laughter and lewd comments hurled at her, face burning with humiliation.

Outside, she flattened herself against a wall and breathed deeply. Then she let it out again in a string of swear-words. Her foster father had known plenty of curses and had never been shy about using them, but just now they seemed hopelessly inadequate.

She rubbed a hand over her face—it was actually as hot as it felt. Gods damn it. She swore some more, and then dusted herself down and walked away as quickly as she could.

*Well, how was I supposed t'know?* she thought furiously. *I couldn't read the damned sign. I was too tired t'notice . . .*

It didn't make her feel any less of an idiot.

She stopped on the corner of the street to wipe the sweat off her forehead. It was completely dark now; how was she supposed to find anything in this twice-damned city?

A hand touched her shoulder. "Lost, are ye?"

Laela turned and saw a couple of men. "Yeah," she said cautiously. "A bit. I'm lookin' for a place t'stay."

They glanced at each other. "Ye could stay with us," said one.

His breath stank of beer. Laela tried not to gag. "No thanks. If ye know where there's an inn or somethin', though . . ."

"We know a good one," said the other man.

"Yeah," said his friend. He hadn't taken his hand off Laela's arm. "C'mon, we can show ye."

Laela tried to pull away from him as politely as possible. "Just tell me where t'go, an' I can find it myself."

"Oh, c'mon," said the other, somehow managing to get behind her without seeming to move at all. "We're all right; just a couple of friends lookin' t'help a nice young lady like yerself. Nothin' t'worry about."

Laela didn't trust them in the least. "All right then," she said, deciding to play along for the time being.

They led her away up the street, keeping uncomfortably close. Laela had the feeling that they were ready to grab her arms if she tried to run. Her heart beat fast. But she didn't want to risk making them angry—they were obviously drunk, and besides, maybe they were just being overfriendly.

She walked as quickly as she could, hoping to outpace them. They sped up, too, not moving away.

"Could yeh move back a bit?" she said at last. "Yer kinda crowdin' me."

"Oh, we're sorry," said one. "We din't mean t'scare ye, girl. We're just makin' sure ye keep safe, like. Wouldn't want anythin' t'happen to ye."

His friend sniggered.

The instant Laela heard it, she snapped. Without a sound, she twisted away from them and ran.

After her first mad dash, she began to look at where she was going, hoping to find somewhere she could lose them. But the crowds had thinned out by now.

And they were chasing her. She could hear their pounding footsteps behind her. Her heart pounded, too, as if it were trying to keep pace with the sound.

She sped up and darted away in a random direction, searching now for a place to hide. But the two men were fit and strong, and she was exhausted after days of long travel and too little sleep. They were gaining on her.

Finally, unable to run any further, she ducked into an alleyway and huddled into a shadow, hoping they would miss her.

She kept as still as she could, scarcely breathing, offering up a silent prayer to Gryphus that he would keep her safe, stop them from seeing her . . .

For a few moments, nothing happened, and she began to think that maybe she had escaped.

"Where are ye, miss?"

The voice came drifting down the alley toward her, full of hateful confidence. Laela felt her stomach twist. She started to edge her way toward the end of the alley, but it was too late.

The two men stepped toward her, leering. They had her cornered now, and the sight of them sent cold despair through her whole body.

But not for long. Laela's eyes narrowed, and she reached behind her and drew the sword.

"Stay away from me!" she snarled.

They backed off a little at that.

"Well, damn me!" said one. "A lady with a sword."

The other looked unperturbed. "I'd put that down if I were ye, girl," he drawled. "Ye don't want t'get hurt, do ye?"

"I want *you* to get away from me," Laela said. "I know how t'use this sword, see? So move away before I show yeh."

The first one pulled a knife out of his belt. "Reckon we're gonna have t'deal with this one together, Aled."

The second, Aled, drew his own knife. "I reckon so, too. C'mon girl," he added, almost gently. "Ye don't want us t'have t'hurt ye, do ye?"

Laela felt her arm beginning to tremble, but she didn't lower the sword. "I don't want to kill yeh," she said. "An' I will if I have to."

"All right, that's enough," said Aled.

He moved forward, along with his friend, and Laela panicked. They were too close, *too close*; she didn't know how to fight like this—

She tried to make a thrust with the sword, but Aled sidestepped the blow and grabbed her by the forearm. He twisted, and pain rifled through her arm. She screamed.

Immediately, a hot, foul-tasting hand closed over her mouth.

"Just shut up," Aled rasped in her ear. "An' it'll all be over soon, see?"

Laela struggled while the other man pulled her belongings off her back and rummaged through them. There was a rattle of oblong.

"By the shadows, look at this!" he said. He opened the bag. "There's got t'be at least two hundred in here!"

Aled, holding Laela with his knife to her throat, grinned disbelievingly. "This is our lucky night! Quick, hide it away in case anyone sees us."

Laela squirmed and bit his hand. He pulled it away for an instant, and she took her chance and screamed for help.

Aled hit her, hard, in the face. "Try that again, an' ye'll crawl out of here with one less ear."

His friend stuffed Laela's bag of money into his tunic. "Hurry it up, will ye? We don't want no guards findin' us."

Aled ignored him. The hand holding the knife crept down Laela's front. She struggled again, harder, trying to scream through the hand still muffling her, but there was nothing she could do. His hand slid inside her dress, down and down to clutch at her breasts, and she felt herself slide into an abyss of pure terror and despair. She was going to die . . .

No. They weren't going to kill her. It would be worse than that, far worse . . .

Aled tensed suddenly, and his hand stopped.

"Who are *ye*?" Laela heard him grate out.

Someone else had appeared in the alley entrance. "What, ain't ye gonna give *me* a go, too?" they asked.

Aled spat. "Sod off."

The stranger came closer. "Selfish, ain't ye? C'mon, give me a piece of the action why don't ye?"

Aled's friend pointed his knife at him. "Get lost, or I'll stick this in yer gut."

The stranger sighed and leant forward, until they were almost face-to-face. Laela heard him say something—she didn't know what. Whatever it was, it had a terrible effect on Aled's friend. The man jerked away from the stranger, paused a moment, and then ran.

That left Aled and the stranger.

"Found yerself a nice prize, haven't yer?" the stranger said, in conversational tones. "Got any t'spare?"

"Clear off," said Aled, though he was beginning to sound uncertain. He pulled his hand out of Laela's dress and pressed the knife against her throat again. "Go on, get out, or—"

"Ye'll do what?" said the stranger. "Ye want to be a murderer, too, do ye? Wanna know what that feels like?"

Aled realised his game was up. He abruptly removed the knife from Laela's throat and thrust her toward the stranger before turning on his heels and running away.

Laela collided with the stranger and fought to get away from him as he grabbed at her, trying to hold her still. He caught her by the wrist, and held on. His grip was cold, and horribly strong.

"Let go!" Laela almost screamed at him, half-mad with fear. *"Let go!"*

The stranger looked past her, to where Aled had disappeared. "Coward," he muttered.

Laela tried to hit him in the face. He avoided the blow easily and pinned her arms to her sides. "Calm down," he said. *"Calm down."*

She stilled, panting. The stranger was . . . she couldn't tell who he was. He wore a hood that hid his face in shadows, and his clothes were all-concealing. He was even wearing gloves. He smelled of cold.

"Let me go," Laela said again. She started to shake. "Please, just let me go."

"Keep calm," the stranger advised. "I ain't gonna hurt yer, see? I just wanted . . . want t'know if ye're hurt."

"I'm *fine*," said Laela. "Let me go."

He did. "I didn't mean none of what I said; that was just cover. Are ye all right? Tell me for true."

Laela backed away from him and tried to pick up her belongings, but her hands were suddenly clumsy, and they slipped through her fingers. She felt tears prickling at her eyes.

The stranger came toward her. "I can help . . ."

"No . . ." Laela tried to pull away from him, but in that moment the last of her strength slipped away, and she started to sob.

The stranger seemed to understand. He bent and gathered up her possessions, wrapping them neatly and efficiently back up in their blanket. "It's all right," he told her. "Ye're safe, see? *Safe.* What's yer name?"

Laela managed to pick up the sword. "L . . . I'm . . . I'm . . . Laela. Laela R . . ." But she broke out in a fresh wave of sobbing before she could finish.

"Here," said the stranger, offering her his hand. "Let me help yer. Can ye tell me where ye live?"

"Not . . . not here," said Laela. "I ain't . . . ain't from here."

"Are ye with anyone?"

"No. I'm alone."

"I see." The stranger straightened up and looked from one end of the alley to the other, apparently checking if the coast was clear. "Well, I'm on my way somewhere . . . If ye want t'come with me I can get ye some food an' a warm place t'rest a while."

Laela was too weak by now to argue, and she clung to her rescuer as if he were her only friend in the world. "Yeah. Yeah. I'd . . . yeah."

# 4

# Wolf

The stranger led her out of the alley and away through the darkened streets. He moved like one who knew the city very well, but he kept to the shadows and the side streets, as if he were trying to hide. Laela followed him, keeping quiet and pathetically hoping that he would protect her as he had claimed he would.

Eventually, he came to a halt outside a modest-looking building. "Here we are. The sign of the Blue Moon. They know me here."

A tavern, Laela realised. She followed him inside more than gladly.

There weren't very many people within, and they showed only passing interest in the stranger—and given his shrouded face and body, Laela took it to mean that they did indeed know him. That reassured her a little.

He walked silently up to the bar and spoke softly to the man on the other side. As Laela came to join him, he turned to her, and said, "I've gotten us a room. Come on."

He took her up a flight of stairs and into a smallish space with a bed and a fireplace. There was a chair in front of it, and he gestured at her to sit in it.

Laela all but collapsed into the chair and stayed there for some time, soaking up the warmth from the fire. The stranger took another chair opposite her and waited in silence while a woman came in with bread, cheese, and a mug.

Laela ate ravenously and drank from the mug, which turned out to be full of beer.

The stranger ate nothing. His face, under the hood, was half-covered by a cloth that concealed everything except his black eyes. But he seemed peaceful enough, sitting there and just watching her.

Laela put down her mug. "Thanks," she said. "Yeh saved my life back there, yeh know . . . more'n that."

The stranger stirred. "Look at me."

Laela had forgotten not to make eye contact. "It's . . ."

He examined her face. "Look at them eyes. Ye're a half-breed, ain't ye?"

Laela wanted to hit him. "Yeah."

"I see, then. Can I ask what ye were doin' wanderin' around the streets in the middle of the night?"

"I travelled here," said Laela. "I'm lookin' for a new home."

"Yer accent ain't Northern," he observed. "Where are ye from?"

"Nowhere," said Laela. "Village in the South. Sturrick."

"Never heard of it. How did ye get here, then? They shouldn't've let ye through Guard's Post."

"Bribed the guards," said Laela. A half-truth was easier.

The stranger chuckled. "Clever girl. Why did ye want t'come here, though?"

Laela's eyes narrowed. "Why should I tell yeh? I don't even know who yeh are. Why's yer face covered up like that?"

"Call me Wolf," the stranger said briefly. "I'm someone who's got a good reason not t'let anyone see his face."

"Why?" said Laela.

He pushed the mug of beer toward her. "Tell me why yer came here, an' I'll tell ye that."

"Deal," said Laela. "I came here 'cause . . ." She paused. "'Cause who in the North is gonna call me a blackrobe or a darkwoman? Nobody so far. I blend in here, right? So long as no-one notices the eyes, I can pretend t'be a Northerner. Me dad died. I din't have nowhere else t'go."

"I see," said Wolf. "Not many people like the King, but he gave a home to outcasts, an' there's not many can say they've done the same. I'm sure he'd be flattered t'hear ye thought enough of his land t'come this far."

Laela shrugged. "Who are yeh, then, Wolf? Why are yeh hidin' like that?"

"Because I just escaped from prison," he said casually. "Don't want anyone recognisin' me; they'd drag me straight back an' make sure I never got out again."

Laela stared at him. "Prison? Why? What did yeh do?"

"Enough for ten death sentences," he said, still calm.

"Aren't the guards after yeh?" said Laela, with the horrible thought that if they were tracking him, they might find her, too, and who knew what they'd do to her?

"No," said Wolf. "They don't know I've escaped yet."

"Are yeh sure?"

"Why, d'ye doubt me?"

"I just *met* yeh," Laela pointed out. "How would I know anythin'?"

He chuckled. "True. Well, don't worry; we're safe. Nobody messes with me if they know what's good for 'em. Anyway . . . so what are ye going t'do now, Laela?"

"I dunno," she mumbled. "Them bastards took all my money. I was gonna try an' find a job . . ."

"Got any skills?"

"Not really. I can cook an' clean, an' I know how t'sew."

"Hm," said Wolf. "I dunno, Laela. Maybe ye can pass as a Northerner at first, but as soon as anyone looks closely at yer, they're gonna notice them beautiful blue eyes."

"But they wouldn't care, would they?" said Laela. "I'm only—"

"Only a Southerner," he said flatly.

"But I never did nothin' wrong!" she almost wailed.

"No, an' nor did most of the Southerners the King's rebels killed here all them years ago. Ye're young, Laela. Ye don't understand what that war meant. Us Northerners had been ground into the dirt by the sun worshippers for centuries. Half the people in this city have collar scars an' memories full of pain an' hard labour in mines an' building sites. That ain't somethin' ye forget in a hurry. An' when they see a blue-eyed Southerner, that's what they think of. An' ye . . . well." He sounded rather sad.

"I know," said Laela. "I know. I ain't just a Southerner. When yeh see me, yeh know one of yer own people bedded a Southerner. Betrayal." She had thought it many times.

Wolf nodded. "It's the mixing of North an' South. Southerners'd see a dirty barbarian, Northerners'd see an arrogant tyrant. Madness, ain't it?"

"Madness!" Laela almost shouted. "What am I supposed t'do? Where'm I supposed t'go? Where . . . ?" The hard but unavoidable realisation that he was right, mixed with the deep shock that had yet to fade away, overwhelmed her, and she began to sob again.

Wolf reached out awkwardly and patted her on the hand. "There, there. Ain't no sense t'be givin' up now, is there? Ye're a brave an' clever girl, ye are. Ye've survived this far; who says ye won't survive even further, eh?"

Laela fought to control herself. "But what can I do? Where can I go? I got no money, no home, no family . . . gods, I shouldn't've ever come here at all."

Wolf regarded her. "Well," he said eventually. "I s'pose ye could stay with me for a while, if ye wanted to."

Laela looked up, tear-streaked. "What? D'yeh have a home?"

"Of sorts," he said. "I'm goin' back there tonight. If ye want to, ye can come, too."

"Would there be room?" said Laela.

"I reckon so. What d'ye say? I'm sure we could find a few odd jobs for ye t'do around the place."

"Where is it?" said Laela. "Is it in the city?"

"Yeah. Ain't too far from here."

"But what about the guards?" said Laela. "Won't they know where yeh are?"

"Oh, don't worry about them," Wolf said carelessly. "They'd never find me. I ain't there t'be found when I don't want t'be."

Laela hesitated. She was still deeply suspicious of this man, whoever he was, even if he *had* saved her. And yet . . .

"How do I know I can trust yeh?" she said.

"Ye don't," said Wolf. "But I didn't have t'help ye, y'know. I was off on my way t'have a good time somewhere, an' I heard ye screamin', so I came t'help ye even though I could've just minded my own business. Guess I'm just soft-hearted." He snorted.

Laela suddenly felt ashamed. "I didn't mean it like that. It's just . . . well, why'd yeh want t'help me anyway? I ain't anybody."

"I'd have helped anyone in that situation," said Wolf. "An' how can I just leave ye to fend for yerself? I know this city, Laela. Ye wouldn't last a day. I ain't that . . . heartless."

*He's only helpin' me 'cause he knows I can't look after myself,* Laela thought bitterly. But what choice did she have? "I'll come with yeh, then," she said.

He nodded. "Good. Finish eatin', an' we'll go. Ye can tell me more about yerself while ye're at it, if ye like."

She wasn't thinking of it, but after a while the silence became uncomfortable as he just sat there and watched her eat, so she talked—giving him her story in bits and pieces.

"Dunno me parents' names. Mother was a Southerner. Lived in the North. Dad said . . . there was this Northerner. Criminal. Raped my mother. Dad was a guardsman; he chased the bastard an' saw him die tryin' t'get away. Then, after I was born, someone murdered her . . . Mum, I mean. So Dad took me away with him out of the North an' raised me himself. But he died." She paused to swallow some beer. "Drank himself to death."

Wolf sighed. "Yes . . . a lot of Southerners ran away out of the North when the war started. An' plenty of Northerners got out of control 'round that time. Wouldn't surprise me t'hear a lot of Southern women were raped like your mother. These things happen."

*These things happen. That's all very well for you t'say.* "Yeah, I'm sure they do," Laela muttered, and drained the beer. "So that's me," she said. "Parents didn't love each other, father was a criminal, foster dad died. Buried him myself. After that, I sold our house an' came North, hopin' t'find somethin' better. An' I found you."

"I wouldn't call myself somethin' better," said Wolf. "Better than those two scum, maybe."

Laela's feeling of shame returned. "Yeh did save me. I don't know what I'd do if I hadn't met yeh, Wolf."

There was a smile in his eyes as she said this. She wondered, suddenly, if his mouth was smiling, too, and what it would look like. She wished she could see his face.

"Are yeh ever gonna take that hood off?" she asked. To her embarrassment, she realised she was blushing.

"Maybe later," he said. His voice was a little muffled by the cloth.

"Right, right," said Laela, looking away from him and wishing she hadn't asked.

Wolf waited politely until she had finished eating. "Are ye ready t'go now?"

Laela stood up. "Ready as I'll ever be. Can I have my stuff back?"

He handed over the blanket roll. "C'mon, then. Stick close t'me, keep silent, do what I do. I ain't taken anyone this way before."

Laela adjusted the sword in her belt. "I'm ready."

"Good." He strode over to the window and opened it. Then, to her astonishment, he climbed out of it. She hurried after him and put her head through the window, but she couldn't see him anywhere on the ground. Where . . . ?

"Up here."

She looked up and saw him perched on the roof. "What the . . . ?"

"I told ye t'keep quiet," he said. "Pass yer stuff up t'me, an' I'll give ye a hand."

Laela pulled herself together and passed up her bundle. He hauled it up and dumped it beside him before offering her his hands. She took hold of them, and he pulled her through the window and up onto the roof though his fingers seemed clumsy.

Up on the roof, Laela straightened up and surveyed the view. Rooftops spread in every direction, studded with chimneys whose smoke drifted in front of the crescent moon.

"The Bear's moon," Wolf murmured. "Protection. Now, pick up yer stuff, an' let's go. Don't put a foot wrong, or ye'll fall."

Laela slung her bundle on her back. "I'm ready." She sounded more resolute than she felt.

Wolf set out. He moved with the balance and certainty of someone who had done this a hundred times, leaping from roof to roof like an alley cat. The gaps were small, but Laela still felt her stomach lurch when she reached the first one. She hesitated, but her companion was already leaving her behind, so she gritted her teeth and jumped.

She made it. Feeling a little more confident, she sped up. Wolf made it look easier than it was, but though she stumbled a few times, she managed to keep up one way or another.

They travelled this way for some time, and eventually Laela

was chilled to the bone. Her legs were trembling with fatigue, and she felt as if she hadn't slept in months.

Wolf stopped and waited for her to catch up. "We're ready t'go back down," he said. "Just follow my lead."

Laela nodded mutely and watched him climb down through the next gap, bracing himself against the walls on either side to stop himself from falling. When he reached the ground, he stopped and waved at her to follow.

Laela sighed grimly and began her own descent.

It was easier than she had expected, but her nerves kept her from relaxing, and she pushed against the walls so hard that once or twice she stopped herself altogether and had to rest before she could make herself continue. By the time she reached the ground, her mind was blank with exhaustion.

Wolf patted her on the shoulder. "Don't worry," he said. "We're almost there. No more climbing from here on."

Laela groaned and fell in behind him. They passed through a gate in a wall, and then had to cross a large, open space before they reached a building. Wolf opened a small side-door with a key, and ushered her inside. Once they were in, he closed and locked the door behind him.

"Now," he said. "Nothing left but a few stairs."

A few!

After the first ten flights, Laela was having fantasies about killing him. Stairs, stairs, and more stairs, up and up and up, on and on and on. She trudged along stoically, until white spots started to flash in front of her eyes. Wolf kindly relieved her of her possessions and went ahead of her, stopping occasionally to let her catch up.

"Nearly there!" he said, more than once.

Laela ground her teeth. She was too tired to say anything, but her mind was full of possibilities, each one ruder than the last.

Finally, Wolf said, "All right, let's stop for a rest."

Laela leant against the wall, then slid down it onto the floor and stayed there.

Wolf sat beside her, hugging his knees. "Take all the time you need. We don't have far to go now."

Laela managed to make a sound of mingled pain and disbelief.

Wolf chuckled. "Yes, these stairs actually do have a top. You've done very well so far, considering how tired you must be."

Laela grunted noncommittally.

"Well." Wolf yawned. "Let's do this last bit together, shall we?"

Somehow or other, Laela managed to drag herself to her feet. "Where *are* we?"

"Nearly home," Wolf said unhelpfully.

Laela muttered curses under her breath as the stairs continued. Wolf seemed to understand, and he didn't hurry her along. That made her like him a little better.

Finally, *finally*, the stairs ended at a modest wooden door.

Wolf unlatched it. "Through here," he said, and pushed it open.

Laela stepped through and into warm firelight. The room on the other side was quite large, and modestly furnished—there was a bearskin rug on the floor, and the walls were lined with wooden panelling. There was a bed there—it looked rather unused—and a very large fireplace. She saw an enormous archway set into the opposite wall, covered by heavy cloth curtains, and wondered briefly where it led to.

There were a couple of chairs in front of the fire, but other than a small writing desk, those were the only other pieces of furniture. Still, it looked like a home. For someone.

Laela collapsed into one of the chairs without waiting to be invited. "Thank Gryphus. I thought . . ."

Wolf put her belongings down on the floor and stretched, rubbing his back. "Argh. Ooh. Ow. Bloody thing. You'd think after this long . . . well." He turned to her. "Home sweet home. What d'you think?"

"It's nice," said Laela. She paused. "What's that smell?"

It was a strange heavy, almost spicy smell. Musty. It made her think of some kind of animal.

Wolf sniffed. "What smell? Ah, this cloth's stopping me from smelling anything. Wait a moment . . . I may as well take it off now."

He pulled off his gloves and tossed them onto the bed, and Laela saw the long, elegant Northern fingers on his right hand as he pulled the hood away and shook out his hair. It was black,

of course—long, thick, and curly. He took off the heavy cloak
that had hidden most of his body, and then untied the cloth from
his face and turned to face her.

He was a young man—probably no older than her. He was
tall and lean like most Northerners, and carried himself with a
certain grace. His face was pale and angular, marred by a long,
twisted scar under one eye, and he wore a neat, pointed
chin-beard.

He shook himself. "That's better. *This* is my face." His eyes
smiled again, but now Laela could see his mouth, she didn't see
it smile, too.

"Er . . ."

Wolf shook his head and turned away. "I'll just get changed
if you don't mind."

Without another word, he took off the tunic he was wearing
and put it away in a box next to the bed. As he straightened up,
Laela felt her stomach lurch.

He was hideously scarred. She had never imagined that anyone could be so deeply wounded so many times and in so many
different places, and still be alive. Pale lines traced their way
over his skin, interspersed with ugly red marks where the cuts
had gone deeper. He looked as if he had been stabbed over and
over again.

The worst of them was in the middle of his back, just to the
left of his spine. It was as wide as her hand, and its edges were
swollen and blackened, as if they were rotting. As he turned
toward her, Laela saw its twin on his chest, over his heart.

*Oh, Gryphus,* she thought, nearly sick with horror. *It went
right through him . . .*

Wolf suddenly looked embarrassed. "Oh, gods, I'm sorry. I
forgot . . ." He hastily snatched up a piece of clothing that was
lying on the bed and slipped into it.

It was a long, black robe, beautifully decorated with embroidered spiral patterns and tailored to fit his slim body. He did up
the fastenings over his chest, fumbling with his left hand. The
fingers on it were twisted and bent at unnatural angles, and the
forefinger looked completely paralysed.

Laela found her voice. "What *happened* to yeh?"

Wolf looked grim. "Too much."

She stood up and came toward him, forgetting her fear. "All

them scars . . ." She reached out to touch his hand, and he let her hold it and turn it over, touching the warped fingers. They were painfully red and swollen around the knuckles, and they cracked horribly when they moved. "Gods. Yer fingers . . . what happened?"

Wolf looked back at her, his expression curiously ashamed. "Laela . . ."

She let go and stepped back, suddenly horrified. "Oh, Gryphus, I didn't mean . . . I'm sorry, I—"

Wolf clutched at his ruined hand. "Nobody's ever touched it like that before," he said. He sounded a little shaky. "Nobody . . . nobody likes to go near it. I know it looks ugly . . . I try to keep it covered up . . ." He rubbed it nervously, until the fingers cracked.

"What happened?" said Laela. "How did yeh get all them scars? What did they do to yeh?"

"My fingers . . ." He wrapped them in his other hand to hide them. "This is what they do to you when they want information."

Laela went cold. "Torture?"

"Yes."

She shuddered. "The King lets them do that to his people? What kind've monster is he?"

"A monster," Wolf snapped. "Hah! The Southerners did that to me. In a cell under this very city. Broke my fingers . . . one . . . by one."

"Griffiners?" said Laela. "Griffiners do that?"

"Always have," said Wolf. "But I was dangerous . . . a dangerous criminal. I had information they desperately wanted. I didn't give it to them. And I made them pay. I made them pay a hundred times. Didn't fix my fingers, though, did it?"

Laela stared at him. Against her will, she thrilled at his words. "What had yeh done?"

"You don't want to know," said Wolf. "Now, as far as . . ."

"Where *are* we?" Laela asked suddenly. "What buildin' is this? Why all those stairs?"

Wolf looked incredulous. "You don't know?"

"Wait. We ain't—"

"We're in the *Eyrie*, Laela," said Wolf. "This is my home. This is where I live and work . . . This is my prison. Of course, my guards don't know I sneak out most nights."

A horrible fear and bewilderment ate away at her. "No. This ain't . . . this ain't . . . Who *are* yeh?"

Wolf tugged at his beard. "I know," he said wretchedly. "I shouldn't have brought you back here, but what was I to do? You needed help, and I couldn't bring myself to leave you . . ."

Laela turned sharply as he suddenly stopped talking and looked to his left.

The curtains over the archway had moved. Laela could hear something stirring on the other side.

"Gods damn it!" Wolf cursed. "Laela, stay behind me."

He pushed her behind him and stepped toward the archway, but too late. They parted, and something pushed its way through.

Laela staggered backward, wide-eyed, and fell.

It was a griffin . . . the biggest griffin she had ever seen—the biggest living creature she had ever seen, or imagined. Its bird-like forequarters were covered in silver feathers, but the magnificent head had a diamond-shaped cap of black and two long plumes over the ears. The hooked beak was black, too, and the eyes, glaring straight at her, were silver.

Wolf reached out to touch the creature, making strange, harsh sounds in his throat. The griffin dipped its head toward him, and he scratched it under the beak, still making the sounds and clicking his teeth every so often.

The griffin rasped something back, and then raised its head to look at Laela again. It took a threatening step toward her, its beak open to hiss.

Laela almost whimpered. "Keep it away from me. In Gryphus' name, don't let it—"

Wolf put himself in the way and made more of those strange sounds.

*Griffish,* Laela thought through her terror. *He's speaking griffish. He's a griffiner. He's—*

The griffin snorted angrily but made no move to come closer. It rasped again and butted Wolf with its beak before abruptly turning away. It went back through the archway, and Laela saw its muscular hindquarters—covered in glossy pitch-black fur.

Wolf breathed a sigh of relief. "You were lucky there. He's in a bad mood tonight."

Laela managed to get up. "What—that was—*you*—"

He turned to her. "That was Skandar. My best friend. My *only* friend, I think."

"But you . . . you . . . in the Eyrie . . . with him . . ."

"Yes." Wolf sighed. "You're right. I am King Arenadd Tara-nisäii, and this is my Eyrie."

# 5

# The Dark Lord

Wolf—Arenadd Taranisäii, the Dark Lord, King of the North—watched Laela in silence, almost as if he were waiting for something.

Laela gaped at him. *No. It ain't possible. It can't be . . .*

But it was. She knew it was him. The black robe, the home in the Eyrie . . . the giant griffin living next door to him . . .

"But yer so *young!*" she exclaimed, finding her voice all of a sudden.

Arenadd scratched his beard. "I'm forty next week. I know I don't look it. Laela, let me explain . . ."

"Explain!" said Laela. "Yer the King! Yeh rule the North— what in Gryphus' name were yeh doin' runnin' about the streets in the middle of the night? An' what do yeh want with me? An' why—"

He waved her into silence. "I sneak out, all right? I go out into the city sometimes. To listen to my people. To have some time to myself. They don't know I do it, and I'd prefer it if you didn't tell anyone about it."

"Then why did yeh bring me here?" said Laela.

"I already told you: because you need help. I can give you a place to live—I can protect you."

"But why?" said Laela. "Why d'yeh care?"

Arenadd's eyes were suddenly cold. "I didn't have to save you, you know. I could have left you to die. I can take you back out into the city and leave you there if that's what you'd prefer."

Laela backed away. "I'm sorry," she blurted. "I'm just . . . well, thanks. I don't . . ."

It was too much. So much had already happened to her, so many terrors, and now this. Now she was seeing *him*. The Dark Lord. The most feared and hated man in Cymria, the most . . .

"Listen," said Arenadd. "It's been a long day, and you're obviously tired. I'll arrange a room for you, and you can get some rest."

"I—" Laela hesitated, not knowing what to say or do.

Arenadd came toward her and touched her on the shoulder. "There's no need to be afraid of me." She recoiled from him, and he withdrew immediately. "I'm a powerful friend to have, Laela," he said abruptly. "Think about that."

Laela managed to nod.

"Then come with me."

The rest of the night passed in a kind of haze. Laela let herself be ushered out of the King's bedroom and into the Eyrie proper, where a couple of servants were unceremoniously woken up and ordered to prepare a room for her. The room in question turned out to be a surprisingly large and well-furnished one—in fact, it looked more decorated than the King's own. The servants efficiently dusted off the furniture and put fresh linen on the bed, and Laela was left on her own to stare at her new quarters in wonder.

The King had somehow managed to vanish without her noticing, so she shut the door behind her and sat down on the bed to rest and try to think. But her mind refused to take in everything that had happened.

*I'm living with the Dark Lord.*

She thought of the deceptively young-looking but appallingly scarred man she had met, trying to reconcile that image with the spectre of the one Southerners called the Dark Lord. The man who had single-handedly started the civil war in the South. The man who had massacred hundreds of Southerners, who had personally killed the pregnant Eyrie Mistress of

Malvern, who had sold his soul to the evil Night God and been given vile powers, who . . .

Gryphus help her, she was *living* with him. She had met him face-to-face, had *touched* him in sympathy, had . . .

It was all too much to take in. But at least, she thought, she was safe now.

Maybe.

In his own room, Arenadd was hardly less agitated than his unwilling guest.

He paced back and forth in front of the fire, his brow furrowed. His heavy leather boots made no sound on the rug.

For a long time now he'd suspected . . . no, had *known* . . . well, everyone knew, didn't they? Saeddryn certainly did. He knew what she'd been whispering behind his back. Everyone was, after all, and who could blame them? Time was turning him eccentric.

"Night God help me, what am I doing?" he mumbled aloud. "She's terrified of me. Why would she want to be here?"

But something about her, *something*, had compelled him to help her. Perhaps it had been just her dire situation. Or perhaps it was her courage.

He smiled to himself. Not many people would have dared to speak to him the way she had. At least, not when they knew who he was. Laela was fearless. He liked that.

He paused and winced, putting a hand to his chest. Gods, it still hurt. After so long, it still hurt. But, then, so many things did.

Arenadd slumped into a chair by the fire. He knew he should probably sleep at least briefly . . . not that he needed to sleep much any more.

Instead, he picked up the jug of wine he'd left on the table and poured some of its contents into a mug, which he drained in a few long swallows. He refilled the mug and drank more slowly, while the familiar, dizzy warmth embraced him like an old friend.

Well, she could stay for a while. She had obviously had a hard life, and it wouldn't hurt her to have some respite. He could give her some work in the Eyrie to justify her presence to everyone else. Yes. That would work.

The wine did its work as he got closer to the bottom of the jug. Yes. She could be a servant, and would have a good enough life—certainly better than she could have expected elsewhere, and he could forget about her and worry about more important matters. Yes.

He emptied the jug and made a good dent in a second one before he fell asleep in the chair. In his dreams, the Night God's voice whispered to him, trying to make him listen. He ignored her.

Laela did sleep that night, and far more deeply than she would have expected. She was too exhausted, both emotionally and physically, to resist the lure of her new bed, and though she was still deeply frightened, she pushed her doubts aside and got into it.

It was wonderfully soft and comfortable, and she drifted off very quickly.

Next morning, she was woken up by a servant.

"Get up an' get dressed; the King wants t'see yer."

Laela sat up sharply, her drowsiness vanishing almost instantly as sick recollection came back. "The King?" she said stupidly.

"Aye, so get a move on, girl—he doesn't like t'be kept waitin'."

Laela dragged herself out of bed and struggled back into her travel-stained wool dress. She also put her sword-belt on, including the sword.

The servant made no move to stop her and stood by impassively while she laced up her boots and dragged a comb through her hair. "Good, now come with me," she said, the instant that was done.

Laela thought briefly of arguing or trying to leave, but only briefly. She was in the Eyrie—probably right at the top, judging by all the stairs she'd had to climb. There would be guards everywhere. The chances of escaping were next to none. She was as good as imprisoned.

Frightened, but a little angry, she followed the servant out of the room.

Now she got a proper chance to see the inside of the Eyrie,

she couldn't help but be impressed. It was a stone building, of course, but the walls were lined with wood, and there were thick carpets on the floor. Tapestries hung on the walls here and there, too, between ornate silver lamps, and she realised she must be in the richest part of the Eyrie.

Another thing she noticed was how *big* the place was. This corridor was easily wide enough for an ox—probably wider, she thought.

She wondered about that as the servant hustled her on. They passed several doors along the way, and those were abnormally huge as well. When Laela noticed that, she finally realised why—they had to be that size so that griffins could use them.

The thought only helped to increase her sense of dread.

Eventually, her guide took her up a ramp and to a door that had a pair of armed guards standing on either side of it. They both glanced curiously at Laela but said nothing and stayed at their posts as the servant nudged her through the door. "In ye go."

Laela hesitated, but the servant had already departed, and the guards shut the door behind her.

She found herself in a fair-sized room furnished with a fire-place and a large table and chairs. And seated at the far end of it was . . .

Her heartbeat quickened.

King Arenadd was already coming to meet her. "Good morning. Did you sleep well?"

Laela swallowed. "I . . . yeah."

"Good. Now, come and sit with me."

It didn't sound like a request. Laela thought he probably wasn't used to having people say no. She walked numbly over to the chair he indicated and sat in it. There was food laid out on the table in front of it.

The King returned to his original seat—directly opposite her. "Help yourself. You must be hungry."

Laela looked uncertainly at the bread, milk, and fruit. For a moment, she wondered if it could be poisoned. But what sense did *that* make? If he wanted her dead, he would have seen to it already.

"Go on," he interrupted. "It's perfectly fine."

*Just do what he tells yeh,* she told herself. *Just play along.*

Arenadd nodded in apparent satisfaction as she helped herself to an apple. "Settling in all right?"

Laela swallowed. "It's nice here, Sire."

"Good. Don't let me interrupt."

He sat in silence and watched her eat, apparently in no hurry to do anything or eat anything himself. He was still wearing the robe he'd put on the previous night, and if anything, he looked even paler and gaunter than he had then.

It was one of the most uncomfortable meals of Laela's life, but she was too hungry to stop. She ate her fill, and then looked uncertainly at her host.

"Finished?"

Laela nodded mutely.

Instantly, Arenadd summoned a servant to clear away the leftovers. "You look a little happier now," he said once they were alone again. "Now then. I was hoping that, while you're here, we could have a little chat."

Laela kept her eyes on his face. "All right . . . Sire. Uh . . . yeah. Sure. Sire."

"Calm down. Now, I was just wondering . . ."

Laela watched him. Where was this going?

Arenadd paused. For a moment, he looked very slightly confused, but the moment passed, and he was impassive again. "You told me last night you'd come from the South. Obviously, going by your accent, you've lived there all your life."

"Yes, Sire."

He sat back. "Do tell me about it."

Laela blinked. "What, the South? Sire?"

"Yes, the South. I haven't been there in a very long time."

Now, hearing his voice and free of the distraction and tiredness of the previous night, Laela finally noticed what was odd about the way he spoke. "Yeh sound like a Southerner," she said, without thinking. "Yeh don't talk like a b— a Northerner. Sire." She felt herself going red. *Gryphus, girl, keep yer damned mouth shut!*

Arenadd's expression did not waver. "I was born in the South," he said evenly. "I didn't come here until after the Night God had chosen me."

Laela shivered internally. *The Night God's creature.* "Well, I . . . uh . . . I was brought up in Sturrick," she stammered. "Sire. Uh . . ."

"Yes? So where is this place, exactly? I don't believe I've heard of it."

"Er . . . well, it's a village, Sire," said Laela. "Bigger than most, but not really a town. Farmers, mostly, but it's on the trade route, so there are some merchants. I'd say it's due t'get bigger some day, Sire."

"I see. How far away is it from the Northgates?"

"Not sure, Sire. Not that far. I didn't take too long t'get there—reckon I could've walked it in a month or two."

Arenadd nodded slowly. "Hm. What did you see along the way?"

"Not much, Sire," said Laela. "Villages, countryside . . . not much else. No big cities 'round there. Didn't see my first one till I got here, Sire. City, I mean. That was Malvern."

"Good, good. No griffiners?"

"No, Sire. Never even saw a griffin till I came here." She thought briefly of the one she had seen by the grave—but why mention it?

"What about the people, then?" said Arenadd. "The ones you talked to. What did they say?"

"About what, Sire?" said Laela.

"The griffiners," said Arenadd. "And what they're doing."

"Oh. Well, I . . . they . . ." Laela trailed off, as realisation finally dawned on her.

"Yes?" Arenadd prompted.

"They, er . . . they . . . dunno much, Sire." She was babbling now, trying to think. "I'm just a peasant girl, Sire," she said at last. "I wouldn't know that much."

"But you might know something," said Arenadd. "What are the people saying?"

Laela thought quickly. "Well, after Eagleholm fell, Canran sent griffiners an' soldiers t'grab some of its lands, an' I heard tell they got a good chunk, but the Withypool gang came from the other way, an' they ended up in a scrap. Canran did well but Withypool got the upper hand somehow, an' in the end Canran's Eyrie burned, an' most of their griffins went over t'Withypool.

That was a while ago, though, Sire. By the time Dad an' me came t'live in Sturrick, Withypool owned that land, but it was all disorganised, Dad said. They couldn't rule so much land from all the way over on the coast, so they was buildin' a new Eyrie further West."

Arenadd leant forward over the table. "Where?"

"Dunno, Sire, but I'd say somewhere where Eagleholm lands used t'be. Probably halfway between Withypool an' where Canran was. Best place to control the lands all around. Sire."

He blinked. "Did you work that out all on your own?"

"Yes, Sire." Laela looked away. "I thought it made sense . . . It was only a guess, like."

"It was a bloody good one," said Arenadd, and the offhand Southern accent and phrasing caught Laela off guard.

"Thanks, Sire. Is that . . . is that everythin'?"

"You tell me," said Arenadd. "Is that all you have to say?"

"I ain't heard nothin' about no plans to attack yeh, Sire," Laela said with sudden boldness. "If that's what yer wonderin'. They ain't strong enough; they're spread all over the place. Too much buildin', too much reorganisin', an' they got no slaves now t'do the work for 'em. An' besides, no-one'd attack *you*, Sire. They ain't mad. They know what yeh can do—they know about yer powers. They're too *scared*, Sire. *I* would be," she added.

Arenadd stared at her, apparently nonplussed. Then he burst out laughing. His laugh was a harsh, humourless thing—one that sounded like it hadn't been used in a long time. "Ye gods!" he exclaimed. "What a find I picked up off the street last night! Traveller, fighter, master negotiator, political strategist, and now a tactician!" He laughed again. "Next I suppose you'll tell me you're a griffiner as well."

Laela gaped at him. "I ain't . . . well, it was just . . . I shouldn't't've . . ." Suddenly, his mocking laughter made anger flare in her. "I've given yeh all the information yeh wanted, Sire, so now yeh've been repaid for yer trouble. Can I go now?"

He stopped laughing. "I wasn't making fun of you, Laela—I was laughing at myself. I wasn't expecting payment, but it was kind of you to provide the information, and I appreciate the free advice. And of course I'll let you go. But there's just one last question I wanted to ask you."

"Yes? Sire."

Arenadd rubbed his broken fingers. "I just wanted to ask . . . does the name *Aeaei ran kae* mean anything to you?"

Laela stared. "What, Sire?"

*"Aeaei ran kae,"* he repeated. "It's griffish, in case you're curious."

"I, uh . . . no, Sire," said Laela. "I don't know any griffish."

"Obviously. Well, then, have you ever heard tell of someone called the Sun's Champion? Gryphus' Warrior? The Chosen One?"

"Oh. Yeah," said Laela. "Of course. Everyone knows about that, Sire."

*"What* do they know?"

Laela hesitated. "Well . . ."

"Go on. I'm listening."

"Well, uh . . ." she plunged on. "They say yer . . . that the Night God chose yeh, Sire. T'fight for her."

Arenadd's eyes were as cold as ice. "I was her assassin and her warlord, yes," he intoned.

Laela drew back. "Yeah . . . yeah, that. Chosen. So they say Gryphus . . . the Day God . . . chose someone, too. A Southerner, t'fight for him against . . . well . . ."

"Against me," Arenadd supplied. "Continue."

"Gryphus' Chosen was like a warrior meant t'fight yeh, Sire," said Laela. "His name was Erian Rannagonson. Erian the Bastard. From Eagleholm. An' he . . . they say Gryphus came t'him in a vision an' gave him a special weapon what he was supposed t'use to kill yeh."

"Hah. And then what?"

"Well . . ." Laela took a deep breath. "So he met yeh in the Sun Temple here at Malvern when yeh came here with yer followers. He fought yeh, an' yeh killed him, an' so the Night God won." She stopped there, having left out the part of the story in which the Dark Lord Arenadd had stabbed the sun's champion in the back.

Arenadd snorted. "I killed him, all right. He put a nice hole in me first, mind you. So that's it, then, is it? The Chosen One found the magical weapon, fought me with it, and died for his trouble? That's all they say?"

"Yes, Sire," said Laela.

"Nothing else to the story?" Arenadd persisted. "Nothing about a *new* champion, or about how the sun shall rise again some day and banish the darkness forever and so on and so forth?"

In fact, there were several such stories, but Laela had recognised them as the wishful thinking they were and shook her head. "No, Sire."

Arenadd stared at her for a long moment, silent and expressionless—as if he were waiting for something. Laela couldn't meet his gaze and kept her eyes on the table instead.

"Well, then," Arenadd said abruptly. "If that's all you have to tell me . . ."

"It is, Sire," said Laela, daring to look up. "I mean . . . I think it is."

"It's enough for one day, anyway," he said. "And I've got other things to attend to, so I'll let you go."

She shivered with relief. "Thanks, Sire."

Arenadd stood up. "I've made arrangements," he said briskly. "There'll be some new clothes waiting for you in your room, and one of the servants will fill a bath for you."

Laela didn't know what to say. "Thanks, Sire."

"No need to thank me," said Arenadd. "Consider this your reward. You can stay in my Eyrie for as long as you want, and I'll see to it that you have everything you need."

Laela opened her mouth to ask why, but all she ended up saying was, "Yes, Sire."

Arenadd nodded formally to her and left the room.

Moments later, she found herself being escorted back to her quarters, where a bath was indeed being filled for her. The servants left soap and a bottle of something they said was for washing her hair, and left her to her own devices.

The sight of the hot, steaming water was more than enough to cheer Laela up, and she lost no time in stripping off her old clothes and getting in. The water embraced her, soaking warmth into her like a blanket that had just been dried in front of a fire.

She sighed, a long, blissful sigh that released all the tension that had been tying her stomach into sick knots, and finally let herself relax.

By the time she'd luxuriated in the water and washed herself as well as she could, she felt much better. And some fresh clothes had been laid out on the bed—a plain but well-made woollen dress, dyed pale blue, and even a new pair of shoes. She put the dress on very gratefully, and sat on the bed, absent-mindedly running her fingers through her wet hair.

*So that's it,* she thought. *That's why he brought me here. For information. He just wanted t'ask me a lot of questions about what's goin' on in the South, because no-one he knows has been there in yonks. Mystery solved.*

But she didn't seriously believe that.

Still . . . looking around at her new home, and still enjoying the feeling of being clean and well-fed for the first time in months, Laela's practical side took over. It didn't matter why she was here—her host obviously had no interest in hurting her, and she had everything she needed. She could recover from her journey, take advantage of everything being offered to her, and consider her next move when she was ready. Simple.

As she got up and went in search of a comb, something else occurred to her.

*Holy Gryphus, I just gave information to the Dark Lord Arenadd. I betrayed my own birthplace.*

She snorted. As if anyone in the South would know, let alone care about what she did. It had never occurred to her to feel loyal toward her birth-nation, and she didn't feel it now. *Anyway,* she added to herself, *I'm nobody. I'd never make a difference.*

# 6

## Living with Shadows

A nd that was how Laela's life in Malvern began.

She spent the first two days as she'd planned to—recovering from her journey. The Eyrie's servants continued to look after her, bringing three solid meals every day and providing her with more new clothes and a bath whenever she asked for one. They were polite but distant with her—apparently interested in doing their jobs and nothing else—and brushed off her attempts at conversation. She saw nothing more of the King during that time, which at first made her feel relieved, but it didn't take long for her to start feeling bored and lonely.

She didn't know how much freedom she had in the Eyrie, so at first she stayed in her room and was careful not to stray any further than the corridor outside. But boredom quickly supplanted caution, and she decided that it wouldn't hurt to wander around a little. With that vague plan in mind, she left her room on the third morning and set out.

She didn't know exactly what she'd been expecting to find when she first left, but in any case, she was disappointed.

The tower's interior looked like nothing but an endless corridor slowly spiralling downward, mostly because that was exactly what it was. Doors lined it at intervals, and every so often she came across an oversized, glassless window—obviously meant for griffins to enter by.

Before long, bored, she began tentatively exploring the rooms—poking her head through the doors that were open.

Most of them led into griffiner lodgings, and some were occupied, but she managed to remain unnoticed. A few people did see her, but she avoided eye contact, and none of them paid her much attention.

Emboldened, and aware now that she was probably the only Southern-born woman able to see the interior of the greatest Northern stronghold in the world, she sped up, turned a corner, and walked straight into a very large griffin.

She halted, frozen in shock.

The griffin paused, too, one enormous forepaw still raised.

As Laela hesitated, a voice spoke in some harsh language, and a woman appeared, walking forward from the griffin's side. She was middle-aged and one of her eyes was covered by a round leather patch. The other eye glared at Laela as she spoke again in that same language. It sounded like a command.

"I don't understand," said Laela, backing away.

The woman's eye narrowed. "I said, get out of the way," she snapped, using Cymrian this time. "Who are ye, anyway? What're ye doin' in here?"

Laela tried not to look at the griffin, which was hissing. "I'm, uh . . . Laela. I'm stayin' here."

The eye narrowed further. "Why would that be? Ye ain't no griffiner."

"I dunno," Laela said honestly.

She had been going to say that the King himself had brought her here, but at that moment the griffin suddenly moved. It came close, brushing the one-eyed woman aside, and sniffed at Laela as the red griffin had done by her father's grave.

Laela cringed away, ducking her head to protect herself. "Please, just let me go. I ain't done nothin'. The King said—"

Without any warning, the griffin reared up violently, beak open. It made a horrible screeching, snarling sound, and at that Laela's nerve broke, and she ran.

An almighty thud came from behind her, and as she ran she heard the rush of feathers and the thump of paws and knew that the griffin was chasing her.

Heart in her mouth, she put her head down and broke into a flat sprint. She had always been fast, and she managed to keep ahead of the griffin, but not far enough ahead to lose it or to duck through one of the doors. She could hear its talons tearing up the floor. And it was gaining on her.

Panic-stricken, she hurtled around another corner and straight into someone coming the other way. Her momentum bowled them both over, and she found herself sprawling on the floor on top of an unpleasantly bony shape. She lifted herself off, and found herself looking into the face of King Arenadd himself.

Laela screamed and rolled off him.

The King sat up, a little dazedly. "Ow. What the . . . ?"

The griffin had halted. Instinctively, Laela hid behind the King as he stood up.

He rubbed his head. "Laela, there you are. What in the gods' names were you doing running around down here?"

The griffin hissed uncertainly but backed off when the King spoke to it in griffish.

A moment later, the woman appeared, huffing with the effort. She stopped when she saw the King, drawing herself up and eyeing him.

"Saeddryn."

The woman stepped closer, gesturing at Laela and speaking rapidly in what she had to assume was the Northern tongue. He replied in the same language, and a brief, rapid conversation took place.

It ended when the woman backed away, wearing a look of complete disgust. She turned it on Laela. "Sometimes I have doubts about ye, Arenadd," she said. "An' ye—half-breed . . . if I were ye, I wouldn't stay long. Ye may think ye're different, but trust me—he'll be the death of ye. Maybe not soon, but one day."

That said, she turned on her heel and walked off. The griffin paused to stare balefully at Laela and followed with a swish of its tail.

Once they were gone, the King turned to Laela. "Oops."

She cringed away from him. "Oh, gods, please, I'm so sorry, I didn't mean t'run into yeh like that, Sire, I . . ."

He smiled crookedly at her. "I'm sure I'll live. What in the Night God's name were you doing down here, anyway?"

"I dunno what happened," Laela mumbled. "I was walkin'

along, like, an' I met up with them two—that one-eyed hag an' the griffin, an' then the griffin just came at me, an' I ran."

Arenadd chuckled. "Yes, apparently he thought you were a spy. I told him you weren't."

"Who was that hag anyway, Sire?" said Laela, calming down.

Arenadd paused to smooth his hair. "The, uh, 'one-eyed hag' would be my cousin, Lady Saeddryn, the High Priestess of the Moon Temple here in Malvern."

Laela blanched. "I . . . uh . . . I . . . didn't know yeh had relatives, Sire . . ."

He chuckled again. "Not many, but Saeddryn and her family certainly count. Anyway . . . I was just going to lunch. Would you care to join me?"

Saying no after knocking him over felt like one rudeness too many, so she nodded.

Lunch turned out to be bread and cheese for Laela, and several cups of wine for the King.

"Aren't yeh gonna have some, Sire?" Laela asked, as he was polishing off the third cup.

He put down his cup and refilled it. "I just need something to keep me going . . . I'm not hungry anyway."

Watching him, Laela felt a sick, sad churning in her stomach. She pushed her plate toward him. "I'm done with this, Sire. If yeh want any."

He stared at her, expressionless. His eyes were fathomless and had no brightness to them. Looking into them for a moment, Laela felt as if she were looking into an empty pit.

She did not look away.

Arenadd put his cup aside and picked up a piece of bread. "Thank you," he said softly, and bit into it.

Laela couldn't help but smile. "I reckoned yeh could do with some feedin' up, Sire."

He finished the bread. "Is that so?" He took another piece. "May as well have some more, then."

She watched him eat. Gods, this was strange—too strange. To be here, with him, seeing him do something as normal as munch on a piece of rye bread. It didn't have much to do with the cackling, blood-soaked lunatic of popular myth. But, then, popular myth had very little to do with real life.

"Sire?" she ventured. "I was wonderin' . . ."

"Hmm?"

Laela stared at her lap. "I can't help but wonder what yeh said to that lady—Saeddryn. Yeh don't have t'tell me, Sire," she added hastily.

The King shrugged. "I told her you were my new mistress."

Laela choked. *"What?* I mean . . . what, Sire?"

He reached for another piece of bread. "I hope that didn't offend you, but it felt like the simplest explanation. Why else would I have an attractive young woman staying with me?"

*Why indeed,* Laela thought. "Uh . . . Sire . . . yeh don't . . . want t'make it like . . . real, do yeh?"

He started. "What? No, Laela. I've had enough lovers over the years. I don't need another one. But you do like staying here, don't you?"

Laela scratched her ear. "I ain't been here long, Sire, but I dunno where else I'd go. I ain't got anyone who'd take care of me, an' I ain't got no money."

Arenadd looked pleased. "Then I have an offer for you."

"What is it, Sire?"

"Laela, would you like to live in the North forever?"

She looked him in the eye. "Yeah. I would, Sire."

"Would you like to become a citizen of my Kingdom?"

Laela started. "Uh . . . what would I have t'do, Sire?"

"Oh, not much. You'd get everything every child of the North gets—you'll be taught how to read and write, how to speak our language. And you'll be taught about the Night God, of course. And once you were done with your education, you'd go through the womanhood ceremony in the Moon Temple."

Outwardly, Laela was expressionless. Inside, she was thinking furiously.

Part of her was filled with fear and disgust. *Live here, forever? Worship the Night God—worship* darkness? *Let the Dark Lord be my ruler?*

But another part—a secret part of her, the part filled with anger and bitterness, whispered a different kind of wisdom. *Do it,* it said. *Go along with it. You ain't never had it so good as yeh do here, girl—see sense! He ain't no Dark Lord—he's just another man. He's a drunk, obviously, an' a nutter, too. He's taken a likin' to yeh for whatever reason—who cares why? He's*

*offerin' yeh everythin' yeh need . . . everythin' yeh want. Who
cares if yeh start worshippin' the Night God? When did Gryphus
ever answer any of yer prayers, anyway?*

Very slowly, she nodded. "I'll do it, Sire. If yeh want me to,
I'll live here an' . . . be a darkwoman."

She felt a secret thrill as she said those words.

Arenadd sat back. "I shall be proud to have you as one of my
subjects, Laela."

Laela smiled at him. "It's nice t'be wanted, Sire."

The next day, Laela was escorted to a large room in the tower,
not too far from the spot where she had encountered Saeddryn.
It was lined with bookshelves.

There was a young man waiting there for her.

Laela regarded him cautiously. "Hullo."

The man stood up and smiled at her. "Ye're Laela?"

"Yeah, I am. Who are yeh?"

The man was perhaps a little younger than her, his black hair
cropped close to his skull. But he had a nice, easy smile. "I'd be
Yorath, son of Yorath. Pleased t'meet ye, Laela."

Laela smiled back at him. "Pleased t'meet you, too, Yorath
Yorathson."

Yorath grinned. "The King's asked me t'be yer teacher in
readin' an' writin' an' speakin' our language. So if ye'd like t'sit
down, we can get started."

Laela sat down at a table with him. "I dunno if I can do it. I
never studied other languages before, like, an' I can't even
really read much in Cymrian."

"Don't worry, I can help ye," said Yorath. "I've done this
before. That's why they asked me t'do it."

"Really?" said Laela. "Who'd yeh teach before?"

"Children," said Yorath. "I work in the Eyrie school. I help
the teachers—one day, maybe I'll be one of 'em. An' I say, if
five-year-old children can learn, so can ye!"

"I'll do me best," said Laela, liking him.

"I trust ye," said Yorath. "Now then, let's start with the
basics . . ."

The first lesson began, and Laela paid careful attention as
her new tutor showed her how to draw the sharp Northern runes,

one by one. He started with just the first few, and made her copy them over and over again until she knew them by heart. After that, he taught her a few simple words in the Northern language—"The 'dark tongue,' some call it."

Laela worked her hardest, and thanks to Yorath's patience and good nature, it was easier than she had expected. She still felt like a child for not knowing it already, but her teacher didn't criticise her, and she let herself relax.

"There!" he said, after a good chunk of time had passed. "Ye're gettin' the idea already."

"They're nice-lookin', them runes," said Laela, looking over the pages she had filled. "It's sorta weird, though, t'think they can mean words."

"It's odd, yeah, when ye think about it," Yorath conceded. "But it serves us well enough, eh?"

"I s'pose."

"Well, it's lunchtime now, an' ye've probably done enough for one day," said Yorath, sitting back. "Take some paper with ye an' practise the runes I taught ye today. Tomorrow, ye can show me how well ye remember them."

"I will," said Laela. She paused. "How long d'yeh think it'll take for me t'learn all this?"

"Hard to say," said Yorath. "The basics shouldn't take too long, but it'll be years before ye're really fluent in our language, an' our writin' . . . well, that'll take a while, too."

She sighed. "Yeh gotta start somewhere, I s'pose."

"Ye're not in a hurry t'go somewhere else, are ye?"

"Doubt it," said Laela.

"There's no hurry then, is there? Now, I'd better be goin'."

He left the library, and she went, too, carrying her precious paper. She thought quickly of talking to him some more—finding some reason they could have lunch together—but he left before she could think of anything, and she went her own way, feeling very slightly depressed.

When she arrived at the dining hall, where she'd been told to go for lunch, she found Arenadd waiting for her.

"Sire."

He got up from his seat and came toward her. "Don't worry, I'm not going to stay too long. How did your first lesson go?"

"Good. I learned some runes. Some words, too."

Arenadd nodded. "Good, good. I'm sure you'll have no trouble learning. I came by here because I had some news for you."

"What is it, Sire?"

"Your friend from the street," said Arenadd. "You may remember him—his name is Aled."

Laela tensed. "Yeah?"

"Last night my guards caught up with him. He's been assaulting women all over the city, it seems. Last night, he made the mistake of trying it behind a tavern where someone saw him and called the guard. He's in prison as we speak."

Laela felt sick. "Oh."

Arenadd reached into his robe and brought out a small bag. "They searched his house after the arrest—I think you might recognise this."

Laela grabbed it. "My money!"

"I think most of it is still there. As for Aled . . . tomorrow night is the Blood Moon."

Laela blinked. "The what?"

"Oh—of course, you don't know what it is." Arenadd's eyes glinted. "The Blood Moon is a very important time for us. A sacred night. It's a time when the Night God is very close to the mortal world. When that happens, her power weakens, and she needs an offering of blood to save her. I thought our good friend Aled would be a perfect candidate."

Laela blanched. "What?"

"Tomorrow night, I have to sacrifice someone," Arenadd explained blandly. "I chose him. I thought you might be pleased to know."

"Yer gonna kill him?" said Laela.

"It's always a condemned criminal," said Arenadd. "As long as it's Northern blood, she doesn't care. Anyway." He drew himself up. "I have things to do, so I'll leave you to have lunch in peace."

# 7

# The Blood Moon

Lying comfortably in his nest, Skandar snuggled deeper into the dry reeds and straw.

"Human sad," he rasped.

Arenadd, sitting near his head, sighed. "Yes."

"Always sad!" Skandar said, in an almost accusing tone. "When *not* sad, human?"

"I don't know."

The dark griffin nudged at him, none too gently. "Why sad? You, me, live together. Have good food—have females, good nest! Have good land. Why sad?"

"Why am I sad?" Arenadd buried his face in his hands. "I don't know; what right do I have? Skandar, I can't live like this. I *can't*."

"Why not live?" said Skandar. He sounded unhappy. "What not right?"

Arenadd raised his head but stopped abruptly and cringed before he could speak. His hand went to his chest, and he groaned. "Ugh . . ."

"Hurt," Skandar said softly.

Arenadd sat very still, teeth gritted until the pain subsided. "Yes," he panted. "Every so often."

"But pain is not why sad," said Skandar.

Arenadd looked away from him, out through the archway at the dark sky. "I can't live without her, Skandar. I just can't. Every day, waking up and knowing she's gone . . ."

Skandar clicked his beak. "Female gone!" he said. "You not gone! Other female come—you Master. Good strong human—all female want!"

"That's different!" Arenadd snapped. "It's not all about . . . *mating*, Skandar. I didn't love any of those women. I loved . . . her. And I . . ." His voice faltered. "I let her die."

Skandar shuffled closer to him and pressed the side of his head against Arenadd's shoulder. "Am not dead," he said. "Am still here. You still here."

Arenadd ran his fingers through the warm black feathers on the top of his friend's head. "I know. I should let her go . . . She'd want me to. She'd want me to move on—but to *what*? I feel like the Kingdom barely needs me . . . Most of the people in the Eyrie certainly don't *want* me—not Saeddryn, that's for sure. And now . . ." His eyes narrowed, and he stilled. "And now *her*. This girl. Why did I find her? Why is she here? Why . . . ?"

"Is female," Skandar said dismissively. "Is another human."

"But there's something about her," said Arenadd. "Something . . . *something*. She reminds me of . . . of something. Someone. But I don't know who, or why. I don't know, Skandar . . . I want her to like me, trust me—but why would she? Why would anyone?"

Skandar chirped. "Not need female. Have me. Have Skandar trust, like."

"Yes. Yes, I certainly do. But I need other humans, too, Skandar."

*"Skra!"* Skandar snorted. "Why need human? Human lie, human weak. I not lie, not weak."

"No. You're the best friend I've ever had, Skandar—and don't let me ever tell you otherwise."

"You do great thing, Arenadd," said Skandar. "Give me all you promise—all I want. You, only human I like. Best human. *My* human."

"I couldn't have done it without you, Skandar. You know that."

"Yes. Know that."

They sat together in companionable silence for a while, each busy with his own thoughts.

"Who *am* I, Skandar?" Arenadd said at last. "Who *was* I? Who died to create me?"

Skandar only stared at him, uncomprehending.

"I was someone before I fell," said Arenadd. "I had another . . . I had a *life*. Before I was dead. Before I was *this*. This thing, this monster, this *Dark Lord*."

"Why want know?" said Skandar.

"Because that was *me*, Skandar," said Arenadd. "If I could only remember . . ."

"Skandar remember," said Skandar. "I live in mountain nest. Look for human. No human talk. One day, you come. See you, think, human different. Human have dark fur, like Skandar. Try and take you, other griffin protect you. White griffin. I kill. Then you—you put me in . . . thing . . . cage. You take me back to place—human nest. I watch you, think you strong. You leave me, other human make me fight. Kill human—many human. Kill griffin. Always wait for you to come back. You special human. Then you come to place . . . fighting place . . . you come back. I catch you, not kill you. Tell you, 'Set me free, or I kill you.' You promise. You come later—night. Set me free, and I kill many human. I fly away from human nest, not know where to go. Hear you call. Find you. Hurt. See you die. Use magic, you wake up. Then you, me, go back to nest. Kill human, griffin. Then we fly away, and you my human. Then come North."

Arenadd nodded. "You told me that much. I captured you, and later on you forced me to set you free. But why did I capture you in the first place? Why was I living in the South if I wasn't a Southerner or a slave? What was my *name*?"

"Not remember human name," said Skandar.

"But I want to know. And I want to know why I forgot."

Skandar yawned. "Maybe Night God know," he said unexpectedly.

Arenadd's fists clenched. "Yes. And I intend to make her tell me."

The Blood Moon ceremony took place the following night in the Moon Temple out in the city. The Temple had been built on the site of the old Sun Temple on Arenadd's orders, as a deliberate sneering gesture at Gryphus, the Day God. He'd always thought the Night God appreciated it.

The witnesses had already gathered by the time Arenadd

made his entrance—alone, as tradition demanded. He came in via the dark wood doors and walked slowly toward the altar, admiring his surroundings along the way.

The Temple had been designed to look like a forest. The pillars that held up the roof were covered in tiny brown tiles that spread onto the floor in the stylised shapes of roots, and here and there lantern-holder "branches' jutted out from them. The lamps they held were silver and had blue glass, so the light they gave off was cool and muted.

There were no benches or seats of any kind, and the gathered worshippers were standing. More than two hundred of them had crammed themselves into the Temple, and more were standing in the street outside. Many of them reached out to touch Arenadd's robe as he passed. He paused to touch some of them in return, sometimes murmuring a few words.

At the centre of the Temple, a hole had been left in the roof to let the moonlight in. It shone on the circular altar, where Saeddryn and the rest of the priesthood were gathered.

As Arenadd approached, Saeddryn came to meet him. She wore her ceremonial silver gown, and a deer mask covered her face.

She silently offered a cup to him.

Arenadd took it and walked toward the altar, while the priestesses formed into a circle around it. They were bare-chested, clad in nothing but simple fur loin-cloths, each one wearing the mask of a different tribe.

Arenadd lifted the cup to his mouth and drank the blood it contained before handing it back to Saeddryn. She gave him the copper-bladed ceremonial knife in return, and went to join her companions, leaving Arenadd to approach the altar alone.

He reached it and stood there, looking impassively at the victim already chained to it. Aled had been gagged, and he stared back mutely.

Arenadd looked upward, to where the moon shone through the roof. It was a perfect silver orb—a Wolf Moon.

*I know you're watching me,* he thought. *If I didn't kill him—if I let you die—what would you do then, Master?*

But he knew that, even now, he didn't have the courage to do something like that.

Around him, the priests chanted, invoking the Night God,

and the worshippers joined in softly. "Night God, bring darkness, Night God, bring death to our enemies. Night God, take the souls of our dead to the stars and let them shine there forever. Night God, guide us, guard us, oh beloved spirit of the moon and the dark and the shadows."

Arenadd knew what he was watching for, and he kept his eyes on the moon. Waiting.

Sure enough, after a few moments, he saw it—saw the shadow begin to cover the moon. The Night God's eye was closing, blinding her to the world and so cutting her off from the strength of her people. Arenadd kept quite still, holding the knife and watching the phases of the moon pass in a single night. The full moon followed by the half moon, the Deer Moon, followed by the crescent, the Bear Moon. After that would come the new moon, the Crow Moon.

As the shadow drifted across it, the moment came. The moon turned red from edge to edge. Inside the Temple, the priestesses moaned and cried out in horror.

Arenadd tore his gaze away from the bloodied moon, and saw the altar and the victim. Aled struggled feebly against his chains. He was actually crying in his terror.

Arenadd felt the same cold calmness he had become so used to over the years, mixed with a terrible excitement—an almost sexual, lustful feeling.

"Join me," he whispered, and brought the knife down with all his strength.

The copper blade, etched with sacred runes, sank into Aled's chest, through his ribs, and penetrated his heart. He jerked and screamed briefly, and then went limp as he died.

The instant that happened, Arenadd saw the world around him fade away.

Darkness came in its place.

He looked around, almost dreamily, and found himself surrounded by a ring of strange beast-headed women. Each one was an animal spirit in human form, and each one represented one of the ancient tribes of his people. He inclined his head toward the wolf-headed woman who represented his own tribe, and then looked upward, to where the mural of stars painted on the roof had become real stars, shining far more brightly than they usually did in a sky that had become the entire world.

Arenadd breathed deeply. "Come to me," he said softly.

Silence answered him.

And then she was there.

Arenadd turned to face her and saw her, standing near him as if she had been there all along. She looked just as he remembered her—young but old, wearing nothing but a mantle of silver fur that left her breasts exposed. In one hand she held a silver sickle, in the other the full moon, somehow balanced on her palm.

*Why have you summoned me, Arenadd Taranisäii?*

Arenadd stepped toward her. "I gave you your blood, just as I did before, Master."

The Night God sighed. *Oh, my sweet Arenadd. How much you have suffered.*

"You know the pact," said Arenadd, stone-faced. "I gave you your blood. Now answer my question."

She ignored him. *Arenadd, you have not listened to me in such a long time. I am not pleased by this.*

"I have a Kingdom to look after," said Arenadd. "That's enough to occupy me now."

*Yes.* She lifted her hand and put the full moon into the hole where her eye should have been. *You have done so well, Arenadd. My people prosper, and I am worshipped as I should be once again. You have done as I asked you, and I am grateful.*

Arenadd's expression did not change. "Good. Now you can tell me what I want to know."

*Ask, and I shall answer.*

"Then tell me this," said Arenadd. "Who am I?"

The Night God smiled. *You are Arenadd Taranisäii. You are the Shadow That Walks. You are the King you deserve to be.*

"I didn't deserve to be a King," Arenadd snapped. "And that isn't what I mean, and you know it. I want to know who I *was*, Master. Who was I before you changed me? Before I was your creature?"

She reached out to caress his face. *Why do you wish to know this, Arenadd? Why can you not let the past rest?*

"I don't know, Master, but I want to know." Arenadd's face creased in pain. "Who did you sacrifice to make me? I know . . . I know I had a life before then. I know I was someone. But I don't know who, or why I died . . . I don't know why I forgot."

*It does not matter,* said the Night God. *Truly. Listen, Arenadd. Our time is short, and I have new commands for you to carry out.*

"Oh, do you?" Arenadd snarled. "What is it now, then? Who else do you want me to kill?"

*You have reclaimed the North in my name,* said the Night God, quite calmly. *Now I would have you deliver Gryphus' ultimate punishment. You must invade the South. Conquer its cities and its Eyries while they are still in disarray. There is confusion and poor leadership there now—take advantage of it. The griffiners' power can be overthrown. If you act quickly, the whole of Cymria may be ours for the taking!*

"So Saeddryn tells me," Arenadd said sourly.

*Then she is right. Destroy the South, Arenadd. I command it. It is in your power.*

Arenadd hesitated. "I don't want to."

*Do it,* she hissed. *I command you.*

"What if I refuse?"

She enveloped him, smothering him in her cold, numbing power. *You know what I can do to you if you do not do as I tell you, Arenadd.*

He shuddered, trying not to show his fear. "I know, Master. I know. But the Southerners aren't a threat any more, and surely . . ."

The coldness around him increased, spreading pain into his limbs. *Surely nothing!* the Night God raged. *I have commanded, and you must obey! The Day God will be an enemy to me until the ending of time itself, and he must be destroyed, or he will destroy me!*

Arenadd cringed under her onslaught. "All right! All right! I'll do it, Master. I'll do it."

She relaxed and took away the pain. *Excellent. You will do as I have told you?*

"Yes. But only if you tell me who I was."

*Why are you so anxious to know?*

"I don't know, but I am. Please, just tell me."

*Very well.* She stood over him, her skin shining like the full moon. *Before you died, you were a young griffiner who went by the name of Arren Cardockson.*

Arenadd felt a shiver go down his spine. "Why did I die?"

*You had a griffin partner who was killed in an attempt on your life,* said the Night God. *You swore revenge upon the one who had betrayed you, but you did not have the strength or the will to take that revenge. Eventually, you attempted to become a griffiner again by abducting a griffin chick, and were sentenced to death for your crime. You were killed as you tried to escape from prison.*

"I fell . . ." said Arenadd.

*Yes. You were thrown from the top of a mountain as you fled from the city guard. The fall crushed every bone in your body.*

"And I died."

*Of course you did. No human could have survived such injuries. Arenadd, I chose you because you were a Northerner who had seen and suffered the cruelties of Gryphus' people yet had the strength and the wit to resist. You alone had been fully trained as a griffiner and had all the knowledge of their ways that you would need to defeat them. When you were in prison, facing almost certain death, you prayed to me in the dark tongue, begging me to save you. I heard that prayer, and it was a true prayer. And as you lay dying, I sent Skandar to you. It was his magic that made you become the Master of Death. My chosen one.*

Arenadd felt strangely blank. "Arren Cardockson. I was Arren Cardockson."

*Yes. But that man is dead now. You are King Arenadd Taranisäii. Kraeai kran ae, as the griffins call you.*

"Your creature."

*Yes. Now, do you pledge to do as I have told you?*

"I do," said Arenadd.

*Excellent.* She caressed his cheek. *You have never failed me before, and I trust you that you shall not do so now.*

"Thank you, Master."

She began to fade. *Arenadd, listen. I have one final command for you.*

"Yes, Master?"

*This girl you have taken into your Eyrie . . .*

"Yes?"

*Protect her,* the Night God said sharply. *Keep her close to you. Make her trust you. Make her worship me, love me. Do not let Gryphus have her.*

"I won't. Master, why is she so important?"

*She has a power she does not know,* said the Night God. *Arenadd, make her mine. Make her a darkwoman. You must do this.*

"I will," said Arenadd. "I promise."

*Good. If she does not become loyal to us—you must kill her.*

"Why?"

The pain again. *Do not question me! She will give her soul to me, or she must die. You will not allow one to live in our land who does not serve us—this is all-important, Arenadd. Do not let her out of your sight, do not let her fall under Gryphus' spell. She will be mine, or she will die.*

"Yes, Master," said Arenadd. "Yes, yes, I understand . . . I swear . . . I'll keep her by me. I already arranged for her to go through the womanhood ceremony here in the Temple under your eye."

*See that she does so with a pure heart,* said the Night God. *There must be no doubt.*

And then she was gone.

# 8

## Secrets

Days passed, and Arenadd's birthday came and went without ceremony. Once, years ago, he'd considered making it a public holiday, but he never had, and by now most people had forgotten what day it was altogether.

Instead, he spent the day in the council chamber, arguing with his officials.

Saeddryn, as High Priestess, had a seat on the council with her partner, Aenae—Skandar's son. Her husband, Torc, wasn't a griffiner, but Arenadd had given him a seat anyway as he was a member of the royal family. The other seats were taken up—very amply—by Lord Iorwerth and Kaanee, the commanders of Malvern's army, and a handful of other officials, most of them griffiners.

As King, Arenadd stood on the platform at the centre of the chamber, which had once been reserved for Malvern's Eyrie Mistress. Skandar sat beside him, powerful and magnificent, with his fur and feathers shining with health and his forelegs adorned with gold and silver bands.

Since it was a formal occasion, Arenadd had put on the crown he usually kept stowed away in his robe, and he stood gloomily and listened as Saeddryn said her piece.

". . . I've talked it over with Lord Iorwerth an' his best commanders, an' they all agree with our assessment, Sire. The people in the street are behind us on this as well. There'd be no outcry; this would be the most popular move we've made in years, Sire."

"The griffins in our city agree with this," Kaanee put in. "Many have come to me and asked me when we shall finally act." He shifted and scratched his head with his pitted talons. "Cymria is ripe for the taking."

"I see," said Arenadd. "Iorwerth, what's your opinion?"

Iorwerth stifled a yawn. "Whatever we do, we have to do quickly, Sire. The longer we wait, the more opportunity we give the sun worshippers to recover. *Now* is the time when they're weakest."

Arenadd nodded. "And what would we have to gain from it?"

"Everything, Sire!" said Saeddryn. "We're Northerners—we were born t'be warriors, not traders an' money-lenders! The Southerners are our enemies, an' they deserve—"

"We must do it to defend ourselves as well, Sire," Iorwerth interrupted. "The Southerners outnumber us, and as soon as they're strong enough, they'll attack us again. Ye know what they're like—how they think."

"Iorwerth's right," said Saeddryn. "Do ye want to throw away all we fought for, Sire? Unless we crush the Southerners first, they'll never let us live in peace. They'll want this land back, an' they'll come in just like they did before. Ye know they will."

Arenadd's mouth narrowed. "And you can't think of *any* alternatives? Not one?"

"There's no negotiatin' with Southerners, Sire," Saeddryn argued.

Arenadd held up his hands. "All right. Please, just be quiet. I've heard your arguments now, and you've made a strong case. And I've been thinking this over for years, long before you first started to petition me."

"An' it's time ye reached a decision, Sire," said Saeddryn. "Past time."

Arenadd resisted the urge to glare at her. "I have."

"Yes, Sire?" said Iorwerth.

The King's brow furrowed and he breathed in deeply. "I'm . . . expecting a visit from the Amorani ambassador soon. He should arrive here in a few days."

There was a stirring from the others.

"Amoran!" Saeddryn said disgustedly. "Dog-eatin' heathens!"

Arenadd fixed her with a cold, unwavering stare. "Amoran is a very powerful country, Saeddryn, and we can't afford to cut ourselves off from the world. *You* may prefer to spend your time enjoying happy fantasies about the so-called golden age, when we solved all our problems by jamming spears in people's throats, but I have the welfare of an entire Kingdom to think about."

Saeddryn choked on her rage. Beside her, Aenae started up angrily but shrank back when Skandar hissed at him.

"Listen," said Arenadd. "I know the Amoranis are different, but they're a fellow nation, and in many ways, they're more powerful than we are. The stronger our alliance with them, the stronger *we* are. And if the South ever does invade again, we can call on them to help us."

"Are ye suggestin' we should let other people fight our battles for us? *Foreigners?* Cursed sun worshippers?"

"Saeddryn, the Southerners outnumber us a hundred to one," said Arenadd.

"All the more reason to attack now, before they can organise themselves against us!" said Saeddryn. "Don't ye see, Sire?"

"Saeddryn, we can't keep doing this!" said Arenadd. "Don't you understand? We cannot keep trying to live in the past. Our people can do more than squabble among themselves and make war on their neighbours—look at how much they've done already."

"We must destroy the South, Sire," Saeddryn said softly. "In the name of the Night God."

Arenadd thought of the Night God's silver moon-eye. "The Emperor of Amoran is sending his best ambassador," he said. "When he arrives, I'll see to it that he speaks with all of you. Until then, I don't want to hear another word about this from any of you. And that includes you, Saeddryn."

She looked him in the eye. "Our ancestors would be ashamed of ye, Sire."

The others there breathed in sharply. Several of the griffins stirred, bracing themselves for a fight.

"Our ancestors lived in a different time," Arenadd said

evenly. "This is *our* time, not theirs. And unless we change as the world does, we'll perish."

That said, he stepped down from the platform and strode out of the council chamber.

Skandar stood up, towering over the entire council, griffins included. "You do as human say," he threatened. "He know what do. Not you."

Iorwerth bowed his head. "Mighty Skandar, do *you* believe we should go to war?"

Skandar clicked his beak dismissively. "This my home nest now. Enemy come here, I kill them. Why leave? Have enough here; territory big enough now. You do as human say, or I drive you away."

His piece said, the dark griffin stepped off the platform and loped away after his retreating partner.


Up in his own room, Arenadd sat down at the desk and began to sort through a heap of paperwork. These days, it seemed everything was about pieces of paper. And arguing. Gods, how had it come to this?

*The Night God gives me immortality,* he thought. *And here I am, spending it doing this all gods-damned day.*

"Well, what's the alternative?" he muttered aloud. "You're a warrior who's lost his taste for fighting. Maybe you don't have any grey in your beard, but you're ageing on the inside."

A sudden, intense feeling of loneliness came over him. He put down his pen and buried his face in his hands. *Gods help me, what am I supposed to do? Everything used to be so simple. What happened to me?*

But things had been simple then because he had known what he had to do. The Night God had ordered him to use his powers to destroy the Southerners and free the North for her people to own once again. She had promised him power and riches in return, and he had them now. But without Skade . . . without his Skade, none of it could make him happy.

*Attacking the South won't bring Skade back, and it won't make me happy. And my people don't need war.*

But the Night God had commanded him to, and if he defied her, even now . . .

He shuddered. *What do I do? What? I know what I must do, but I don't want to do it.*

For some reason, he had imagined that finding out his old name would answer the questions that had been spiralling endlessly in his head for the past few years. But now he had the knowledge, nothing felt any simpler.

"Arren Cardockson," he repeated to himself.

The name stirred nothing inside him. It could have been anybody's name. It certainly wasn't his. Not now. No, whoever Arren Cardockson had been, he was gone now. His short life had ended a long time ago, and perhaps his soul was at rest now.

"For your sake, I hope it is, Arren," he said. "And I hope you never did find out who would use your body after you died. No matter what you did in life, you didn't deserve that."

His misery and anxiety were making him feel sick. He wanted to scream.

Instead, he breathed out slowly and picked up his pen again. *Control yourself. You have work to do.*


Laela returned to her room after dinner, tired but happy. She had spent the entire morning in the library with Yorath, learning more runes. She could draw all of them by now, and once she'd practised the last of them and could write them down in their proper order, she could begin learning a few simple words.

After the lesson, Yorath had surprised her by offering to show her around the Eyrie. She'd accepted, and after they'd had lunch together, he took her through the five towers—showing her the armoury, the treasury, the kitchens, and the Hatchery, where unpartnered griffins lived and bred. They couldn't actually enter the Hatchery since unpartnered humans weren't welcome inside it unless they worked there, but Yorath showed her to a window, where she could look through and see the huge space, teeming with griffins, fighting, eating, or sleeping.

"'Course griffins weren't really meant to live this close together, but they manage," said Yorath. "Takes humans t'keep 'em peaceful-like. If a griffin kills a human, he's likely t'be brought up on murder charges. Same goes if a human kills a griffin. It's different if a human attacks a griffiner, mind. Then the griffin's within his rights t'kill the bastard. Ye don't have much t'fear if yer a griffiner. Probably why everyone wants t'be one." He grinned.

"I'd be damned scared having one of them things followin' me around," said Laela.

"Oh, me, too," said Yorath. "Wouldn't happen, though. Griffins, they're picky. They only choose the best humans."

"Still," Laela said wistfully. "Flyin' would be somethin' else."

"Oh, yeah, wouldn't it just," said Yorath. He sighed. "I used t'dream of flyin' a griffin, when I was a lad." He tugged at her elbow. "C'mon, anyway—there's one last thing t'show ye. I saved the best part till last."

They returned to the largest tower in the Eyrie, which Yorath had said was called the Council Tower.

"An' this is why they call it that," he said, pushing open a huge pair of doors.

Laela stepped through them and into the biggest chamber she had seen so far.

It must have taken up more than one entire level of the tower, and had the same rounded shape. High above, the ceiling was an enormous dome, painted with a mural of griffins flying in a dark, star-studded sky dominated by the phases of the moon in a ring.

The only furniture in the room was in the middle of the floor, where a ring of huge benches surrounded a platform shaped like a full moon. Above, ringing the inside of the chamber, were an enormous series of ledges, obviously designed for people and griffins to sit on. In fact, when Laela squinted, she could see a solitary old woman asleep up there.

"Probably didn't realise the meeting was over," said Yorath, behind her. "What d'ye reckon?"

Laela walked slowly toward the middle of the chamber, almost speechless at the sheer size and magnificence of it. "What *is* this?" she managed.

"The council chamber, of course," said Yorath. "This is where all the highest officials meet an' talk with the King. They met here just today. Everyone was here—very important things going on just now."

Laela stepped onto the platform, noticing the deep cuts in the wood. "Is this where the King stands?"

Yorath nodded. "The Mighty Skandar, too." He knelt and ran his fingers over a row of marks at the edge of the platform. "Ye can see where his talons've been. Griffins have got a bad habit of tearin' things up like this. They do it when they're angry or upset about somethin'."

Laela examined the cuts. "Dear gods, the strength that beast has got. I saw him once up close, an' I never want t'do it again."

"Ugh, me neither," said Yorath. "He's an unpredictable creature, that Skandar. He wasn't brought up in a city, see. Word is he was born wild—an' ye can't change a wild griffin for love nor money. My father says that in the war, he'd tear a man's head clean off in one go. An' what he did when the griffiners attacked at Fruitsheart . . ."

"He's got magic, ain't he?" said Laela. "Griffins've got magic."

"So they do," said Yorath. "I've even seen one use it a few times. They don't do it often, mind. But when they do . . ."

"What do they use it *for*, anyway?" said Laela.

"All kinds of stuff. Every griffin's got a different power, see?"

"Really?" Laela had never heard that before.

"Oh, yeah. Some are more powerful'n others. Skandar, now . . . his magic won the war, really."

Laela shivered in pleasant anticipation. "What's his power?"

Yorath looked solemn. "The power of death. The power of shadows. They say the Night God gave it to him, and to the King as well. Lord Iorwerth—he's the commander of the army—he told me he saw it used in battle. Skandar an' the King can both disappear—turn 'emselves into shadows. That's why they call the King the Shadow That Walks. An' the Mighty Skandar, well . . . Iorwerth told me that in Fruitsheart, when the griffiners came, the Mighty Skandar breathed black magic at them. An' everyone that magic touched—even the biggest of the griffins—died."

Laela felt cold inside. "Oh, Gryphus . . ."

Instantly, Yorath's friendly face darkened. "Gryphus!" he said. "Ye don't worship *him*, Laela. Ye don't, do ye?"

"What?" Laela started. "Gryphus? No . . . I don't think so, not really."

"Good." Yorath's mouth twisted with hate. "Nobody can worship Gryphus here, on pain of death. The Day God . . ." He spat. "A demon, he is. Only filthy Southerners worship him. The light an' the day . . . it's disgustin'. Who'd want to worship the *sun*, anyway? It's a ball of flames—it can't do anythin' except burn. There's no beauty in it, an' no subtlety, either."

Laela stared at him. "Ye gods, Yorath, calm down. I never said nothin' about worshippin' Gryphus."

"Sorry." Yorath looked embarrassed. "It's just . . . well, the Day God's our enemy. He's the one sent his people here in the first place, an' they oppressed us in his name. An' I just hate the idea that ye'd ever worship him, Laela. I like ye, see?"

Laela looked at his earnest face and felt inexplicably sad. Her father had always taught her that Gryphus was her protector—the guardian of the South and its people, the giver of life. But the Night God—Scathach, Southerners called her—was different. A god of lies and deceit, a god of darkness, a god of death, worshipped by barbaric Northerners, who slaughtered men on her altar.

And yet . . .

"I prayed to Gryphus once," she said softly. "I'll admit that."

Yorath scowled. "An' what did ye ask him for?"

"I asked him to make my father well again."

"An' did yer father get well?"

"He died," said Laela.

Yorath moved closer and touched her shoulder. "I'm sorry about that, Laela."

"He was real sick," Laela admitted. "It was probably just his time."

"Then the Night God answered yer prayer," said Yorath. "She comes in the night, when a man is deathly sick and suffering, an' she takes away his life an' lets him sleep forever. Life is suffering, but the Night God gives us rest."

Laela nodded. "I like that."

Yorath smiled. "I'm sorry I got angry. Ye'll come t'know the Night God better once ye start learnin' from the priesthood. They'll teach ye about her. She protects her people. That's why she sent the King—to be her warrior an' fight for us."

Laela thought of Arenadd, the night he had rescued her. "I know."

Yorath looked at the floor. "Ye know . . . ye're beautiful, for a—"

"—Half-breed?" said Laela.

Yorath reddened. "That's not what I meant."

Laela grinned at him. "An' you're not bad-lookin' for a blackrobe."

For an instant, Yorath stared at her as if she had slapped her. Then, suddenly, he laughed. His laugh was a warm and genuine thing, and wonderfully spontaneous. "I wouldn't use that word in front of anyone else if I were ye. It's a quick way to get yerself in a fight. Anyway, I ain't a blackrobe."

"I know," said Laela. "Yer wearin' a tunic."

"That, an' I was born free," said Yorath. "An' so was my dad. He was a peasant boy around the time the war started. He went t'join the rebels with a runaway slave. Good ole Garnoc . . . they're best friends now. Ye don't call him a blackrobe to his face, though. Not unless ye want yer teeth broken."

"I'll remember it, then," said Laela, but she wasn't really thinking about that. She was watching Yorath. She *did* like him, she thought. And he . . . "Do yeh really think I'm . . . well, good-lookin'?" she asked shyly.

"'Course I do," said Yorath. "The King's lucky to have ye."

"Oh." Laela deflated somewhat. Of course, he must think she was the King's property. He'd never dream of . . . well . . .

Yorath suddenly looked embarrassed. "It's gettin' late, an' I'd better get home. Can ye find yer way back to yer quarters from here?"

"Yeah, I know where it is," said Laela. "Thanks for showin' me around."

"It was my pleasure," said Yorath. "Here, let me walk ye back."

He accompanied her back to her room despite her few token protests and inclined his head toward her when they arrived at the door.

"I'll leave ye here, then, an' see ye tomorrow."

Laela smiled at him. "I'll be sure to practise them runes."

"Yeah." He moved close to her. "Listen, I don't want t'sound nosy or anythin', but I was wonderin' . . ."

"Yeah?"

"How long are ye plannin' to stay here?" said Yorath.

Laela stared at him. "I dunno. I got a good place here . . . I wasn't thinkin' of leavin'—why?"

He looked uncomfortable. "It's not my place to ask ye; I just was wonderin'. If ye're stayin' with the King an' all . . ."

"He let me stay here for nothin'," said Laela. "I owe him that, don't I? He's not askin' anythin' of me."

"I know," Yorath said hastily. "But listen—how are ye feelin'? Are ye . . . well?"

"'Course I am," said Laela. "What sort of question's that?"

Yorath looked even more uncomfortable. "Just . . . if ye start feelin' sick or somethin', then tell someone."

"I will," said Laela, by now thoroughly lost. "Why—there ain't some sickness goin' around here, is there?"

Yorath hesitated, and muttered a Northern curse under his breath. "Damn this—ye've got the right to know." He glanced over his shoulder, and then hustled Laela into her room and closed the door behind them. "Listen," he said urgently. "If anyone asks, I didn't tell ye this, understand?"

"Lips are sealed," said Laela. "What's this all about?"

"The King's had mistresses before ye," Yorath said. "Ye're the first in a while, though."

Laela shifted. "Ah . . . I see . . ."

"Do ye know what happened to the others?" said Yorath. "The ones before ye?"

"No," said Laela.

"They died," said Yorath. "All of 'em."

Laela gaped at him. "What? *All* of them?"

"At least four of the poor things, from what I heard," said Yorath. "They were fine when they came here, but none of 'em survived. Some lasted longer'n others, but in the end . . ."

An image flashed into Laela's mind—Saeddryn, narrow-eyed and contemptuous . . . *if I were ye, I wouldn't stay long. Ye may think ye're different, but trust me—he'll be the death of ye. Maybe not soon, but one day.*

"He kills them," she breathed. "He takes mistresses, then kills them."

"What? No!" Yorath looked horrified. "No, no, it's not like that. He never killed any of 'em. He wouldn't do that. No, no-one knows why they died. It was like a sickness. They'd just sort of . . . fade away, like they'd lost the will to live."

"For gods' sakes, why did they keep comin' to him?" said Laela. "If they knew they'd die . . ."

"They didn't, did they?" said Yorath. "Would *ye* believe it? They all came in thinkin' they were invincible—not weak like the others. Maybe the King believed it, too. But that must be why he never married. In the city, they say he's cursed never to love a woman for more than one full moon. Everyone thought the last mistress would *be* the last, but now . . . ye've come along."

Laela felt dizzy. "Don't worry," she said. "If I ever feel sick or anythin', I'll leave. That's a promise. Nothin's good enough to make me die for it."

Yorath smiled. "Good. I'm glad t'hear ye say it. Now I'd better go. Don't want the King thinkin' we're up to somethin'." He hastily opened the door and checked that the coast was clear.

"Thanks for tellin' me," said Laela. "It's nice t'know yeh care, like."

Yorath inclined his head politely. "Always, my lady."

He smiled at her again and hurried away, leaving Laela to watch him until he had gone.

Alone again, she closed her door and collapsed onto her bed, where she lay on her back and stared at the ceiling.

Her head was spinning.

Gods, no wonder Saeddryn had made that threat. And no wonder people had been avoiding her since she'd come into the Eyrie. She'd thought they were keeping their distance for fear of offending the King, but if they all believed she was going to drop dead in a matter of months . . .

To her surprise, she felt a pang of sadness on the King's behalf. She couldn't imagine what it would be like to see so many young women die so quickly simply because he had touched them.

She wondered if he had cried for any of them.

*He's so alone.*

The thought surprised her.

# 9

# The Tomb

That night, she had a strange dream.

She was standing in a meadow, surrounded by flowers and lush, green grass. Butterflies drifted through the warm air. Above she saw the huge, graceful shapes of griffins soaring. Their feathers were brown, patterned with gold that shone in the sun.

But there was no sun in the sky.

Laela wandered through the meadow, breathing in the rich, flower-scented air, and saw someone else there.

It was a man. He was tall and muscular—the most-powerful-looking man she had ever seen. His skin was tanned brown, and he had a mane of thick, red-gold hair flowing over his shoulders. A strong beard covered his chin, and he wore a golden crown. Below it, his features were strong and stern, dominated by blazing blue eyes.

He walked toward her, barefoot and graceful. His only clothing was a bright yellow-and-orange cloak, and she could see his manhood, long and thick between his legs.

Laela tried not to stare at it. "What is this?" she said aloud. "Where am I?"

The man towered over her, smiling. *My child. My sweet Laela. Walk with me.*

"Who *are* yeh?" said Laela, falling into step beside him regardless. Everything seemed too bright, too unreal.

*I am light,* said the man. His voice was deep and strong. *I am warmth. I am the day. I am life and health and happiness.*

"Yeh look like a man to me," said Laela.

He laughed—a deep, magnificent laugh. *Humans gave me my shape, Laela, and what better for a man to worship than another man?*

"Worship?" said Laela. She felt sleepy and bewildered.

*Yes, worship—many do,* said the man. *I am the god of the South, the god of the day. There are some who call me Gryphus.*

"Gryphus!" Laela grinned at him. "But this is all a dream, ain't it?"

*Yes. But I am here, nonetheless. Laela, I am the god of your people, and you have been in my grace all your life.*

"I ain't," said Laela. "I never been in anyone's grace. I'm a half-breed, an' I get what I'm given, an' nothin' an' nobody's ever answered *my* prayers."

*But you did pray to me once,* said the man—Gryphus. *A prayer offered up in terror and despair, but a true prayer nonetheless. I hear all the prayers of my people, if they are true.*

"Yeh never answered it," Laela said flatly.

*Didn't I?*

"No." Laela looked around at the meadow. "Beautiful place, this."

*Thank you. It is a place where I am at home. When my followers die, they come here.*

"What'm *I* doin' here, then?" said Laela. "I ain't dead."

*You are here for . . . a visit,* said Gryphus. *Laela, listen to me. You are more than a half-breed. You are from the line of Baragher the Blessed, and though your hair is black, you have the blue eyes I blessed him with. You are both Northerner and Southerner in looks, but what your nature is is for you to decide. You were not born to either Scathach or myself. Whom you worship is your choice.*

"I never thought about it much," Laela confessed. "What'd you want me for, anyway?"

*You are stronger than you know,* said Gryphus. *And your spirit is great. Put your trust in me, and you can do great things.*

"What things?" said Laela.

*You could take back the North,* said Gryphus. *Avenge our people. Overthrow the Dark Lord, who has caused so much suffering in the name of the Night God.*

"I couldn't do *that!*" said Laela.

*With courage, and faith in me, you could do anything.*

Laela spat. "Faith! What did faith ever do? I had faith my father'd protect me, an' he died. Left me with nothin'. I never had nothin'. The Dark Lord took me in, gave me a home— why'd I want to hurt him?"

*He seeks to corrupt you to darkness, in his mistress's name,* Gryphus growled. *Stay with him, and you will give her your soul. Then you will be lost to me forever.*

"Maybe that'd be a good thing," said Laela. "Maybe the Night God would care about me. Maybe *she'd* help me when I was in trouble."

Gryphus' blue eyes blazed. *If you would know what the Night God would do for you, see how she has treated her most loyal follower.*

"She gave him a Kingdom," said Laela. "And how are *you* any better? Did yeh ever answer that prayer yeh heard me send yeh?"

His expression softened. *You prayed to me for protection. Pleaded to be saved from the scum who sought to hurt you.*

Laela looked him in the face, and the truth dawned on her. "I was saved," she said.

*Yes. You prayed for help, and help came.*

Her mouth curled into a smile. "I see it now, Gryphus. I prayed, an' I was answered."

*Then I have your faith?*

"What do yeh want me to do, anyway?" said Laela.

The meadow seemed to vanish. All she saw now was him, filling her whole world, his voice booming in her ears. *The Dark Lord must die,* he said. *He must be destroyed, so that our people may take back the land they own by rights. The Night God's people are not fit to live upon this beautiful land of Cymria. They must be driven from it and cast back into the darkness from whence they came. You, Laela, are in a place where you may do this. Where my chosen warrior failed, you may succeed.*

"But how?" said Laela.

*You must find his heart. It is his only weakness. Laela, there is something you must know. He killed*—And then, without warning, she woke up.

She turned over in bed. "What?"

"Laela. Are you awake?"

She realised the room was full of light, and sat up hastily. "Who's there?"

"Calm down," said a voice. "It's just the Dark Lord."

Laela woke up very quickly, but not before she'd got out of bed in a hurry. "Sire . . . ?"

Arenadd was standing over her bed, holding a lantern, which he put down on a table. "I didn't mean to wake you up," he said. "I just wanted to talk to you."

Laela grabbed a cloak and put it on over her night-gown. "It's fine, Sire," she babbled. "I can always . . . What's up?"

"I wanted to talk to you," the King mumbled. He was swaying slightly.

"What about?" said Laela.

Arenadd gestured at the hearth, where a fire was still burning. "We can . . . can sit down if you want."

Laela took a chair and watched in alarm as he staggered over and half-collapsed into a second one.

"What's goin' on, Sire?"

Arenadd waved a hand, a little wildly. "Oh, it's nothing . . . nothing, just wanted someone to talk to, really."

"Well . . . all right, Sire. Talk about whatever yeh like."

He looked unsteadily at her. "D'you know, it was my birthday not long ago."

Laela stifled a yawn. "Really?"

"Yeah." He sighed. "Forty years old. I look good for my age, don't I?"

"I didn't know it was yeh birthday, Sire," said Laela.

"Almost no-one does," said Arenadd. "I don't celebrate it any more. Why bother? I died . . . a long time ago. You don't celebrate a dead man's birthday."

Laela watched him sadly. "Everyone should celebrate his birthday, Sire."

Arenadd slumped in his chair. "I'd only celebrate mine if I had someone to celebrate it *with*. If she were here . . . maybe. Skandar cares, but he's a griffin, and griffins don't care about birthdays. *She* would have . . ." He shivered. "She cared about me. She always did."

"Did she?" said Laela, wondering who he was talking about. One of his mistresses, perhaps?

Arenadd nodded. "Always. You see, I never realised until it was too late. I didn't see that she was the only one who cared about me. Skandar cares about me because I'm his human, and I give him what he wants. But she . . . she . . . loved me."

"She did?" said Laela. She was being polite, but inside she was deeply curious, and surprised as well.

Another nod. "Oh, she did. She loved me so much, and I loved her. I could talk to her about anything. She would have cared that it was my birthday. Nobody else does, you know. Not Saeddryn, that's for sure. She hates me."

"Who loved yeh, Sire?" said Laela. "What was her name?"

His gaze was distant. "Skade," he said softly. "My sweet Skade. Oh, gods, how I wish she was here . . ."

Laela had already caught the stench of wine on his breath. "Where is she, Sire?"

To her surprise, his response was to jerk out of his chair. "You want . . . want to see her, do you?"

"Sure," said Laela, still playing along.

"Well." He dragged himself out of his chair. "Well, come with me, then. I'll show you."

Laela stood, too. "All right, Sire."

Bleary-eyed, barefoot, and not a little frightened, she followed him out of the room, and then on a long journey through the Eyrie. Arenadd walked a few paces ahead, weaving slightly but apparently confident about where he was going.

Where he was going, Laela quickly saw, was down.

They followed the corridor that lined the tower, down and down, only pausing once when Arenadd stopped to rest. But he quickly recovered and went on until they had passed all the parts of the tower Laela had seen. She kept close to her companion, though not too close, sometimes wondering if she should try and support him or suggest that he stop.

Finally, they reached a point where the passageway became dark and cold, and a door opened onto a narrow flight of stone stairs. Arenadd started down them without hesitation, clutching a torch taken from the wall.

Laela followed, but reluctantly. She had already realised they were going underground.

The staircase was horribly cramped, and she began to feel the first hints of irrational panic before they had gone very far. But it ended soon enough, and as she hesitated at the bottom, Arenadd went ahead into the room it led to and lit the torches.

When the place had been lit up, Laela saw a large, stone space with a low ceiling. The air was still and smelt of earth.

Ahead, two large, stone blocks had been placed side by side, the gap between them just large enough for someone to walk through. Arenadd had already gone to the nearest of them and was standing over it, unmoving.

Moving as quietly as she could, Laela went to stand by him, and her heart fluttered when she realised what she was seeing.

It was a tomb.

The stone block—actually a hollow box intended to hold a body—had a lid decorated with a highly detailed, life-sized statue of a woman lying on her back. The woman wore a long gown, and her hair flowed over her shoulders. She had sharp, hard features, and her mouth was set into a stern line. Laela thought she looked strange and unfriendly.

Arenadd, shoulders hunched and heaving slightly, caressed the cold stone face. "This is Skade."

Laela looked at the face again. The eyes were open but without pupils, and stared blankly at the ceiling.

"Who was she, Sire?" she ventured.

Arenadd lurched suddenly, and almost collapsed over the tomb. "She was . . . someone very special," he mumbled. "She was a . . . she was the most beautiful woman I ever met. The most wonderful."

Laela blinked. "She looks fierce."

He laughed softly. "She was. Fiercer than Saeddryn. Fierce as a griffin. Gods, how I loved her."

Those simple few words had an incredible effect on Laela. For a moment she felt faint. She looked at the Dark Lord, his eyes now fixed on the statue's face, and felt as if her heart had swelled inside her.

Arenadd didn't seem to notice her any more. "She was the only one who knew me. The only one I could talk to. She knew all my secrets. She had my heart, Skade did. My poor, dead heart. Such a worthless thing, but she wanted it, she did, and she protected it . . ." He looked at her suddenly. "You see, I always knew that when I drove the Southerners out, I would rule Malvern. My followers would demand it, and the Night God had promised it. I wanted that." He breathed in shakily. "I wanted the power. And I always planned that when I was King, I would make her my Queen. Only she could rule with me. And on the last day, when we came here, she and I, and Skandar . . . I told her. And she said she would. We could have been so happy, I *know* we would have, I . . . I could have loved being King, with her there beside me."

Without even realising what she was doing, Laela moved closer to him. "Who was she, Sire?"

"Sire!" He spat the word. "Don't mock me, Laela."

Laela started in fright. "I wasn't mockin' yeh, Sire, I was only askin'—"

He was breathing strangely. "I have a name. Arenadd. That's my name. So call me that. Let me be a man, not a King."

Laela had backed away, but now she dared move closer. "Arenadd?"

He calmed down. "That's better."

"Who was she, then, Arenadd? This woman yeh loved."

Arenadd looked at the tomb again, and shuddered. "Who was she? Just a woman I loved. I've had lovers since she died, but I never *loved* any of them. There was only ever one woman for me. Just her, just Skade. And my lovers all died. My touch killed them. It took longer for some of them, but in the end . . . it was me, you see. My curse. I am the Master of Death. All I know how to do is kill. I can never create."

"Yeh made a Kingdom," said Laela.

"Oh yes." He snorted. "My precious Kingdom. All I do day in and day out is care for it. It gives me a reason to . . . live."

"At least yeh got a reason," said Laela, trying to sound upbeat. "Plenty of people ain't."

He didn't seem to be listening. "I killed Aled a few days ago, like I said I would."

Laela shivered. "Yeh did?"

Arenadd nodded. "I sacrificed him on the night of the Blood

Moon. Gods, I forgot how much I missed killing. You know—
d'you know . . ." He had begun to sway. "D'you know . . . when
you . . . when it's the Blood Moon, when the sacrifice is made,
it summons the Night God. It did last time, before the war. That
was when she told me who I really was."

Laela gaped. "It what?"

"Summons the Night God." Arenadd nodded unsteadily.
"The blood brings her. I'd been . . . been planning for it a long
time. I wanted to ask her things, and I knew when the Blood
Moon came, I could do it. When she came, she told me . . . told
me . . ."

"What did she tell yeh, S—Arenadd?"

Arenadd rubbed his eyes. "She told me she wants me to
invade the South."

Laela bit her lip. "She wants . . ."

"Invade the South," Arenadd repeated. "She . . . she's my
master. She always knows what I should do. And Saeddryn
wants me to do it, too. It's not enough to take back the North. If
we attack while they're in disarray, take advantage of it, we
could take the whole of Cymria for ourselves. For the Night
God. My power—and Skandar's—could do it."

Laela felt sick. Images flooded her mind, images of Northern
warriors in Sturrick, burning the houses and slaughtering everyone in the village. She thought of the Dark Lord's armies, carrying destruction into all the city-states until there wasn't a
single Southerner left in the country. And she thought of the
Dark Lord himself, riding Skandar into battle—the dark griffin
unleashing his magic and visiting death on anyone in his way.

"Yeh can't do it!" she burst out, unable to stop herself. "The
people—all them ordinary people—in the country, just tryin'
to keep their farms goin'—what'd happen to 'em? An' everyone
else, too . . ."

Arenadd grimaced. "Yes. But . . . sweet shadows, to fight
again . . . I haven't gone into battle in such a long time, and gods
I miss it. I haven't felt so alive since then."

"But yeh've got yeh Kingdom here, ain't yeh?" said Laela.
"Ain't it enough?"

"It's not as simple as that," said Arenadd. "Laela, the Night
God is my master. I *must* do what she tells me. If I don't, she
could do terrible things to me. You don't know how powerful

she is. She has my soul. She owns me. Without her, I wouldn't exist. How can I disobey her?"

"I . . . I dunno," Laela stammered.

"And besides . . ." Arenadd turned back to look at the tomb. "I know what happens when I hesitate. When I falter. If I had killed the Bastard's sister as the Night God told me to, instead of holding back, then Skade would still be alive. She killed her, you see."

"Who?" said Laela.

"I was ordered to kill her," said Arenadd. "The Night God told me that there were three people I must kill. One was the Bastard—Erian Rannagonson. I killed him in the Sun Temple, the poor fool. After that, I had to kill his sister as well . . . Flell, her name was. But when I found her, she was trying to defend her child from me—a child I was also ordered to kill. I didn't want to do it. I hesitated. Skade attacked her instead, and she killed her. Killed her in the same room you're staying in now." He looked up. "But that was my punishment, you see. The price I paid. If I hadn't held back, if I'd only obeyed the Night God, then Skade would be here with me now."

The sick feeling in Laela's stomach increased. "What'll happen if yeh don't invade the South?"

Arenadd looked her in the eye. "The Night God will take away my powers," he said.

"Do yeh need them, though?" said Laela. "If yer only runnin' a Kingdom . . ."

He gave a hollow laugh. "I need them. And my Kingdom needs them."

"Then . . . are yeh gonna do it?" Laela asked in defeated tones.

Arenadd looked away. "I met with the council today and Saeddryn petitioned me to invade. So did Iorwerth. The entire damn Kingdom wants me to do it."

"What did yeh tell 'em?" said Laela.

He looked at her again. "I told them no."

Laela stopped. " 'No'?"

"I refused the petition," said Arenadd. "The gods alone know why. Maybe I've turned into a coward over the years, but going to war again . . ." He shook his head. "I can't do it. I won't do it. It isn't what the Kingdom needs. It isn't what *I* need. Truth be told, I'd rather try and engage in trade negotiations with the South. Not that I've got the spine to say *that* in front of the council."

Laela hid a grin. "Yeh ain't gonna do it, then."

"No." Arenadd touched the statue again. "Ah, what would Skade say if she were here? She'd say I'd lost my nerve."

"No, she wouldn't," said Laela.

"Oh, she would have," said Arenadd. "She always chose fighting, Skade did." He smiled wistfully.

"She'd be proud of yeh," said Laela.

Arenadd gave her a look that was almost pitiful. "Would she?"

"Yeah," said Laela.

He became serious. "Listen, Laela. An ambassador from Amoran is coming here soon. I haven't told anyone yet, but he's coming here to talk to me about my going to Amoran to speak with the Emperor himself."

"Yer goin' to Amoran?" said Laela. "Ye gods, isn't that over the sea?"

"Yes. Skandar and I will both be going. Do you want to come with us?"

Laela stared at him. "What? Go to *Amoran*?"

"Yes."

There was a long silence.

*"Why?"* Laela said at last.

He smiled that crooked, joyless smile. "I'll be a long way from home. I wouldn't mind having a friend with me."

Laela backed away from him. "We ain't friends."

He started as if she had slapped him, and then his eyes narrowed. "But we could be. D'you . . ." He lurched and grabbed onto the tomb to support himself. "Don't you know why I saved you? Why I looked after you? Why I like spending time with you?"

She wanted to run away. "Why?"

He grinned manically. "You remind me of myself. That's why. And the more time I spend with you, the more I feel it."

Laela snapped. "I ain't like you. I ain't *nothing* like you."

He turned his back on her. "Hah. Who'd want to be like me, anyway? Of course you don't. Go, Laela. Just go. Leave me."

Laela stared at him a moment longer and stumbled away.

# 10

## A Price

Back in her room, Laela slumped onto the bed. She couldn't stop herself from shuddering.

*He was drunk,* she told herself. *He was talkin' nonsense. I ain't like him. And I ain't goin' to Amoran with him, either.*

The dream came back to her, and she shivered again. Gods, but it had felt so real. And what if it *was* real?

No. The idea was ridiculous. Why would Gryphus want to talk to her, anyway?

*An' even if it was real, it's still ridiculous,* she thought. *Me, kill the Dark Lord? How'd I even do it?*

And she didn't want to do it, either. She was afraid of him, true—horribly afraid. But she couldn't bring herself to hate him. He was too . . . sad to hate. Deep down, she had long since realised that the man she was living with wasn't the warrior of darkness people saw him as. Not any more. He was past his prime: weak and indecisive, full of regrets he was obviously trying to drown in wine—and failing. She couldn't hate a man like that, and killing him felt like little more than cowardice.

Assuming it was even possible.

As she lay there, thinking it over, she remembered something Gryphus had said to her.

*But you did pray to me once. A prayer offered up in terror and despair, but a true prayer nonetheless . . . You prayed to me for protection . . . and help came.*

A slow smile spread over her face. "Yeah," she said aloud. "I prayed to yeh for help, an' help came. But not from you."


After Laela had fled, Arenadd staggered back to his private chambers. He felt sick and dizzy, and once or twice he nearly fell over, but he made it back and locked himself up in his room, where he sank into his chair and poured himself another cup of wine.

It made him feel a little better.

He sat forward, resting his forehead on his hand.

Why would she want to go to Amoran with him, anyway? There was no reason for her to want to. And there was *certainly* no reason for her to want to be his friend.

He picked up his cup and wandered into Skandar's nest. It was empty, and he clambered over the nesting material and out onto the balcony.

Alone, he looked up into the sky and saw the half-moon glowing among the clouds.

"Damn you," he growled. "Damn you. I served you, and you betrayed me. You took Skade. You sent me back. All I wanted was for you to let me die, but *you sent me back*. Sent me back here, trapped me in this hideous body again. You betrayed me."

He hurled the cup away with all his strength, at the sky—at the moon.

*"You betrayed me!"* he screamed. *"Damn you, let me die!"*

There was no reply, but he clenched his fists and continued to shout, hurling his curses at the moon with all his strength until something in him snapped, and he simply screamed.

The scream went on for a long time, a primal sound, full of agony and hatred.

Afterward, the silence seemed deafening.

Arenadd fell to his knees, as if his exhaustion were forcing him to abase himself before his mistress once again.

"Damn . . . you," he gasped. "I won't do it. I won't. I don't care what I told you. I won't invade the South. I won't kill any more. I don't care what you do to me."

He fell silent, panting as he calmed down.

Then, without any warning, a slow and horrible grin appeared on his face.

"I'll have my revenge on you," he said softly. "Oh yes, I'll make you pay. I can do it, and now I know how."

The grin widened, and madness gleamed in his eyes as it all unfolded in his mind—as if it had been there all along, just waiting to show itself.

"Yes," he hissed to himself. "Oh yes. Yeeesss . . ."

And he laughed.

"Oh I know what to do now. I know how . . . oh yes. *She's* the key."

He stood up and dusted himself down in a dignified fashion before returning inside.

There, he picked up the wine jug, took it out onto the balcony, and poured the contents off the edge.

After that, he took the wine-barrel from under the bed, rolled it out into the audience chamber, and left it there. The servants could remove it in the morning.

"No more wine," he told himself. "No more drinking. No more trying to hide."

Back in his room, he took off his boots, robe, and trousers and put them aside before opening a chest and bringing out a nightshirt.

He hadn't worn it in months, and the cloth smelled stale, but he put it on anyway and snuffed out the lamp before climbing into his bed. It, too, was dusty and unused.

It felt more comfortable than he remembered its ever being in the past.

He snuggled down under the blankets, his mind exploding with ideas as it had not done in many long years. He even felt excited.

"You'll come with me to Amoran, Laela," he murmured to the darkness. "You'll come because I'll order you to come. And after we get back, you'll stay with me. Every day, whether you like it or not. I'll see to it that you learn all you need to know. And the Night God won't be able to stop us, and neither will Saeddryn."

He grinned wolfishly to himself and drifted off to sleep.

Arenadd's new feeling of determination and purpose was still there when he woke up, and it made the day feel much brighter. He enjoyed his customary bath and gave his hair the usual thorough brushing and combing before neatening up his beard and dressing in his favourite robe. That done, he called some servants to remove the wine-barrel, and then went for breakfast. The servants looked openly surprised when he asked them for food, and again when he ate it.

After he'd eaten, he went to see Laela. The girl looked frightened and resentful at the sight of him, but he had rehearsed what he was going to say and wasted no time in saying it.

"Listen, I'm sorry about last night," he said. "I haven't been myself lately. And quite honestly, I drink too much. Now, about Amoran—"

She avoided his eyes. "Yes, Sire?"

"You're coming with me," he said. "And that is not a request. Also," he went on, as she opened her mouth to protest, "I'm going to arrange for some more lessons for you. These won't be as . . . cerebral as the ones you're having now."

"What are they, Sire?"

"You're going to learn how to fight," said Arenadd. "You mentioned that you already know how to use the short sword you brought with you, and that's good, but if you're going to become a Northerner, then you need to learn how to use one of *our* weapons. And you'll find that the sickle handles quite differently. You'll also learn how to use a bow, and how to fight hand to hand. I won't have my new companion be helpless when there's danger."

Laela's blue eyes gleamed. "That's fine by me, Sire. I mean, I'd like to learn how t'fight, like."

"And you will. I'll assign someone to do that once we get back from Amoran."

"Yes, Sire." She paused. "Thanks, Sire. I'm grateful for that. An' I'm sorry how I was last night. I was rude, an' I shouldn't have been."

"Ah, don't worry about it," said Arenadd, waving her into silence. "How should I have expected you to react? You saw a side of me I wish you hadn't, and for myself I'd rather not talk about it any more."

"Yes, Sire," said Laela.

"Good. And you can call me Arenadd. I'd prefer it, if it's all the same to you."

"All right . . . Arenadd."

* * *

The conversation improved Arenadd's mood even further, and that good mood persisted until well after he had shaken off the last of his hangover and enjoyed a hearty lunch.

After he'd eaten, he visited several of his officials whom he hadn't spoken to in some time and enjoyed their obvious surprise when he called on them out of the blue to ask them about how their various duties were going and whether there were any problems.

Even when there was nothing significant to talk about, it still felt reassuring just to talk and refresh his memory.

After that, he managed to track down Skandar, and the two of them spent a lazy afternoon flying over the city together, just enjoying the feeling of being in the air.

Arenadd felt more alive than he could ever remember.

After dinner, he retired to his room to catch up on some paperwork, but that didn't last long before he felt bored and put it aside.

His gaze drifted toward his sickle, resting on its pegs over the bed. He lifted it down and gripped the handle, thrilling at how perfectly it still fitted into his palm. How long had it been since he'd used it? Five years? Ten years?

He took up a fighting stance and flicked the weapon back and forth so that the blade flashed in the fire-light. It followed his every movement, almost dancing in the air, the wickedly sharp point curving back toward him in an imitation of the crescent moon.

Arenadd ran his broken fingers over the blade, with its etching of the triple spiral, and smiled to himself.

"By gods, I've missed you," he said. "I've missed seeing you in battle . . . how the Southerners fell under you."

He smiled, remembering. The sweet smell of blood and the sound of screams, like music in his ears. Oh, how he'd thrilled to it. How could anyone ever say that killing was wrong or evil, when it felt so good?

He realised he was standing very still, almost salivating at the thought of it.

*If you went to war, you could feel it again,* an inner voice whispered.

He shut it out, and returned the weapon to its place. No. No matter how much he wanted it, he would not do the Night God's bidding. There was nothing she could offer him that he wanted, not any more. Even killing wasn't worth it.

He felt the familiar thirst for wine nagging at him. He hadn't had so much as one cup all day . . . how long had it been since he'd gone an entire day without a drink?

*Maybe I could have just one. Just a quick one . . .*

"No!"

He grabbed his broken fingers with his other hand and twisted them until they cracked, and his eyes watered. The pain helped to bring him back to his senses, though, and he berated himself internally. *No more wine. You're a King—act like one! You're degrading yourself—making yourself look like a fool. You can live . . . you can exist . . . without drinking yourself to sleep every night.*

The room had begun to feel like a prison. If he stayed in it much longer, he knew he would crack and call for the servants to bring him a jug.

But there was a solution to that.

He went to his clothes chest and lifted out the black tunic, the hood, and the cloth to wrap around his face. He'd visited his officials—now it was time to visit his people as well.

He put on the disguise of Wolf with practised speed and stuffed a money-bag and a long dagger into his belt before slipping through the concealed door into the secret passage and away, toward freedom.


The Blue Moon tavern was as quiet as it usually was. Arenadd slipped in via the back door and took his accustomed seat in a shadowy corner. There, carefully ignored by the other drinkers, he sipped at a mug of water and listened to the conversation around him.

". . . going to join up," one man was saying. "The instant it's made official."

"For sure? The money won't be so good . . ."

"It ain't for the money!" The first speaker sounded a little overexcited. "It's for the glory! I was way too young when the war was on, but my dad always told me about the fightin'. He said how he went into battle once under the leadership of the

King himself! An' afterward, he picked up all sorts of loot. He's still got a gold cup from a griffiner's bedroom."

"Who says we're invadin' the South, anyway?" someone else called out.

"Not me," Arenadd muttered under his breath.

"'Course we will," said the first man. "The King'll lead us there. He'd never let the sun worshippers go."

"I dunno," said someone else. "If we were goin' to invade the South, wouldn't we have done it by now?"

"Well, obviously the King's had other stuff on his mind," the first said defensively. "Ye don't build a Kingdom overnight, do ye?"

"*I* heard he's gonna make more trade deals with Amoran," said someone else.

The others made disgusted noises.

"I don't believe that," said the first speaker. "He wouldn't do somethin' like that."

Arenadd groaned to himself. *Gods, listen to them whine. They all think they can read my mind.*

He was interrupted in his listening at that point by something nudging his elbow. He started, reaching automatically for his knife, but it was only the barmaid.

She pushed a tankard toward him. "That'll be four oblong."

"I didn't order that," Arenadd snapped.

She gave him a condescending look. "No-one stays in 'ere unless they buy a drink. Four oblong."

He growled and fished in his money-bag. She took the oblong and walked off.

Arenadd picked up the tankard and sniffed its contents. Beer. Well, maybe just one drink would do him some good. It would certainly be better than listening to this poor fool brag about joining the army to march off to a war that wasn't going to happen.

He carefully lifted the cloth away from his mouth and sipped at his drink. It wasn't bad, especially considering he didn't like beer much.

The conversation around him continued, but it was fairly noisy in the tavern, and he let it wash over him without much effort, drinking his beer while he soaked in the atmosphere. Gods but it felt good to be surrounded by people who didn't know who he was and didn't stare at him. True, he attracted a few curious glances because of his shrouded face, but the regular drinkers at the Blue Moon were used to him by now—and all of them knew that he wasn't a person to be interfered with.

It had taken him a while to establish himself at first—the owner had found his appearance unsettling and started to ask suspicious questions, but a bag of money and a few threats had made it clear to the man that *this* drinker preferred to be left alone. And at least the Lone Wolf (as people had started calling him) always paid for his drinks and never got into fights. It was enough to keep them quiet.

Normally, he enjoyed being here, but listening to the conversation and the barmaid's sneering attitude had left him feeling out of sorts, and he decided to move on. There were other haunts he could visit.

He downed the last of his drink and pulled the cloth back into place before quietly slipping out of his seat and making for the door.

As he crossed the threshold, a sick, dizzy feeling hit him, and he staggered and nearly fell.

He clutched at his head. "Oooh . . ."

The dizziness increased sharply. He blinked several times to try and dispel it, but that only made grey spots flash in front of his eyes.

His stomach roiled.

"Ugh, what is *wrong* with me?" he mumbled, leaning against a wall as he tried to recover himself.

The sick and disoriented feeling only got worse, and frighteningly quickly. It made him feel something he hadn't experienced for as long as he could remember: fear.

*Oh, holy gods,* he thought suddenly, as the world spun around him. *I've been drugged!*

His first instinct was to go back into the tavern and confront the barmaid, but he quickly realised that would be the worst thing he could do. He couldn't possibly fight like this—even walking would probably be very hard.

Realising that, and now very aware of how much danger he could be in, he struck out toward the Eyrie as fast as he could. He had to get back to safety—had to get somewhere protected, where he could sleep off the drug. In the morning, he could return to the Blue Moon—or better still, send the city guard.

But even that plan began to look impossible as he weaved back and forth along the street, staggering hopelessly this way and that. He couldn't tell which way was which. His vision was turning grey and hazy. He felt so tired, he wanted to lie down and sleep in the middle of the road.

He forced his eyes to stay open and took deep breaths to clear his head.

*Find a guard,* he told himself. *Find one and tell him who you are—it doesn't matter that they'll ask questions tomorrow—you'll be safe!*

But he couldn't see any guards, or indeed see much at all. The entire world was turning dark. His feet felt like a pair of granite blocks. When he thrust out a hand to try and support himself, he half-expected it to touch the sky. Meanwhile, people around him were bumping into him, sometimes painfully. He wanted to ask them for help, but his head was in a whirl, and none of them seemed to stay long enough to speak to. Finally, one of them ran into him hard enough to send him staggering sideways and into a wall. He hit it, and then groped his way along it until he found a corner, and peered around it. It looked dark, and he could see another wall, but he couldn't tell whether it was another street, or even if it was an open doorway.

A hand grabbed him by the arm. He resisted, but the hand didn't let go, and he stumbled after it until it released him and something shoved him violently in the chest, sending him to the ground, which he hit with a bone-jarring thud.

An instant later, something heavy pinned him down and he saw a face looking into his, wavering sickeningly through the haze. It looked small, but the mouth was twisted and horrible, the eyes staring.

Arenadd groaned and mumbled something.

The stranger reached down and took hold of the cloth wrapped around his face. "Now let's see who's behind the mask," a voice rasped.

The cloth came away, and Arenadd felt air on his face. "Let go of me," he managed. "I . . . order you . . ."

The stranger's leer widened, turning his face into a hideous mask. "At last," he breathed, and his voice was a strange lisping thing. "At last, I've found you."

Arenadd shoved at him, but all his strength had gone. "Leave me alone. I swear, if you don't let me up and call the guard, I'll make you suffer."

A laugh. "Too late!" the voice almost screamed. *"Too late!"*

And then something hit him.

It felt as if he'd been punched in the chest. But only for a moment.

The stranger rose, breathing harshly. "This time, no-one will be there to take it out," he said. "Not this time. In Gryphus' name, *die*."

Arenadd's breath came in short gasps, and he reached up and clutched feebly at the dagger embedded in his chest. Blood bubbled up between his teeth, and he coughed and moaned. If he could only take it out . . .

But he didn't have the strength, and he could feel it sapping his energy, shutting down his senses. The last of his vision faded to black, and his ears filled with a roaring sound that blotted out all else.

He felt his attacker roll him onto his front and tie his hands behind his back. His ankles were tied, too, and after that, something was stuffed into his mouth. The blood welling up in his throat had nowhere to go now, and he choked on it, gagging and retching. It was filling his lungs . . .

Above the roaring in his ears, he heard the stranger say something.

*"For Gryphus. For Lord Erian. For justice."*

After that, he fell into the void.

# 11

# Learning

Laela had had a long day. The morning had been spent with Yorath, as usual, learning to write her first words. He had also taught her several more Northern phrases—she was learning how to ask for food and how to say "I am the King's companion." Yorath had told her she had very good pronunciation, which surprised her.

Once the lesson was over, Yorath began to excuse himself as he usually did.

"Wait," said Laela.

He stopped. "Yes?"

She resisted the urge to stare at her boots. "I'm goin' for lunch now, an' I was wonderin' if . . . er, if yeh'd like to come an' have it with me, like."

Yorath looked uncertain. "I dunno . . ."

"Yeh don't have to come if yeh don't want," Laela said in a rush. "I just . . . sorta . . . thought I'd ask."

"Oh, I want t'come," Yorath said, just as quickly. "It's just that . . ."

"Why? Yeh got somewhere else to be?"

"Well, no, but—"

"Come, then," said Laela. "I'll be eatin' on me own otherwise."

Yorath scratched the back of his neck. "Well . . ."

"The King won't mind," said Laela. "He really won't. He

told me I could do whatever I wanted." This wasn't actually true, but she said it anyway.

"I thought he'd be eatin' with ye," said Yorath.

"No, he never does," said Laela. "C'mon, hurry up—I'm hungry."

He paused a moment longer, and then smiled. "All right. I'll be glad to."

Laela smiled back, and they left the library together, side by side. Up in the dining hall, food had been laid out for her as always, and the serving-woman, seeing Yorath, silently left to bring a plate for him.

Laela sat down, gesturing at him to sit beside her.

He did, looking around at the room. "I've never been up here before, ye know."

"Really?"

"Yeah, usually only the King an' his officials use it," said Yorath. "Teacher's apprentices like me'd never come up here. Not without an invitation, anyway."

"I gave yeh one," said Laela. "Want some beer? It's not bad."

"Thanks."

They drank together in companionable silence.

Laela's heart was pounding. *I wonder what's goin' on in his head. What does he really think about me? I'd never get him to tell me . . .*

She paused, holding her cup. *Well, be damned with that.*

"Yorath?"

"Yeah?"

Laela put her cup down and looked him in the face. "What do yeh think of me?"

The question obviously caught him off guard. "What do I think of ye?"

"Yeah," said Laela. "I mean, yeh got yerself a good job tutorin' me—probably got yeh some favour with the King an' all—an' yer nice to me, but that's probably just 'cause of me livin' up 'ere with the King. So I was wonderin'—what do yeh actually *think* of me?"

"Look, Laela—"

"C'mon," she said more softly. "I ain't gonna bite yer head off. I'm just . . . curious."

He brightened slightly as he looked her in the face. "Ye're direct, ain't ye?"

"Er—"

"I like that," he added. "I always liked that about ye, Laela, since the first day we met."

Laela smiled. "Me dad always said that the best way to get somethin' off someone is to stop foolin' around an' just *ask* for it, 'cause it's amazing what people'll do if yeh put them on the spot."

Yorath took a sip from his cup. "That's very true. I'm curious myself, though."

"About what?"

"*Everyone's* curious," said Yorath. "About ye. Where ye really came from. Seems ye just appeared in the Eyrie one day, an' no-one ever saw ye come in or knows how ye got into the King's favour so fast."

"Oh." She had a feeling he had wanted to ask her about it for some time.

"Ye don't have to tell me," Yorath added. "I just thought I'd ask."

The rest of the food arrived at this point, and Laela had a few moments to think while they ate. Well, why not just tell him the truth? She couldn't think of anything else to tell him, anyway, and she didn't want to be rude to him.

"I came 'ere from the South," she said eventually, and braced herself for the reaction.

He started. "The South? *Where* in the South?"

"Nowhere special," said Laela. "Little village not far from the Northgates. Sturrick, it was called."

Yorath was looking at her with a new interest. "I thought yer accent sounded . . . different. But if ye were born in the South, how did ye get here? An' why did ye come?"

"I bribed the men at Guard's Post," said Laela, as casually as she could.

Yorath stared at her, and then laughed. "Ye gods! An' then ye came to Malvern, eh?"

"Yeah."

"Why, though? I mean, why come North if ye had a home?"

"I didn't," said Laela. "I grew up there with my dad . . . well, he was me foster father, really. Never knew me mother. Then he died, so I sold our house an' came North."

"Shadows, that's rough," said Yorath.

Laela shrugged. "These things happen. I ain't got it so bad."

"So why did ye come North?"

Laela tried to smile. "'Cause I'm a darkwoman, that's why. An' where else can a darkwoman go?"

"True." Yorath smiled again. "How did ye end up in the Eyrie, then?"

"I got into some trouble in the city," said Laela. "An' the King rescued me."

"*What?* The *King*?"

"Yeah. He was passin' an' saw me."

Yorath looked surprised but not overly so. "Didn't know he'd been down into the city. He doesn't do that much any more."

Laela tore a piece of bread in half. "He brought me back here, anyway. We talked a bit, an' he asked me a bunch of questions about what's goin' on in the South, an' I told him what I knew, an' afterward he said I could stay here."

"That's all?"

"More or less," said Laela. "He just took a likin' to me."

"Huh." Yorath rubbed his chin. "Well, he's got eccentric over the years, no-one'd argue with that. I guess maybe he was impressed about how ye'd come all this way just t'live in his Kingdom."

"Yeah, he said that," said Laela.

"It's just a bit odd, though," said Yorath, half to himself. "All the mistresses he's had before, they were all . . . well, high-born. An' they were . . . well . . ."

Laela gritted her teeth. "I know. Yeh can't understand why he'd be wantin' a peasant girl now. One with filthy *Southern* blood in her."

Yorath jerked as if she had slapped him. "Laela—oh, gods, please, I didn't mean—"

"Well, don't worry about it," said Laela, more sharply than she meant to.

Silence.

"Listen," Yorath said eventually, "I'll go. I didn't mean . . . I'm sorry. I'll leave ye."

Laela grabbed his arm. "No. Stay. Yorath, I'm sorry. I didn't mean to yell at yeh, I'm just . . . feelin' a bit out of sorts, like."

He looked thoroughly awkward and unhappy to be there. "Gods, what would my dad say? He was over the moon when I told him I'd been asked to be yer tutor. Said it was the best opportunity I'd ever had. Told me a hundred times, 'Don't say anythin' out of turn! Be polite as ye can! If ye put one foot wrong, ye could lose it!' "

To her own surprise, Laela took him by the hand. "Yorath, listen. Yeh've got it wrong. I ain't angry with yeh. I . . . well, I like yeh."

He tried to pull away, but gently. "Laela, don't. We can't—"

"Yeah, we can," she said impulsively. "Look, it's fine for us to spend time together. The King won't care."

"Laela, if I do somethin' to make him angry—"

"Yeh won't," said Laela. "Yorath, it ain't . . . we ain't sharin' a bed. The King an' me ain't lovers. Actually . . ." She looked shyly at the tabletop. "Actually, I ain't never had a lover. Never. Who'd bed a half-breed?"

Yorath gaped at her. "What? But the King said—"

"He was lyin'," said Laela. "An' yeh've got to keep it a secret. He told me never to tell anyone else. He said if I wanted to stay 'ere an' be looked after, I should pretend t'be his mistress, 'cause it would be simpler, an' everyone would leave me alone. I asked him if he wanted t'make it . . . real-like, an' he said no."

"I'll . . . I'll keep quiet," Yorath promised.

"Thanks." Laela let go of his hand. "The King an' me ain't . . . well, we ain't lovers, an' we ain't friends. He just decided he wanted t'take care of me. I dunno why."

*You remind me of myself.*

She shut the memory out.

"The King doesn't have friends," said Yorath. But he looked less surprised now, and more . . .

Laela blinked, puzzled. He looked oddly . . . disappointed . . .

"What's wrong?" she asked.

"What? Oh . . . nothin'."

"Yeah, there is," Laela said firmly. "So tell me. I hate liars."

"It's not important," said Yorath. "I was just thinkin'. . ."

"What?"

"The King's done a lot for ye," said Yorath. "Ye do know that, don't ye?"

"Of course I do," said Laela, more than a little taken aback.

"Do ye?" He looked her in the eye. "Do ye really?"

"Well—"

"He's never done somethin' like this before," said Yorath. "An' if he's done it for ye now, without askin' for anythin' in return . . ."

"What?" said Laela. She felt the same sick, frightened feeling in her stomach that she had felt the night before, by the tomb.

"I dunno," Yorath said abruptly. "It just seems like . . . maybe he *is* expectin' somethin' back from ye. An' if it's not yer body, then I dunno what it could be."

Laela didn't reply, and the rest of the meal passed awkwardly, with neither one of them seeming to know what to say. She wanted to talk more—about things other than the King— but a strange feeling of guilt and shame had come over her, and it was so powerful, it made her keep her silence.

When the meal was done, they took their leave of each other and began to go their separate ways. But at the last moment Yorath stopped and hurried back.

"Laela!"

She started. "What?"

"I nearly forgot—ye're supposed to go to the Moon Temple after lunch."

"What? Why?"

"So ye can start learnin' about the Night God," said Yorath. "There should be a priestess waitin' for ye up in yer room— hurry up there, they don't like to be kept waitin'."

Laela cursed and darted off.


Sure enough, when she entered her room, she found a woman sitting by the fireside with a slightly bored expression.

The woman rose when Laela came in, saying, "There ye are. I was about to come looking for ye."

Laela smoothed down her skirts. "I'm sorry, I didn't get told yeh were here until just now."

The woman shrugged. "There's no great hurry. I'm Aderyn. And ye would be Laela, the half-breed?"

Laela growled. "Yeah. Do I go to the Temple with yeh?"

"Yes." Aderyn was already moving toward the door. "Let's go."

Her new companion, who was stoutly built and looked about thirty, took Laela down the endless ramps and stairs to the ground floor of the Eyrie, where an impressively large door took them out of the building. Laela hadn't come this way before and looked around with interest as they crossed the open court-yard to the outer wall. The gates set into it had a pair of alert and well-armed guards stationed on either side of it, but they stood aside immediately when they saw the priestess coming, and she and Laela passed out and into the city.

It looked different in the light of day, and Laela thought it looked friendlier, too, now that she was more or less one of its citizens.

Aderyn walked briskly toward a building that Laela saw almost instantly, mostly because it was the largest one in the city that wasn't the Eyrie. It had a domed roof and looked much like one of the Sun Temples in the South. Laela had never been inside any sort of Temple before, and she felt deeply excited to be going into one now. The fact that the Night God was said to be a cruel and savage deity only added an extra thrill.

The doors had been carved with a massive triple spiral that had been inlaid with silver, and the handles were also spirals—double spirals, in this case, made from what looked like bronze. Aderyn grasped one and pulled one of the doors open.

She gestured at Laela. "Go in."

Laela hesitated ever so briefly on the threshold. *Gryphus is your god,* her memory whispered. *To flirt with any other god— even to enter a heathen temple—is to risk the corruption of your soul by evil.*

She took a deep breath and went in.

Inside, the Temple was dark—but not gloomy. There *was* light in there, but it was dim and cool, and she quickly spotted the blue glass lamps that produced it.

She had an impression of the enormous space around her, and she saw the strange pillars made to look like trees. The floor was covered in a mosaic of leaves of all kinds, picked out here and there with silver and chunks of crystal. It was like standing in a forest, but an othewordly forest. Perhaps a forest in the afterlife.

A memory came to her without any warning—a memory of her dream of Gryphus, in the field of flowers and sunlight, and she had the strange but absolute certainty that while Gryphus had his sunlit meadow, this moonlit forest belonged to Scathach.

In its way, it was just as beautiful.

Aderyn came up behind her. "What do ye think of it, Laela?"

"It's incredible," said Laela, and she meant it.

The woman smiled for the first time since they'd met. "It took our people nearly ten years to make. This was a heathen temple once. Built by sun worshippers. When we took this city, we took the temple, too, and remade it to serve the Night God. There has never been a Temple like this for her."

"Really?" said Laela, genuinely surprised.

"Yes." Aderyn nodded. "In the past, we worshipped the Night God in the open air, under the stars. Our temples were stone circles, built by our ancestors long ago. When the sun worshippers came, they knocked down our stones and commanded our people never to worship the Night God again. Those of us who defied them were burned alive."

Laela shuddered. "*Why?* What'd they done that was so wrong?"

"The Day God hates our people, and our beautiful god," Aderyn said solemnly. "To follow her is to be his enemy. He commanded his followers to destroy us. They were our oppressors for centuries, until the Night God sent her greatest follower to us. Her warrior." She smiled. "The Master of Death, blessed by the Night God and given her power. He destroyed the Southerners in her name, and set Tara free."

"Tara?"

"The North's true name," said Aderyn, sounding slightly annoyed at the interruption. "We were given this land by the Night God, and now we have it again, and the Shadow That Walks rules over us, as she commanded."

*The King,* Laela thought.

"Now," Aderyn went on. "Come with me, and I will show ye the altar."

They went to the middle of the floor, where a circle of upright stones had been arranged in a ring. Laela, looking at them, instantly realised what was going on—the Temple's interior had been decorated to look like a forest, and here was the stone circle that would have been erected at its centre. They had built a new Temple to recreate the old.

In the middle of the stone circle was the altar, which was covered in spiral patterns and had a silver bowl set into its top.

"This altar is where the High Priestess, Saeddryn, comes every night to offer our prayers to the Night God," Aderyn explained. "And on very special occasions, the King himself comes here. He came here only a few days ago, on the night of the Blood Moon, to make the offering of blood."

"He told me the Night God needs blood to survive," Laela volunteered.

Aderyn nodded. "True. Now, the King has commanded for ye to learn the ways of the Night God, but first I must ask ye some questions."

"All right."

The priestess gave her a slightly irritated look. "Ye are a half-breed," she said bluntly.

"Yeah," said Laela, trying to sound polite.

"How were ye conceived?" said Aderyn. "Who was yer mother, and who was yer father?"

Laela reddened. She almost snapped at the woman. "My father raped my mother," she said stiffly. "My mother was a Southerner livin' in the North, an' my father was a darkman criminal."

"What was his name?" said Aderyn, unmoved. "Do ye know?"

"No," said Laela. "All I know is he got out of prison an' died tryin' to escape." *An' good riddance to him.*

"What clan was he from?"

Laela looked blank. "What?"

"What clan was he from?" Aderyn repeated patiently. "Do ye know?"

"No," said Laela. "What do yeh mean, clan?"

"There are four clans," said Aderyn. "Once, there were others, but they were lost, and only four are left. Bear, Wolf, Crow, and Deer."

"Oh, all right," said Laela. "What does that have to do with anythin'?"

"The fact that yer father was a Northerner means that ye, too, are a Northerner," said Aderyn. "Since ye were born out of wedlock, ye should be glad, half-breed. If it had been yer mother who was a Northerner, ye could not be initiated. Now, if ye knew what clan yer father was from, ye would become part of that clan when ye were initiated. But since ye don't know . . ."

Laela wanted to hit her. "What does that mean?"

"It means ye'll have to find out which clan ye should be part of. Tell me, do ye know what phase of the moon it was when ye were born?"

"No."

Aderyn sighed. "That makes it even harder, then. Ye understand—we have a priestess for every one of the clans. If ye were a Bear, ye'd be taught by that priestess. If ye were a Deer, the Deer priestess would take care of ye. But since ye don't know, ye'll learn from me until we find out."

"How do yeh find out?" said Laela.

"Our guiding phase always finds us," Aderyn said primly. "We don't find them. Now, move close to the altar."

Laela did. "What do I do?"

"See the water in the bowl?" said Aderyn. "Look into it and don't look away."

Laela obeyed. The water was clear and silvery in the muted light.

As she stared, the priestess dipped a finger into the water and moved it in a circle. Once, twice, three times . . .

"Repeat the words," said Aderyn.

*Plentyn yn tyfu'n ddyn,*
*Gorffennol ddaw'n bresennol,*
*Rhaid i amser fynd rhagddo*
*Arglwydd tywyll y nos, gweddïaf*
*Cwyd len y nos, rho i mi ond trem*
*Yn y nen, tair lleuad lawn ar ddeg,*
*Pob un yn fywyd blwyddyn,*
*Llygad y nos, agor led y pen,*
*Dangos fy nhynged i mi.*

"Say them. Keep your eyes on the water."

Laela obeyed. The words felt clumsy, but she repeated them doggedly, watching the water closely and trying not to feel too embarrassed. What in the gods' names was this supposed to do?

Aderyn continued to swirl her finger in the water, slowly and methodically, and Laela kept on repeating the Northern words and watching the water. Finally, Aderyn withdrew her hand. Laela was about to look up and ask her if she could stop now, but then . . .

But then she saw the shapes in the water.

Her eyes widened.

The visions were faint, but not so faint that she couldn't recognise them.

Something moving, something . . . something . . . some animal . . . a griffin! A griffin, wings spread, rearing up on its hind legs. A man, reaching out to her. A great globe, flaming and terrible . . . the sun. And another globe, this one shrinking to nothing. The moon. And something else . . . it looked like a ring.

The visions faded as quickly as they had come and left Laela blinking in confusion.

When she looked up, it was into the eyes of Aderyn.

"Did ye see anything?" the priestess asked softly, but she sounded as if she already knew the answer.

"Yes!" said Laela. "I saw . . . saw things in the water. There was a—"

"Don't tell me," said Aderyn. "Don't tell anyone. What ye saw was for ye. Not for anyone else. What ye do with it is yer own business."

"*What* did I see?" said Laela. "What *were* them things?"

"Ye've seen yer future," said Aderyn. "Every Northerner can see her future in the water, just once. Normally, ye would have to wait until the moon was shining on the water, but in the Temple, no."

Laela's heart was pounding. "I saw . . . I saw the *future*? *My* future?"

"Yes. With luck, ye'll be able to understand what the vision meant." Aderyn looked pleased. "But the fact that ye saw anything is very important."

"Why?" said Laela.

"I told ye already," said Aderyn. "Every *Northerner* can see their future. Ye saw it, and that means that ye are a Northerner. A darkwoman. One of us."

"One of . . ."

"There's no need to look so scared!" said Aderyn, and her voice had lost that distant, formal quality it had had before. "Ye are one of the Night God's people by birth, Laela. And that's something to be proud of!" She reached out and touched Laela's hair, stroking it gently. "See this beautiful black hair ye have. These fine delicate fingers. See how tall and graceful ye are, see how pale yer skin is, see how sharp and clever yer face is. These are the Night God's gifts to her daughter. She chose ye, Laela. She loves ye, like all her children."

"But I ain't . . ."

"I know what people have said about ye," the priestess said, cutting across her. "In the South. Don't look so surprised—I know ye came from the South, the King told me. People always called ye sly and deceptive. They said they could never tell what ye were thinking or what ye were going to do next. They did, didn't they?"

Laela gaped at her.

Aderyn smiled knowingly. "Those are a darkwoman's qualities, Laela. Ye're one of us. Do ye see that now?"

Very slowly, Laela nodded. "In the South, they always called me a darkwoman."

"And that's because ye are," said Aderyn. "If ye want to be an adult—if ye want to be one of us—ye must accept that, and so accept the Night God."

Laela thought of Gryphus. *You offered up one true prayer. You prayed for protection, you prayed . . .*

She nodded. "I see it."

"Then ye want to give yerself to the Night God?"

"I want t'learn more about her," Laela confessed.

"Then ye will. Listen, and learn."

# 12

# Rude Awakening

Laela spent the rest of the day in the Temple, with Aderyn. The priestess told her a lot—about the Night God and about the Temple. She explained that there were twelve priestesses, and that Saeddryn, as High Priestess, made the thirteenth—one for each full moon of the year. The four who represented the four clans were more senior—only one step below Saeddryn in rank. Aderyn herself was only a minor priestess.

"But hoping to be more senior one day," she confided. "I'll teach ye to begin with, until ye find yer tribe."

Once she'd taught Laela about the hierarchy and shown her around the Temple, describing some of the more important rituals that happened in it, they sat down in a back room and shared a drink while Laela heard the first and most important tale of the Night God.

"Long ago," Aderyn began, "when the world was young, the two gods ruled side by side. The Day God and the Night God. But the Day God became arrogant and believed that he alone should rule. The Night God, wishing to avoid an argument, suggested that they break time into two, and that each of them would have their own time to rule in. He agreed, and his time became Day while hers became Night. In those days, the moon was full every night, and the sun neither rose nor set. But Gryphus still wasn't content. He began to steal the Night God's light from her while she slept in the day, and he became brighter and brighter. And the night became dark. Knowing that the Night

God would realise what he had done, Gryphus used his powers to create the griffins. He gave them the ability to draw on the magic that made up the world and use it however they pleased. They became his creatures. When the Night God saw what he had done, she realised that one day he would send the griffins to destroy her. She did not have the power to create, as Gryphus had done. So she turned to the humans who roamed the earth. She chose some of them—the cunning, the brave, the subtle, and the graceful. They turned away from the day and worshipped only her, and she blessed them with beautiful black hair and black eyes, to match the night sky. And she sent animal spirits, made from starlight, to teach them how to hunt and fight."

Laela had heard this story before, or thought she had. But not like this.

"When Gryphus saw what the Night God had done," Aderyn continued, "he knew she was preparing to fight him, and he was angry and jealous at the wonderful race she had blessed. And so he created his own race, and he gave them yellow hair like sunlight and blue eyes like the day-time sky. He made them arrogant and angry like himself and filled them with his burning belief that only he should rule. The Night God's children saw them, and were frightened, and they turned to her and begged for her protection. She told them she would not make them fight the Sun People; she would fight for them, to protect them. So she crept up on Gryphus while he was asleep, and she took the sickle moon from the sky and stabbed it into his back. His blood made the sunrise, but he survived. They fought all that long day, and neither one was strong enough to win until Gryphus took his own sword and stabbed out the Night God's eye. Her own blood made the sunset, and she fled back into the night. Then Gryphus summoned his griffins and commanded them to join with his people and attack the Night God's people. And so they did." Aderyn paused to take a long drink from her cup. "The Day God and the Night God never fought each other directly again. Instead, their people fought each other in their names. And until the Dark Lord came, we were suffering under Gryphus' hatred. Now, we are free. And the Night God still watches over us."

Laela stared into her empty cup. *That wasn't how Dad told*

*it. He always said the Night God attacked Gryphus out of jeal-*
*ousy an' that she chose her people from the outcasts an' mur-*
*derers an' liars.*

"What are ye thinking, girl?" Aderyn interrupted.

Laela looked up. "They tell a different version of that story in the South."

"Of course." The priestess nodded. "Gryphus would never let his people think of him as a tyrant."

"Well," said Laela. "It's just that I was wonderin'—there's two versions of the same story. How do yeh know which one's the right one?"

"When it comes to the gods, there are two truths," Aderyn said firmly. "This truth is ours. Theirs is theirs."

Laela scratched her chin. "I'm sorry, but that doesn't make a lick of sense to me."

Aderyn chuckled. "It will one day. Now, we've probably done enough today. I'll see ye here again tomorrow."

Laela left the Temple deep in thought, with a guard as an escort and guide. She *had* enjoyed learning about the Night God and how her rituals and Temple worked . . . and seeing her future—if that was what it was—had thrilled her. And yet she couldn't help but feel a sense of guilt, deep down. A feeling that, in going into the Temple and listening to the priestess, she had betrayed someone or something.

Gryphus, perhaps? Had she betrayed *Gryphus*? Did he know what she was doing—did he know about her newfound curiosity in the night's dark goddess?

Her foster father had taught her that people who betrayed Gryphus were always punished. And she was turning away from Gryphus now—turning away from her father.

*No,* she told herself. *No. It doesn't matter what I worship—I'll never stop lovin' him or rememberin' him. Day God or Night God—it won't change nothin'.*

And she was a darkwoman. She knew that now. She'd come to the North, she'd chosen to live there, and now she had performed a ritual to the Night God and been shown her future. She'd never even been into one of Gryphus' temples. She'd never been a part of any of his rituals.

But there had been the dream . . .

*Dream's a dream,* she thought, almost sternly. *An' that's what it was. The gods don't talk t'people like that. Everyone knows it.*

She couldn't help but wonder what it would be like if the Night God came to her. What would *she* be like? How would she react to a half-breed living in her land? Would she welcome her as one of her followers, or would she be angry?

Laela sighed. *Gah, what's the point? Think about somethin' else.*

Her empty stomach provided a helpful distraction, and she turned to thinking about dinner, which was waiting for her when she returned to the Eyrie. Tonight there was roasted goat, flavoured with wonderfully tart cymran juice.

Now *that* was something she could love about her new life. Cymran fruit was horribly expensive—only the rich could afford the stuff, and here she was, eating cymran-juice sauce with her dinner, as if she were a griffiner!

That cheered her up enormously—the very good wine they'd given her helped—and she went back to her room afterward feeling thoroughly happy.

When she opened the door, the first thing she saw was that the lamp was already lit. That surprised her.

When she saw that it was lit because there was someone in there waiting for her, she forgot about the lamp very quickly.

"Yorath!" She shut the door and strode toward him. "What are yeh doin' here?"

Her tutor stood up. He was dressed much more finely than usual, and his tunic hung partly open, revealing the elaborate spirals tattooed over his chest.

"Laela."

She relaxed slightly. "Good gods, yeh gave me a fright. What's up?"

Yorath looked nervous, but confident as well. "I wanted to see ye. Is this a bad time?"

"Oh . . . uh, not really. I've just come back from dinner."

He smiled. "I just wanted to tell ye somethin', that's all."

"What is it?"

"Well . . ." He scuffed at the floor with his boot. "I just wanted t'say . . . I like ye."

She felt as if a floodgate had opened inside her chest. "Yorath!"

He shrugged. "I just do, that's all. An' I wanted to tell ye."

"Yeh picked an odd time t'do it," said Laela, her mind racing.

"I know," Yorath confessed. "I just felt like I *had* to do it tonight. But I'll go now, if ye want . . ."

He didn't move.

"Yorath, I like you, too," said Laela. "I've liked yeh since the day we met."

His eyes lit up. "Ye do?"

"Yeah." She smiled. "No-one here seems t'like me much . . . It's nice t'know at least one of yeh looks forward t'seein' me an' smiles when he does."

Yorath came closer—so close they were almost touching. "Ye're lonely here, ain't ye?"

"Yeah, I am, I guess," Laela mumbled. "I never really thought about it. I ain't really had no-one to talk to since Dad died."

"I know it must be hard for ye," he said softly. "My dad used to tell me about how it was here before the King came. We weren't allowed t'have weapons, we couldn't worship our own god—we couldn't even speak our own language. That's why we all know Cymrian—once, that was all we could speak. The King tried t'pass a law sayin' we couldn't speak *Cymrian* after he was crowned, but most of the common people can't remember the dark tongue at all. So he passed a law that all children have t'learn it. The Southerners knocked down the stone circles an' buried them, an' we couldn't tell the old legends or wear the manhood tattoos. We were forgettin' our own ways. They made us second-class in our own land—anyone who fought back or broke any of their laws was killed, or sold as a slave. It was a crime just to be born dark."

He said it with so much sincerity, and with such quiet sadness, that it made Laela's heart ache. "Gods, I'm so selfish," she muttered. "Always moanin' about *my* lot in life, when I know what happened to yeh. To a whole *people*."

Yorath smiled slightly. "Ye walk down the street, tryin' to hide yer face. Ye pretend not to hear, but ye do. Ye always hear it. Hear 'em shout after ye. 'Blackrobe, moon lover, darkman, heathen scum.' All ye can do is keep quiet an' hope they'll leave ye alone. Because if they decide t'come after ye, ye're dead, an' no-one's going to help ye."

Laela touched his arm. "Yorath . . . I'm sorry. I should've known it from the start."

"Oh, it never happened to *me*," said Yorath. "But it happened to a lot of people. I've heard it from some of them face-to-face. It happened to the King, too, once, most likely. But he never talks about his past."

"That used to happen t'me," said Laela. "I never went out into the village on me own, but even when I went with Dad, I'd hear it. The other kids never wanted anythin' t'do with me once they got old enough t'see I was different."

"It shouldn't've been like that for ye," Yorath said fiercely. "It *shouldn't*. Ye never asked for it, an' ye don't deserve it, either. Ye're a beautiful woman, Laela. Beautiful an' clever an' wonderful, an' . . . an' yer eyes . . ."

She squeezed them shut. "I know . . . these blue eyes of mine . . ."

"They're beautiful eyes," said Yorath. "So don't hide them away like that. Let me see them."

She obeyed. "Dad always said I got them from me mother."

"Well then, she must've been a beautiful woman, Southerner or no," said Yorath. "Laela—"

"Yeah?" she murmured, almost pressing herself against his chest by now.

"Are ye . . . are ye really sure the King doesn't want to bed ye?"

"Yeah, I'm sure," said Laela. "An' even if he did, I'd say no. I'm his guest, that's all. I got no interest in sharin' his bed."

He looked her in the face. "Who *would* ye bed, then?"

"Bold, aren't yeh?" Laela couldn't hide a grin.

"Dad always said I got that from him," said Yorath, unbothered. "I always reckoned I just don't know when to shut my mouth."

Laela giggled, which was most unlike her. "Yeah, I'd bed yeh," she said archly.

Now it was his turn to be taken aback. "What?"

"C'mon, that's what yeh really wanted t'know," said Laela. "Why, ain't yeh interested?"

"Oh, I am," he mumbled. "I just wasn't . . ."

"Well, like Dad always said, say what yeh mean an' mean

what yeh say. I like yeh, Yorath. An' I would've said so before, only . . . well. Lots of reasons, really."

He grinned. "Can ye keep a secret?"

"Yeah, I can keep a secret just fine."

"A *big* secret?"

"Little secret, big secret . . . they're all the same. I can keep 'em all. Why, what did yeh have in mind?"

"This," he said, and kissed her on the mouth.

She stiffened and drew back at first, but he came after her, and she shook off her surprise and her nervousness and pressed herself against him. She'd never kissed anyone before, but she did it now—clumsily, but eagerly. His lips felt wonderful.

When he pulled her toward the bed, she let him do it. She didn't care if it would hurt, or if she was ready, or . . . or anything. She wanted him.

Afterward, Laela snuggled in Yorath's arms. His skin was deliciously warm.

"Gods, I had no idea," she murmured.

"Was I any good?" he asked. He almost sounded anxious.

Laela laughed softly. "I'm a virgin . . . *was* a virgin, Yorath. What'd I know? But it was amazin'."

"I didn't hurt ye?"

"No. Well, maybe a bit. But I don't care." She yawned. "I love yeh, Yorath."

"An' I love ye, Laela."

She yawned again. "I saw me future today, y'know. In the water, at the Temple. Aderyn showed me how—the priestess what took me there. Have you ever done that?"

"No. What did ye see?"

"A griffin," she said sleepily. "Saw a griffin. An' I saw somethin' looked like a ring. Aderyn said I might be able t'figure out what it meant. I got no idea, though."

Yorath chuckled. "A griffin, eh? That's somethin' special t'see. Wonder what it could mean?"

"Yeah, me, too."

"Maybe it means ye'll be a griffiner," he teased. "Eh?"

She nudged him. "Stop that."

"Sorry."

"It's all right."

A moment later, she fell asleep.

She didn't dream of Gryphus that night. In fact, she didn't dream at all.

She jerked back into the waking world abruptly, and terrifyingly.

*"Get up! Move!"*

Hands were dragging her out of bed, none too gently, and she came awake a moment before she hit the floor. It was daylight, Yorath was gone, and a couple of powerfully built guardsmen were hauling her to her feet.

Laela struggled. "What the . . . ? Let go of me!"

One of them shoved her toward the bed. "Get dressed. Now."

She grabbed the dress she'd left on the floor and pulled it on as quickly as possible and managed to get her feet into her boots before they took her by the shoulders and marched her out of the room. They completely ignored her protests, and when she tried to break away, one of them silently caught her by the wrist and twisted her arm behind her back so hard it made her eyes water.

Her first thought was that she was being taken to the King, and the panicked thought crossed her mind that he knew about Yorath. He'd found out somehow. But what was he going to do to her now? Had she finally pushed him too far?

But the guards didn't take her to the dining hall or any of the other places where she'd met the King before. They took her downward instead—down and down to the ground floor, and then into a passage that went underground. Laela thought they were taking her to the crypt instead, but she quickly realised that this was a different passage than the one the King had shown her. Gods help her, where was Yorath?

They hadn't gone very far along this new passage before she realised where they were.

Her heart thudded painfully. They were taking her to the dungeons. The same dungeons where the worst and most dangerous criminals were taken—the same dungeons where the King had been tortured long ago.

Laela began to struggle violently. "No! Stop! I ain't done nothin' wrong! *Let me go!*"

The only reply was a blow so powerful it snapped her head sideways and slammed her teeth together with an audible thump.

Dazed, with blood dripping from her nose, she staggered on in the direction her guards chose. Her ears were ringing so badly, she only just heard the brief conversation with another guard they met along the way. A barred door opened, and they passed into another passage so narrow they had to walk along it in single file. There, the guard in front of her unlocked a door and pushed it inward. His comrade shoved Laela through it, and she stumbled forward and collapsed onto a hard stone floor as the door slammed behind her.

She lay on her stomach, her blood dripping softly onto the stone beneath her. Her face hurt so badly, she thought she was going to pass out, but her mind was clear enough to know what was going on, and she didn't have to look up to know that she was in a cell.

*What happened? What did I do?*

It would be a long time before she would find out.

She spent the rest of the day in her cell—a tiny, cold, stone-lined thing whose only furniture was a narrow wooden bench bolted to the floor and an oversized jar in one corner meant to serve as a lavatory. A guard eventually brought her a jug of water but ignored all her questions.

She drank some of the water and used it to wash the crusted blood off her face and bathe her swollen eye. Her jaw still hurt badly—she was fairly sure she had at least one broken tooth, and another one was threatening to fall out. And her eye was swollen so much it was almost completely impossible to see out of. The guard must have had a very strong arm.

She was too frightened to spend much time feeling sorry for herself. Lacking anything else to do, she paced back and forth in her cell and agonised. Had the King got bored with her? Was this some cruel game he was playing with her before he disposed of her? Was she going to be executed—or tortured? Would they break *her* fingers, too?

But why would he do this to her? He'd made her one of his subjects, she'd started learning so many things on his orders— why would he suddenly change his mind?

Yorath.

That was why. It had to be. He must have found out that she'd shared her bed with him, and that must have made him angry with her. Maybe he was jealous . . . Maybe he didn't want a half-breed dallying with one of his people . . . Maybe she'd broken some Northerner rule she didn't know about. But *how* had he found out? Had he been watching her? People said he could make himself invisible . . . hide in the darkness . . .

Or had Yorath told him? Gods forbid, had he betrayed her?

Laela slumped onto the bench, face in her hands. *Oh, help me.*

She lifted her head. "Help me," she said aloud. "Please, help. Help me get out of this, please . . ."

Silence answered her, and she stared into the darkness. Who had she been pleading with? Who was she praying to—Gryphus, or the Night God?

Her eyes gleamed.

"Night God," she said aloud. "Scathach. Can yeh hear me? I'm Laela. Laela Redguard. I dunno if yeh know about me. I'm a half-breed. My father, he was a Northerner. They told me that means I'm a Northerner, too. Yesterday I saw visions in the water, an' they say that means I'm one of your people, too. I ain't never prayed to yeh before. I always prayed to Gryphus. But he never did answer any of my prayers. Maybe that was because I'm a darkwoman. Didn't want t'think of myself that way. But maybe I should. I'd like a god of my own. Just t'know who was watchin' over me, if anyone really was. I prayed to Gryphus, but he never helped me. So I'll tell yeh this—Night God—I'll believe in yeh. I'll pray to yeh. Just help me. Protect me like they say yeh do. Stop them from hurtin' me—get me outta here, an' I'm yours. That's a promise, like."

She nodded to the invisible presence and lay down to try and get some rest.

Maybe she slept—she was never sure about that—but it felt like almost no time later when her cell door opened and a guard came in. He was carrying something, which he put on the bench before backing out of the cell and closing the door again.

Laela sat up and reached for the thing he'd left—it was a small loaf of bread, and she bit into it immediately.

"Eat that fast an' smarten yerself up," the guard said brusquely. "Lord Torc is comin' here to see ye."

Laela swallowed quickly. "Who's that?"

The guard had already gone. But his message had given her some hope, and she ate the rest of the bread and did what she could to neaten her hair and clothes. If the person coming to see her was a lord, then she'd have to look as tidy as possible to make a good impression on him. It couldn't hurt.

She'd retied her boot-laces and used some of the leftover water to flatten her hair when she heard the jangle of keys outside her cell and looked up as a guard called to her.

"Get away from the door, half-breed—sit at the end of the bench an' stay there."

She did it straightaway, and waited tensely while the door was unlocked and opened to let someone through. The someone stood by while the guard came in with a torch and put it in a holder on the wall. It lit the cell quite well, and the guard bowed to the visitor, and then left.

Laela looked at the man she could only assume was Lord Torc, trying to get the measure of him. He was in his thirties and not very tall, but he had a wiry look to him. He had a neat beard, and his clothes were fine but plain.

"Ye're Laela?"

She debated whether to stand up and decided to stay where she was. "Yeah, that's me. My lord."

He looked her up and down, unreadable. "I'm Lord Torc," he told her. "Master of Law. Do ye know why ye're in here?"

"No," said Laela. "Look—my lord—just talk to the King. He can tell yeh I'm allowed t'be in the Eyrie an' that—he gave me a home here. We're . . . well, he trusts me. Just tell him I ain't done nothin'—let me talk to him, I can tell him . . ."

"Ye won't be talking to the King," Lord Torc said coldly. "And he won't be talking to ye, either."

"But look, I ain't done nothin'!" said Laela. "Please, just tell him—"

"Can ye tell me where ye were last night, Laela?" he said, cutting across her.

"What? I was in my room," said Laela. "Where else would I have been?"

"I'll ask the questions, thanks," said Torc. "Can anyone confirm where ye were?"

"I—" Laela hesitated. Her instincts told her that bringing Yorath into this wouldn't help her. "I dunno," she said lamely.

"I see. Ye didn't see the King, then?"

"Just once, in the morning, real quick," said Laela.

"Ye didn't see him any later in the day?"

"No."

"Are ye sure?"

"Yeah, of course I am!" said Laela. "The King ain't someone yeh just forget about. Why does it matter, anyway?"

"Considering ye're his mistress, I would've expected ye to be with him last night," said Torc.

"Well, I wasn't," said Laela.

"Can ye prove that?"

"I dunno. Wouldn't someone've seen me go in his room?"

He didn't react to that. "Had ye seen anything in the Eyrie that was odd? Strangers? Anyone acting differently?"

"I've only been here a week or so," Laela countered. "I dunno much've what goes on around here. What looks odd t'me might be totally normal to you."

"No strangers, then?"

"Not that I saw."

"Ye haven't been talking to anyone different?" Torc persisted. "Anyone who wasn't one of yer tutors, or one of the servants?"

"No," said Laela.

"So I take it ye don't know anything about what happened last night?"

"I doubt it, because I got no damn idea what that was," Laela said flatly.

He leant closer. "Last night, the King vanished out of his bedroom. No-one has seen him since. Every guard and griffin in the city has been looking for him, but so far none of them have found a thing. And so far we don't know of anyone in the Eyrie who could have had something to do with it. After all— who here would want to harm the King?" He paused. "But the thing is, there *is* someone in the Eyrie who might want that. Someone who came from the South, where everyone hates our ruler. Someone with every reason to resent us and want revenge.

Someone who just so happened to be in the Eyrie last night, with no way of proving she *wasn't* anywhere near the King when he went missing."

Laela's mouth had fallen open. "I—"

Torc straightened up. "I suggest ye think hard, half-breed. Because unless ye can come up with some way of proving ye *were* in yer room all last night, then I'll have no choice but to assume ye know more than ye're saying, and then ye'll face the same thing all traitors face."

"Death?" Laela managed.

"Of course not," said the Master of Law. "If ye are guilty, then ye know where the King is, and we must find out, and soon. By any means necessary."

"I didn't do nothin'!" Laela burst out. "I swear, I ain't done nothin'! I didn't know the King was missin' at all until yeh told me—I swear!"

Torc clutched his throat as if it were hurting him. "I was a slave until the King set me free," he said quietly. "I owe him everything. And I don't care what I have to do to ye to find out where he is now. I will find him. And ye'll help me, or die. Think about that."

Then he was gone.

# 13

# Back at the Blue Moon

Laela didn't sleep that night, even briefly. She didn't *want* to sleep, even if it would mean an escape from her fear and hunger.

Whatever happened from here on, she knew her life in the Eyrie was over. She'd already decided that when they came for her in the morning she'd tell them about Yorath. Whether they'd believe her was another question. The memory of Torc's hostile face gave her the grim feeling that they wouldn't believe her and would probably torture her regardless. And . . . what then? What would she tell them?

Nothing, that was it. She'd tell them nothing, because that was what she knew. And if they had nothing to torture out of her, then they'd have no reason to stop.

She knew what happened to people who were tortured. Her father had told her. It didn't matter whether they talked or not; they always cracked in the end. After that, they died. If not by execution, then from infected wounds, or insanity.

She spent that night pacing again, her mind in a whirl. Thoughts of the fate ahead of her mixed with thoughts of Yorath and his sweet smile, and she felt sick to think she'd have to betray him to get out of this situation. He'd asked her over and over again to keep it a secret; he'd been so frightened that he might make the King angry, even now.

But the King was gone, and Laela knew that betrayal was her only chance.

To her surprise, she realised that, mixed in with her fear for herself, was worry about the King. Arenadd.

What could have happened to him? Was he hurt—had he been kidnapped?

Maybe he had run away.

She remembered the bitter way he'd talked about his Kingship—how depressed he'd seemed. Maybe he'd killed himself.

But she remembered seeing him the morning before he'd vanished, and noticing how energetic he seemed all of a sudden. Cheerful, even. That wasn't the look of a man planning to kill himself that night. It had been closer to the look of a man who had something completely different on his mind.

He'd looked like someone who had something planned—something important and special.

*He's run away*, she thought. *Must have done. He decided to do it yesterday or the night before, an' he did it that night, after he'd talked about Amoran to throw me off.*

But where could he have gone? And would he really run away from his responsibilities like that? He hadn't struck Laela as the sort to abandon something as important as an entire Kingdom. But maybe she'd judged him wrong.

It was too much for her to figure out, and she sighed and drank the last of the water.


Morning saw her sitting hunched on her bench, staring at the floor with blank, dead eyes. She had no idea what time of day it was, but it felt like morning. It had to be.

The by-now-familiar jingling of keys made her look up, her tiredness vanishing as her heart leapt into her mouth and started pounding furiously.

A solitary guard came in, leaving his friend outside to watch the door. "Get up."

She did. He stepped forward and shoved her toward the door, and she went meekly enough though her mind was racing as much as her heartbeat. She desperately wanted to speak up and tell them about Yorath, but something held her back. Part of it was her final reluctance to expose him, but it was also a more practical thought—that the guards were just guards and wouldn't want to hear anything she had to say. They had no power to set her free anyway. If she told anyone, it would have to be whoever interrogated her.

The guards took her along the same narrow passage as before—she was befuddled by her lack of sleep and couldn't remember which direction they had been going in when they'd arrived and whether they were following it now.

They reached a door at the end, and once the guard in front had identified himself to his comrade on the other side, it was unlocked, and they went through. Not, as Laela had expected, into a torture chamber, but into a small space that looked like a guardroom. Numerous guards were in it, relaxing at a table and sharing gossip and a game of some sort. Most of them barely glanced up.

Laela's own guards escorted her to the other side of the guardroom and through another door. That took them to a set of stairs that led them straight upward, and as Laela reached the top, she squinted as light hit her eyes. This wasn't right . . .

At the top of the stairs, the guards pushed her out and into a much more ordinary corridor, where a man was waiting for them. He wore armour like the guards, but carried himself with more authority than they did, and her two escorts bowed their heads to him.

"Who are yeh?" Laela demanded. "What's goin' on?"

The man looked distastefully at her. "I've been ordered t'pass this onto ye by Lord Torc."

Her heart quickened. "What?"

"Yer tutor came forward this mornin' and told the Master of Law he was with ye all last night an' there's no chance ye could have gone anywhere else without him seein'. Since there's no proof he's lyin', the law says ye must be set free."

Laela felt warm all over. "They're lettin' me go?"

A nod. "However, the Lady Saeddryn, as actin' ruler of the Eyrie, has ordered that ye cannot stay here. Ye're t'leave the Eyrie immediately, an' if ye come back, ye'll be thrown back into the dungeons for trespassin'. Is that clear?"

She nodded dumbly.

"Good. Now get goin'."

Laela walked past him with as much dignity as she could

muster, and followed the corridor around until she reached the door leading out into the city.

Where Yorath was waiting for her.

Laela stared at him for an instant, then threw herself into his arms. *"Yorath!"*

He returned the embrace. "Laela, thank the Night God ye're safe! They didn't hurt ye, did they?"

She realised she was on the verge of tears. "No. They were goin' to, but they didn't. Yorath, yeh saved me. They was gonna *torture* me in there—if yeh hadn't . . ." She hugged him more tightly.

"Well, I couldn't just sit by an' do nothing!" said Yorath. "I knew ye hadn't done anythin' wrong. An' besides . . ."

Laela pulled away to look him in the face. "Yeah?"

He hesitated. "Never mind. Laela . . . look, I'm sorry. I did what I could for ye, but Lady Saeddryn's in charge now since she's the King's oldest blood relative. I can't go against what she says."

"I know," said Laela. "It's all right; I ain't blamin' yeh. I don't wanna stay here anyway. Not with the King gone. Gods, Yorath—what happened to him? Where did he go?"

Yorath shrugged helplessly. "No-one knows. He just vanished out of his room, an' no-one saw him go in or out. The whole city's in an uproar. Skandar's half-mad."

"Wait—Skandar?"

"Yeah. Well, of course he's gone bats. He's lost his human—do ye know how shameful that is for a griffin? If the King doesn't come back soon, he could lose everything. The other griffins won't respect him any more if he hasn't got a human."

Laela barely heard him. *The King vanished, but Skandar didn't. Why in the gods' names would he run away an' leave his griffin behind?*

"Listen," Yorath interrupted. "I'm so sorry about this, but I can't let ye stay any longer. Here." He pressed her sword into her hands. "I got this back for ye. An' this."

Laela took her bag of money and tied it to her belt. "Thanks, Yorath. This sword was Dad's, y'know. He left it to me."

"I know; ye told me. Now, go. Get out of here, Laela—an' good luck."

She smiled to hide her real feelings, and tapped the sword-hilt. "I don't need luck when I got this."

Yorath darted forward and planted a kiss on her cheek. "Go, Laela. An' may the Night God watch over ye."

She kissed him back. "I think she does," she said, and walked out of the Eyrie.


A renadd. Arenadd . . .
    The voice drifted toward him through the currents, and he struggled to reach it. His own voice felt weak, but he tried his hardest to call out to her. "Master . . . help . . ."

*Arenadd.*

"Help," he whispered. "Help me . . . please, Master . . ."

*My help . . . is no help,* she said.

He tried to speak, again, but his throat was full of something he couldn't cough up. His mind was full of vague memories of a scarred and horrible face looking down at him with terrible malice and pain.

*Skandar,* he thought, *I need Skandar. Need him to help me. I need . . .*

"Where's . . . Skandar . . . ?"

*Arenadd,* the Night God said again. *You are weak, uncertain . . . I sense it in you. Why is this? Why do you waver?*

He said nothing but tried to drag himself toward her, wanting her comfort and strength.

*I cannot sense you,* she said, and for the first time, she sounded uncertain. *You are weakening . . . your faith in me is weak . . . your devotion, weak. Why? What have you done to make this happen?*

"Don't," he managed. "Don't want . . . Where's Skandar? Make him come, send him to help, help . . ."

*BELIEVE!* The Night God roared. *Believe in me, Arenadd Taranisäii! You are my creature, you cannot turn away from me. Without me, you are nothing. You—are—nothing! Is that what you wish? Do you wish that? To be nothing, know nothing? Would you cast yourself into the void?*

His voice was coming back. "No. Please, no. Not that."

*Then listen to me.*

"I will." He felt stronger now, more lucid.

The confusion and the greyness faded, and darkness came. And the Night God was there, as always, her face stern but sad. *I know that it is difficult for you, Arenadd. You have been steadfast for so long.*

He gritted his teeth, his insides almost boiling with rage and despair. "I—don't—*want* to be steadfast! Understand? I've had enough! I've come so far—you've *pushed* me so far—and what do I have to show for it?"

*Only power, only wealth. Only the immortality I promised. Only the loyalty and love of thousands. Only that, Arenadd. Only my favour.*

He said nothing.

*Behold,* she whispered. *I have brought something with me.*

"What . . . ?"

She smiled. *On the night of the Blood Moon, you asked me to tell you who you were. But when I told you, you did not seem content. Perhaps I did not give you what you truly wanted. Therefore . . . see what you have forgotten.*

As she spoke, she reached upward—upward to where stars shone in their millions. Her fingers closed around one star. Just a small star. It wasn't particularly bright.

*See it,* she said, bringing her hand down toward him. *See him.*

Her fingers uncurled, and the star drifted away from her palm and toward him, to hover between them. Then the Night God leant forward, and blew softly on it. Her breath came out as silvery-white mist, and it gathered itself around the star, soaking up its light.

The mist spread out once again, but it didn't drift away. The star lit it up from within, as it formed itself into a shape around it—a shape that grew larger and larger until it was man-sized.

And man-shaped.

Arenadd found himself looking into a pair of eyes—pale, transparent eyes.

The mist had taken on the shape of a boy. He looked no older than nineteen and had the same height and build as Arenadd did. He was silvery-white all over, but Arenadd could tell from his angular features that the mop of curly hair on his head must once have been black.

The boy was simply clad, and though he had a brash, self-confident smile on his face, his eyes were sad.

Arenadd reached out toward him. "Who are you?"

*Don't you know?* The spirit's voice was fainter than a whisper and echoed slightly.

"No . . ."

The boy reached out in return, until his ghostly finger-tips almost touched Arenadd's. *This was what I looked like, when I was alive,* he whispered. *Before Eluna died. Before I met Dark-heart. Before my face was torn by the griffin chick I stole.*

"Who were you?" said Arenadd. "What was your name?"

The boy didn't seem to hear him. *A griffiner, I was. A Northern griffiner. So many people thought it was wrong, but they couldn't stop it. I was so close! So close to having everything. They were going to put me on the council—make me truly one of them! They tried everything to stop us, but we wouldn't go away, Eluna and me, and we were so clever and careful . . . We worked hard and people liked us . . . I was Master of Trade, I was.*

"Master of Trade," Arenadd muttered. "A Northerner, Master of Trade in a Southern city?"

*Oh, I was, I was.* The boy smiled beatifically. *Eluna was so proud of me.* He looked up abruptly, his smile fading. *I was wrong. I was wrong! WRONG! Listen, listen—you've got to understand. Northerners can't live in the South! We can't be like them, understand? They hate us, hate us . . . oh, gods, what did I do? All I wanted was to show I could be more than just a blackrobe, but Lord Rannagon betrayed me. Betrayed me! The dark griffin killed Eluna. I lost everything, everything! And then they killed me. Killed me! I was murdered. They shot me full of arrows, pushed me off the edge of the city. Oh, gods, not falling, not that, not that . . . oh, gods save me, I fell . . . fell so far . . . oh, gods, the pain. All my bones, my whole body broken, and it hurt . . .*

The ghost was hysterical, his face a mask of horror. Arenadd thought he could see the marks of wounds appearing on his body as he screamed—a phantom arrow, protruding from his chest, and another from his leg. Blood ran down his face from just beneath his eye, as if he were weeping.

"I'm sorry—"

The ghost lurched toward him, wild-eyed. *Who will avenge me?* he demanded in a terrible voice. *Who? Rannagon betrayed me, his griffin cursed me to die! They killed me! Who will avenge me?*

"I did," Arenadd whispered.

*You? Who are you?* The ghost's eyes had gone wide in sudden fear. *Who are you? Why do you look like me? WHO ARE YOU?*

Arenadd backed away. "Leave me alone. I don't know you, I don't know . . ."

The ghost stopped dead, holding his hands upward as if to tear a hole in the sky. *I am Arren Cardockson, curse you! I am Arren Cardockson, and I was murdered!*


When Laela stepped through the outer gate in the wall surrounding the Eyrie and back into the city, she knew exactly where she had to go. Even if it came to nothing, she had to be certain, at the very least for the King's sake. He'd been so kind to her, done so much for her—he deserved her help.

She was taking no chances this time. Keeping her sword at her side and her hand on the hilt, she approached the nearest person. "Oi, you. Yeah, you."

The man looked vaguely annoyed at first, but became wary when he saw the sword. "What can I do for ye, girl?"

"I'm lookin' for the tavern called the Blue Moon," said Laela.

"Oh, is that all? Well, it's easy enough t'find. It's on this street—just follow it westward until ye see it. It's a bit shorter'n the ones around it, an' there's a nice big sign over the door."

"Thanks." Laela nodded and went on her way.

She had already noticed how different the city was now. For one thing, guards were stationed on nearly every street-corner, heavily armed and looking tense and watchful. The people around and about had a nervous look to them, too, and avoided the guards as much as they could. Laela avoided them as well. She'd become somewhat disenchanted with guards.

A shadow passed over her, and she looked up sharply and gasped.

The sky was full of griffins. She'd seen them before, of course—they seemed content to spend most of their time flying aimlessly over the city—but now they had an intent look about them. This wasn't the lazy circling of griffins who had nothing better to do; this was the deliberate motion of a group of hunters. And they were hunting for something they were desperate to find.

But not as desperate as Skandar.

Laela saw him, too—massive compared to the others, even at that height. He circled close to the Eyrie, his huge wings beating slowly. As Laela watched him, she heard his cry echo over the city.

She had heard him call before, but not like this. It was a plaintive cry—almost a wail. It made her think of a lost child calling for his mother. She had never imagined that an animal so huge and powerful could sound so forlorn.

Laela tore her eyes away and walked on, shoulders hunched in determination.

The street was a long one, but she followed it doggedly, pausing to examine every sign. Finally, she came across one that made her heart leap. It hung over the door of a building that looked squat despite its two storeys, and featured a faded picture of a blue moon.

She examined it, and her eyes narrowed. This was the place he'd taken her on the night they had met. This was the place he went when he snuck out of the Eyrie. *They know me there.*

Laela gripped her sword more tightly and went in.

The tavern was almost deserted today—there were only one or two drinkers in it, one of whom was asleep in a pool of vomit. Laela ignored them and strode up to the counter, where she thumped the solid wood until a man appeared on the other side.

"What d'ye want?"

Laela reached for her belt and opened her money-bag. "I'm lookin' for someone."

"Anyone in particular?" the bartender said cautiously.

She reached up to the bartop again, and slowly placed a silver oblong on it. "I'm lookin' for a man who comes here a lot," she said, choosing her words carefully. "Yeh probably remember him pretty well."

"I've got plenty of regulars here," said the bartender, not taking his eyes off the money.

"This one's different," said Laela. "He keeps his face covered an' never shows it to anyone."

The man's expression changed. "Look, I don't mess with him, all right? No-one does. He minds his own business, an' so do I."

"But he was here two nights ago," said Laela. She pushed the oblong toward him. "Wasn't he?"

The bartender took it. "I ain't interested in helpin' ye, understand? What he does is his own business, an' it's more than my life's worth t'go talkin' about it to anyone who just walks in here."

"I ain't just anyone," said Laela. "An' I don't want t'know where he goes or anythin' like that, see?"

"Well then, go away an' stop botherin' me," said the man. "I've got enough troubles of my own as it is, what with the serving girl disappearin'. The Lone Wolf's brought enough bad luck here already without bringin' any more."

Laela dug out another oblong. "Just tell me one thing. Just one thing, all right? That's all I want t'know. An' I'll make it worth yer while."

"What do ye want to know?" he asked cautiously.

She put the oblong on the table, keeping it trapped under her fingers. "Was the Lone Wolf in here two nights ago?"

"I dunno, we had a lot of people in then . . ."

Laela lifted the oblong between her finger and thumb, holding it up where he could see it. "Was he in here?" she repeated. "Did yeh see him?"

"I might've," said the bartender, staring at the oblong. "Memory's not what it used t'be."

She sighed and tossed it to him. "Now is it what it used t'be?"

He frowned, scrunching up his eyes. "Two nights ago . . . he hadn't been here in a while . . . sorta got used to him not being here. But I ain't sure . . ."

Laela reached into her bag one last time. This time, the oblong she brought out was gold. *"Was—he—in here?"* she said, very slowly and deliberately.

The bartender reached over the counter and snatched it from her. He backed away before she could take it back. "Yeah, he was in here," he said, stuffing it into his pocket. "Didn't stay long. Had one drink, an' then left. He was took funny—must've been to another tavern, 'cause he looked pretty out of it to me."

"That was two nights ago?" said Laela.

"Yeah. Now push off an' don't come back."

She left the tavern, her heart pounding. *He was here. I was right. But then where . . . ?*

It was a start.

She sat down with her back to the tavern wall, deep in thought. If the King was drunk, where would he go? A whorehouse, maybe? Or maybe back to the Eyrie to sleep it off?

The second possibility felt more likely to her. She couldn't see him as the sort to visit whores. Not when he could choose any one of the women in the Eyrie.

She stood up and began to walk back along the street toward the Eyrie—maybe he'd decided to go home. She moved slowly, still thinking—this time, recalling the night he'd taken her to the Blue Moon.

She stopped abruptly. *Of course! He wouldn't use the street—he'd want t'stay hidden an' all that. He'd have used the roofs like he did with me—must've done!*

Excited now, she hurried back to the Blue Moon and walked around the outside, looking for the window they'd climbed out of. She found it—there was a broken brick just above it that had provided a handhold.

The tavern backed onto the canal that ran through the city, and she walked along it, hoping to find a clue. She couldn't help but wonder whether the King would be capable of running along those blasted rooftops while he was drunk. Then again, if he'd been doing it for years, maybe he could. He must have done it before while he was drunk.

As she walked along, keeping her eyes on the rooftops, her boot caught on something and she pitched forward and fell flat on her face.

She got up, muttering, and walked on, watching the ground now. A few steps later, she saw something that made her pause.

It was a strange dark stain. What made her pause when she saw it was its shape; it was long—reaching all the way to the edge of the canal. It looked like it had been left by something that had been dragged there.

Her throat tightened.

She knelt and examined the stain more closely. It had soaked into the dirt, and when she ground some of it between her fingers, she saw the brownish-red colour of it.

By chance, she glanced at the edge of her skirt, hanging over her leg near her hand. It had been light blue, but it was dirty now—she had used it to clean her face after her nose bled, and now the cloth had an ugly brown-red stain on it.

*It's blood,* she thought, almost calmly. *The colour's the same. And it's been here long enough to dry out.*

It was a clue, maybe, and she decided to investigate.

She stood up, looking back toward the buildings in the direction the thing must have come. There was an alley behind her, and she walked slowly toward it, examining the ground.

There were more bloodstains here. They led her to a spot just inside the alley, where more blood had been left on a wall. She found nothing else there.

Very frightened now, she almost ran back to the canal and looked down into it. The waters were murky brown and sluggish, with nothing to suggest that there was anything beneath them. But she knew there had to be.

She sat down and pulled her boots off. Making sure there was no-one watching, she stuffed her money-bag inside one of them and hid the sword under a heap of garbage.

Then she dived into the water.

It was cold, and much deeper than the stream near Sturrick where she had swum as a child. The current tugged at her clothes, trying to pull her away downstream, but she fought against it and struck out for the bottom.

Relying on instinct more than anything else, she thrust downward with all her strength. She risked opening her eyes, but couldn't see much beyond the vague impression of light filtering through the water. She closed them again and swam on.

Her dress hampered her badly, and it didn't take long for her to start running out of air. She kept on doggedly, despite her fear, determined not to give in until she absolutely had to.

Finally, just as she was on the point of turning back, her outstretched hand brushed against something. She jerked in fright and almost breathed in a lungful of water, but quickly thrust out her hand again, searching for whatever she'd touched. She found it, and after a few tries managed to catch hold of it.

Cloth. It was cloth. She tugged at it, but it was attached to something else and refused to move. But she grabbed at it again, and fear stabbed at her when she felt something soft underneath. At that, lungs bursting, she gave in and swam for the surface.

Once she had reached the open air, she checked to make sure no-one had stolen her belongings and dived again.

It took her a few more tries to find the cloth again, and several more to feel her way around it, but her heart thudded painfully when she realised that there was something underneath it. She tried several more times to pull it to the surface with her, but it was stuck fast, and she eventually realised that there was a rope tied around it that had to be anchoring it to the bottom.

She returned to the surface yet again, and climbed out of the canal. There she rested and considered her next move.

She nodded to herself, got up, and checked yet again to make sure no-one else was around. All was quiet. Satisfied, she moved close to the nearest wall and stripped off her wet dress. Naked, she spread it out in the sun to dry and fished her sword out from its hiding place. She took it out of its scabbard and tucked it under her arm before slipping back into the water. Its weight dragged her down, but not too badly, and she stuck it between her teeth and dived.

The sword's added weight was an advantage now, and she reached the cloth bundle, swam underneath it and, anchoring herself by holding onto the rope, took the sword and started to cut through it. The blade wasn't that sharp, but it was not as blunt as a long sword or something else meant for warfare, and as she sawed at the rope with it, she could feel it working.

She had to return to the surface again, but when she returned for another go at it, she felt the rope fray, then snap. Above her, the bundle, set free, started to drift away. She hastily transferred the sword to her teeth again and grabbed the thing before it could escape. Then she set out for the surface once more.

It was easier said than done. The bundle was far heavier than she had expected; it felt as if it were actively trying to pull her back to the bottom. Desperate for air, panicking a little now, she struggled with all her might, trying to pull it toward the canal's brickwork bank so she could use it to drag herself upward. The bundle barely moved, but she didn't dare let go of it—she knew that if she did, she'd never find it again. Not in this water.

Red lights were flashing in her brain by the time she found the side and dug her fingers into a gap between the bricks.

They helped her, and she groped her way upward as well as she could, the rough surface bruising her fingers. But her thin fingers were just thin enough to fit in the gaps between the bricks, and her confused mind was full of sudden gratitude. *Thank gods I got Northern fingers . . .*

By the time she reached the surface, her head was pounding with pain. She opened her mouth to gasp in air, and the sword instantly fell into the water. She made a grab for it, but started sinking again the instant she let go of the wall.

The sword vanished into the murky depths. Gone.

She stared dully after it, chest heaving.

Once she'd caught her breath, she began to climb out of the canal. She needed both hands for that, but she solved the problem by taking hold of the loose bit of rope still attached to the bundle while she climbed. It was just long enough to keep hold of once she was on land, and she used it to drag the bundle out after her and dump it on the ground.

Once it was high and dry, she fetched her dress and put it back on before returning to examine her find.

It was smaller than it had seemed underwater, but still big— nearly as long as she was tall. Whatever it was was entirely wrapped in cloth . . . no, a sack, she realised.

Feeling sick with apprehension, she turned it over until she found the opening, and fumbled with the trailing rope that held it shut. It came away after a few tries, and she opened the sack and began to pull it away.

A boot-clad human foot appeared, and she screamed and backed away.

The bundle didn't move. She inched back toward it, able now to see the shape of a body inside it. *Oh gods, I was right.*

She almost ran away to find a guard but stopped herself. She'd found it, and now she would have to finish it, for better or worse.

Grim-faced, she knelt and pulled the rest of the sack away, and the body flopped onto the ground.

It was Arenadd.

Laela stared at him for a long, long time, not quite able to take in what she was seeing.

The King had been bound hand and foot. The hilt of a dagger protruded from his chest, and his head was thrown back, the once-neat hair and beard soaking wet. His eyes were closed, and his skin was a sickening blue.

Very slowly, she leant over and placed two fingers against the side of his neck.

There was no pulse. As she'd expected.

A sudden, terrible rage and horror came over her. Furiously, she turned him on his side and undid his bonds. They had been tied so tightly they had cut into his skin. She threw the cords aside and laid him out as gently as she could with his arms by his sides.

Then she grasped the dagger, and pulled it out. It was long . . . horribly long . . . it came out coated in gore, and she could feel it scraping against bone as it came. She retched, but kept pulling until the blade was in her hand, and then threw it aside.

The wound it left behind was ghastly.

She moved the King's head, tilting it forward so it looked more comfortable, and hesitated.

Something had been stuffed into his mouth; she could see it poking out. She pulled it out.

It was a piece of cloth. As she moved to throw it away, she noticed something, and gingerly spread it out on the ground. It looked like an ordinary piece of linen, probably cut from a bed-sheet or something similar. But someone had drawn on it with charcoal.

She shivered involuntarily when she saw that, even though it was a picture she knew well. A circle, with three curling lines that met in the middle spreading out from it. A sunwheel. Gryphus' symbol.

She looked at the King's face again, and a terrible sadness spread through her chest.

"Oh, gods, what did they do to yeh?" she whispered. "Why? Yeh poor bastard . . ."

Memories flooded back into her mind. The King, coming into that alleyway on the night they met . . . She'd stumbled into him after the would-be rapist had pushed her . . . He'd felt so thin, but so strong, too, as if nothing could ever knock him down. She remembered the way he'd looked at her, when she had finally realised who he really was—that look she had been too panic-stricken to notice then, but remembered and recognised now—that sad, yearning look. The same look he had given her that night by Skade's tomb. *You remind me of myself . . . Why would you want to be like me?*

She put her hands on his chest, over his silent heart. "Sire . . . Arenadd . . . oh, gods, I'm such an idiot! Yeh did so much for me, an' all I ever did was treat yeh like rubbish. I was scared . . . didn't know what was goin' on, what yeh were interested in me for . . . but I know it now. Yeh just wanted me t'be a friend to yeh, didn't yeh? That's all yeh were askin' for . . . Gods, if I'd only . . . if I knew who'd done this . . ."

She looked down at his white face. *Gods, to spend all those years alone, with no-one there who loved him, no-one to talk to except his griffin . . . an' knowin' the woman he loved was dead. No wonder he took to drink.*

When she was younger, she'd seen her foster father drink, too. He'd stay sober for a few days, but in the end the wine or the beer would come out, and he'd drink until he was asleep. Sometimes he'd get angry, but he'd never hit her . . . Most of the time he was silent, and sometimes he even cried. One day she'd asked him why he did it, and she'd never forgotten the answer.

*It's yeh mother, girl. I miss her, an' I can't stand it.*

She wanted to laugh. "It's just the same, ain't it?" she said aloud. "Just the same."

Then she *did* laugh—but it was a broken, ugly kind of laugh, and when she laughed again, it broke again, and before she knew it, she was crying.

The tears were for her father, but they were for Arenadd, too. Poor, drunken Arenadd, who frightened her so much but only wanted her friendship, and who had come to such a pitiful end in this dank place, all alone.

*He wasn't no Dark Lord,* she thought as she sobbed. *He was just a man.*

## 14

## Destiny

L aela was too exhausted to cry for long.
Common sense told her she should leave, and soon—if
someone found her with the King's dead body, she would be in
unimaginable trouble. But she couldn't bear the thought of leaving
him there, so cold and vulnerable. She lifted him into her
arms and held him, cradling him against her chest.

"Night God, help him," she prayed. "Please, help him. Yeh
helped me. Now help him. Please . . ."

She sighed and bowed her head.

As if that were a signal, an instant later Arenadd's body
twitched. Laela gasped and nearly dropped it, searching
urgently for any sign of movement. For a moment it looked like
she'd imagined it, but then he twitched again, then gave a violent
jerk. His mouth gaped wide open, and horrible wheezing
sounds came from his throat. Then he jerked again and started
to cough.

Laela let go of him and pulled on his shoulders, moving him
into a sitting position. He gagged suddenly, making an awful
gurgling sound, and then vomited blood and water.

Once the last of it had escaped, he slumped back onto Laela's
lap and was still.

Laela patted his face. "Sire! Sire—Arenadd! Arenadd, are
yeh . . . all right? Breathe! For gods' sakes, breathe in!" She
thumped on his chest. "*Breathe*, damn it!"

His mouth opened, and he gasped in a breath and coughed. More water came up, and he coughed again, but then he breathed, deeply and shakily, and again and again until it had steadied and the colour began to come back into his face.

Laela sobbed. "Oh, thank gods. Thank gods. Thank . . . thank the Night God." She looked skyward, and cringed when the sun hit her eyes. "Thank the Night God," she said again, more loudly, looking back at Arenadd's face.

He was breathing much more strongly now, and the blue had left his face. Laela could scarcely believe it.

She touched his face. "Arenadd. Arenadd, can yeh hear me?"

He stirred and moaned, and his eyes flickered open. They had a glazed look, and didn't focus on her face.

Laela waved a hand in front of them. "Arenadd," she said again. "Arenadd, please, wake up. Say somethin'."

He coughed weakly. "Skade . . ."

"I ain't Skade," said Laela. "Arenadd, yer hurt. I dunno how bad . . . Can yeh hear me?"

His eyes slid shut. "Skade, he's killed me. I'm sorry. I should have listened to you. He had the . . . the sword . . . Gryphus gave it to him . . . I can still feel it in me . . . Skade . . . please, don't cry. I was . . . I was already . . . already dead."

Laela hugged him to her. "I ain't Skade. I'm Laela. Arenadd, listen—I gotta get yeh back to the Eyrie, so they can help yeh."

He stirred. "Skade, I can't feel my legs."

"I can carry yeh, then," Laela said sternly. "Just wait a moment." She laid him down and went to fetch her boots—he reached weakly after her and made a sound that might have been a sob.

Laela put her boots back on as quickly as she could, and tied her money-bag to her belt. She paused briefly over the now-empty scabbard, and then sighed and threw it into the canal. No point in keeping it.

Then she returned to Arenadd's side and touched his forehead to reassure him. "It's all right, I'm here. I've got yeh."

He grabbed at her hand. "Take me out of here, Skade. I don't want to die in Gryphus' temple."

"Don't worry; I'll take yeh back," Laela soothed. She slid her hands underneath him, and awkwardly lifted him. He was heavier than she'd thought, but she slung one of his arms over her shoulders and straightened up. His legs dragged uselessly, and his head lolled forward.

Laela gritted her teeth and set out back toward the Eyrie, following the canal.

They made slow progress. Eventually, Arenadd revived somewhat and tried to help her by using his free arm to support himself on the walls of the buildings they passed. But he showed no sign of trying to walk under his own power.

The path beside the canal was completely deserted, and they got almost all the way back to the Eyrie before a heap of garbage forced Laela to turn away into an alley and back onto the main street. There were plenty of people there, of course, but none of them paid too much attention to the girl and her soaking-wet and apparently crippled companion.

Laela's shoulders were aching horribly. She wanted to lie down and sleep for a year, but she gritted her teeth and forced herself on over the last stretch.

There were guards posted at the gate. "Oi!" one of them shouted when she was close enough. "What're ye doing back here? Who's that?"

Laela raised her head. "I've got the King!" she shouted back. "I found him!"

After that, it was as if the entire world went mad. The guards came running, saw the King's face, and went white. One of them sprinted back through the gate to alert the rest of the Eyrie, while the other stayed with Laela and asked a rapid succession of angry questions.

"Where did ye find him? What happened to him? Why is he all wet? Is he hurt?"

Laela did her best to keep up. "Found him in the canal. Someone tied him up an' threw him in. That's why he's all wet. Yeah, he's hurt, but I dunno how bad."

"What d'ye mean, someone threw him in the canal?" the guard growled. "Who? How did ye find—"

Laela didn't have to answer that because people were already running out of the gates toward her. She braced herself and opened her mouth to begin her explanation, but nobody was interested in hearing it. The King was torn out of her grasp so fast and eagerly it almost knocked her over, and before she knew what was happening, someone had taken her by the arm and pulled her through the gate and back to the Eyrie.

There was no point in trying to argue. She did her best to keep up and stood as tall as she could, trying to see where the King had gone. She caught a brief glimpse of him being lifted onto a stretcher and rushed inside, and then he was gone, and she had her own predicament to deal with.

The guard who had seized her seemed at a loss as to what to do with her, but an authoritative-looking middle-aged burly man Laela didn't recognise stepped in and said, "I'll take her. Come with me, girl."

She followed him, grateful that at least he didn't decide to drag her after him. He took her into what looked like a storeroom, which was at least out of the way of the crowd.

"Right," he said. "Who are yer?"

"Laela Redguard," said Laela. "I'm the King's companion."

"The half-breed who was thrown out of the Eyrie on suspicion of havin' somethin' t'do with the King's disappearance," he summarised.

"Yeah," Laela gritted out. "That'd be me."

"An' now yer come back with him, badly hurt."

"Yeah." Laela paused. "Who are yeh, an' why should I tell yeh anything anyway?"

"I'd be Garnoc, Commander of the City Guard," he said. "An' you'll tell me the truth, or I'll make the world a painful place for yer."

"Then listen," said Laela. "I didn't have nothin' to do with the King vanishin', got that? He was a good friend to me. Saved my life, gave me a home—he was kinder to me than I deserved. Then he vanishes an' everyone's sayin' I did it. Well, I ain't done nothin' wrong. They threw me out, so I went lookin' for him myself, an' found him. Then I brought him back here where he'd be safe."

"Right," said Garnoc. "So how did yer find him, when my men've been lookin' for two gods-damned days and found nothin'?"

Laela thought quickly. "'Cause I knew where he'd have gone, that's why."

"*How* did yer know?"

Laela explained.

Garnoc's eyes were narrow. "I see."

"Look," Laela added in desperation, "if I did that to him, why in the gods' names would I have brought him back here where there's all these guards what hate my guts an' think I did it? I ain't as stupid as I look."

He looked at her for another long moment. "We'll get to the bottom of this later. Go back up to yer room an' stay there. I'll send someone up with yer t'make sure yer don't go anywhere."

She nodded resignedly. "Fine."

Garnoc summoned a guard, who took her back up to her old quarters. They hadn't changed in her absence. The guard ushered her inside and locked the door behind her.

Laela didn't particularly care about being locked in. It was still better than being in the dungeons, and she needed her bed, and badly.

She stripped off her wet clothes and hung them in front of the fire, dried herself off with a handy towel, and climbed under the blankets very gratefully indeed. In virtually no time at all, she had slid away into peaceful, dreamless sleep.

She slept for a long time, and when she woke up she found a tray of food waiting for her. She put on a clean set of clothes, and then ate everything on the tray. It tasted delicious.

Outside, the sun was beginning to sink. She'd slept most of the day. Everything that had happened that morning felt hazy and unreal.

She found a comb and sat down to try and do something about her hair, which was full of dried mud and other bits and pieces it'd picked up in the canal.

As she was untangling a particularly stubborn knot, she heard the door open and looked up to see a young woman peering in at her.

"Laela?"

She stood up hastily. "What's goin' on?"

The woman coughed. "The King is awake and asking for you."

Laela threw the comb aside. "I'm comin'."

The guard was still outside, but he let them pass without

comment. Laela walked beside her new companion. "How is he?"

"Better," the woman said shortly.

She was walking too fast. Laela sped up. "Don't think I've seen yeh before—what's yer name?"

The woman glanced at her. "Arddryn Taranisäii."

"Taranisäii?" Laela repeated, unable to hide her surprise. "Related to the King, are yeh?"

"His cousin Lady Saeddryn is my mother," said Arddryn.

Laela scratched her head. "Didn't know she had children. Are yeh the heir to the throne, then?"

Arddryn's lips pursed. "My brother Caedmon should be the next in line."

*Should be,* Laela noted. She thought of asking more, but Arddryn's manner was distinctly unfriendly, and she decided not to push her luck.

Arenadd was in a different tower, in a part of the Eyrie Yorath had shown her and said was the infirmary. There were several different rooms in it, and Arddryn led her into the largest. There were guards stationed outside, both grim-faced.

As Arddryn opened the door, Laela caught a snatch of conversation from within.

"—getting too damned over-confident by half." The King's voice.

"I had a duty t'do somethin'—what would ye have *preferred* me t'do?"

"Not throwing an innocent girl into prison would have been an excellent place to start!"

"All the evidence—"

Arddryn coughed politely, and the voices stopped. A moment later, Laela heard a muffled curse, and she and Arddryn had to stand aside as a very-angry-looking Saeddryn strode out of the room. Laela watched her leave the infirmary and felt very slightly smug.

"Laela?" Arddryn was beckoning to her. "Go on, go in."

Laela walked past her and into the room, and heard the King's voice call her name.

He was tucked up in bed, looking pale and tired, but alert. "Laela," he said again.

She went to his side and tried to smile. "Hullo, Sire."

He frowned. "Call me Arenadd. I think you've earned the right by now. Please, sit down."

There was a chair by the bed. She took it. "How are yeh feelin', Arenadd?"

"Better. And you?"

"Pretty tired," Laela admitted. "It's been a long day."

"You can say that again." He smiled at her with his eyes.

"I thought yeh were dead," said Laela.

"A common mistake. I've survived worse, trust me."

She thought of the scars. "I believe yeh. Arenadd . . ."

"Yes?"

"It's all right about Amoran. I mean, I'll go with yeh. If yeh want me to."

He groped for her hand, and clasped it weakly. "Laela . . ."

She couldn't look him in the eye. "I'm sorry," she mumbled. "What I said to yeh before. I shouldn't've said it, it was cruel. You were just tryin' t'be open with me an' that."

"You saved me," he said matter-of-factly. "If you hadn't pulled me out of that canal, no-one would ever have found me."

She said nothing.

"Why?" said Arenadd. "Why did you come looking for me? I didn't . . . well, I didn't think you cared about me."

Laela paused. "I . . . well . . ."

"What is it?"

"I had a dream," she said. "I dreamt about Gryphus. He said I prayed to him once—a true prayer, an' he said that prayer was answered."

He was looking keenly at her. "Oh?"

"I thought about it the next day," said Laela. "It's true. I prayed once. In that alley, with them two bastards. I prayed t'be saved from them. An' I was saved. By you."

"I heard you," said Arenadd.

"Don't yeh see, though?" said Laela. "It wasn't *Gryphus* what answered my prayer, it was *you*! Gryphus never answered any of my prayers. I prayed for him t'save Dad, an' Dad died. Yorath told me that means the Night God took his pain away, by makin' him die."

"Laela—"

"They say you're the Night God's avatar," Laela went on.

"Her Chosen One. She sent yeh to fight her enemies. Now I've made four prayers in my life. I prayed for Dad, an' the Night God answered. I prayed t'be rescued, an' she sent you. I prayed t'her t'get me out of prison, an' I got out."

"And the fourth prayer?"

"I asked her t'help yeh," said Laela. "When I thought you was dead. An' then you woke up."

Arenadd watched her closely. "So what have you decided?"

"That I belong to the Night God," said Laela. "An' I think she wants me t'stay with yeh, Arenadd. But I don't care. I want t'stay with yeh anyway. So I'm going to."

His face crinkled into a smile—the first true smile she had seen him wear. "Thank you, Laela."

She smiled back. "It's no trouble. Someone's got t'keep an eye on yeh."

"Yes." He sighed. "It certainly looks that way."

O ver the next few days, she kept close to him, visiting him as often as she could. He slept a lot and looked tired and weak most of the time, but she could see he was recovering . . . far too fast.

That frightened her more than she was willing to admit, and that fear only increased when he calmly said, "The feeling's coming back in my legs. I think they're getting better."

Laela breathed deeply. "That's . . . good."

He looked at her. "What's wrong?"

"I still don't understand why yeh ain't dead," she confessed. "I mean, yeh must've been in that canal for . . . what, two nights an' half a day? An' with a dagger in yeh . . . I mean . . . I pulled yeh out of there, an' yeh weren't breathin', yeh heart wasn't beatin' . . . How can yeh have survived? I mean, it ain't possible!"

His expression saddened. "You don't think I'm an ordinary man, do you?"

"Well, no, but . . ."

"Touch my neck," he said softly. "Do it."

Laela obeyed. "Yeh feel a bit cold . . . What'm I meant t'be lookin' for?"

"Keep your hand there," he advised. "You'll realise it soon enough . . ."

She frowned. "That's weird . . . I can't find a pulse."

"I know," said Arenadd.

Laela took her hand away sharply. "What? Why can't I feel one?"

"Because there isn't one. They don't call me the Man Without a Heart for no reason."

She bit off an incredulous laugh. "Don't be—that's ridiculous! Everyone's got a heartbeat!"

"I don't."

"But that's . . . that ain't . . ." She trailed off.

"My heart has only beaten twice in twenty years," Arenadd said quietly. "The first time was when I kissed Skade. The second was when I first set foot on Northern soil. It hasn't made a sound since."

Laela's eyes had gone wide. "But . . ."

"I am the Dark Lord," he intoned. "No mortal weapon can kill me. The Night God's power is in me, protecting me."

Laela stood up. "I should—"

His hand shot out, catching her by the wrist. "Laela, I can't die. I *can't*. I can't age, I don't need food or sleep. I can be injured, but I can never be killed. Not by weapons, or poison, or suffocation, hanging, drowning . . . nothing. Not even the Bastard's sword could kill me. You can't kill someone who's already dead."

In an instant, all her old terror of him returned. "Stop it!"

He let go of her and lay back as if the effort had exhausted him. "The Night God needed a warrior to fight for her and defend her people," he muttered. "She can't fight for herself . . . She's weaker than anyone knows. In the South, a Northern boy was betrayed and murdered. The Night God sent Skandar to him, and he filled the dead boy with his magic . . . *her* power. Only a griffin could channel it. That was how she made her champion. But when I died, I lost my heart. Lost my soul. For a while I thought I could get them back, but now I know I can't. I don't even remember what it was like to be alive. All I do is what the Night God wants me to, and when she finds out I've defied her . . ."

The fear in his voice was so palpable that Laela's own began to fade. "Arenadd . . ."

He glanced toward the door. "Laela, I want to tell you

something. No-one else in Tara knows it. Not even Skandar knows, but I think plenty of people suspect. I trust you to keep it a secret."

"I will," said Laela. "I swear on my heart."

"Lean in close," said Arenadd. When she had, he spoke again, in an undertone. "I have no heir because I can't father children. I've had lovers over the years, but the only thing I ever planted in them was a curse. It killed them all. None of them ever had so much as a miscarriage."

Her heart ached with sadness. "I'm so sorry."

"I'd be a terrible father anyway. But keep it to yourself, all right?"

"I will." She paused. "Why tell me, though?"

He smiled. "We're friends, aren't we?"

"Yeah, we are," said Laela. "An' yeh can trust me."

Arenadd stifled a yawn. "I'm tired, so I think I'll rest a bit. But I'll see you again soon. I should be able to walk again before long."

"I hope so." Laela left the room, her mind in a whirl.

A nother person she saw a lot of during that time was Yorath. Her tutor kept visiting her—to continue their lessons, he claimed, but she knew better. They shared meals together, and talked, and Laela enjoyed his company more and more.

They spent nights together, too. She had no more fears about that, and neither did he.

"I really do care for ye," he told her one night.

Laela pulled him closer. "I must just be a bitter girl," she said. "I always thought I'd spend my life alone after Dad died. I never did think anyone'd ever love me."

"Well." He chuckled. "Ye aren't the easiest person t'get close to, I'll say that."

"When I was tiny, Dad taught me to trust no-one," said Laela. "He said, 'Laela, girl, yer a half-breed. Yeh can't just pretend otherwise. Never think I love yeh less for it, but the world won't be kind to yeh. It's tough enough for the rest of us, an' it'll be doubly tough for you. Remember that, an' rely on yerself an' no-one else. Sometimes, that's the only way t'live.' "

"Mm," Yorath grunted. "I don't think I'd be able to. I've

always had my family t'look out for me . . . I can't imagine what it'd be like without them."

She paused. "Yorath?"

"Yeah?"

"What tribe are you from?"

Yorath yawned. "Deer tribe."

"I dunno what my tribe'd be," said Laela. "The priestess what teaches me about the Night God said I'd belong to my father's tribe, but I don't know what it was, so she said we'd have t'just sort've . . . find out."

"Ah, ye'd be Crow," said Yorath. "For sure."

She looked curiously at him. "Why?"

"The Crow has no moon, only darkness an' the stars," said Yorath. "He's secret and mysterious; he lives in darkness an' his black feathers hide him from anyone who tries to know him. He goes where he pleases an' follows his own star, an' nobody knows where he comes from or where he goes. That's ye, Laela. All over."

She turned it over in her mind, and then smiled. "I s'pose it is. Crow. Huh. I like that."

"How's the King?"

"Better," said Laela.

"Are ye sure?" He sounded worried. "They were saying things . . . Everyone's sayin' he's been crippled."

Laela stirred. "He said he'll walk again, an' I believe him."

# 15

# Griffins

Arenadd's prediction had been correct. Within two days, he was able to move his legs again, and on the day after that, when Laela came to visit him, she found him out of bed and walking slowly around the room with the help of a stick.

He grinned at her. "There. I told you I'd get better. Now, I think it's time for an outing."

Laela did her best to look calm. "Are yeh sure yer ready t'go anywhere?"

"Yes, yes, of course," he said, waving her into silence. "Now, let's go. Skandar will want to see me."

Ignoring the protests of the healers, he limped out of the room. Laela followed.

"Keep close to me," he said. "I might need you to support me again."

"I will."

It was a slow journey up to the King's chamber, but Laela kept pace with him as patiently as she could.

"Sire—Arenadd, I mean—can I ask yeh somethin'?"

"Of course you can."

"Do yeh know who did it?" she said. "Who attacked yeh—did *that* to yeh?"

Arenadd winced as he took another step. "No. And he won't be easily caught. He planned it very well."

"We've gotta catch him, though," Laela said in angry tones.

"What he did to yeh was unspeakable. If I could find him, I'd have him hung an' quartered."

"Would you now."

"Yeah, I would. Did yeh see him, though? Do yeh know what he looked like?"

"He was working with someone at the tavern," said Arenadd. "I know that much. I only had one drink while I was there. One. And trust me, it takes a lot more than one drink to do that to me. It *must* have been drugged. By the time the bastard caught up with me, I could barely see straight. I only saw him very faintly."

Laela shivered. "What'd he look like?"

"Scarred," said Arenadd. "Horribly scarred, on the face. I heard him say something—he said the name Gryphus."

"An' later he shoved a bit of cloth with a sunwheel on it in yer mouth," said Laela. "I pulled it out."

Arenadd paused. "I see. So I wasn't imagining it. Well, a sun worshipper could easily have done something like that. There's not one single man or woman among them who doesn't hate me. But how he managed to hide in my city . . . that's another question."

"He'd be easy t'find, though, wouldn't he?" said Laela.

"Not necessarily. He'll have left Malvern by now, for certain. I already sent guards to the Blue Moon to ask some very blunt questions, but it seems the woman who gave me the drug has suddenly disappeared, and the owner hasn't the slightest clue where she went or whether she had anything to do with what happened. So unless we find some other clue, it looks like our would-be assassin has escaped."

"We'll find him one day," said Laela.

"I hope so." Arenadd's mouth tightened. "I have a few things I'd like to share with him. Most of them are sharp. But not too sharp."

When they got to Arenadd's chamber, he paused only very briefly to change into a fresh robe and boots, and then led the way out through the curtain that Skandar had appeared through on that first night.

Laela followed, intrigued.

On the other side of the curtain was a griffin's nest. She had seen a few by now, but this was something else.

It was full of straw, of course, and there were stray feathers scattered about the place. But there were heaps of gold coins and gemstones heaped in the corners, and sumptuous tapestries and banners hung from the walls. It was ten times more luxurious than the King's bedchamber—in fact, it was the most over-decorated room Laela had seen in the entire Eyrie.

She waded over to the water trough and nudged it with her foot. "Is this thing made out of *gold*?"

"Gold-plated wood," Arenadd said absently. "He demands the best, Skandar does. And I make sure that he gets it."

"I noticed," said Laela. "Good gods, all this for a—"

"Skandar isn't just an animal," Arenadd said sharply. "Never let me hear you say that again, Laela. No, he's not human, and he's not the brightest star in the sky, but he's as much of a person as I am. I owe him a lot, and so does this city. A little luxury isn't much to ask in return."

Laela drew back. "I'm sorry, I was just surprised."

"I suppose you've got every right to be," he admitted. "Now then, let's see where the old rogue's got to."

He limped away through the opening in the opposite wall and out onto the balcony. There, he tucked his walking stick under his arm, cupped his hands around his mouth, and let out an unearthly shriek.

Laela cringed. It sounded like he was trying to mimic a griffin's cry—in other words, it was a horrible noise that made her want to cover her ears. When he followed it up with another shriek, she did just that.

Arenadd continued to send out his call for some time before he lowered his hands and took a few steps back. Laela, venturing closer, heard an answering shriek from somewhere outside.

A moment later, Skandar arrived—landing on the balcony with a thump that shook the floor and nearly made Laela throw herself flat to save herself.

The giant griffin folded his wings and rushed at Arenadd, so fast and violently that it looked as if he were attacking. But a moment later, Arenadd was scratching his partner under the beak and talking rapidly to him in griffish, while Skandar cooed and nudged at him, like a cat asking to be petted.

Laela watched them with a bemused expression that vanished when Skandar suddenly looked up at her.

The griffin's eyes were silver and full of untamed ferocity.

"Stay calm," said Arenadd, as Skandar took a step toward her. "He just wants to look at you. Stand still and let him. He won't hurt you unless he thinks you're an enemy."

Laela stood as still as she could and kept her jaw clenched while the giant griffin sniffed her up and down. His breath was hot and smelt of old meat, mingled with the musty smell of his feathers. He shoved her carelessly while he sniffed, and she could feel the immense strength in his touch.

Apparently satisfied, Skandar raised his head and looked down on her, inscrutable.

"Touch him," said Arenadd. "Be gentle."

Laela glanced at him and reached out very carefully. Skandar tensed but didn't move, and she stroked his chest as lightly as she could. He didn't react. Emboldened, she combed her fingers through his feathers, feeling their soft warmth.

*Good bloody gods, it's like touching a giant chicken,* she thought suddenly. *If a chicken could rip yer head off, anyway.*

Skandar tapped her on the back of the neck with his beak. He did it lightly, but she felt a chill go down her spine, realising that if he wanted to, he could break her back as easily as if it were a twig.

She took her hand away.

Skandar's head descended to her eye-level. His own eyes focused on her face, and he rasped at her.

"What does that mean?" Laela asked, not without fear.

"He said, 'Skandar glad you save human,'" Arenadd supplied from somewhere behind the griffin's bulk.

"Tell him I said it was no trouble," said Laela.

Arenadd clicked and rasped a griffish phrase. Skandar kept his eyes on Laela and grated a reply.

"He said, 'You good friend to human. Give Skandar back human, so friend to Skandar, too.'"

Laela smiled. "Thanks, Skandar."

*"Krrree an oo,"* said Skandar, and turned away abruptly.

"He said, 'Not eat this one,'" said Arenadd.

Laela's smile vanished. "Er—"

"Don't worry; he was just joking," said Arenadd.

He spoke to Skandar some more, and Laela watched as the two conversed briefly.

"Settled, then," Arenadd said afterward. "Are you ready to come with us?"

"Where to?" said Laela.

"Well, to the Hatchery, of course," said Arenadd. "I think it's high time you saw the inside."

"What? Oh." Laela paused. "Why?"

"You've done a great service to the Kingdom," said Arenadd. "And you've done a great service to Skandar and me. This is the least we can do in return."

"What is?" said Laela. "Showin' me the Hatchery?"

"Showing *you* to the griffins," said Arenadd. "I think they might just be interested in you, Laela."

The Hatchery was even noisier and looked more dangerous than she remembered, and she probably would have refused to go in if Arenadd and Skandar hadn't been with her. The King unceremoniously shoved the doors open and limped in, upsetting the few human beings present.

"Sire!" one of them blurted, dropping her broom. "What . . . ?"

"Don't mind me," said Arenadd. "I'm just visiting."

Skandar came in after him, and the effect on the griffins was astonishing. Before, they had been all over the place—flitting in and out of the rafters, squabbling with each other, eating, sleeping, or screeching at each other for no apparent reason. But when the great black-and-silver griffin appeared in their midst, they went silent almost instantly.

They stopped what they were doing. Some lay flat to make themselves look smaller; others bowed their heads. Some actually fled, flying out of the openings in the roof or using the hatches at floor level.

Skandar held his head high and looked majestically at his inferiors, like a King watching his subjects.

Arenadd took Laela by the arm and muttered to his friend in griffish. Skandar rasped back. Then he turned his attention to the griffins. They raised their heads to listen as he said something to them. Whatever it was, it sounded vaguely like a command, and that idea was proven to be correct when they stood up and began to come forward.

Arenadd pushed Laela toward them. "Stand in front of me,"

he said. "Let them see you; you're being presented to them. Skandar's telling them about you. They'll come forward to inspect you; keep still and let them. *Don't show fear.* Don't. They don't have any respect for someone who shows them she's afraid."

"Right," Laela muttered back, and stumbled forward.

The griffins were all staring at her. She felt dizzy. To be surrounded by so many of them . . . each one horribly strong and full of magic . . .

She kept still and stood as tall as she could, raising her chin and trying her best to look fearless and dignified.

Skandar stopped speaking, and a horrible silence fell while the griffins regarded her, their eyes full of cold curiosity.

Finally, one broke away from the group and loped toward her. It was one of the smaller griffins, fortunately—its head was level with her face. Laela stood still, heart pounding, and the griffin circled her, sniffing at her clothes. It pushed at her a few times with its beak, and then peered at her face.

After a few moments, it made a dismissive noise and walked away. Several other griffins left with it.

After some hesitation, another one came to look at her, but it, too, left. So did the next.

As if that was a signal, the group suddenly began to break apart and wander off. Laela watched them go, crestfallen. It wasn't that she wanted to be a griffiner that badly, but it was such a clear and obvious sign of rejection and disinterest that it hurt her more deeply than she would have expected.

Arenadd stepped forward. *"Kree!"* he shouted.

Many of the griffins stopped to look back at him.

Arenadd came to Laela's side and spoke in loud and rapid griffish, emphasising whatever he was saying by thumping his stick on the floor.

Some of the griffins hesitated a moment longer at this; some turned away and left regardless, but others stayed.

Finally, one of them came closer. It was small—barely bigger than a large goat—but it had the same aura of danger that all griffins had. It came to sniff at Laela, and Arenadd quietly moved away while it did.

Laela braced herself while the griffin examined her up and down and looked her in the face. Then, without warning, it reared up onto its hind legs and planted its front talons on her chest. Keeping still then was much harder, especially given that the thing's weight nearly pushed her over, but she managed it somehow, and squeezed her eyes shut while it sniffed at her face. Gods, its breath was awful . . .

The griffin moved away and dropped back onto its forelegs. When Laela opened her eyes again, she found it staring at her in a way that made her more than slightly nervous.

"What do I do?" she hissed out of the corner of her mouth.

"Just keep still," said Arenadd. "Don't panic, no matter what—"

The griffin kept staring at her. It looked like it was going to pounce on her, like a cat with a mouse. And a heartbeat later, it did exactly that.

Laela had never imagined that a creature so big could move so fast. One moment it was crouching back and staring at her, and the next it had sprung straight at her, wings open and talons spread. She yelled and backed away, but it came after her, screeching. It caught up with her without any effort at all, and hurled itself at her. Its talons caught in her clothes and pulled her toward it, and its beak opened wide, ready to strike . . .

*"Help me!"* Laela yelled. "For gods' sakes, do somethin'!"

A moment later, she had fallen over, and the griffin was on her. It bit her, using its hooked beak to tear at her as if she were food. Its talons wrapped around her body, holding her tight. Any moment they would go through her clothes and sink into her flesh.

She struggled wildly. "Get off! *Get off me!* Arenadd, get it off me!"

But the griffin continued its attack, and neither Arenadd nor Skandar appeared to help her. It loosened its grip on her and reared up, its beak aimed at her face . . .

Instinct pushed Laela into action. She freed her arm, and punched it square in the throat.

The griffin backed off, hissing furiously. She managed to get up—before it attacked yet again. It knocked her over and bit and scratched at her until she managed to free herself, only for it to come at her again a moment later. She tried to take shelter behind Skandar, but he had moved to the other side of the room, and Arenadd was nowhere to be seen.

She started to panic.

The griffin attacked a fourth time, but it was at this point that she realised that, despite its greater strength and apparently murderous intent, it hadn't seriously injured her at all. It was just toying with her, maybe to get as much fun out of her as it could before it killed her.

She grabbed it by the beak and pushed hard, forcing it away from her. "Get off!" she yelled. "Get away, or I swear t'gods I'll kill yeh!"

The ridiculous threat had no effect whatsoever on the griffin, of course, which struggled to free itself and dug its talons into her even more painfully than before. Desperate now, she let go of it with one hand and jammed her thumb into its eye as hard as she could.

The griffin screamed.

The talons let go instantly, and it backed off, shaking its head violently and hissing. Laela got up and tried to run out of the Hatchery, but a knot of griffins were in the way, and when she turned back, she found the one she had hurt still there, its eye swelling and probably making it even more violent than before.

But it didn't attack. It sat back on its haunches and rubbed its head against its flank, and then settled down to groom its feathers as if nothing had happened.

Laela checked herself for injuries, and was frankly astonished when she found nothing more than a few scratches and a shallow gash on the side of her neck. Her clothes were torn, but other than that, the griffin hadn't done anything to her at all.

She looked around for Arenadd, but couldn't find him.

"Arenadd? For gods' sakes, where are yeh? What's goin' on? Get me out of here! I ain't jokin'!"

There was no reply.

The griffin finished its grooming and stood up. It came toward her, but slowly this time.

Laela backed away. "Keep away, or I'll get yer other eye next, yeh overgrown parrot."

It ignored her and came on until it was only a few paces away from her. Then it stopped, sat down on its haunches, and dipped its head toward the floor. It said something in griffish.

Laela blinked. "What?"

"She said, 'You are a half-breed human, but you saved the King's life,'" said Arenadd, from behind her.

She turned sharply. "What?"

The griffin spoke on.

" 'You are clever, to have come this far and climbed so high from such beginnings,' " the King continued. " 'With help, you could go much further.' "

The griffin came closer, but it looked placid now. It lifted its head toward her face and said something else.

" 'I have tested your courage, and found you worthy,' " Arenadd translated. " 'I will go with you now and make you my human until one of us is dead.' "

Laela blanched. *"What?"*

The griffin nudged at her hand and made an odd cooing sound.

"Touch her," said Arenadd. "She'll let you do it now."

"I ain't touchin' that thing!" Laela exclaimed. "The damn thing nearly killed me already; it'll take my hand off!"

Arenadd chuckled. "Laela, if she'd wanted to kill you, you'd be dead already."

"Well, it attacked me, anyway," said Laela. "I ain't gonna *pet* it, that's for damn sure."

"She was testing you," said Arenadd. "To see if you were brave and strong enough to fight her off."

Laela eyed the griffin. Its own eyes were a brilliant green and contrasted with its tawny feathers. It didn't look as if it were going to attack again. "That was a *test*?"

"Nearly all griffins do that," said Arenadd.

Laela looked at him. Then she looked at Skandar. "Did *he* do that?"

"Yes."

She looked at the griffin again. It still hadn't moved. Very slowly and carefully, she reached toward it. The griffin made no move. Finally, Laela put her hand on its head and left it there. The griffin's only response was to blink.

"Stroke her," said Arenadd. "You don't have to be too gentle; she won't mind."

Emboldened, Laela began to move her hand—running her fingers through the griffin's head feathers. The griffin closed its eyes and crooned.

"You see?" said Arenadd. "She likes it!"

Laela kept her hand on the griffin's head as she looked at him. "Yeh mean this griffin's . . . mine?"

"Don't ask me, ask her," said Arenadd.

Laela looked at the griffin. "Are yeh . . . uh . . . are yeh my griffin?"

The griffin rasped back.

" 'You are mine,' " Arenadd translated. " 'From this day, you shall go where I go and do all that I ask, as a human should. You shall clean my talons, bring me my food, translate for me, give me treasures, and clean my nest.' "

"Oh yeah? An' what do I get back?" said Laela, hiding her bewilderment with sarcasm.

*"Eee-an oo,"* said the griffin.

" 'Everything.' "

Laela gave up. "This is . . . this is ridiculous. I can't be a griffiner!"

"Why not?" said Arenadd.

"I ain't no noble, I ain't rich, I ain't powerful—I ain't nobody!" said Laela. "That's why! I only just learned how to say 'my favourite colour is blue,' for gods' sakes!"

"But you're very high in the King's confidence," Arenadd pointed out. "You're obviously a girl who's going somewhere. And with a griffin beside you, you'll go a lot further. And you showed a lot of courage. She likes that."

Despite herself, Laela felt a blush of pride on her face. "Well." She looked at the griffin again, with a new appreciation. "What's yer name, griffin? I'm Laela."

The griffin stood taller. *"Ooooeeek-a,"* it chirped.

"Oeka," said Arenadd. " 'Greeneyes.' "

"Oeka," Laela repeated. "Oeka."

The griffin clicked its beak at her. *"Leeeeaela."*

Laela grinned. "That's Lady Laela now, Oeka."

# 16

# How to Care for Your Griffin

Laela left the Hatchery and felt a deep and wonderful thrill of excitement when Oeka followed her. With the small griffin at her heels, she went back toward her quarters.

On her way, she ran into someone she recognised—and recognised in a way that made her feel sick with fright.

She halted. "Lord Torc."

He eyed her cautiously. "Laela. Where are you going . . . ?" He trailed off as Oeka appeared around a corner. The tawny griffin came to stand beside her human, and a look of open bewilderment showed on the face of the Master of Law. "What . . . ?"

Laela's mouth curled. "This is Oeka," she said, savouring every word. "My griffin."

Torc's eyes had gone wide. "*You* have a *griffin*?"

"That's right," said Laela, brazenly putting her hand on Oeka's head. "Now, we've got t'get goin', if yeh don't mind." That said, she pushed past him and went on her way with her head held high.

She passed other people on her way—servants, mostly, but also one or two of the royal officials, all of whom gaped, and then bowed low. Laela watched them, first with wonder, but before long she felt her pride and confidence soar. *Oh, my gods,* she thought, over and over again. *Oh, dear gods . . .*

It was probably the greatest moment of her life. By the time she reached her room, she was almost strutting.

She had talked to Arenadd before she left the Hatchery and knew what to do. She opened the door and let Oeka go in ahead of her. "This is my place," she said. "Our place now. Make yerself comfortable while I go an' get yer nest ready."

Oeka acted as if she hadn't heard her at all. She padded into the room and began to explore, shoving furniture aside and poking her beak into nooks and crannies. Laela left her to it and crossed the room to the wall opposite the door. There was a large tapestry hanging there, and she tore it down to expose the arched opening on the other side. Laela went through it and found a huge, bare, stone room. There was a water trough and some mildewed straw on the floor, but that was it. The other side had another arched opening, this one leading out onto a balcony without railings.

Laela took it all in and nodded in satisfaction. A griffin had lived here once, and now Oeka would. But she would have to find someone to bring more nesting material.

She went back into her room, where she found Oeka standing in the middle of the floor and giving her an impatient look.

"I've opened up the nest for yeh," Laela told her. "Come an' look."

The tawny griffin yawned and came toward her. Laela let her pass, and watched hopefully while she walked around the nest, flicking the old straw aside with her feathered tail.

"It ain't much now, but once we've got some new straw in . . ."

While she spoke, Oeka turned dismissively and walked back through the archway, pushing past her without a backward glance.

Laela followed. "I know it ain't pretty, but we can soon— *hey!*"

Oeka reached the bed, and casually climbed up onto it.

"That's my bed!" said Laela. "Yeh can't just . . ."

Oeka gave her a look, and Laela's indignant tones faded away.

"Uh, I mean . . . well, I guess yeh can use it," she stammered. "I'll go an' see about the nest." She backed out of the room as quickly as she dared.

The servants, obviously used to this sort of thing, brought several baskets full of freshly cut dry reeds and grass, clay jugs of water, and a newly slaughtered pig carcass. In very little time, they'd made the nest fit for a griffin, and when Oeka smelled the food, she got up off Laela's bed and sauntered into the nest.

Deeply relieved, Laela opened her wardrobe and took out a new set of clothes—the one she had on had been utterly ruined by the griffin's talons. She checked herself after she had stripped, and marvelled at the fact that she had nothing but cuts and a few bruises. If she had wanted, Oeka could have torn her to pieces—Laela had no illusions about that.

Frightened, but awestruck as well, she dressed and sent a servant to bring her some food.

By the time it arrived, Oeka had wandered back into the bedroom. She sat down by the fireplace and watched as Laela settled down to eat.

The griffin's silent stare was deeply unnerving. Laela did her best to look relaxed as she picked up a piece of bread. "So how do yeh like yeh new home? I can make it better, like. Over time an' that."

Oeka, of course, said nothing, but she was obviously listening.

Laela swallowed a mouthful of food. "Look, I dunno how to say this, so I'll just say it . . . uh . . ." She hesitated. "Thanks for choosin' me. I mean, it's . . . well, it's an honour. I dunno if I'll make a good griffiner, but I'll do my best."

Oeka shifted and clicked her beak.

Laela put her cup down. "I won't let yeh down, Oeka," she said. "I promise. Whatever yeh want from me in return for choosin' me—I'll give it. Even if I ain't got much."

The tawny griffin put her head on one side. Finally, as if she had made a decision, she stood up, snatched a wedge of cheese off Laela's plate, and strutted away.

"Yer welcome," Laela said weakly.

Fortunately, Oeka didn't seem to want anything else. She threw her head back to swallow the cheese and left back through the arch. Laela got up to see what she was doing, and saw the griffin go out onto the balcony and launch herself into the air.

Laela felt oddly relieved.

Once she had finished eating, she sat back in her chair and thought. What should she do now?

*Well, what do yeh want to do?*

Tell Yorath, of course. She wanted him to hear the news from her first. With that in mind, she got up and left the room, her heart pounding with newfound excitement.

Yorath sat back. "Tell me ye're lyin'. Please."

Laela grinned. "Can't. That'd be a lie. I never was that good at tellin' lies anyway."

He looked her in the face. "Ye. *Ye* are a griffiner."

"Yeah, I am."

Her blunt reply obviously threw him off. "What's the griffin like?" he asked eventually.

"Only small," said Laela. "Well, not that small. Arenadd—I mean, the King—says she's got big paws. That means she'll be very big when she's grown up."

"What's her name?"

"Oeka. Means 'Greeneyes.' "

"So what're ye going to do now?" said Yorath.

"How d'yeh mean?"

"Well, ye've got to be trained. An' after that . . . griffiners have big responsibilities, Laela."

Nervous heat touched her cheeks. "Well. I already got the trainin' sorted out . . . dunno about the responsibilities, but I know I'm meant t'look after her an' that . . ."

"Trainin' is sorted out, ye say?" Yorath raised an eyebrow. "Who are ye apprenticing with?"

"What's that mean?" said Laela.

"Who's going to train ye?" said Yorath. "Teach ye griffish an' the rest of it?"

"Oh. Well, the King said he's gonna do that himself," said Laela.

The effect on Yorath was amazing. He lurched as if she had hit him and recovered himself with an obvious effort. "The King," he said very slowly. "Ye . . . are going t'be apprenticed to the *King*."

"Yeah, I am," said Laela. "He said he'll teach me griffish an' fightin' an' how to fly on a griffin's back. An' some other things, he said."

Yorath rubbed a hand over his face. "I don't believe this," he said. "Ye're apprenticed to the *King*. First he vouches for ye in the Hatchery—makes ye a griffiner, in other words—an' now he's going to train ye himself."

"Yeah," said Laela, but some of the confidence had left her voice.

"How in the Night God's name did ye get so close to him?" said Yorath. "Takin' ye in is one thing, but this . . ."

"Well, I did save his life," Laela pointed out.

"Seems he really took that to heart," said Yorath. "Well." He sighed. "I s'pose that means I'll have t'go back to regular work from now on. Ye won't be needing me to teach ye any more."

Laela took his hand. "Don't be daft; I'm nowhere near knowin' how to speak Northern. Anyway, we'll still be seein' each other, right?"

"If ye want to . . ." Yorath looked uncomfortable.

It took Laela by surprise. "What's up with you?"

Yorath stirred. "I'm sorry, Laela. But now ye're a griffiner, a commoner like me . . ."

Laela stared at him for a moment, and then burst out laughing. "I'll tell yeh what, Yorath," she said once she could control herself again. "I'm gonna pretend yeh never said that. Now." She stood up. "My room smells of griffin, an' I've always wanted t'know what yer own place looks like. Mind if I come visit?"

L aela returned to her quarters much later, drunk on a mixture of excitement and the rather good mead Yorath had shared with her.

The alcohol ran its dizzy race around inside her head, filling her with a warm and wonderful sense of invincibility and pride. "Lady Laela," she repeated to herself, several times. "Lady Laela, griffiner of Malvern. Lady Laela Redguard." She laughed and sped up, almost dancing up the ramps and staircases toward her home, her head full of images of herself flying on Oeka's back with a shining sword in her hand.

By the time she reached her own door, the rush had worn off somewhat, and drowsiness had set in. She went in and gratefully walked toward her bed, intending to collapse on it.

It was already occupied.

Laela paused. It was too dark to see more than the huge

mound on top of her bed—she prodded it carefully, and found herself touching straw. Bewildered, she picked up a lantern and went to light it with a taper from the fire.

Its light showed her utter chaos. For a moment she stood there, frozen in disbelief as the reality of what she was seeing slowly sank in.

The bed had been torn apart. Blankets had been shredded, the pillows ripped open. The mattress had been disembowelled and the straw inside pulled out. The ruins of bed and bedding had been piled up into a crude nest, and Oeka was asleep in the middle of it.

Laela put the lantern down and put her hand over her eyes. "Oh, holy gods . . ."

After a few moments, tiredness and the fading effects of the mead fuelled her temper enough to let her put her caution aside. She strode toward the bed. "Oi!"

Oeka stirred but didn't wake up.

Laela poked the griffin in the head. "Oi! What are yeh doin'?"

A green eye slid open.

Laela took a step back. "This is my bed," she said. "Yours is next door, remember? *Oi!*"

Oeka yawned and tucked her head under her wing.

Defeated, Laela slumped into her chair by the fire and wondered what to do. She was so tired that sleeping in the chair looked possible, so she snuffed out the lamp—thinking that even if she couldn't, there was no point in wasting the oil.

Her exhaustion notwithstanding, sleeping in the chair proved to be impossible. She sat there in the semi-darkness for a long time before finally giving up and getting out of the chair to pace back and forth, debating internally. Her training was meant to start in the morning, and she knew she'd be useless unless she got some sleep.

Tired anger finally won her over. This was ridiculous. She was a griffiner now; a member of the nobility, and she had been turfed out of her own bed by an animal.

"Gryphus burn that," she muttered, and moved back toward the bed. She found Oeka's wing and pulled, hard.

A split second later, she staggered away from the bed, too shocked even to cry out, her arm cradled against her chest. She backed toward the wall, preparing to run away, but Oeka didn't come after her and she realised that the griffin hadn't even left the bed.

Blood ran down to her fingers and dripped onto the floor. She hastily covered the wound with the hem of her dress, and watched with a mixture of terror and disbelief as Oeka curled up in her new nest and went back to sleep as though nothing had happened.

Laela ran away through the archway and into the griffin's chamber. There she knelt by the trough and tried to clean her wound with the water.

It continued to bleed stubbornly no matter how many times she dabbed it dry, so she wrapped it up as well as she could and lay down on her side in the straw.

Eventually, the shock wore off, and she whiled away the rest of the night listing every curse-word she knew.

Morning came in a haze of tiredness. Laela sat up and peeled the fragments of straw off her blood-caked arm. The wound was smaller than she had thought, but it still hurt horribly. She did her best to clean it, and then walked stiffly back into her own room.

If her wound looked better than she had thought, then the bed looked far worse. Oeka was still asleep in the ruins.

Holding her wounded arm with her other hand, Laela crept toward the door. She reached it and took hold of the handle without incident, but at that moment the bed rustled. Oeka's head came up. Before Laela could decide whether to just run away, the griffin had jumped down from the bed and sauntered toward her, yawning.

Laela did her best to look harmless. "Mornin', Oeka. Did yeh sleep well?"

Oeka yawned. Her beak made an unpleasant *clack* sound when it shut.

"Well," Laela said weakly. "I'm gonna go an' see the King now. I'll be back later." That said, she opened the door and made her escape.

She was barely in the corridor outside when she heard the soft clicking of talons and turned to see Oeka following her.

Laela knew better than to argue with the griffin, so she gritted her teeth and set out toward Arenadd's audience chamber with Oeka in tow.

Arenadd was waiting for her. He was wearing a particularly nice robe trimmed with red, and there was a gleam in his eyes that Laela was too tired and upset to notice.

"Good morning, Lady Laela. Did you sleep well?"

Laela glanced at Oeka. "No."

"Too excited, eh?"

"Too deprived of a bed," Laela said sourly.

Arenadd raised an eyebrow. "Oh?"

Now she was in the King's presence, Laela felt bold enough to say exactly what she was thinking. "I don't want this," she said.

"Don't want what?"

"Don't want *that*," said Laela, pointing straight at Oeka. "I don't want t'be a griffiner. She's goin' back to the Hatchery today, an' that's flat."

Oeka backed away from her finger, hissing.

Arenadd looked nonplussed. "Laela, what are you talking about? You can't—"

"I don't want t'be a griffiner!" said Laela. "I ain't gonna. Not if it means livin' with a griffin."

Arenadd glanced at Oeka. "Why, what's she done?"

"She took my bed," said Laela. "She tore it apart, an' then slept in it! An' then, when I tried t'make her get out of it, she did *this* to me." She held up her arm, displaying the deep gash.

Arenadd gave it a cursory glance. "Is that all?"

Laela couldn't take it any longer. "Is that *all*?" she nearly yelled. "The damn thing bit me, for gods' sakes! She destroyed my *bed*! I had to sleep on a heap of straw all night!"

Oeka pushed forward and rasped in griffish.

"She said she didn't like the nest you gave her," said Arenadd. "The straw was mouldy."

"She didn't have t'go an' bite me!" said Laela.

"She said you pulled her wing."

"Yes, because she was sleepin' in my bed!" Laela tried to keep herself under control. "I ain't livin' with that thing," she said. "It's vicious."

"Laela. Calm down. Listen to me."

Laela folded her arms. "I'm listenin'."

Arenadd sat down on the white marble plinth that rose out of the middle of the chamber and gestured at her to do the same.

Laela sat beside him. A moment later, Oeka got up beside her and settled down on her haunches. She nudged Laela with her head, like a cat. For a moment, Laela wondered if the griffin was asking to be petted as a cat would, but when she looked, Oeka had turned her head away and was staring aloofly at the ceiling.

Arenadd watched them with the hint of a smile. "Oeka is a griffin, Laela, and griffins demand our respect."

"I'm a human, an' I ain't seen much respect from *her*," said Laela.

"You have to *earn* a griffin's respect, Laela. And then you have to keep on earning it. You impressed her, but unless you keep on pleasing her, she'll take what she wants. A griffin doesn't *have* to have a human, you know. If she wants to, she can leave you and look for a human she likes better."

"Good," Laela said viciously. "Let her go, then."

"What, and lose everything you gained when she chose you?" said Arenadd. "Stop being a griffiner?"

"Yeah, whatever. I don't care."

Arenadd sat back. "Oh dear," he said mildly. "And there I was, planning to give you an official position. Oh, well. I suppose I'll have to find someone who isn't so easily discouraged."

Laela choked. "Official position? Me?"

"Yes. I can't give titles or responsibilities to a *commoner*, now can I?"

There was a pause.

"All right," Laela said eventually. "I see what yer tryin' t'do. Don't know why yeh care so much, though."

Arenadd's black eyes glittered. "So are you ready to start learning how to be a griffiner?"

Laela looked at Oeka. Once again, she was struck by how beautiful the griffin was. "But she bit me," she said again, rather lamely.

Arenadd sighed and rolled up his sleeves. "Yes. Griffins do that."

Laela saw his exposed forearms, and breathed in sharply

when she saw the maze of scars on them. "Skandar did that to yeh?"

Arenadd pulled his sleeves down again. "Look on the bright side. At least Oeka was born and raised in the Hatchery. Skandar was born wild. When *he* looked for a human to choose, he ate the ones he didn't like."

Laela shuddered. "Oh, gods."

"Yes. So, are you willing to give it another try?"

Laela paused. "What's this official position yeh gonna give me?"

"Master of Wisdom," said Arenadd.

"What's *that*?"

Arenadd smoothed down his hair. "That's just the official title. The Master of Wisdom is the foremost advisor to the Eyrie Master. In this case, me."

Her eyes widened. "Advisor? Me? But . . . what would I be doin'?"

"More or less what you're doing now," said Arenadd. "Letting me confide in you. Giving me advice. Only I'd be paying you to do it. But you have to be a griffiner," he added. "I can only give official positions to nobles."

Laela grinned. "How much money are we talkin' about?"

"Oh, I don't know. About five hundred oblong a week, I think, is the official amount. I can ask the Master of Gold, if you like."

"No, I think that's enough," Laela said slowly.

"So you'll do it?"

Laela reached up and tentatively touched Oeka under the beak. The griffin lowered her head, and Laela rubbed her fingers back and forth as she'd seen Arenadd and other griffiners do. Oeka closed her eyes and cooed in response.

"Yeah," said Laela. "I'll do it."

"Excellent!" Arenadd stood up. "Now, I'm afraid our first lesson is going to have to wait because I need your help with something else."

Laela stood, too. "What is it?"

"Come with me. I've got something very special to show you."

Laela followed him through the door and into his own room.

The moment she stepped through the door, she winced. "Holy gods, it's like an oven in here!"

Arenadd rolled up the sleeves of his robe again. "Yes, I'm sorry about that, but it was necessary."

There was a roaring fire in the fireplace, and dozens of braziers had been lit around the room to add to the heat. Laela, already sweating, looked at Arenadd. "Why?"

"Because of that," said Arenadd, pointing.

Laela followed his finger. "What in Gryphus' name is *that*?"

The creature perched on a table by the fire looked like a bird at first glance, but Laela instantly decided that if it was a bird it was very, very wrong.

It was about the size of a chicken, and more or less shaped like one, with a small, lean body perched on two legs, with long talons shaped for gripping branches, and a pair of wings placed just below the base of the neck. But the neck ended in a big, muzzled head topped by a pair of stubby horns, and the tail was long and serpentine and had a diamond-shaped membrane on the end.

And where a bird had feathers, this thing had pale green scales.

Arenadd took a step toward it, but the creature backed off, opening its mouth to reveal dozens of sharp, silver fangs. The King moved away from it, shaking his head. "It won't let me go near it, but it should let you—it's probably well trained."

Laela hadn't moved. "What *is* it?"

"It's a dragon," said Arenadd. "From Amoran. They use them to carry messages."

Laela's mind reeled. *A dragon!*

Everyone knew about dragons, of course—there were dozens of stories about them. But as far as she'd ever known, they were myths, or maybe something that had existed once but not now. Seeing one here was unbelievable.

"I thought it'd be bigger," she said at last.

"As far as I know, that's about as big as they get," said Arenadd. "Now, can you do me a favour? See if you can get close enough to take the message from it."

Laela started. "What?"

"Look there," said Arenadd. "On its back."

Laela ventured a step closer and finally noticed the small brown cylinder strapped to the dragon's back. "It's got a message from Amoran?"

"Yes. It arrived early this morning. It should let you take it."

"It won't bite me, will it?"

"No; it's perfectly tame. Dragons aren't very aggressive anyway."

Very carefully, Laela reached out toward it. The dragon came closer to her and sniffed her fingers. Wary of its teeth, she tried to touch its head. It let her do it, and even thrust its snout at her, asking to be petted. Laela noticed the bristly ears and scratched them. The dragon hooted and put its head on one side, asking for more.

Laela smiled despite herself and scratched more vigorously. The dragon hooted again. Then it leapt. Laela jerked away, but she was too slow. Before she knew what was happening, the dragon had jumped onto her arm and was perched there, talons gripping.

Specifically, gripping the half-congealed wound.

Laela let loose with a stream of curse-words, and groaned in relief when the dragon decided to shuffle further along toward her elbow. The wound still smarted, but the pain faded quickly enough.

"Go on, take the message," Arenadd urged.

Laela pulled herself together. Once the dragon had settled down on its new perch and begun to nibble at its wing, she wiped the sweat off her forehead and reached tentatively for the cylinder on the creature's back. The dragon glanced at her, and then went back to its grooming.

Laela fiddled with the cylinder for a few moments before she figured out how to take the cap off the end. It came free easily enough—there was a wax plug underneath it. She put it aside and reached inside the cylinder and pulled out a thin scroll of paper. It was covered in tiny, neat runes, and, unable to stop herself, she had a go at reading them. She could decipher a few words here and there, and smiled proudly as she handed it to Arenadd. "Here yeh go."

He took it. "Thanks. Now, let's see . . ."

Laela, the dragon now perched on her shoulder, watched with interest. "What's it say?"

Arenadd scanned it briefly. "Excellent. Just as I thought—it's from the Amorani ambassador."

Laela glanced at Oeka. The griffin had been grooming herself, apparently uninterested in what was going on, but now she looked up as if she were as interested as her human.

"What's it say?" Laela persisted.

Arenadd looked up. "You know, this *is* a confidential message from the head diplomat of the Emperor of Amoran."

"Yeah, so yeh shouldn't share it with anyone except yer most trusted advisor," said Laela.

The King smiled again, with his eyes. "Indeed." He rolled up the message. "This was sent from Maijan—that's an island away to the east that the Amorani Empire controls. Apparently the ambassador is there right now—or was when he sent this message, anyway. He's on his way here now, and he says he should be here in a matter of days."

Laela grinned and petted the dragon. "What's his name?"

Arenadd checked the message again. "Uh . . . Lord Vander. His griffin is called Ymazu. From what I'm told, he's a reasonable man, and an extremely good negotiator." He frowned. "This isn't going to make me any more popular, you know—this treaty with Amoran."

"But it's for the best," said Laela.

"Yes. It would be a lot easier if the Amoranis weren't so different from us. And if they weren't sun worshippers."

Laela started. "They're sun worshippers?"

"Yes. In fact, some people believe that Gryphus was born in Amoran. That's probably partly because it's eastward and the sun rises in the east, but also because the Amorani were worshipping a sun god before Cymria was even inhabited by humans."

"They worship Gryphus?" said Laela.

"Actually, their god is called Xanathus," said Arenadd. "But they also believe that the sun is his eye, and that he's the father of all life. Most Northerners hate the Amoranis for that. But the truth is, we in Cymria have been copying them for some time." His expression hardened. "The slave collars that my people used to wear—those were invented in Amoran. Still, you're right—a treaty with Amoran is exactly what we need."

"Are we still goin' there?"

"Probably. If my negotiations with Lord Vander go well. In fact, if everything goes to plan, we'll probably go back to Amoran with him." He paused. "Are you excited?"

"Yeah," Laela confessed. "How long're we gonna be there?"

"Well, first we'd have to travel to the coast . . . then a few months of sailing to get to Maijan . . . We'd have to follow the entire island chain, and then cross the Amourfish Sea to get to Amoran itself, and then when we get there, the negotiations with the Emperor would take some time, and we'd have to stay a bit longer to be polite . . ." Arenadd trailed off.

"How long?" Laela pressed.

"Probably more than a year."

She stared at him. "A *year . . .* ?"

"That isn't going to be a problem, is it?" said Arenadd. "I'm sure I can teach you a lot while we're on our way."

"I guess so," Laela mumbled.

"And you haven't really been here long enough to have to worry about homesickness, so what's the problem?"

"Yorath would . . ." She trailed off.

"Yorath?" Arenadd put his head on one side. "Oh yes, your tutor. What about him?"

Laela started. "Oh. Uh . . . it's not important. Never mind."

Arenadd gave her a knowing look. "You *have* been spending a lot of time with him after classes, haven't you?"

"Well . . ." Laela felt inexplicably ashamed.

"Not to worry," Arenadd said briskly. "I'm sure he can come along with us. After all, I won't have time to teach you *everything* myself."

Without even thinking, Laela stepped forward and hugged him around the neck. The dragon shrieked and leapt off her shoulder, but she didn't pay any attention.

Arenadd jerked away from her, as if in fright. "Laela!"

She let go and backed off. "I'm sorry—"

He shook himself. "It's all right. Sorry, I didn't mean to . . . You took me by surprise."

"Haven't been hugged in a while, have yeh?" said Laela.

"No," said Arenadd, his tone as matter-of-fact as hers. "Dark Lords aren't very huggable. So," he added, suddenly awkward, "are you ready to start your first lesson?"

Laela went to stand by Oeka. "Yeah, I am."

# 17

# The Amorani Ambassador

Laela spent the rest of that morning with Arenadd, learning her first lessons. To her surprise, Arenadd wasn't her only teacher—Oeka taught her, too.

Arenadd began by lecturing her about the habits of griffins—what they liked to eat, the best materials to give them for nest-building, and even the times when they preferred to go to sleep and wake up. Oeka then helped him show her how to clean her partner's talons, how to treat fleas, how to remove a bone lodged in the throat, and a dozen and one other things about griffish health and medicine.

Laela took it all in, paying close attention not just because of her renewed interest in becoming a griffiner but also because most of it was fascinating. Learning so much about griffins made her feel like she was being brought into a secret circle of knowledge, seeing things only a select few were allowed to see. That feeling of pride and excitement kept her so enthralled that she didn't even realise how much time had passed until Arenadd announced that they should stop for lunch.

After lunch, Laela had to go to the library again for another lesson with a wary Yorath, but the next morning she was with Arenadd again. Now he began teaching her something she was particularly determined to learn—the language of griffins.

It was much harder than she'd thought. Griffins had a completely different language structure than humans, and the sounds they used were far away from anything humans used. Arenadd explained that griffish was a primitive language that had never really been meant to express complicated ideas, and that humans weren't built to speak it. The best that Laela would be able to manage would be a crude approximation of griffish sounds, but the important part of knowing griffish was learning how to interpret what Oeka said. Griffins could indeed understand human languages even if their beaks stopped them from speaking them properly, but they preferred to be spoken to in griffish.

As far as Laela was concerned, knowing griffish was another and even more important part of being a member of the secret world of griffins and griffiners. One day, she would be able to talk to Oeka and know what she was thinking and what she wanted. And maybe then they could be friends.

On the second night after they had become partners, Laela returned to her room with Oeka, but without the sense of dread she'd had before. On the way she paused briefly to give a few orders to a servant, who hurried away to make arrangements. By the time she and Oeka had eaten, a hammock had been hung near the fireplace.

"There," said Laela. "If yeh like that bed better, then keep it. I don't mind."

Oeka watched her while she spoke, and Laela imagined that she could see satisfaction in the griffin's face. There was definitely a new air of energy about her as she picked over the bones of her dinner and went next door for a drink before returning and climbing into her new nest.

Laela watched her rearrange the shredded blankets and snuggle down, and felt an affection toward the griffin that hadn't been there before. She was dangerous; Laela wasn't about to doubt that now, but she was appealing, too, with those bright green eyes and the fluffy feathers on her chest. Laela wouldn't have gone so far as to call her cute, but she was nice to look at, and there was something endearing about her slightly awkward, leggy frame and the way her head bobbed up and down when she walked.

With that pleasant thought, Laela snuffed out the lamp and climbed into her new hammock. She'd never slept in one before, but she was so tired that she was convinced she could sleep anywhere.

She was wrong. The hammock was uncomfortable and

swung back and forth alarmingly whenever she moved too much, and the shock always woke her up. She tried what felt like half a dozen different positions, hoping to find one that would let her sleep, but none of them changed the fact that the hammock didn't support her back and kept on threatening to tip her out.

Finally, after spending what felt like half the night trying to sleep in the wretched thing, she got out of it and padded over to the bed, rubbing her back along the way. She could just see the outline of Oeka in the middle of her nest. She could hear her, too—cheeping softly in her sleep.

Laela didn't even think about trying to make her move. But maybe there was another solution.

She took a deep breath and climbed into the nest. Oeka stirred and clicked her beak warily, but she didn't attack.

"It's only me," Laela told her. "Mind if I join yeh?"

There was a rustling as Oeka moved away, leaving a warm hollow where she'd been lying. Laela grinned and took it. Instantly, the musty smell of feathers enveloped her.

It wasn't that bad.

The nest was surprisingly comfortable, and Laela quickly felt her tiredness take hold. As she started to drift off, she felt Oeka snuggle against her.

She smiled to herself and went to sleep.

The Amorani diplomat arrived two days after his message, his griffin coming in to land at the top of the Council Tower. Arenadd gave him the rest of the day and that night to rest, so they didn't actually meet until the following morning.

Arenadd put on his best robe and the crown he usually avoided wearing, and met his guest in the audience chamber that had once belonged to Lady Elkin. It still had its old white marble floor, but the walls were covered by richly woven tapestries. Dozens of beautifully made, straight-bladed Southern swords hung there, too—trophies from the war.

Arenadd had managed to persuade Skandar to be there, and the giant griffin grudgingly stepped up onto the marble platform intended just for him. Arenadd sat on a cushion between his partner's talons and waited.

Lord Vander came into the chamber, with only his griffin

beside him. He was a short, middle-aged man with a thin grey moustache, and most of his body was covered by an enormous cloak covered in feathers that had probably come from his griffin. She was small, as Amorani griffins generally were, and had dark brown feathers with a patch of scarlet on the throat. Her legs and beak were yellow, and she wore an elaborate head-dress.

Arenadd stood to receive them but said nothing and stayed where he was while Skandar stepped down off the platform. The ambassador stepped aside, and waited while his partner went to meet her own host.

If anything, the dark brown griffin looked even smaller next to the hulking Skandar, but she moved with a grace and confidence that impressed Arenadd. She bowed her head until her beak nearly touched her talons and waited submissively while Skandar walked around her, sniffing her up and down and nudging her none-too-gently with his beak. This would have been enough to provoke most griffins, but this one held still until Skandar moved away. When he was at a respectable distance, she raised her head—not too high, Arenadd noted—and spoke rapidly. She was using the faster, more basic version of griffish, which most humans were too slow to understand.

Skandar was also too slow. He waited until she had finished, and grated back.

This time, Arenadd understood perfectly, and he smiled to himself.

"I am Ymazu," the ambassador griffin said at last.

"Am Skandar." He turned to look at Arenadd. "This one not fight," he said, and lumbered back to the platform. "Will mate with her later, maybe," he added, and settled down to groom his wings.

The griffish formalities over with, Arenadd finally stepped forward to meet his human guest. "Welcome," he said. "I'm honoured to have you in my Kingdom, Lord Vander."

Lord Vander folded his hands together and bowed his head. "The honour is mine, Sire."

Arenadd raised an eyebrow. "You speak Northern. I'm impressed."

Vander smiled. "As an ambassador, I am expected to know

the languages of the places I visit." He spoke the dark tongue very well though with a pleasantly rounded accent.

Arenadd extended his good hand. "As one griffiner to another, my lord."

Vander hooked his fingers with Arenadd's, and tugged briefly in the traditional griffiner gesture of greeting. "I see that your fingers are in better condition than I expected, Sire."

Arenadd held up his maimed hand. "Not these ones, I'm afraid."

"Ah." Vander inspected it briefly. "Yes. So that story of you is true."

"Story?" Arenadd couldn't help but be intrigued. He gestured at the seat by the platform as he spoke.

"Yes," said Vander, taking it while Ymazu settled down beside him. "In my homeland, they call you the King with the Broken Fingers. It is said that you snapped the bones with your teeth to prove to the chiefs of your people that you did not feel pain."

Arenadd rubbed the fingers in question. "I wouldn't dream of ruining such a great story by saying anything about that. So tell me, my lord—I'm curious—where did you learn my language?"

"From one of your people, Sire," said Vander. "You may know that there are black-haired men in Amoran who do not have our skin."

"Yes," Arenadd said gravely. "I know that. I'm surprised you were prepared to learn from a slave."

Vander ran a delicate finger along his thin moustache. "How else could I have learned their language, Sire?"

"Most people think they're above even talking to slaves, my lord."

Vander touched his neck. "I am not, Sire."

"And neither am I." Arenadd leaned forward. "My lord, I'm sure you're aware that my main condition for making this alliance with Amoran—apart from promises of military support— is that I want those slaves to be returned to their homeland."

"I do know that, Sire," said Vander. "And I expected it before I knew. After all, the freeing of slaves is something that you have become famous for."

Arenadd touched the collar scars on his neck. "We all need

to be set free, in one way or another. Now, is the Emperor willing to accept that condition?"

"I think so," said Vander, slowly and deliberately. "If the conditions are agreeable, Sire."

"And what conditions would those be?"

"Conditions," said Vander.

Arenadd resisted the urge to drum his fingers. "Be more specific. What does he want? Lower trade taxes? Money?"

Vander paused. "Tell me, Sire—are you still planning to come to Amoran?"

"If all goes well with our negotiations," said Arenadd. "A courtesy visit to the Emperor would be expected of me."

"The Emperor would like to see you, Sire," said Vander.

"Is that so?" Arenadd scratched his beard. "Did he say why?"

"Between us, I suspect it is partly curiosity," said Vander. "All of us in Amoran have heard your story; many would be astonished to see you in person."

"But there's another reason, isn't there?"

Vander shifted. "There is," he admitted at last.

"Tell me, then."

"I have forged many alliances between my country and others," said Vander. "And with such a major treaty, it is expected for the ruler that suggested it to make a gesture more meaningful than a few agreements and proclamations."

"A gift, perhaps?" said Arenadd, not liking the diplomat's indirect manner.

"A gift," Vander nodded.

"I'm sure I can find something," said Arenadd. "Is there anything in particular he wants?"

"Griffin eggs."

Arenadd paused at that. "Griffin eggs?"

Vander stroked his partner's shoulder. She chirped in response and nibbled at his ear. "Our griffins in Amoran are strong and cunning, but smaller than those in Cymria," said the diplomat. "This request comes not from the Emperor himself, but from—"

"But from the griffin who chose him," Ymazu interrupted. "Wise Zaerih." She flicked the crest that decorated the back of her head. "Those in Cymria have never stayed in Amoran, but we believe that a mingling of blood would benefit us all. If a nestful of hatchlings from your Eyrie were to come to us, we would be most glad."

Arenadd shook his head. "This isn't a question for me to answer. Skandar?"

Skandar blinked and raised his head. "What say?"

Ymazu stood. "Mighty Skandar," she said, bowing her head to him. "We ask if you would give us eggs from your females. Young griffins, to live with us."

Skandar jerked his head forward and snapped his beak loudly. "I give egg!" he boomed. "I give to you!" He made an odd, purring noise deep in his throat. "Come see. I give Mighty Skandar egg! Hatch big chick!"

Ymazu fluttered her wings and purred back. "I would be honoured."

Arenadd hid a smile. "That answers that question."

Vander was openly grinning. "If Skandar comes to Amoran, I am certain that plenty of females will be willing to submit to him. That should please the Emperor enough."

"Then that's settled," said Arenadd. "Is that all he wants?"

"No, Sire," said Vander. "There is one other thing."

"Name it."

Vander's dark brown eyes gleamed. "There is another way in which the mingling of blood could be . . . useful to us all, Sire."

"Human blood, this time," Arenadd surmised. "Yes?"

"The Emperor has a daughter," said Vander. "She is young—very pretty, too, if you ask me."

Arenadd groaned internally. "I see. An arranged marriage."

"You are not married, Sire," said Vander. "I know that already. If the women of your own country do not please you, then perhaps an Amorani princess would."

There was no way Arenadd could tell Vander why the idea horrified him, so he settled on a compromise. "I'll go to Amoran," he said. "And talk it over with the Emperor. I'm sure we can come to some agreement."

Vander smiled. "I am glad to see that you are a reasonable man. Those in the South would not be pleased to know that I am speaking with you!"

"Ah, yes, and what about the South?" said Arenadd, relieved at the change of subject.

"Bah." Vander flicked his fingers dismissively. "The South would not ally with us in a way that satisfied us, and by now they are nothing. By now the North is the only part of this land that is wealthy and peaceful. Thanks to you, Sire," he added, fixing his eyes on Arenadd's face.

Despite himself, Arenadd felt flattered. "I did what I had to do."

Vander said nothing. He kept looking at Arenadd, studying him in a way the King found very disconcerting.

The silence drew out uncomfortably, until Vander finally broke it. "I never thought I would see you again," he said. "And never in a place such as this. Truly, the gods work in mysterious ways."

Arenadd's forehead wrinkled. "'Again,' my lord?"

Vander smiled. "You do not remember me? Disappointing, considering that I saved your life, Arren."

Arenadd went cold all over with shock. "I'm not sure I know what you're talking about, my lord," he said, keeping his face carefully blank.

Vander ignored him. "When we last met, you were only a boy," he said. "It was in Eagleholm, before the war. I was there to treat with Lady Riona. A long time ago by now, but I remember you well. And I remember you," he added, looking at Skandar. "I saw you fight in the arena. Darkheart, they called you."

Skandar blinked lazily at him.

Vander, however, was still looking at Arenadd. "Forgive me, Sire," he said. "But if I saw you today as I saw you then, I never would have dreamed that one day you would be a King." He paused. "But I would have easily accepted that you had the strength and the will."

Arenadd didn't know what to say.

Fortunately, Vander took his silence as modesty. "My masters always taught me to be truthful, Sire. You could have fled that night—taken your escape while your enemies did not know you had broken free of your prison. But you returned. Ymazu told me everything. You stayed to free another prisoner." He looked at Skandar again. "And I see that he was grateful."

Arenadd shivered internally. *Dear gods, he was there. He knew me . . . knew Arren.*

"Ancient history, my lord," he said airily. "Right now I'm more interested in the here and now."

"Understood, Sire," said Vander. "I apologise if my idle reminiscences were not appropriate."

Arenadd longed to ask him more, but he knew he couldn't. "Thank you for . . . what you did for me back then, my lord."

Vander smiled. "I considered it a parting gift to the masters of Eagleholm. But I doubt they even thought of it after they had suffered your own. Now." He leaned forward. "We have talked long enough, and I am tired. Perhaps we should speak again, this evening, or perhaps tomorrow."

"Agreed," said Arenadd.


Saeddryn was not amused. "*Amoran?* Ye're goin' to Amoran?"

Arenadd folded his arms. "A courtesy visit to the Emperor. I'm sure the Kingdom will be fine in your capable hands."

She took a deep breath. "I see. An' ye didn't think it would be a good idea t'say somethin' to us beforehand?"

"Actually, I'm pretty sure I mentioned it more than once," Arenadd said calmly. "In fact, if I recall, I said something about it last week."

"Well, yes, but I didn't think that was anythin' more than idle speculation . . ." Saeddryn trailed off, eyeing the other councillors. None of them looked about to support her, so she shifted her gaze to Laela, who had begun attending council sessions.

Laela noticed the thinly concealed hatred in Saeddryn's expression, but she only raised her chin and looked back smugly.

The High Priestess looked away. "An' ye'll be away for a year."

"At the very least."

The councillors looked uncomfortable.

"A year, Sire?" said Lord Iorwerth. "Without ye?"

"I'm afraid so."

The tough commander straightened up. "No, Sire. We can't let ye go. Not that far. Not for that long."

"I agree," said Torc, from beside his wife. "Too far, too dangerous."

Arenadd raised his eyebrow. "I don't know what I'll tell the ambassador, then. He came a very long way to negotiate this visit."

"Sire," said Iorwerth. "Think of this." He rubbed his head. "Ye are what's stopping the South from invading us again. Fear of ye. With ye gone for a year . . . what would we do if they came back? Without our protector . . ."

Arenadd cast an amused glance at Laela. "I think the Master of Wisdom can help us here."

Laela stepped forward, aware of all the eyes on her. Oeka came with her, to stand by her side, and Laela put a hand on her head. The griffin didn't object, and Laela felt warm confidence fill her from end to end.

"No offence to yeh, Lords an' Ladies, but yeh ain't been in the South," she said. "I have. I seen what's goin' on there, an' let me tell yeh, there ain't no invasion comin'. Not now, not for ten years. South's in turmoil. In the place where I grew up, we had a new Eyrie Master every other spring. Griffiners over there're too busy fightin' each other t'even think about comin' up here."

Arenadd nodded as if that settled it. "Well said, Lady Laela. Now." He turned his attention back to the council. "The South is in no condition to fight us, and even if they were, I doubt they'd ever dare set foot on my soil again. And how would they even know I was away? We're miles away from them, we have no communications with them—there's no way they'd ever find out. And besides," he added wickedly, "I hope you're not implying that you don't think you could fight them off if they ever came sniffing around our borders."

The King's jab had the right effect; Saeddryn looked irritated, and several of the griffins hissed at the insult.

Iorwerth's partner, the scarred Kaanee, spoke out. "Then we have no argument against your plan, *Kraeai kran ae*," he rasped. "But if you are right, why do you care so much about Amoran? Those griffins are small and strange, and the humans are not of your kind."

This was Arenadd's moment. He stepped forward, his face suddenly full of rage. "What in the Night God's name is wrong with you?" he demanded. "We're Northerners, aren't we? Didn't we fight to give our people back their homes? Didn't we stand up against the enemy to set our brothers and sisters free? Didn't *I* come into this city, alone, and fight to protect you all—didn't I lead the slaves back to the North? Have you forgotten that?"

Iorwerth's fists clenched. "I would never forget that, Sire. Never."

"Well then, remember *this*," Arenadd snarled. "Remember that there are still Northerners living in slavery. And they're out there." He pointed a thin finger eastward. "They're in Amoran, building giant statues of the Day God. Cleaning his temples. Serving his worshippers." Arenadd wiped a hand over his forehead. "You think I care about *military* benefits? *Trade agreements?* No. I care about our people, and unless I make an agreement with the Emperor, and please him enough to make him want to repay me, then there's no way I can bring those people home." He paused. "That's my duty. It's always been my duty, ever since the Night God handed it down to me. And if I never do anything else while I'm King, I'll fulfil that duty to the very last."

Silence followed the King's speech. The councillors glanced at each other.

Laela almost gaped at her protector. She'd thought she knew him better than anyone else aside from Skandar, but she'd never imagined that he could be so eloquent, or so passionate.

For the first time, she began to see why so many people had been prepared to follow him—and still did.

Finally, Saeddryn spoke out. "Sire," she said. "I apologise. I was too hasty. If going to Amoran is what it'll take to bring the rest of our people home, then so be it. I'm sure we can look after the Kingdom while ye're gone."

"Agreed," said Iorwerth.

"I agree as well," Torc said solemnly. He touched his neck. "I haven't forgotten what slavery is like, and I never will. And I'll never forget who it was that set me free. Go to Amoran, Sire. Bring our brothers and sisters home."

Arenadd smiled with his eyes. "I will, Lord Torc. I promise."

"There's only one other thing left to decide," Saeddryn cut in. "An' that's who ye're going to leave in charge of the council while ye're away."

Arenadd stroked his beard. "You mean who's going to sit on the throne in my place, Saeddryn?"

"If ye want to put it that way, Sire, then yes."

"You, of course," said Arenadd. "Who else would I leave in charge but the eldest member of my family?"

Saeddryn's expression was inscrutable. "Who indeed, Sire."

Laela, watching closely as Arenadd had told her to, had the odd feeling that there were other meanings and other words hidden behind what had just been said. But just what that was she couldn't tell.

"She's happy about bein' left in charge," she observed to Arenadd afterward, as they were leaving together.

Arenadd walked slowly, still limping slightly from his injury. "Of course she is. You know, she never forgave me for coming back."

Laela kept pace, with Oeka close behind. "Comin' back how?"

Skandar hadn't bothered to come to the meeting, but Arenadd glanced over his shoulder as if expecting to see the giant griffin behind him. "Oh, well, when we stormed Malvern, after the fighting was more or less over, I . . . well, it's a long story, but I was out of it for a few days afterward. They took me for dead, and Saeddryn took charge. She would have been happy about that; after all, she always saw it as *her* revolution, and she didn't much like it when I took charge. Anyway, I came back to my senses and walked in on her just as she was telling everyone how I would've wanted them to demolish the city and go back to living in huts. I put a stop to it quick smart, but I'll never forget the look on her face when I walked into the room." He paused. "Now I'll give her a taste of ruling here while I'm gone, and we'll see how well she enjoys it. Not too much, I hope."

"Yeh really think yeh can trust her?" said Laela, recalling Saeddryn's hostile expression.

"Of course I do," said Arenadd. "She might be a bad-tempered old stick, but she's still my cousin. And besides, I'll have Iorwerth keeping an eye on her. Now that's a man you can trust to the ends of the earth." He put a peculiar emphasis on that last part.

"Well, yeh got 'em t'let yeh go, anyway," said Laela.

"Oh, I'd have gone even if they hadn't 'let' me," said Arenadd. "They might be the highest officials in the land, but I'm still the King, and I have the final say in everything we discuss. All they can hope to do is talk me out of it. Now—"

"Yeah?"

"I'm on my way to have lunch with the ambassador," said Arenadd. "As my advisor, you should definitely meet him, so would you care to come with me?"

Laela glanced at Oeka. The griffin had perked up and was looking as interested as her partner. "'Course I'll come!" said Laela. She grinned. "I never met an Amorani before. Do they really have hair all over their faces?"

Arenadd choked on a laugh. "I don't know about the rest of his people," he said, recovering his dignity, "but Lord Vander's got a lot less hair on his face than I do. I'd love to know how he keeps his moustache so neat even when he's travelling . . . I should ask him what his secret is."

Laela hid a giggle and did her best to keep close to Oeka and look important as they entered the dining hall.

When she saw the Amorani ambassador for the first time, she was almost disappointed. He was short and slight, and aside from his brown skin, he could easily have passed himself off as a Northerner, with his dark hair and eyes.

Aside from the moustache Arenadd had admired, his face was hairless, and lined. Laela thought he looked shrewd but not unfriendly.

"My lord." Arenadd nodded.

The ambassador stepped forward, speaking in Northern. Arenadd replied, glancing at Laela.

"Very well, then," said Vander, using Cymrian this time. He looked at Laela with an interested expression. "I am Lord Vander, of Amoran," he said, holding out a hand. "And your own name?"

Laela hesitated for a moment, but then linked fingers with him and tugged, as Arenadd had taught her. She bowed her head briefly. "I'm Lae—*Lady* Laela," she corrected, adding with pride, "Master of Wisdom."

Vander looked her up and down, then looked at Arenadd. "So this is the famous Laela," he said. "Forgive me, Sire, but I was not prepared . . ." He glanced at Laela again. "I did not know that you had a daughter."

Laela and Arenadd both stopped and looked at each other.

For Laela, it was as if Vander's remark had lifted a veil. She looked at Arenadd's face as if for the first time, taking in

the angular features, the long, curly hair . . . features she knew
she had, too—features that had made her look so sharp and odd,
and not how a woman was supposed to look.

*No,* she thought. *That's just stupid. There's no way. Yer real
father's dead. An' Arenadd wouldn't . . . he'd never . . .*

No. She shook herself, pushing away the unwelcome thought.
Arenadd was her friend, and he was a good man; she believed
it with all her heart. He would never rape a woman, not even a
Southern woman. Never.

Arenadd laughed humourlessly. "You're mistaken, my Lord.
I don't have any children. Laela here was born in the South,
anyway."

Vander looked at Laela again. "Forgive me—" He stopped
abruptly, and his expression changed. "Ah. I see. Of course.
Forgive me; I did not mean to imply that you would ever father
a . . ." He trailed off.

Arenadd glanced at Laela, his look suddenly embarrassed
and defensive. He tried to shrug it off with another laugh. "Well,
let's hope not, my lord. I mean, could you imagine? The Shadow
That Walks—with a *Southerner*?" He grimaced as if the very
idea was disgusting.

Laela actually took a step back. She froze, staring at him as
if she could hardly believe what he'd said.

Arenadd looked at her. "Laela? What's the matter?"

She could feel her shoulders trembling as she straightened
up. "I was born because a Northerner raped my mother," she
said, in a voice like ice cracking. "One of *your* people, Sire. She
was barely older'n me, an' she never did nothin' to anybody. It
happened in the war. So it was your fault."

Arenadd's face fell. "I didn't mean—"

Laela couldn't stand it a moment longer. She turned and
strode out of the room.

# 18

# The Box

Oeka darted ahead into their chamber and lay down peacefully on the bed, apparently oblivious to her human's emotions.

Laela stomped over to the fireplace and almost threw herself into a chair. She buried her face in her hands and did her best not to shout exactly what she was thinking.

Up until now, she'd never really thought about the full meaning of living with Arenadd and becoming a Northerner through and through. She'd thought about how accepting that side of her heritage was a betrayal of Gryphus, and her foster father, in a way.

But she had never thought about how it would also be a betrayal of her mother.

Bran had often talked about her, and even if he never said what her name was or gave any details about her life and where she came from, his stories had built a picture in Laela's mind—and that was a picture of a woman who was brave and strong and kind-hearted. A woman Bran had loved, and whom Laela had come to love in a way as well. But when Laela had come to the North and accepted Arenadd's offer to become one of his people, she'd forgotten about that woman.

Now the King's casual remark had suddenly brought the full meaning of that home to her. It had also revealed something she hadn't realised or thought about, but which caused her pain now.

*He doesn't care about her,* she thought. *What happened to her. She was just a Southerner. An' he does look down on me because I'm a half-breed.*

That realisation, that Arenadd did, after all, think she was inferior because she was a half-breed when she had thought he was the only one who didn't, slammed into her like a physical blow. With a sinking heart, she realised that she couldn't put it behind her. She never would be able to, no matter how long she lived.

She stood up and walked toward the fireplace. The weather outside was cold, and there was a fire burning. She stared into the flames, and took a deep, shuddering breath. "I'm sorry, Mum," she mumbled. "I ain't forgotten about yeh . . ."

The silence that followed felt accusing. Laela snarled and smashed her fist into the copper panel that framed the fireplace.

As the noise died away, she caught a strange, faint rattling sound.

Curiosity dulled her anger slightly. She banged on the copper again, and listened. The rattle came again. After several more blows and some careful listening, she had an idea.

"Something on the other side," she said aloud.

The fire made it too hot to investigate, so she put it out with the jug of water from the night-stand and waited a while before thrusting an arm up into the space just above the fireplace. There was a little ridge there, where two copper sheets joined together. Thinking the noise might have come from a loose rivet, Laela felt around it. Her fingers closed around a small metal box, and her heart skipped a beat.

She brought the box out into the light and examined it with fascination. It was covered in soot, but when Laela rubbed it, silver showed through. She cleaned it with her sleeve and found vine-and-leaf designs all over it.

"Well, ain't this nice?" she said aloud, forgetting her bad temper for a moment while she turned it over in her fingers.

Oeka came over to investigate. She sniffed at the box when Laela held it out to her, and gave her an inquiring look.

Laela smiled and tapped the lid. "Let's see if there's anything inside."

It took her a few moments to figure out how to undo the clasp, but the lid came up without any trouble, and she looked inside. To her disappointment, all she saw was a scrap of grubby cloth.

"That's it?" she said, pulling it out. "What's this—*oooh!*"

Underneath the cloth there were several other things, and the one she had just noticed was a jewel. Grinning, Laela picked it out. It was about the size of a grape, and the fact that it was black only made her more excited. She'd never seen a black gemstone before, and the thought crossed her mind that this one could be very rare.

She stuffed the stone in her pocket and sat down to investigate the other contents of the box. No other gems, unfortunately, but she did find a lock of hair wrapped with a piece of thread, and the withered remains of a flower or two.

"Probably someone's secret treasures," she remarked to Oeka. "Wonder who stashed it up there?" She paused. "Looks like it's been there a long time, so I might as well keep it. Maybe I can use it as a jewellery box. Once I get some jewellery, I mean." She dug the stone out of her pocket and rolled it on her palm, admiring it again. "Bet I can find someone to set this for me. In a ring, maybe, or a necklace or somethin'." She put it back into the box and closed the lid.

As she stood up to put it on the shelf over the fireplace, she noticed the scrap of cloth on the floor and bent to pick it up.

She was about to throw it into the fireplace when she noticed some odd marks on it, and stopped to turn it over, examining it critically.

"Looks like writin'."

The words were charcoal, and badly faded, but she recognised some of the letters, and frowned to herself, suddenly feeling guilty at having pried into someone else's belongings—even if the original owner was long gone.

Oeka thrust her beak at the piece of cloth, rasping in her throat.

"It's got somethin' written on it," Laela explained, showing it to her. "A letter, I'll bet. Got no idea what it says. Maybe I should show it to Yorath."

Oeka stared at her. Laela couldn't read the griffin's expression, and looked away awkwardly. "It's probably not very interesting anyway," she mumbled, and went to stuff it back into the box.

As she lifted the lid, she heard the door open behind her. Oeka started up aggressively but backed down a moment later. Laela's eyes narrowed.

"If yeh ain't come to apologise, then yeh can go away," she said, without turning around.

Arenadd stepped into her field of vision. "I have, actually."

Laela closed the box and turned to face him. "Is that so?" She folded her arms. "Well, that's good, because the next time yeh insult me *or* my mother, I'm leavin'. Understand?"

Arenadd rubbed his forehead. "Yes, perfectly. But listen, you don't—"

"Yeah, I'm a half-breed," Laela interrupted. "I think we all know that by now. But I thought it didn't make a difference to you."

"It doesn't, Laela. Honestly."

"Well, that ain't the way it looks to me right now," said Laela. She took a deep breath, to stop herself from outright shouting at him, but it only half-worked. "How dare you go sneerin' at my mother like that?" she snarled. "Yeah, she was a Southerner, an' I get that you don't like 'em, but that doesn't give yeh any right to be like that about it."

Arenadd winced. "I know. I'm sorry. I was . . . I shouldn't have joked about it like that. I was embarrassed."

"Why, because the ambassador thought I was yer daughter?" Laela hesitated. "I . . . I'm not, am I?"

"No," said Arenadd. "I can't father children; you know that. And I'd never—"

"Never go with a Southern woman," said Laela, more sharply than she meant to.

"I would never rape a woman," Arenadd said in icy tones. "No matter who that woman was."

Laela relaxed slightly. "I'm sorry. I'd never think about yeh like that. I swear."

"I know." Arenadd hesitated. "Laela, I was embarrassed because Vander isn't the only one who thinks you're my daughter."

Laela frowned. "He ain't?"

"Half the Eyrie thinks it," Arenadd said baldly. "Haven't you been listening? It's everybody's favourite piece of gossip."

"Is it?" Laela didn't know whether to be amused or horrified.

"Trust me; I make a point of listening to what people are saying," said Arenadd. "But it's an explanation that makes sense to people. Where did the King find this strange girl who looks like him, and how did she get to such a powerful position so quickly? Obviously, it's because she's his secret child. His secret *half-breed* child, which is why he won't admit it to anyone."

Laela's heart sank. "Gods, I'm sorry. They must be sayin' awful things about yeh."

"They are," said Arenadd. He smiled slightly. "You've made me quite unpopular."

All of Laela's anger toward him vanished and was replaced by embarrassment and a strange feeling of shame. "Should I just go, then?"

"No!" Arenadd shook himself. "No. I need you here."

"Why?"

He hesitated, just for a moment, and then smiled—genuinely, this time, and put his good hand on her shoulder. "Where would I be without my chief advisor?"

In the end, Laela didn't show the letter to Yorath. On the evening after their argument, Arenadd sent her a brief message, to the effect that the negotiations with Vander were done and that he and Laela would be leaving with him in four days.

When she went to visit Yorath that night, all she could talk about was Amoran.

"Isn't it amazin'?" she exclaimed, bright-eyed. "We're goin' all the way over the sea! Half the people I knew when I was a girl thought Amoran was just a legend—it's that far away an' whatnot. An' I get t'go there! An' I'll stay in the Emperor's palace, an' meet all his officials, an' they'll give me gifts an' show me all sorts of amazin' things, I just know it! I can't hardly wait!" She stopped herself with an effort and looked at Yorath. "Ain't yeh excited?"

He smiled uneasily. "I'm excited for ye, Laela."

Laela took his hand. "But yeh get to see it, too, don't forget."

"I'm not coming, Laela."

All her excitement drained out of her. "What? What d'yeh mean yeh ain't comin'? The King said—"

"He asked me to come," said Yorath. "But I said I'd prefer

not to, an' he said it was fine an' if I felt that way, he'd teach you your lessons himself."

"But why don't yeh want t'come?" said Laela. "Yorath, I'm gonna be away for a year an' all—how can yeh want t'just stay home?"

"I want t'come, Laela," Yorath said unhappily. "I do, an' I'll miss ye something terrible, I know. But I can't go away for a year, even if I'm paid well for it. My dad needs me to look after him. He's not well, Laela."

A quick memory of her own father flashed into her mind. "Well," she mumbled. "If that's how it is, then I guess yeh'd better stay."

"Please, don't be angry with me, Laela," said Yorath.

She smiled and caressed his hair. "I ain't, yeh daft bugger. I looked after my dad when he was sick, too, an' I know what it's like. I'd never want t'make yeh leave him."

Yorath smiled back, with more than a little relief. "It wasn't easy for me to decide. I don't know how I'll cope without ye for so long."

"As long as yer waitin' for me when I get back, I'll be happy," said Laela. She moved closer to him, her hand still on the back of his head. "Have a little somethin' to remember me by, why don't yeh? I got time."

Yorath was more than happy to oblige, and they fell back onto his bed, pulling at each other's clothes.

Laela loved it; she'd loved it more every time. Yorath's touch helped dull the pain of knowing they would have to part, and she thrust the knowledge aside and lost herself in his body yet again.

Four days later, she and Arenadd were ready to leave. Laela had long since packed, and waited while the King got his affairs in order—appointing different people to take up his various duties, giving orders for what they should do if certain things came up, and so on and so forth. Laela had to go with him and listen while he did all of that; it was incredibly boring most of the time, but she went along dutifully, and learnt a fair bit about the things a ruler had to do. A lot of it was surprisingly mundane.

On the last morning before they were due to leave, Arenadd and Laela took some time for a final lesson in the audience chamber. That was mostly because Laela had asked for it; she was bored to death of talking to an endless list of officials and wanted to spend more time with Oeka and learn about her.

"Tell me about magic," she told Arenadd. "I want t'know how they use it an' that."

Arenadd paced back and forth, idly flourishing his sickle. "I can't tell you too much, I'm afraid; griffins don't like to talk about magic. Not to humans. It's almost their religion."

"What *can* yeh tell me?"

He threw the sickle upward with a quick flick of his wrist and caught it easily by the handle. "Every griffin has its own power, as I think you already know by now, but they aren't born knowing how to use it. As far as I know, each griffin discovers his or her particular gift when they're at least ten years old—in other words, when they're big enough and strong enough to deal with the strain of using it. Magic takes a lot out of them, you see. It taps directly into their life-force. Using too much can put them in a coma for days, or even kill them."

Laela rubbed Oeka's head. "What's your power, then, Greeneyes?"

Oeka clicked her beak.

"She probably doesn't know," said Arenadd. "She's only about seven years old, by my guess."

The tawny griffin rose suddenly, pushing Laela's hand away. *"Eeee kree oo eia,"* she said, slowly and deliberately.

Arenadd put his sickle back into his belt with an interested expression. "She said, 'I will show you my magic.' "

Laela stood up. "Show us, Oeka!"

The small griffin stood for a moment, tail swishing. She lowered her head, and a strange stillness came over her.

"Look out," said Arenadd. "She's about to—*ggngh!*"

Laela yelled and put her hands over her head as pain lanced through it. As she fell to her knees, she saw Arenadd step backward and slump onto his seat, both hands grabbing at his own head.

The pain rose sharply, and Laela heard a strange, harsh voice.

*This is my power.*

A moment later, the pain vanished. Laela got up slowly, feeling her arms tremble. "What in the gods' names was *that*?"

Oeka looked calmly at her and lay down on her belly, blinking and apparently tired.

Arenadd shuddered and gave the griffin an icy look. "Colour me impressed. But don't try that again when Skandar's about, or the servants will have to mop you up off the floor."

*"Ae en'oo, keeeekaree,"* said Oeka, apparently unbothered.

"What was that?" Laela said again. "Oeka, what did yeh just do?"

Arenadd rubbed his broken fingers. "It would seem that your partner is a telepath. Not a common power."

"A what?"

"She can get into people's heads," said Arenadd. "Break into their thoughts, probably. Even send messages from her mind into yours. It's not very useful for that sort of thing, though, mostly because the pain stops anyone from thinking very clearly. But it's a powerful weapon." He smiled thinly. "I doubt anyone would interfere with her if they knew she had the power to make their heads explode."

Laela eyed the griffin. "Tell her I said she'd better not use it on me."

Oeka got up and came to her, rubbing her head against Laela's hip. *"Ooo ae oo,"* she cooed.

" 'Never,' " Arenadd translated.

"It's a deal, then," said Laela. She scratched Oeka's ear, the way she liked it. "I'm terrible for sayin' it, but I almost hope someone tries t'mess with us just so I can see what happens next."

"Let's hope it doesn't come to that," said Arenadd. "But—"

There was a sound of running feet from beyond the archway, and a guard came running in. "Sire!"

Arenadd stood up. "What is it?"

The guard came to a halt and bowed hastily. "Sire, I've got urgent news."

"Out with it, then," said Arenadd.

"It's the assassin, Sire. The one who tried to kill ye. They've caught him, Sire."

Arenadd's hand went to the handle of his sickle. "Where is he?" he said sharply.

"Down in the cells, Sire. Lady Saeddryn told me to come tell ye immediately."

"I see." Arenadd glanced at Laela. "You don't have to come if you don't want to."

Laela was already halfway to the archway. "Oh, I'm comin', Sire. No way I'm missin' this."

Arenadd ignored her and strode out of the room.

It gave Laela an uneasy feeling to be back in the prison under the Eyrie, even though this time the guards bowed and stood aside when they saw her coming. She even saw the very same guard who had dragged her out of her bed on the morning of her arrest, but when he saw her, he bowed his head to hide his face from her and made a hasty exit at the first opportunity.

Arenadd paid no attention. He followed the head of the prison guard along a corridor, his hand resting on his sickle all the while. Laela, keeping close behind him with Oeka on her heels, thought he walked with a terrible purpose. She pitied whoever was waiting for them in the cells.

Ahead, a familiar figure was waiting for them by a cell door.

"Lord Torc." Arenadd came to a stop. "What's happened?"

The Master of Law inclined his head. "Sire. We've got him in here."

"When was he caught?" Arenadd said curtly. "Where?"

"They found him trying to break into the Eyrie," said Torc. "Very early this morning. He was put into the cells straight-away, but after I happened to see him, I realised he fitted your description of the man who attacked you."

"Has he been interrogated?"

"Briefly, yes, but . . . we won't get anything out of him, Sire." Torc's face was pale.

"We'll see about that," Arenadd growled. "Open the door."

"Sire—"

Arenadd freed his sickle. *"Do it."*

Torc silently opened the door. It was well lit beyond, and Arenadd went in.

The prisoner was hunched on the wooden bench provided, but he looked up when Arenadd entered.

His face was small and round, but whatever more definite features it might have had once were impossible to recognise. Something had left three deep slashes at an angle from his forehead to his chin, cutting through his nose and twisting his mouth into a permanent snarl.

Even Arenadd faltered at the sight of him. "You." He pointed the sickle at the man's horrible face. "I know you. I *knew* I knew you, you son of a bitch!"

The scarred man's dark eyes had gone wide. His mouth opened as if he were going to speak, but he made a sick, gurgling sound instead, and blood splashed onto his chin.

Arenadd's own eyes glittered with hate. "I saw you in the war," he said. "You stabbed me five times in the chest. I'd remember those scars anywhere. I thought you died in the fire. And *then*—" He ran his fingers over the sickle blade, almost lovingly. "Then you stabbed me again and threw me in the river. Don't you ever give up?"

The scarred man said nothing.

Arenadd moved closer, until the point of the sickle was almost touching the man's deformed nose. "How did you get into the city?" he asked softly. "How did you hide for so long? *Answer me!*"

Still no reply.

"Answer me, damn you!"

The mouth opened again, the lips trying to form words, but all that emerged were hideous wet garglings. The man stopped suddenly, choking, and lurched forward. Blood had matted the front of his tunic, and more coated his lips.

Arenadd stopped. "What . . . ?"

"Sire." Torc appeared behind him. "Sire, I told you there's no point. He can't speak."

"Something happened to his mouth?" said Arenadd, not taking his eyes off the shaking figure in front of him.

"He's got no tongue," said Torc. His voice was low with revulsion. "It's been torn out, Sire."

Arenadd didn't flinch. He looked at the prisoner's hands—bloodied, pawing uselessly at his mouth. "His fingers are gone. So he can't write anything down, either." He turned at last, and his eyes met Torc's. "How did this happen?"

"I don't know, Sire. He was like this when we took him."

"Then how in the gods' names could he break into the Eyrie?"

"I don't know, Sire," said Torc. "But look at him."

"I already have, Torc. There's nothing we can do to him that hasn't already been done."

"He's insane, Sire," said Torc. "If he wasn't before this happened to him, he is now. A man can only take so much before he snaps."

Arenadd touched his twisted fingers. "I know, Torc."

"Arenadd?" Laela's voice interrupted. "What's goin' on? Is it him?"

"Get out of here, my lady," Torc said sharply. "This isn't—"

"No." Arenadd put a hand on his shoulder. "Let her see. Get out of the cell, Torc. I don't need you here just now."

The Master of Law hesitated. "Yes . . . Sire."

As he went out through the door, Laela came in. "What's . . . ? Oh, *shit*." She lurched away as if someone had punched her in the stomach. Recovering her balance, she leant against the cell wall and breathed deeply, swearing.

"It's all right," said Arenadd. "He can't hurt you. I thought you should see this."

Laela turned to him, a look of open horror on her face. "Who did that to him?"

"I don't know, Laela. Laela—" Arenadd took her by the chin, turning her head. "Look at him. *Look at him*. You have to see this."

She did, and immediately tried to look away again. "No. I don't want—"

"It's not a question of what we want or don't want," Arenadd said harshly. "You wanted to see him, so look at him!"

Laela stared at the prisoner and retched. "Oh, gods help me. His hands . . . his face—"

"This is the man who stabbed me and threw me in the river," said Arenadd. "And if you hadn't come along, I would have stayed there. Apparently he was caught early this morning, trying to break into the Eyrie. Seems he must have heard I wasn't dead."

"But what happened to him?" said Laela. "Who would have done that? Why?"

"Torc swears he had nothing to do with it, and I believe him," said Arenadd. "As for who else could have done it . . . or ordered someone else to do it . . . ." His eyes narrowed. "I do know that someone didn't want him to talk. It could well have been himself. If he's part of some kind of resistance group, then he wouldn't want to betray his friends."

The prisoner slumped against the wall, blood dripping from his mouth, and let out a pitiful moan.

Laela shuddered at the sound of it. "Can't yeh do anythin' for the poor bastard?"

"Yes, I can." Arenadd strode over to the bench and pressed the tip of his sickle into the underside of the man's chin, forcing him to raise his head. The prisoner, unable to spit out the blood from his mouth with his head tilted back, gagged and began to cough, his useless hands dabbing at his throat.

"Arenadd, put him down!" Laela shouted. "He's suffocatin'—"

Arenadd ignored her. He leant forward and whispered something in the prisoner's ear. Then the sickle flashed, just once.

Laela stared in disbelief, as the prisoner's body crumpled to the floor. "Yeh just killed him! Why . . . ?"

Arenadd wiped the sickle clean on his robe, without even glancing at the body. "Well, that was an utter waste of time. But at least I finally showed the bastard what happens to people who stand against me."

"But . . . yeh just killed him," said Laela. "Just like that! Shouldn't he at least've had a trial?"

Arenadd actually looked surprised. "A trial? What for?"

"Well, because . . . everyone should have a trial?" Laela said, rather lamely.

Arenadd put the sickle back into his belt. "All *Northerners* are entitled to a trial here," he corrected.

"But shouldn't everybody get one?" said Laela.

"I don't give Southerners fair trials, Laela," said Arenadd. "I kill them. That's what I was made to do." He saw her look, and added, "They didn't give me a trial, you know. When I was a prisoner here. They tortured me for information, and then sentenced me to death."

Laela shivered. "How did yeh get away?"

"Simple," said Arenadd. "I waited until after they hanged me." He grinned wolfishly. "I'll never forget the looks on their faces."

# 19

# To Amoran

The day after the assassin's death, King Arenadd left Malvern. He took an escort of several griffiners with him—most of them underlings of Lord Iorwerth, who had been left behind to help Saeddryn run the Kingdom. After the war, most of Arenadd's best warriors and commanders had been chosen by griffins after he had given them important positions and awarded them with wealth stolen from dead or exiled Southerners. They were the new nobility of the North, and Arenadd had chosen the strongest and most loyal of them to go to Amoran with him.

As the newly appointed Master of Wisdom, Laela would naturally be expected to go as well. Nobody had questioned that, but she was convinced she had seen more than a few people cast dark looks at each other when she appeared at the King's side that morning.

Skandar was there, too, of course, up on the flat top of the Council Tower. Arenadd had persuaded him to wear a harness for once—a magnificent thing decorated with rubies that gleamed in the early sun.

Oeka, too small to wear the silver leg-bands due to the griffin whose human was Master of Wisdom, stood by Laela's side and watched while her fellows prepared to leave—harshly reminding their humans how to lean and balance in the air, or standing patiently while their harnesses were adjusted.

Laela glanced at Oeka. Next to the rest, her own partner

looked much smaller. But there was a solid, determined look to her as well, Laela thought. She didn't look like a griffin who would back down easily. Laela grimaced and touched the bandage on her arm—she didn't need to wonder about *that*.

Over near Arenadd, Lord Vander placed a hand on his partner's neck and easily slid up onto her back. Ymazu shifted, re-balancing herself to compensate for his weight, and then settled down, blinking serenely.

Arenadd was on Skandar's back a moment later, despite the giant griffin's irritable clicking. Laela glanced around and saw the other griffiners mounting up. She cast an uncertain look at Oeka—nobody had told her how she was going to keep up. She'd assumed they'd be travelling by cart or horseback, but how was she supposed to fly . . . ?

"Hey."

Laela turned and saw Arenadd reaching down toward her from Skandar's back. "Are you coming, or what?" He grinned.

Laela stared. "What, am I supposed to—"

"Hurry up, take my hand," said Arenadd. "Everyone's waiting."

He grasped her hand and pulled her up onto Skandar's back. Embarrassed and more than a little nervous, she sat down behind Arenadd.

"Put your arms around my waist and don't let go," he advised.

"But—"

*"Don't let go,"* said Arenadd. "We've got a long way to go today, and I don't want to watch them scrape you off the ground. Do you feel secure back there?"

Laela had put her arms around the King's bony body. "I think so."

"Good," said Arenadd. "Now hold oooooon . . . !" The last word turned into a whoop of excitement, as an impatient Skandar charged away over the stonework like a runaway horse. Other griffins scattered out of his way.

Laela bounced up and down with every thud of the griffin's paws and talons, holding on to Arenadd for dear life. She thought she was going to be sick.

Then Skandar reached the edge of the tower, and hurled himself into the air.

Laela felt as if her stomach had dropped through her spine.

She clutched at Arenadd's robe, anchoring her fingers in the rough cloth, but the panicked thought went through her mind that he wouldn't be able to hold on with her pulling at him, and she nearly let go in a moment of stupidity. Luckily, Skandar levelled out a moment later, and she thumped back into place on his back.

Riding the griffin was frightening, cold, and noisy, but she got used to it fairly quickly, and once she felt a little safer, she risked a look back and saw the other griffins taking to the air after their master. She couldn't see Oeka anywhere, but a moment later the small griffin drew level with Skandar. She came close enough to make sure Laela was safe, and then fell back to ride on the dark griffin's slipstream.

Laela could hardly believe what had happened. She was riding the Mighty Skandar, and in front of half the King's court. And Skandar had let her get on his back! Arenadd must have persuaded him, but she knew the haughty griffin would have needed a lot of persuading.

It didn't take her long to feel embarrassed as well as proud—Skandar was enormous, but there wasn't that much room on his shoulders, and she had to sit pressed up against Arenadd's back, with very little room to move. Being this close to him made her feel as if she was intruding on him in some way. And despite his thick robe she could feel how painfully thin he was underneath it, and that didn't do much to make her feel better.

*Well, he invited me to sit here, so he doesn't mind,* she told herself.

She still felt embarrassed.

They were in the air for a long time, and making conversation was more or less impossible. Laela occupied herself with looking at the view and watching the other griffins when they came into view, but holding on took more effort than she'd expected. It was tiring, too.

They had been flying long enough for her to start worrying that she was going to fall off, when Skandar abruptly came down to land. He touched down in a large open field, and did it with enough of a thump that Laela fell off him, hitting the ground in a painful and humiliating heap.

A moment later, Arenadd had appeared and was hauling her to her feet. "Are you all right?"

Laela rubbed her numb legs. "Legs've gone t'sleep."

"Yes, that happens on long flights. Walk around a bit; that should wake them up again."

She looked around at the field, where the other griffins were landing, too. "Where is this?"

Arenadd stretched. "Somewhere in Lady Hafwyn's lands, if I'm any judge."

"The Governor of Warwick," Laela recalled. "Why have we landed here? This just looks like farmland t'me."

"So the griffins can rest, of course," said Arenadd. Behind him, Skandar had lain down and was idly grooming his wings. "They're not built to fly long distances, especially with a load on their back. We'll set out again when they're ready."

At that moment, Oeka landed lightly on the grass beside her human. She nudged Laela's hand roughly, and chirped. Laela rubbed the griffin's head with her knuckles. Oeka pushed back briefly and then looked away, observing the other griffins.

"How long'll it take us to get to the coast?" Laela asked.

"Hm? Oh, not long. A day or so at most. We'll stop at Warwick tonight. So, are you excited about seeing the sea?"

Laela nodded and grinned. "It's the part I'm lookin' forward to the most."

"There's Amoran still to come," Arenadd pointed out.

"Yeah, I've decided to get excited about that once I'm done with the sea," said Laela. "If that's all right."

Arenadd chuckled. "Planning your own levels of excitement ahead of time—now that's good organisation."


They spent most of the rest of the day like that—flying, resting, and then flying again, following the River Snow. That evening, they reached Warwick, a big, walled city built by the river and surrounded by thick, fortified walls—a relic of wars older than the one that had made him King, Arenadd said. At Warwick they were greeted by Lady Hafwyn—an old, silver-haired griffiner who Arenadd said was a veteran of the Dark Wars and one of the first to join his cause.

"Technically, I joined *her* cause," he added over dinner. "Hafwyn was one of the rebels who survived the uprising led by Saeddryn's mother, Arddryn senior, and hid in the mountains with her. They'd been there for years, waiting for their opportunity to fight again."

"An' then you came along," Laela supplemented.

Arenadd nodded. "Skandar and I, and Skade. Fugitives from Southern justice. We were hoping to hide in the mountains, and we found someone had already done it."

Laela looked up, immediately interested. "What had yeh done, that you were runnin' away from?"

Arenadd picked up his cup. "I committed murder," he said, quite calmly.

She faltered at that. "Why . . . ? I mean, who was it?"

"Man called Lord Rannagon Raegonson," said Arenadd, still casual. "He was one of the leaders who put down Arddryn's rebellion." He paused. "He was the first man I ever killed. I slit his throat with a broken sword."

Laela withdrew from him very slightly while he spoke. *It's too easy,* she thought grimly. She watched him as he ate, pausing briefly to exchange a few words with the man on his other side. So normal. *Too easy, to forget what he is. What he's done. He acts . . . he doesn't act like a murderer.*

Laela paused at that. *How's a murderer supposed to act, anyway?* her inner voice wondered.

"So, yeh found Arddryn in the mountains," she prompted.

Arenadd turned his attention back to her. "Yes, and she told me she'd been waiting for me. Another Taranisäii—her younger brother's grandson, come back out of the South to find her. Or so she thought."

Laela had heard of the famous Arddryn Taranisäii by now, from various people back in Malvern. "What was she like?"

"Very old," said Arenadd. "But she was as tough as her daughter. She had a missing eye, and a horrible scar across her face. Courtesy of Lord Rannagon's sword," he added. "Of course, the fact that I had killed him made the rebels like me very, very much. Isn't that right, Hafwyn?"

"Eh?" the elderly Northerner looked up from her food.

"I was just telling my young apprentice here how pleased you and your friends were when you found out what I did to Lord Rannagon," said Arenadd, raising his voice.

Hafwyn grinned, showing numerous missing teeth. "So we

were!" she said. "None of us'd forgotten *that* old bastard. How could we, seein' what he did to Arddryn's face every day?"

Several others there had been listening, and now one of them raised his cup. "To Lord Rannagon!" he said. "May he stay dead forever!"

The other diners cheered raucously, many yelling what sounded like curses in Northern.

Arenadd raised his cup, too. "To Lord Rannagon," he repeated, and drank. "And to his son, and to his daughter," he added in an undertone.

Laela had heard him. "So Arddryn wanted—"

"She expected me to take her place and start a new rebellion, with Saeddryn at my side. I was reluctant at first, but . . . well, those mountains—at Taranis' Throne—that was where I first saw the Night God, and she told me what my purpose was. That was when I knew what I had to do."

"And Arddryn?"

"She died," said Arenadd. "Not long after I came. She thought . . . well, that's a story for another time. Her partner is still alive, though. She lives in the Hatchery and teaches the youngsters griffish lore. Remind me to introduce you to her when we get back."

They ate in silence for a while.

"Arenadd?"

"Yes?"

"Yeh said somethin' about Lord Rannagon havin' a son an' a daughter," said Laela.

"Yes, what of it?"

"You killed their father," said Laela. "Didn't they . . . wait a moment, wasn't . . . ?"

"Yes, one of them came after me," said Arenadd. "His bastard son, Erian. He wanted revenge, and he came all the way to Malvern, looking for it."

"An' you killed him."

"Yes. His sister, too."

"His entire family," Laela muttered. "Sweet gods."

Arenadd sighed. "Not his entire family, actually. Not quite. The Night God wanted it, but . . ."

Laela finally recalled the rest of what he had said that awful night. "Flell had a child. Yeh didn't kill it."

"No, and the Night God never forgave me for it," said Arenadd. He looked her in the face, his expression serious. "He'll be back one day, you know."

"Who?"

"The child. He's out there, somewhere. He'll be a man by now. Sometimes, I wonder what he looks like and whether he has his uncle's bright blue eyes." Arenadd's own eyes narrowed. "He must know what I did to his family. What I am. And one day, he'll come looking for me. Just like his uncle; some young fool with a sword, looking for glory."

"An' what will yeh do if that happens?" said Laela.

"Kill him, of course," said Arenadd.

She grimaced. "That's not very—"

"As long as he stays away from me, I'm happy to leave him alone," said Arenadd. "I won't look for him. But if he comes to me . . ."

"He won't," said Laela, hoping like mad that she was right.

The King and his escort left Warwick at dawn the next day, and after the second day of travelling, Laela had settled into the routine of it.

One thing she grew to enjoy was watching Oeka. The green-eyed griffin was the smallest in their party, but she had enough self-confidence for two adults, and Laela loved the way she strutted around the other griffins, sometimes provoking one with a nip to the tail and then easily dodging the angry response. The only griffin she never dared annoy was Skandar—but that was more than understandable. Arenadd had told her that the giant griffin had killed more than one of his fellows for annoying him one time too many.

Most of the time, though, Oeka preferred to stay with Laela. During the journey, Arenadd continued teaching her griffish whenever they landed to rest, and it was in this time that Laela began her first, clumsy conversations with her new partner.

Oeka listened to her human's attempts at griffish with amusement bordering on disinterest, and was kind enough to offer some feedback.

" 'Your griffish is terrible,' " Arenadd translated.

"Tell her I said I'm workin' on it," said Laela.

Oeka only ruffled her feathers and huffed by way of an answer.

Finally, after another day of travelling, the sea came in sight.

By that afternoon, they were standing on the shore. They had landed at a small Eyrie built by the sea, where a port housed the ship that would take them eastward.

That evening, Arenadd and Laela went down onto the rocky beach together and watched the moon rise over the water.

Laela thought she'd never seen anything so magical in her life.

Arenadd said nothing, and seemed content to let her take it in while he kept his eyes on the moon, apparently busy with his own thoughts.

The griffins had stayed at the Eyrie to rest after a long day's flight, and the King and his companion were alone.

Eventually, when the moon was high and yellow in the sky, Laela sat down on a rock. Arenadd sat beside her, hugging his knees. "So," he said. "Is it how you imagined it would be?"

It was almost an effort to reply. "No," said Laela. "It ain't." She held a hand out, gesturing at the sea with her long fingers. "Who's got the imagination to come up with somethin' like that?"

"Someone, somewhere," said Arenadd. "The gods, presumably."

"Well, of course," said Laela.

Arenadd reached upward, tracing the outline of the moon with his finger-tip. "The Night God is the mistress of the sea. They say sometimes she lives deep inside it, where the sun can never reach, and the night lasts forever."

"It goes that deep?" said Laela, shivering.

"So they say. She controls the sea, my master does. When her eye is fully open and her power is strongest, the sea comes higher up the land, trying to reach her. They say that's why the sea moves that way, when lakes and rivers don't—its spirit can see the moon in the sky and reaches toward it, wanting to have its beauty and its light."

Laela looked at him. "Is that true?"

"I don't know." Arenadd paused. "I never asked her."

She watched him for a while in silence. "Yeh really saw her, then? Like, face-to-face?"

He looked her in the face. "Yes."

Laela said nothing.

"You think I'm mad, don't you?" said Arenadd.

"No! I never—"

"I wouldn't blame you. Plenty of people don't believe me. Sometimes I think even my own family likes to think I made it up." Arenadd stretched. "But they can't close their eyes to my power, and that makes them believe. Or keeps them from saying otherwise."

Slowly and carefully—almost fearfully—Laela reached out to touch his hand. Arenadd started, and looked at her in surprise.

"What's she like?" Laela asked softly. "What's she look like?"

"To me?" said Arenadd.

"Uh . . . yeah. To you."

The Dark Lord closed his eyes. "To me she looks like a woman. Not old, not young. Ageless. She looks like one of us. Beautiful black hair, and one black eye."

"So she really does only have one eye," said Laela.

Arenadd's own eyes opened. "I think she can look like whatever she wants. But when I see her, she has one eye. The other is . . . gone."

Laela tried to grin. "She sounds a bit like Saeddryn."

"Oh, no," said Arenadd. "She's not like . . ." He trailed off.

"Arenadd?"

He shook himself. "Saeddryn lost her eye to an arrow—she was lucky not to lose more than that. But the Night God . . . she doesn't have a scar, or wear a patch. Her eye is just . . . gone. There's nothing there, just a black hole in her face."

Laela grimaced. "That's horrible."

"I suppose it sounds horrible," said Arenadd. "But somehow . . . it doesn't feel that way. Anyway, haven't you heard the legends? About her eye?"

"Gryphus took it," said Laela.

"Supposedly. I never asked her that, either. But the stories also say she puts the full moon into the empty place where her eye was. And it's true."

"Oh."

"That's why people love Saeddryn so much," said Arenadd.

"Because of her missing eye. A one-eyed woman is thought to be very close to the Night God. I've heard tell of more than a few priestesses who put out one of their own just so they'd have some extra credibility with the masses."

Laela sniggered. "That's just stupid."

"You wouldn't do something like that for your god?" said Arenadd, unexpectedly serious.

"What? No!" Laela was taken aback. "Why would I?"

Arenadd picked up a rock. "Because this life is fragile," he said. "Temporary. I know that better than anybody ever has. But the gods are forever. What are we next to them? Nothing. *Nothing.*"

Laela felt cold despair.

"And everything," Arenadd added softly, and hurled the stone into the sea.

## 20

## Over the Sea

Early the next morning, the King and his travelling companions went down onto the docks and boarded the ship that would take them to Amoran. The vessel, called *Seabreath*, was the first ship Laela had ever seen, and she stared with slight bewilderment at the masts.

"What in the gods' names are those for?"

"To catch the wind," one of the griffiners explained.

"Yeh can't 'catch' wind!" said Laela. "It ain't solid."

The griffiner looked slightly uncertain at that. "Well . . . that's how it's meant t'work. Don't ask me; I'm not a sailor."

The concept of "sailors" was another new one to Laela, but the helpful griffiner had already gone up the ramp ahead of his partner, and she decided to follow everyone else and try to work things out as she went.

Oeka hesitated before stepping onto the thick planks connecting the ship to the dock. Laela gave her a puzzled look, which was met with one of the griffin's impenetrable green stares. "It's all right," she told her. "I think."

Oeka hissed and stepped onto the ramp after her human.

The decks were bustling; Laela, discomfited by the rocking motion of the ship, leant against a mast and watched the group of men whom she assumed were the "sailors" run here and there, trying to avoid the agitated griffins while doing various strange and mysterious things with ropes. Most of the griffiners looked slightly bewildered—Laela guessed they'd never been

on a ship, either. Arenadd, calm as always, was talking to the
man who looked as if he were in charge. Skandar, less collected
than his human, crouched in the middle of the deck, ignoring
the sailors who were less than happy about it and hissing to
himself.

Eventually, some kind of order returned after Arenadd called
Skandar over and a couple of men opened the large trapdoor
he'd been sitting on. Underneath was a ramp leading down into
what looked almost like the inside of a barn. Laela couldn't
believe that there could be a space *inside* the ship—when she'd
first seen it, she'd assumed the whole thing was a solid lump of
wood. She wanted to go and have a look, but stayed by the
mast—everyone around her was speaking either griffish or
Northern, and she felt more than a little lost.

Arenadd seemed to be trying to persuade Skandar to go
down inside the ship. After a while, the giant griffin huffed
irritably and loped down the ramp—the space was large enough
for a couple of oxen walking side by side, but Skandar only just
fitted. The other griffins followed him with obvious reluctance—
one or two refused outright and instead took off to circle over
the ship, safely out of reach.

Laela glanced uncertainly at Oeka. "Are you supposed to go
with 'em?"

The griffiners were leaving too, now—using another, smaller
trapdoor set closer to the pointed end of the ship.

"Am *I* supposed t'go with *them*?" Laela mumbled, as if hoping someone would answer.

"My lady?"

"Huh?" Laela turned distractedly. "You talkin' to me?"

The speaker was one of the junior griffiners—Laela thought
his name was Penllyn. He bowed to her. "My lady."

"Yeah, what?"

Penllyn looked slightly bewildered for a moment, but pulled
himself together. "The captain says yer quarters are ready
for ye."

"Oh, good. Where are they?"

"Toward the . . . back of the ship. The captain's standing next
to the door—see?"

The back of the ship had a raised section on it, as if a small
building had been put on top of it. Steps led onto the "roof," but

there was indeed a door. Laela made for it without another thought, already excited to see what would be on the other side.

The captain, a heavyset Northerner, bowed low, and said something in Northern.

Laela tried not to grimace. "Is it through there?"

He gave her a slightly affronted look. "Yes, my lady. There should be room enough for all of ye."

" 'All'?" said Laela. "Why, am I sharin' with someone?"

"There's only one cabin other than the captain's and Lord Vander's, my Lady, an' the King insisted ye be allowed t'share it with him."

Laela went red. "I ain't—" She stopped herself. "Right." She waited until the captain had opened the door for her and went in, with Oeka skittering after her.

The cabin was surprisingly roomy, and even more surprisingly well decorated. There were even tapestries hanging on the walls.

Laela noted that there was only one bed. What was Arenadd playing at?

The King was sitting at a small table by the fireplace with his feet up. "Ah, hello. Nice quarters we've got, eh?"

Laela folded her arms. "What's this about?"

"What's what about?"

"We're sharin' a room all of a sudden. What are yeh thinkin'?"

Arenadd looked surprised. "There's only one cabin. I thought you'd prefer this to sleeping belowdecks with everyone else. They're all packed into bunk-beds with the sailors. They won't like it much, but we didn't have any other options."

Laela caught herself mid-anger. "I—oh."

Arenadd glanced at the bed. "I'll put up a hammock. I don't mind. It's not as if I sleep much any more anyway."

"Well. What about Oeka, then?" said Laela, embarrassed. "Where'd all the other griffins go, anyway?"

Arenadd took his feet off the table. "This ship was meant to carry livestock to Maijan. We've had the stalls modified for griffins. But Oeka's small enough to stay here with us if she'd prefer. It'll be easier for when we start our lessons again."

"Suits me fine," said Laela.

Oeka flicked her tail and rasped briefly.

"She said—"

" 'I am happy,' " Laela interrupted.

Arenadd grinned. "You're a fast learner, aren't you?"

The *Seabreath* set sail not long after its passengers had settled in. Laela went up on deck with Arenadd, and the two
of them watched his Kingdom slowly fade into the horizon.

"I'll be back, Tara," Arenadd murmured. "Don't lose faith
in me."

Most of the griffins had come up out of their stalls, but there
was nowhere near enough room for them all on deck, so they
took to the sky instead, lazily following the ship as a healthy
wind drove it eastward over the waves.

Arenadd pointed northward. "Hey, look at that."

Laela squinted. "Looks like a . . . blob."

"It's land," said Arenadd. He frowned. "I didn't know there
was an island there. Oh well, it's probably nothing important.
Now, where were we?"

"I dunno," said Laela. "I don't think we'd started whatever it
was yet."

"Oh, that's right," said Arenadd. "I remember now." He
flicked his sickle out of his belt and flourished it. The blade
flashed in the sun, and he grinned.

"Whoa, hey, wait a moment—" Laela backed off, holding up
her hands. "What're yeh doin'?"

Arenadd raised the sickle. "Catch."

It flashed through the air, straight toward her. Instinctively,
Laela lashed out at it to protect herself. The handle bounced off
her wrist, and she grabbed for it and managed to catch it.

"Good reflexes," said Arenadd. "Don't lose it."

Laela turned the weapon over, admiring it. The handle was
made from some dark reddish wood, reinforced with gold
bands. The blade, notched in places and slightly tarnished, was
etched with a triple spiral surrounded by five small stars.

Laela gingerly touched the edge, wanting to test its sharp-
ness. "It's beautiful. I can't believe—*gah!*"

"I should have warned you about that," said Arenadd. "Are
you all right?"

Laela rubbed her bleeding finger on her dress. "Fine. What'm I meant t'do with it?"

"What I tell you to," said Arenadd. "It's time you started learning how to fight."

Laela spent most of that day with the sickle in her hand, practising the different blows and blocks Arenadd showed her.

"Do it over and over again," he said. "And then do it some more. Do it until it's second nature—until your body remembers how to do it. Muscles have memory."

Laela set to work.

By evening, she was exhausted and irritable—something that wasn't helped by the constant, sickly rocking of the ship. She and Arenadd retired to their cabin, where food had been laid out for them. Before she ate, Laela had to feed Oeka—taking the bloody haunch provided and cutting strips off it. The finicky griffin had refused to take it any other way and wouldn't take food from anybody else. At first, Laela had found this cute and flattering, but by now she'd realised what it really was: the griffin's way of showing her exactly where she stood.

Still, it was a small enough price to pay. For now, at least.

Afterward, Laela washed the gore off her hands and sat down with Arenadd—who had politely waited for her before beginning to eat.

"Yeh didn't have t'do that. It's probably gone cold by now."

Arenadd shrugged and reached for the cheese. "Eat up. We're ready to move on to something a little less tiring now."

Over dinner, he resumed teaching her griffish. Laela, who had never been formally educated until her adoption into Malvern, was beginning to find it boring, but she said nothing and persevered—knowing the eventual reward would make it worthwhile. And she was far too proud to even think of how humiliating it would be if she were the only griffiner who couldn't speak griffish. Not knowing Northern was bad enough.

Oeka gulped down the last of her food and listened with interest. Now she'd been taught some respect, the human was working hard at being a worthy griffiner. Oeka was pleased. She'd already done well by claiming the human before one of the larger griffins did; Oeka knew that being a youngster meant it was harder to take the best humans without being challenged. But the others in the Hatchery knew better than to interfere with her—she'd discovered her power early on, and once they knew what it could do, the others left her alone.

*I have come far in little time,* Oeka thought. *As my power means I should. This human will serve me well.*

The small griffin's eyes narrowed on Laela, awkwardly stumbling her way through a griffish phrase. At first she'd disliked the idea of leaving Malvern for so long, but by now Oeka had decided it was for the best. Better to have time to break her human in, unmolested. By the time they returned, she would have her well trained and ready to take all the Kingdom had to offer.

# 21

# Kissing the Snake

Three months passed.

The ship reached Maijan and docked there to take on fresh supplies. The Amorani-controlled island was big enough to support two small cities and even a few griffiners. Lord Vander went ashore with Ymazu to speak to them, and Arenadd went, too. Laela went with him, more than happy to have solid ground under her feet again.

They spent two days in Maijan, and Laela took the opportunity to explore the port-town where they'd docked, with Oeka by her side. The locals were a friendly enough lot—obviously used to visits from their pale neighbours. Most of them spoke some Cymrian, and they received Laela with great interest, many of them pointing out her blue eyes and chattering animatedly among themselves. At first, Laela was offended, but she quickly realised that their interest was nothing but friendly curiosity, and after that she began to find it vaguely enjoyable.

Once the supplies were on board and Arenadd and Vander had completed their business on the island (and Skandar had taken the opportunity to acquaint himself with the handful of female griffins who lived on it), the *Seabreath* departed.

For the next few weeks, they followed the chain of small islands that Maijan belonged to, anchoring beside one or two of them so the griffins could go ashore. Most of the human passengers went, too, Laela among them, though she spent most of her time on dry land training with Arenadd in the art of the sickle. She could feel herself getting better at it all the time.

She was almost sad when the time came to leave the islands behind and strike out over the Armourfish Sea.

The weather had been growing steadily warmer and warmer as they sailed further east, and by the time they were a month out of Maijan, it was sweltering.

The Northerners, used to cold, looked as if all their energy had been drained out of them. They stayed belowdecks, moaning and grumbling among themselves and trying to cool down by soaking their clothes in sea-water. Laela, too, suffered in the heat, which grew unbearably as the weeks dragged by. She couldn't believe that any place could possibly be this hot, and almost dreaded what it would be like when they were actually in Amoran.

But as unhappy as they were, nobody looked as miserable as Arenadd did.

The King scarcely moved during the day, and was pale and tight-lipped whenever he was awake. He became snappish and irritable during Laela's lessons, and only sheer exhaustion stopped them from outright arguing.

Eventually, after what looked like a very unpleasant struggle, Arenadd gave up and took his robe off—going bare-chested like the other men on board. His scars looked even more hideous under the harsh sun and attracted plenty of morbid conversation, which he obviously didn't appreciate.

Skandar wasn't much happier than his human. Laela started visiting him with Arenadd as an excuse to get out of the sun, and she was shocked when she saw how thin the huge griffin had become. Whoever had made the stall he was living in had done his best, but it just wasn't big enough for him. His fur and feathers had become dull and matted from too little grooming. His stall hadn't been cleaned out properly and stank, but though he'd been lying in it so long that he was developing pressure sores on his paws, he refused to go out into the blazing sun.

By the time Arenadd intervened, the dark griffin's temper had snapped, and he had begun lashing out at anyone who came close.

Laela, too sensible to try and go too close, hung back and watched while Arenadd did his best to calm his friend down. Eventually, Skandar groaned and laid his head on his talons,

and Arenadd could go in and clear away as much of the mess as
he could.

Laela realised he was swearing. "We've got t'get him out of
here," she said. "He needs—"

"I *know* what he needs," Arenadd growled without turning
around. "That doesn't mean he'll look for it. Go back up on deck
and see if you can find someone who knows where to find some
ointment for these sores."

Laela nodded brusquely and left.

As she and Oeka climbed the ramp back to the deck, Laela
heard shouting. "What's goin' on up there?" she mumbled.

Outside, there was furious activity. The captain was yelling
orders at his men, most of whom were already dashing off to
follow them. There were some griffiners about, most of them
looking anxious and uncertain.

Laela squinted irritably in the sun and stumped over to the
nearest person. "What's goin' on? Why's everyone shoutin'? I
already got enough of a bloody headache."

"There's another ship coming this way," said the man—one
of the sailors.

She perked up at that. "Who is it?"

"We're not sure. They're not close enough to tell. But we
have to be ready, in case . . ."

"In case they ain't friends?" Laela hazarded.

"Yes. Just in case."

"What, how likely is it that they're wantin' to attack us?"
said Laela.

"There are plenty of trading ships in these waters," said the
sailor. "Which means—"

"—It's probably one of them?"

"Which means there are also pirates," the sailor said grimly.

"What in the gods' names are they?"

"Bandits. Thieves."

"Ah. Right." Laela's grip on his arm slackened. "I'd better go
tell the King, then."


Arenadd took some time to emerge from belowdecks, and
when he did, it was obvious what had taken him so long.
He walked slowly, pausing every few moments to look back.

Skandar was following—limping slightly and hissing. Several times he tried to turn back, but Arenadd kept talking softly to him, and he gave in to his friend's coaxing and stepped up onto the deck. There he opened his wings, put his head back and stretched luxuriously. Someone brought a bucket of water and a brush, and Arenadd set to work cleaning the griffin's flanks. Skandar cooed, obviously enjoying it, and deigned to lift his paws one by one so Arenadd could scrape the muck out of his talons and clean and dress the sores.

Laela, watching, found the scene so strange and weirdly amusing that she almost forgot about the oncoming ship.

"Don't yeh have people t'do that for yeh?" she asked eventually.

Arenadd glanced up. "He won't let anyone else touch him. I wouldn't ask them to, anyway."

"Well, yeah, they might lose an arm or somethin'."

Arenadd picked up the sharp tool he used to scrape out the inside of Skandar's talons. "I may be a King, but I'm a griffiner as well, and doing this sort of thing is part of my duties as Skandar's human. Yes, what do you want?"

The sailor who'd been trying to get his attention bowed hastily and spoke in Northern.

Arenadd's expression changed. "How close?" he asked, using Cymrian for Laela's benefit.

The reply came in the dark tongue—Laela understood a few words here and there, but had no idea what the man was saying. She gritted her teeth in frustration.

Arenadd nodded curtly and went back to his work, speaking to Skandar now. After three months of daily tutoring, Laela was pleased to find that she could understand parts of this, at least.

". . . enemies . . . dangerous . . . fighting . . . many."

Skandar raised his head and stared out over the sea. His tail began to lash back and forth.

Laela turned, and her face froze. "What?"

The strange ship had come so much closer since she'd last seen it that it was as if it had appeared out of nowhere. Now she could see that it was at least as big as the *Seabreath*—and far more heavily manned. At least a hundred men were up on the decks—Amoranis, all of them.

Many of them were carrying bows.

"Pirates, Sire," one of the griffiners said. "They have us outnumbered."

From the other ship, a thickset man brandishing a spear yelled out a sneering challenge in Amorani.

"Fools," said Lord Vander, appearing from somewhere as if by magic. "They have no idea that they are up against griffins. Sire—" He turned to Arenadd. "You need not concern yourself with these scum. If you wish, I will go at once and tell the griffins belowdecks. They will deal with them quickly enough."

Arenadd didn't look at him. He kept his eyes on the oncoming pirate ship. There was a very strange look on his face. Not angry, not frightened, but strangely . . .

Laela stepped closer to him. "What's up, Arenadd?"

The Dark Lord was pale, and his eyes were gleaming. He was breathing heavily and his fists clenched. He let out a long, slow sigh. *"Oh . . ."*

Laela nudged him. "Sire? Arenadd?"

The ship was very close by now—so close Laela could see the intent expressions on the bandits' faces.

Fear put a tight band around her chest. She moved closer to Oeka and tried to look calm. Strangely, her mind—addled by the heat and now by apprehension—threw up a memory that seemed to have nothing to do with the situation. She was a child back in the village, listening to the miller's sons singing a taunting song at their sister. *Pretty maid, dressed in yellow, went upstairs to kiss a fellow. By mistake she kissed a snake—*

Laela glanced at Arenadd, in time to see a horrible grin spread over his face.

"Sire?" Vander was still hovering nearby, looking slightly anxious.

"Those fools," Arenadd breathed. "They have no idea."

"Not yet," Vander said grimly. "Ymazu and I—"

"No." Arenadd held up a hand. "Stop. *Stop!*"

The people around him, who had been hurrying to organise the defence, stopped in their tracks.

Arenadd's hand went to his belt and freed his sickle. "There's no need for you to risk your lives here. Leave this to us."

The griffiners glanced at each other. "But, Sire," said one of the younger ones, "there's no need for—"

Arenadd drew himself up to his full, impressive height.

"Quiet, Arawn." He gripped the sickle. "I may have been a King for twenty years, but underneath I am still *Kraeai kran ae*." He looked at the pirates again. "And I think it's time I reminded myself of that."

Laela gaped at him. "Yeh ain't gonna—"

Arenadd laid a hand on her arm. "Sorry, Laela," he said. "But today you're going to see a different side of me. Skandar!"

Skandar, who had been lying on his belly, stood up and limped toward his human. The ship actually leaned to one side under his weight, and several people quickly ran to the opposite side to try to balance it.

Over on the deck of the pirate ship, the crew stopped their jeering. Laela saw their faces slacken with dismay as they saw the giant griffin.

Arenadd went to the railings and held his arms out, his hair blowing in the wind. *"You fools!"* he roared. "You think you can stand against me? You dare to challenge the Dark Lord? Look on your deaths and shudder!" and he laughed like a madman.

Behind him, Skandar spread his wings and screeched.

The pirates had already realised their mistake. They dropped their weapons and scattered, desperately trying to turn their ship around. Laela saw them tug on ropes to adjust the sails, shouting at each other in panic.

A handful of them were more collected. They leapt onto the railings, balancing there with incredible ease, and aimed their bows.

The captain of the *Seabreath* shouted a warning, and everyone, including Laela, dropped flat.

Everyone except for Arenadd and Skandar.

Laela heard Arenadd grunt as an arrow buried itself in his hip. As she stood up, he yanked it out and hurled it into the sea with a contemptuous laugh. Skandar hadn't been hit at all, and Laela suddenly realised that the arrow had been aimed at the giant griffin's chest.

Arenadd had put himself in the way.

That was the final straw for Skandar. He stumbled forward and launched himself clumsily into the air. For a moment, it looked as if he were going to go after the pirate ship alone, but once he had gathered momentum he came swooping back and scooped Arenadd up in his talons. Laela stood up and watched, open-mouthed, as the giant griffin flew straight for the fleeing bandits. He paused to deposit Arenadd on the deck, and then landed himself.

Arenadd had already attacked.

On the *Seabreath*, sailors and griffiners alike ran to the railings to watch, expressions of disbelief slowly spreading over their faces.

For Laela, it was beyond imagining

Skandar rushed over the decks like a massive wave, all claws and talons and enormous beak. Men fell in front of him like blades of grass. Most of the time, the dark griffin didn't even bother to kill them—he simply knocked them over and then crushed them under his paws as he charged on, straight at the wheel and the man holding it. The man in question made a run for it the instant he saw Skandar coming, but there was nowhere near enough room to dodge, and for his size, the griffin was astonishingly fast. He caught up with the fleeing Amorani and his beak snapped shut around the man's chest.

Laela heard the sound of breaking bones from all the way over on the deck of the *Seabreath*.

But Skandar didn't have the fight all to himself. Arenadd was at the other end of the ship, apparently oblivious to his partner's slaughter. A gang of pirates had rushed him, obviously hoping to overwhelm him by sheer weight of numbers. For a moment Arenadd disappeared among the press of bodies, and Laela feared the worst.

Then she saw the pirates begin to fall. Arenadd appeared, standing on a dead man's chest, his sickle scattering drops of blood as he flicked it expertly at another man's throat. He fought with unbelievable speed, but methodically, like a man who was immune to excitement or fear. He took several blows but didn't react to them at all.

The ship, listing crazily as Skandar unbalanced it, drifted closer to the *Seabreath*, and Laela could hear the screams.

Then, as quickly as it had begun, the fight was over. The surviving pirates dropped their weapons and fell to their knees, holding up their hands in surrender.

Laela relaxed. "My gods," she said. "He's done it. He's . . ."

Her voice faded away. Arenadd stepped off the dead man

and walked slowly toward the cowering pirates. Skandar, bloodied but apparently unhurt, came to join him. Arenadd spoke to
him, pointing at his prisoners. Skandar rasped back.

Arenadd nodded, and with a quick, graceful blow, slashed a
man's throat from ear to ear.

"No!"

Laela's shout was drowned out by the screams and yells.

The defenceless Amoranis were trying in vain to escape,
screaming what had to be pleas for mercy. Arenadd chased
them and cut them down one by one, pausing occasionally to
torment one with the point of his sickle before finally slitting his
throat.

Laela realised that he was laughing.

Skandar joined in the sadistic game, lolloping after the vic-
tims like an oversized kitten chasing butterflies.

When it was over, and not one single man was left alive on
deck, Arenadd went into the cabin and then belowdecks. Left to
his own devices, Skandar settled down and began to eat the
corpses—tearing at them as if they were no different than the
goats and sheep Laela had seen him dismember back at Malvern.

Afterward, when Arenadd returned to the *Seabreath*, Laela
didn't recognise him at all. His hair was matted with blood, and
more blood had stained his bare torso. It dripped from his sickle
onto the deck. And from his fingers.

But it wasn't the blood she noticed. It wasn't the blood that
made him unrecognisable.

His eyes, normally so cold and calm, were burning. The
impassive face was locked into a fierce and terrible smile. He
looked alive in a way that he never had before. But he didn't
look like a man any more, either.

Laela backed away from him, her inner voice locked into an
endless nonsensical loop. *By mistake she kissed a snake, by
mistake she kissed a snake . . .*

Arenadd didn't seem to notice her. "The ship's ours," he said
to Lord Vander, quite casually. "Mostly intact, too, along with
its supplies. They've got a lot of valuable loot in the hold. Consider it a gift for the Emperor from me."

Vander's expression was guarded. "Thank you, Sire. We had
better send men over to clear away the bodies and attach the
ship to ours."

"Of course." Arenadd nodded. "Now I'm going to go and clean myself up." He walked off.

Laela couldn't help it—she went over to the other ship once the sailors had pulled it closer with ropes and made a makeshift walkway between the two vessels.

Once there, she walked around the deck as if in a dream.

In many places, it was slippery with blood.

Belowdecks, she saw far worse. There had been other people down there—wounded men and others unable to fight. Some of them looked as if they had been prisoners of the pirates.

Arenadd had killed them all.

Laela's numbed mind managed to note that no-one around her looked particularly bothered. Only some of the younger men showed signs of unease. The older ones—the ones she knew must be veterans of the war—acted as if nothing unusual had happened.

They must have seen this kind of thing before.

Laela couldn't bear to see any more, and went back up onto the deck, where Oeka was idly grooming.

The green-eyed griffin gave her the keen look she had come to know so well. "You are pale. Did you see things you did not like?"

Laela strained to understand her. "Everyone . . . is . . . killed . . ." She gave up, and reverted to Cymrian. "Everyone down there's dead. Even the people locked up in the little prison thing. He killed 'em all."

Oeka flicked her tail in displeasure. "I have told you to use griffish when you speak to me."

Laela ignored her. She noticed the cabin—its door hanging open as Arenadd had left it. Nobody had gone in there yet.

She knew it was a bad idea, but once again she couldn't help herself. She walked toward it, bracing herself for what she might find inside.

The inside of the cabin wasn't that much different from her own quarters back on the *Seabreath*. Somehow, that made the sight of it so much worse. She took in the furniture and the decorations—all made in unfamiliar styles that she knew must be Amorani. They were strange, but beautiful.

She wondered what colour the rug had been, before it had been dyed with blood.

There were two bodies there, one lying near the door and the other slumped over the table. Both of them had had their throats cut.

*They died quickly,* Laela thought distantly. *He killed them quickly. He didn't . . .*

Her inner voice died away as she saw the lumpy object by the fireplace, covered in blood.

There was more blood nearby, leaking out of what looked like a wooden cage.

Laela never knew why she looked closer, or where she found the will, but she looked.

She never looked more closely at the thing by the fireplace. Not once she had seen the wisp of hair and the tiny ear showing through the blood.

She left the body of the child and investigated the cradle.

The baby inside had been cut almost in half.


W hen Laela returned to her cabin she found Arenadd there. He had cleaned the blood off himself and put on fresh clothes, and was sitting by the empty fireplace and peacefully reading a book.

"Hullo!" he said, in cheerful tones. "Have you looked at the treasure yet? If you see anything you like, feel free to take it— I've told them you're allowed to."

Whatever she'd meant to say fell out of her brain when she saw him, looking so normal and happy. "I . . . ain't looked yet."

"Well, go ahead if you want to." He paused. "Something you want to talk about?"

Laela found her voice again. "Why did yeh kill the baby?" she said. "An' the child?"

Arenadd looked blank. "What?"

"I went on the ship," said Laela. "I saw it." Her face twisted with anguish. "I know they was gonna attack us an' that, an' it was amazin' how yeh killed all them bandits, but . . . why did yeh have t'kill the rest, too? The prisoners down in the hold? The children? Why did yeh have t'kill the *children*? The baby? They weren't no harm."

Arenadd's face fell. "You shouldn't have gone on that ship."

"Well, I did," said Laela, her voice cracking. "An' I saw what yeh did. I saw it all. I saw the dead baby. Why did yeh do it? *Why?*"

He put down the book. "Laela, you don't understand—"

"Yeah, I do." Laela felt fear twist inside her and become anger. "I understand just fine." She took a step closer to him. "I never understood before, but now I do. This is why they call yeh the Dark Lord. This is why they're afraid of yeh. This is why they say yeh ain't got no heart. It's because of this. Yeh did things like this in the war."

"Yes," Arenadd said quietly. "I did things exactly like this in the war."

"But why?" said Laela. "Why the baby? Why kill a baby, an' a child? Why kill people who didn't have no weapons, people who wanted . . ."

Arenadd sighed. "Oh, gods. I knew I should have kept you away from this. Laela . . ."

"What? Tell me. Tell me why."

"Your foster father," said Arenadd.

"What?" Laela started. "What about him?"

"You told me he drank himself to death, yes?"

"Yeah, I did. So what?"

"He couldn't stay away from it," said Arenadd. "He knew it was hurting him, but he kept on drinking."

Painful memories came back to her. "Yeah . . . he knew it. I told him, too. I begged him t'stop. But he never could stop."

Arenadd nodded. "He couldn't live without it. Couldn't live without that feeling that drink gave him. And I . . ." He sighed. "I'm the same as him. I kill, Laela. I love to kill. It gives me a feeling . . . I can't describe it. When I fight, a madness takes hold of me, and then all I can do is kill. Kill as many people as I can, it doesn't matter who. I didn't even know I killed a baby. I swear."

Laela couldn't think of anything to say.

Arenadd closed his eyes and sighed. "Gods, it's been such a long time since I've had a reason to fight. You can't imagine how wonderful it felt to do it again."

There was a long silence, while Laela stood and looked at him. Arenadd looked back, with a hint of uncertainty.

"I thought I knew yeh," Laela said at last. "But I don't, do I?"

"I am what the Night God made me," said Arenadd.

"Yer a monster," said Laela.

He stared at his broken fingers. "I know."

L aela couldn't eat anything for the rest of that day even though the sailors had brought over enough new supplies for an impromptu feast. She managed to get her hands on the carcass of one of the live goats that had been on board, and gave the choicest part to Oeka. Once the griffin was satisfied, Laela spent the evening skulking in the shadows, avoiding Arenadd and drinking spiced Amorani wine.

She put off returning to the cabin as long as she could, but eventually everyone else had gone to bed except for the sailors who were on watch, and Oeka was becoming impatient.

Drunk and exhausted, Laela stumbled back into the cabin. Arenadd was in his hammock, apparently asleep, and she pulled her boots off and flopped onto the bed, her head spinning. Oeka curled up beside her as usual, and went to sleep.

Laela couldn't sleep.

She lay awake for most of the night, not wanting to close her eyes. Whenever she did, images of dead children would flash behind her eyelids, and her addled brain convinced her that if she went to sleep, they would follow her.

Her head flopped sideways on the pillow, and she stared at the vague shape that was Arenadd. He wasn't moving at all, and she imagined him sleeping peacefully, without any nightmares. How could anyone rest that well when he'd done what he had— and *liked* it?

The memory rose up again. "Pretty maid, dressed in yellow, went upstairs to kiss a fellow. By mistake she kissed a snake . . ." Laela murmured the words to herself several times, trying to remember how the rhyme ended.

She couldn't remember.

Arenadd stirred and sighed in his sleep.

*By mistake she kissed a snake,* Laela thought, and rolled over.

She had been lying like that for some time before she realised she was hearing something strange. She stilled and concentrated, her heart beating faster.

It sounded like a voice.

Laela rolled over again and sat up, tense now. The voice was coming from somewhere to her right, and she relaxed very slightly when she realised what it was—it was Arenadd, talking in his sleep. The words were mumbled and difficult to make out, but Laela listened intently, wondering what someone like him would say in his sleep.

When she finally did realise just what he was saying, she flinched and put a hand to her mouth.

". . . help me . . ."

Laela shivered.

"Help me," Arenadd repeated. "Please, someone let me out, please . . . help . . ."

Laela put her head under the pillow and fought to make herself sleep.

# 22

## Amoran

Two days after the slaughter of the pirates, the *Seabreath* came within sight of Amoran. Arenadd, to the silent horror of everyone on board, put his robe back on before spending half a day grooming in his cabin. Laela, still trying to stay out of his way, found herself hustled back into their quarters shortly before they were due to reach land.

"What do yeh want?" she asked, unable to hide her unease around him.

Whatever new energy Arenadd had gained from his killing frenzy had worn off by now, and he looked grim and solemn, but businesslike. "We're going to follow the river from here, and we should dock in Instabahn tonight."

"So?"

Arenadd rolled his eyes. "Laela, can you just for one moment forget your utter inability to stand on ceremony and take it into your head that the Emperor and his entire court are going to be waiting for us there?"

Laela blanched. "What'm I gonna have to do?"

"Look respectable for once," Arenadd said shortly. "I've got an outfit picked out for you. But first we're going to do something about that hair."

Instinctively, she clutched at it. "What's wrong with . . . ?"

Arenadd prodded her curls. "What's wrong with them? They're a tangled mess, that's what's wrong with them. When was the last time you even combed? Dear gods, girl, curly hair takes looking after! Take it from someone who spends most of his private time trying to stop his from turning into a rat's nest! Now come here, and I'll show you a few things that can help . . ."

Laela trundled after him and listened with vague hopelessness as he showed her various bottles of lotion and different combs and brushes, and explained how they should be used and in what order. Outwardly, she looked bored and irritated, but inwardly she was fighting against her own confusion. *He killed so many people yesterday,* she told herself. *He cut a baby to pieces. He looked me in the eye an' told me he loved doin' it. He . . .*

But she couldn't keep reminding herself of that while that same man was waving a bottle of softening conditioner in her face and proudly extolling its detangling virtues.

All of a sudden, she had to stop herself from laughing. This was insane.

". . . have you got all of that?"

Laela pulled herself together. "Er, yeah, I think so . . ."

"Good, then I'll leave this by the tub for you—there's already plenty of water in there. Now, time to show you your outfit. I think you'll like it."

Laela had expected a new dress. What she found instead was something she recognised but had never thought she would wear herself.

"Dear gods, is that . . . ?"

"Of course," said Arenadd. "I had my tailors make it. You're entitled to wear it."

It was a griffiner's ceremonial outfit. It looked as if the tailor who'd made it had started with a fairly ordinary gown made from a rich brown-gold fabric, before they'd added a patch of brown fur attached to a long "tail" that reached almost to the ground, and had sewn hundreds of small feathers onto the bodice until it was as fluffy as a bird's chest. The shoulders and sleeves had been decorated with more feathers, but these were definitely griffin feathers—huge, long, strong wing feathers that formed a kind of cape. They were brown, too.

"Not Oeka's," Arenadd told her. "Normally, she'd have to donate the feathers, but she's too young for hers to be long enough, so we found a griffin who was about her colour and collected some from his nest."

Laela fingered the outfit, noting the green gems sewn into the fabric and the embroidered vine designs. "This is . . ."

"How do you like it?" said Arenadd.

Laela caved in. "I can't wear this! This is . . ."

"You don't like it?"

"It's magnificent," said Laela. "I can't wear somethin' like this! I'm just a—"

"You're a griffiner," said Arenadd. "You have to wear it. I'll be wearing mine."

"I s'pose so." In fact, Laela was dying to try it on.

"Clean yourself up first," Arenadd advised.

After he'd left, and she had some privacy, Laela bathed and washed her hair—following his instructions as well as she could remember. She was surprised to find that the lotions worked as well as Arenadd had claimed, and after using them and the various combs he'd left, her hair was clean and neater than it had ever been.

Once she was dry, she put on the ceremonial outfit. It made her feel so important that she didn't even notice how hot it was. She walked around the cabin, trying to get used to the feeling of the feathers on her shoulders.

Oeka darted excitedly around her. "A true griffiner at last!" she chirped. "We will be an impressive sight to the Amoranis."

Laela understood her well enough to catch the gist of it, and she grinned. "Griffins are impressive, an' now I'm dressed up like one." She fingered the patch of feathers on the front of her gown, and wondered how long it must have taken someone to sew them all on. And Arenadd had had it all prepared, just to surprise her.

A chill disturbed her good mood. Not for the first time, she wondered helplessly how someone could be so kind and generous one moment, and so utterly depraved the next. The man was a walking contradiction.

As if reading her mind, Arenadd appeared at that moment. "How d'you like it?"

"It's amazin'," said Laela. "Perfect fit."

Arenadd looked her up and down. "Well, I never. You actually look like a lady now. Who would have thought it?"

Laela grinned and shoved him. "Yeah, well, I'm still waitin' for the part where *you* start lookin' like a King."

"You don't think I do?" he asked, unexpectedly serious.

"Not really," said Laela. "I s'pose I think of yeh as a man first an' a King second."

Arenadd's face creased into a smile. "And that's why I like you so much."

Laela smiled back without thinking. Somewhere inside at that moment, she realised that no matter what he'd done, she couldn't hate him.

"Something on your mind?" Arenadd inquired.

"Nah, just wonderin' how long it'll be till we're there," said Laela. "How long's it been since we left home, anyway? I lost track."

"Just over four months," said Arenadd. "We made pretty good time. Now, I'd better go and talk to our fellow griffiners and make sure everyone knows how they're expected to conduct themselves. The Amorani have different expectations than we do, you know."

Laela did know. During the voyage, she'd spent some time listening to Vander describe how she would be expected to conduct herself in Amoran. Their laws and customs sometimes sounded weird to her, but at their root they weren't that much different than the ones she knew.

"Ain't this excitin'?" she said to Oeka. "Amoran, at last!"

Oeka clicked her beak. "Soon, we shall meet a mighty ruler indeed."

"Yeah," said Laela. "An Emperor, eh? Fancy that."

"And his human, of course," Oeka conceded. "Now, I think that while we have time, you should fulfil your duty as my own human."

Laela guessed what she was getting at quickly enough—this "duty" was one Arenadd had taught her about, and she'd practised it several times. She went into the cabin and fetched the brush and the talon-cleaning tools. When she returned, she found several adult griffins already on deck, being groomed by their humans.

"Little room for us," said Oeka. "Others will take their place once these have done. We shall go back into our nest."

Laela nodded and retreated, not wanting to be around that many large griffins anyway. In the cabin, she spent a good chunk of time brushing Oeka's furred hindquarters, going over each patch until the fur was smooth and glossy. After that, she had to go through her feathers, looking for parasites and removing any dead or damaged feathers. Oeka didn't like that much, and hissed warningly once or twice, but she kept still and let her finish before obligingly lifting her forepaws one by one so that Laela could clean the talons.

Once that was done, Laela took a bottle of very expensive scented oil and rubbed some into Oeka's beak—making it shine as if it had been polished.

After that, she could rest and have something to eat, while the griffin groomed her wings herself.

When she was fairly sure the grooming up on deck was over (she waited until the ship had stopped rocking so much), she went back outside. Sure enough, only one or two were left, and the rest were in the air, following the ship as it drifted up the mighty River Erech.

From the deck, Laela could see the faint lights of buildings on the riverbank, and her heart began to flutter. She was seeing the first tiny parts of Amoran—a country that, among their party, only Vander had ever seen, one so far away that most Cymrians believed it didn't even exist except in legends.

Oeka, of course, looked completely unflustered. "Amorani griffins are smaller than us," she remarked. "I shall feel very much at home, I think."

"Yeah." Laela was finding her partner easier to understand all the time.

There didn't seem to be much more to say after that, and girl and griffin stood together in silence on the stern, watching as the lights of Instabahn came into view at last.

Laela knew they were there when the griffiners assembled on deck. All of them were wearing their ceremonial outfits. Laela, sweating horribly in hers, went to join them.

Arenadd was there, also, and he, too, was in his ceremonial clothing. His, however, rather than being a tunic enhanced with feathers and fur, was based on a robe. It looked more or less like one of his customary black robes, but the area over his chest was covered in Skandar's silver feathers, and the wing feathers on his shoulders and sleeves were a mix of silver, black, and white. The patch of fur below the feathers on the chest was white, and the end of the "tail" had been decorated with a fan of more feathers in imitation of a griffin's own.

He was wearing the crown, too.

"Okay," said Laela, coming to stand beside him as he'd beckoned her to. "Now yeh look like a King."

"A King ready to meet an Emperor," Arenadd murmured. "Now, remember your manners, Laela. I'd rather you didn't embarrass me."

Laela nodded sternly and stood a little taller.

Instabahn's harbour came in sight. The ship angled toward it and came to a sedate halt as the sailors dropped the anchor and threw ropes to the waiting Amoranis.

A few moments later, the sailors had thrown down a wide ramp, and Arenadd walked down it with Oeka and Laela in step beside him. She had been aboard ship for so long that she stumbled a little, and her head spun before she managed to recover herself.

The moment Arenadd set foot on solid ground—the Mighty Skandar came down to land by his side as if from nowhere. He, too, had been groomed, and his gleaming feathers and fur only made him look more magnificent.

Arenadd walked on without missing a step, ignoring the other griffins, who landed as their own humans stepped off the ramp.

Ahead, the great court of Instabahn was waiting for them— dozens of men and women, dressed in their strange finery, most with griffins beside them.

At their head was a bald man of indeterminate age, wearing nothing but a yellow-and-blue-striped kilt, a pair of sandals, and a heavy collar decorated with dozens of tear-shaped jewels.

Arenadd walked straight toward him, halted, put his hands together, and bowed. Then he spoke—in Amorani.

The bald man smiled and put his hands together and bowed before he replied in the same language.

"An honour," said Arenadd, using Cymrian now. "Great Khalid, Master of Amoran."

The bald man smiled again. "I am sorry that I do not speak your own language, Great King," he said in very good Cymrian. "If I did, rest assured I would use it."

"Your courtesy is not in doubt," said Arenadd. "I am honoured merely to meet you at last. Sacred Ruler, this is my partner, the Mighty Skandar, greatest of all griffins in my Kingdom."

Khalid bowed deeply to Skandar. "It is a great joy of my life that I have met such a magnificent griffin," he said—using griffish now.

Skandar peered at him, and snorted. "Furless human!" he declared.

After a moment of painful silence, the Emperor burst out laughing. "Observant, indeed, Mighty Skandar!" he said.

Arenadd smiled slightly. "My partner has a habit of saying just what he thinks, Great Emperor."

"So I have noticed," said the Emperor. "Now, who is your companion, who looks so much like you?"

Laela panicked for half a heartbeat, and then imitated Arenadd's bow. "I am the Lady Laela," she recited. "Master of Wisdom and chief advisor to the King. And this is Oeka, a very powerful griffin."

Oeka moved closer to her to show her pleasure. "We are both honoured to meet you, Sacred Ruler."

The Emperor looked at Laela with interest, and then he looked at Arenadd. "I see the ability to rise to great power is in your family's blood, Great King." He paused briefly, before his smile returned even more warmly than before. "Now, my own family and I are happy to welcome you to our home, and to invite you to come and share food and wine with us."

"We shall be honoured to accept, Sacred Ruler," said Arenadd.

The Emperor paused for a moment, and his smile became much more genuine. "My lord Vander!"

Vander came forward, bowing low. He greeted his master in formal-sounding Amorani, but the Emperor laughed and embraced him. Vander returned the embrace while Ymazu—now heavily pregnant—looked on approvingly.

Laela smiled to herself. Amoranis weren't so different after all.

After that, they were ushered away from the dock and walked with the Emperor and his court along a paved road lined with enormous stone pillars and into a large building.

Inside, it was warmly lit, and dozens of low tables filled the space. *A hall,* Laela thought.

But while a hall in Malvern would have had wooden beams and probably some spears or hanging animal skins by way of decoration, this one was so rich it took Laela's breath away. The walls and roof were completely smooth, as if they had been made all in one piece. The room was made all in sensual curves and elegant domes and arches, and everything had been painted. Laela saw images of brown-skinned women dancing and playing instruments, griffins using magic to cover a pillar in swirling patterns of red and green, and a massive flower opening to reveal a golden man with a serene smile.

Flowers were everywhere, in elaborate gold holders on the walls and on the pillars that held up the ceiling. More decorated the tables—ornamental vines, lush with blooms, flowing over the wood.

Laela realised her mouth was hanging open. She shut it again, so she could use it for a disbelieving grin.

Even Oeka looked taken aback. "Such magnificence!" she chirped. She spread her wings and fluttered them a little, as if trying to calm herself down. "What power humans possess!"

"What power *these* humans possess," said Laela. "This place must be the most magnificent building in the country!"

"I wouldn't count on it," said Arenadd from behind her.

"Argh!" Laela turned sharply. "I *hate* it how yer always doin' that!"

Arenadd grinned. "Call it a bad habit. Now, let's mingle, shall we? I think the Emperor will want to introduce me to his daughter in a moment."

The other griffiners had already spread themselves around the room and were beginning to mingle with their hosts—using griffish to talk to them.

"Everyone in Amoran speaks griffish," said Arenadd. "It's a sacred language to them—apparently they believe that Xanathus only listens to prayers spoken in it."

Laela was about to ask who Xanathus was, but remembered in time. "Should make it easier for us here, eh?"

"Definitely."

The Emperor was already seated at a table with a group of people who looked to be his family. Arenadd went to join him, with Laela and Oeka following. Skandar, typically uninterested, was wandering here and there, busily intimidating other males and making suggestive remarks to the females.

The Emperor received Arenadd with his usual smile. "So, how do you like our hall, Great King?" he asked. He had a gold ring in his nose, Laela noticed.

"A very beautiful place indeed, Sacred Ruler," Arenadd said smoothly. "Your people are very skilled."

The Emperor inclined his head. "This is only a minor hall—I apologise that I could not receive you in the Hall of Suns in our capital city, but I thought you would prefer not to sail up the River Erech for another moon's turning, and I was in Instabahn regardless."

*Only a minor hall!* Laela wondered if this Hall of Suns was made out of solid gold or something.

"No offence is taken, Sacred Ruler," said Arenadd, inclining his head in return.

"Excellent." The Emperor's startlingly white teeth flashed. "Please, allow me to introduce the Imperial Family, Great King."

The table had strange round cushions around it instead of chairs. Laela tried to get comfortable on hers, and listened while the Emperor named the other people with him.

"Aznaran, my first wife." This was a middle-aged woman whose ears sagged under the weight of a pair of enormous gold hoops. Her face had been painted to make her dark eyes look bigger. Laela thought she looked how a mother should look.

"And Ilya, my second," the Emperor added. This one was younger, and was openly staring at Arenadd's pale skin.

"And this," said the Emperor, "is my youngest daughter, the Princess Nyria. No doubt you have been longing to meet her."

Unlike the other women there, the Princess wore a veil over her face—but it was thin enough for Laela to get an idea of what she looked like. She had a small, pretty face, and wore a gown covered in golden beads, and she stared silently at the table while she was introduced.

Arenadd smiled at her. "I have indeed." Then, to the

apparent surprise of the Imperial Family, he reached toward her with his good hand. "Nyria. You're as beautiful as I imagined you would be."

There was an awkward silence, and Laela knew he'd broken some kind of Amorani protocol. But Arenadd looked unembarrassed, and, a moment later, the Princess touched his hand in return. "I am awed to meet you, Great King," she said softly. "You are far more handsome than I imagined."

At that, the Emperor burst out laughing. "I see you are to my daughter's liking! I hope that she is to your own!"

"She would put any Northern woman to shame," said Arenadd.

"You shall have plenty of time to see," said the Emperor. "Nyria, if you would like, then perhaps you could visit your betrothed in his quarters tonight, so that you can come to know him better."

The Princess bowed her head toward him. "I would be glad to, Father."

"Just be careful the Mighty Skandar doesn't eat yeh!" Laela joked.

The Emperor and his family looked at her with slightly shocked expressions, but then they laughed.

"It would seem that your own daughter has a fine tongue on her," the Emperor remarked to Arenadd. "As fine as your own, Great King."

Laela decided that she quite liked this strange bald-headed man. "I ain't his daughter, Sacred Ruler," she said.

The Emperor paused at that. "She looks very much like you, Great King," he said. "I am sorry if—"

"She does," said Arenadd. "In more than looks, let me assure you. But she is not my daughter. I am unmarried."

The Emperor's eyes gleamed. "Of course. Please excuse my mistake, Great King."

After that, he and Arenadd chatted about this and that, trying to put each other at ease. The women didn't try to join in.

Laela supposed they weren't allowed.

In the meantime, food was brought in for the Amorani court and its guests. Naturally, the Emperor's table was served first, and Laela was shocked when she saw who brought the food to it.

They were men, pale-skinned and black-eyed. Their hair had

been shaved off, and they wore nothing but plain white kilts. All of them had heavy metal collars clamped around their necks.

Slaves. *Northern* slaves.

Laela had never seen a slave before. Now she could scarcely believe her eyes. To be treated like that, to have all your hair cut off and be forced to work all day, to be a piece of property instead of a person . . .

What upset her most was the way the Emperor and his family reacted to them. They didn't even look at the slaves as they put platters of food and jugs of wine on the table before retreating.

Even Arenadd didn't react much. He gave one of the slaves a lingering look when he came near, but his expression didn't change, and he didn't say anything. It was as if nothing had happened.

But Laela kept her gaze on them, and she didn't take it away. She kept on watching them, ignoring the food they'd brought despite her hunger. They moved slowly, their faces blank, as if they had nothing to feel or think about. But the more she looked at them, the more she began to realise the truth.

*This is what they were fightin' for. Arenadd and his rebels. It wasn't about power. It was about* this. *It was about stoppin' this.*

She took in every detail of them, seeing their long fingers, their narrow shoulders, the hints of black hair on their heads.

*My people. They're my people. Our people.*

She felt like she was waking up. All of a sudden she was angry—angry toward the likeable Emperor, toward his family—toward his entire country that put these people in bondage and treated them like animals.

But they had to be friends, she realised. Arenadd had to *make* them his friends, so that they would let these slaves go home. Even if it meant his marrying this Princess he didn't know and taking her to live in a place that would be as foreign to her as Amoran was to Laela.

Eventually, hunger won through, and Laela ate. The food was strange and spicy, but she barely tasted it. She ate as if in a dream, letting the conversation wash over her.

By the time the meal ended, and the visitors were ready to be shown to their quarters, Laela found she had a new respect for Arenadd—even admiration. He'd left his Kingdom in someone else's hands for a year, just so he could come all this way to gather these last few Northerners who still had to be brought home. Cymria's slaves had been freed, and now these were all that were left.

*An' it's up to me t'help him,* she thought. *I'm his right-hand . . . woman now. It's my duty.*

She'd never thought of it that way before.

Her quarters turned out to be a set of rooms in another building attached to the great hall. They were close to Arenadd's and Skandar's, but though Laela had wanted to talk to Arenadd before bed, he had the Princess with him and was obviously more interested in having some time with his bride-to-be instead.

Laela managed to catch him for a moment anyway. "I saw the slaves."

"Of course you did," Arenadd said tersely. "They weren't exactly easy to miss."

"I can't believe the Emperor actually had them poor buggers serve us like that," said Laela. "What was he thinkin'?"

Arenadd glanced at the Princess, who was waiting for him. "Possibly he just didn't think of it, but he seems much too intelligent to make that sort of blunder. I think the intention was to remind us of just what we're asking him for here. And maybe to warn us."

Laela cringed. "What, they wouldn't make *us* into . . ."

"We can't assume anything just now," said Arenadd. "Listen; I've got things to do, and you should get some rest. Tomorrow I'll be in talks with the Emperor, so you probably won't see much of me."

"What'll I do, then?"

"You'll be shown around the city, most likely—they'll want to entertain you, try and impress you. And to keep you busy as well."

"Yeh don't think they're gonna try anythin' on, do yeh?" said Laela.

"It seems unlikely, but that's no reason not to be careful," said Arenadd. "Keep Oeka with you. *Never* let her out of your sight. If something happens, she's the best defence you've got. Don't accept any food or drink you're not certain about."

"Right. But what should I do for you?" said Laela. "To help yeh?"

He smiled very slightly. "I'm pleased you asked. I want you to be my eyes and ears, Laela. Remember everything you see and hear. Note anything you think could be important. I'm counting on you."

"Gotcha." Laela grinned and retreated into her chambers after Oeka, where she dumped the small travel bag she had brought with her and stopped to look around.

Her quarters were large and airy, and simply but richly decorated. There was another of those low tables with cushions around it, and a brass bowl full of strange fruit. The bed was a strange, flat straw mattress covered in fine fabric and had nothing in the way of bedding aside from a single thin sheet and an odd-looking long, thin pillow. Oeka had been provided with a nest in an adjoining room, and a beautifully carved water trough.

Fine netting had been draped over the nest, and over Laela's bed as well. Laela had no idea what it could possibly be for, but she was too tired to care. She pulled off her boots and ceremonial outfit and lifted it aside to get at the bed.

It looked unfamiliar, but it was comfortable, and she curled up under the sheet and was asleep in moments.

# 23

# In the Streets of Instabahn

Morning, when it came, brought a painfully hot blaze of sunshine in through the high, narrow window. Laela woke up feeling sick and dried-out. She rolled over and groaned.

It felt like a hangover, but she was sure she hadn't been drunk the night before . . .

She lay on her back in the unfamiliar bed, feeling sorry for herself for a good while before she noticed something odd.

Dawn had come and gone, judging by the amount of sunlight, but Oeka hadn't woken her up to demand food.

Laela got up in a hurry, suddenly afraid. If Oeka wasn't commanding her to bring meat at once, then something was badly wrong. *Maybe she's sick,* she thought as she fumbled for her clothes. *Or worse . . .*

Her ceremonial costume wasn't where she'd left it. She groped around, sick and confused, and nearly screamed when she realised there had been someone standing silently by the table the entire time.

*"Who* are *you?"* she yelled, trying to cover her nakedness with her hands.

The stranger bowed low. "Please, don't be alarmed, my lady. I am your servant. Here, take these clothes."

They were unfamiliar—a strange, bead-encrusted blue thing that looked vaguely like a tunic that had had most of it cut away, and a skirt made of the same material. "I ain't wearin' these," said Laela. "Where's my dress?"

"They're Amorani clothes, my lady," said the strange person who'd offered them. "I was asked to give them to you. Every Amorani woman wears something like it."

"Well." Irritated and confused, but desperate for anything to cover herself up, Laela put on the skirt. The other piece took some fumbling, but she worked it out even though it only covered her breasts, a tiny patch of her back, and not much else. "I can't go out in public wearin' this; I'll look like a whore!"

The stranger's expression didn't change. "I assure you that nobody in the city will look twice, my lady. Here, I have breakfast waiting for you."

Sure enough, there was food on the table. Scowling, Laela sat down and picked up something that looked like a cake. "Who're you then?"

The stranger wore nothing but a plain white kilt, a piece of cloth around the chest, and a heavy collar.

Thanks to that and the shaved head, it took Laela a good while to realise that the slave was a woman.

"My name is Inva," the woman said. "I have been assigned to be your guide and personal servant during your stay here, my lady."

It was deeply bizarre to hear a clearly Northern woman speak with a broad Amorani accent. "So you'll be showin' me around the city, then?" said Laela.

Inva inclined her head. "If it pleases you, my lady."

"I ain't sure I like the idea of bein' waited on by another Northerner wearin' a collar like that," Laela muttered. "Where's Oeka?"

"Your partner has been fed and is being attended to by her own servant, my lady," said Inva.

Laela blinked. "She got a . . . good gods."

"My lady?"

"Nothin'." Laela went back to her breakfast. Eating made her feel better.

A few moments later, Oeka swaggered in. She had another slave following her, and for a moment Laela didn't recognise her. She was wearing an elaborate headpiece decorated with brightly coloured feathers and beads, and had a gold sheath on her beak, studded with jewels.

Laela stood up. "Oeka! What the . . . ?"

The small griffin sat on her haunches and raised one fore-paw, flexing the talons. They'd been painted gold. "At last, you and I receive the treatment we deserve!" she said, without a trace of irony. If griffins could grin, she would have been doing so.

"Well," Laela said weakly. "Ain't that special."

"Indeed," said Oeka. "Finish your food quickly; I am eager to explore the city."

Laela almost lost it at that point; Oeka looked so much like a feathered Queen holding court with her personal assistant beside her that it was all she could do to keep a straight face.

"The Emperor has asked that we see to your every wish, my lady," Inva said smoothly. "I will arrange your hair for you when you have finished eating."

She made good on that promise, and in spades. Laela had expected her to brush it, which she did—after she'd spent what felt like half the morning combing it. After that, she combed it some more, adding some oil that smelt like ancient spices and made Laela's hair lie flat for the first time in its entire existence. After the oil came what looked like an entire basket of gold and coloured glass beads.

Then came the make-up. And then Laela had to sit there while her nails were filed and stained red with some kind of crushed stone. Inva did the same thing to her toenails, after she'd washed both feet with scented water. *Then* she was finally allowed to put on a pair of fine leather sandals. And a gold anklet, and a heavy gold necklace. And a ring with a huge blue stone.

Laela, who normally hated pampering, was so overwhelmed by all this that she sat there meekly and let Inva do her work with the speed and grace of someone who'd done it hundreds of times before.

Eventually, though, she said, "All right, *now* can we go?"

Inva smiled. "You look magnificent, my lady." She paused. "And yes, we may go now."

Laela caught a glimpse of herself in a mirror on the way out, and nearly swore with the shock. "That ain't me," she mumbled. "Tell me that ain't me."

Oeka was already leaving. "Come! We have a city to impress!"

A few moments later, she and Laela had left the building with their escorts, and the city of Instabahn was before them.

Laela stepped out into the street, all embarrassment over her new outfit forgotten.

Amoran was a dry country, beaten down by the same blazing sun that had been so exhausting while they were out at sea. By now, Laela was used to the heat, and she took in the paved, sand-covered walkways, the strange trees that looked like erect griffin-tails, and the people—ye gods, the people. The place was packed, with Amorani citizens everywhere. There were shops and stalls lining the streets, a little like in Malvern, but most of the trading seemed to be taking place in the open air. Cloth canopies provided some shade. People crowded among them, arguing over prices, carrying boxes of cloth or fruit, driving goats, leading small donkey-carts, or just trying to get through the press of bodies to somewhere else.

It looked like a nightmare, but to Laela's amazement, she and her companions had no trouble at all. People stood aside when they saw Oeka, bowing low and muttering respectfully. Inva and her fellow slave went ahead, each one carrying a pole decorated with feathers and tassels.

Laela kept close to Oeka's side, remembering Arenadd's advice. She didn't have to pretend to look important for very long.

Inva had been right—her new outfit didn't make her stand out. Or at least not in the way she'd expected. The people around her were as scantily dressed as she was; the men in light kilts, the women more or less the same, aside from some extra cloth to hide their breasts. Laela's own clothes stood out by virtue of being far gaudier, and once the surprise had worn off, she lifted her chin and strutted along beside Oeka, enjoying the sights as a lady on a day out should. She even started to enjoy all the stares being directed at her.

The buildings were different here, she noticed. Their roofs were flat—but of course, they didn't have to shed snow. Laela wondered if it ever even rained here. All of them were made in the same way as the hall; they looked like stone, but they were smooth, without a single join anywhere. Laela finally caved in and asked Inva outright why they looked like that.

Her guide looked surprised. "They are made from clay," she said. "Bricks, with a coating of clay."

"Oh." Laela felt slightly stupid.

The other people in the street were quick to stand aside, but that didn't mean they stayed away. Plenty of them followed Laela, trying to get her attention and holding up various bits and pieces they obviously wanted her to buy. At first she ignored them, but one man finally caught her eye—he came up unexpectedly on her left, thrusting a piece of jewellery at her. Oeka hissed and made a move to chase him away, but Laela looked at the offering and paused. It was an elaborately crafted necklace—all twisted gold tendrils like a metal vine with many-coloured jewelled fruits.

The man holding it saw her interest and grinned hopefully. "You like?" he asked, in fractured Cymrian.

Laela's other guide raised his pole and snapped something in Amorani.

"No, stop," said Laela, taking the necklace. She turned it over in her fingers. "It's beautiful! Did you make it yerself?"

The man nodded rapidly. "Make all myself," he said. When Laela tried to give the necklace back, he pressed it into her hand, saying, "Keep. Free."

Laela smiled and put it on. "Ta." She paused. "Listen . . ." She glanced at Inva, appealing to her for help, and then groped in the little bag she'd brought with her. After a moment she found the black jewel she'd found in her room back at Malvern, and which she had brought with her as a treasured possession. The jeweller's eyes widened when he saw it. "I was wonderin' if you could make somethin' for this," said Laela.

Inva translated. The jeweller replied, holding out his hand for the jewel.

Laela made sure there was no escape route for him and handed it over. "I thought a ring, or somethin'."

The jeweller examined it expertly, muttering to himself. Finally, he looked up and smiled ingratiatingly as he spoke in Amorani.

" 'A gem unlike any I have ever seen,' " Inva translated. " 'I can make a fine setting for it. For a price.' "

There had been some Amorani money in her chamber,

apparently meant for her. Laela had no idea how much it was worth, but she nodded anyway. "Give it the setting it deserves," she said.

The jeweller grinned even more widely and led them to his own stall, where he showed off his tools with an expansive gesture and explained that it would take two days for the job to be finished.

Laela nodded in response and promised to be back.

"No, no," the jeweller said, inclining his head toward her. "I bring."

"All right, then," said Laela.

She left, feeling excited, wondering what it would look like when it was done. The only thing she'd asked for in particular was that he use silver. It would suit the stone better.

After that, she wandered around the marketplace some more and bought a couple of trinkets before Inva suggested going back to her quarters before noon brought the worst of the heat.

Laela, sweating badly by now, agreed.

Back in her own room, Inva caught her unawares by saying, "Shall I bathe my lady before the food is served?"

Laela went red. "What? Er . . . well—" She thought wistfully of cold water and pulled herself together. "A bath'd be nice, but I reckon I can do it on my own."

Inva bowed. "As my lady commands."

"My lady" went on to command that she be left alone to enjoy the stone tub full of scented water, and dressed herself while Inva and her colleague got the food ready.

While Laela was enjoying a light lunch of fruit, nuts, and flatbread, she found herself watching Inva with more and more curiosity.

"So what's yer story?" she asked eventually.

Inva glanced up. "My lady?"

"The name's Laela. I was just wonderin' about yeh."

Inva looked politely bewildered. "What were you wondering, my lady?"

"Well, yer a slave," said Laela. "How come yeh speak Cymrian so well? Yer better spoken than I am, for gods' sakes."

Inva smiled very slightly. "I am a slave meant for the nobility, my lady. I can read and write, and know many of the finer arts."

"Oh." Laela paused. "To be honest, I ain't never seen a slave until I came here, but back in my part of the world, slaves were just used for buildin' houses an' suchlike."

For a moment, a hint of emotion showed through Inva's reserve. "You're from the land called Tara, my lady?"

"Yeah. The North, most of us call it."

"Tell me, I . . ." Inva broke off quickly and bowed her head. "I am sorry, my lady. I did not mean—"

Laela bit off a mouthful of bread. "Listen, Inva, I was brought up in a peasant village, an' I don't stand on ceremony," she said, with her mouth full. "Just say it. I ain't gonna bite yeh when I got bread."

Inva smiled. "What is it like, my lady?" she asked. "The North?"

Laela thought about it. "Cold," she said eventually. "I dunno how you people can live here. It's like a bloody oven!"

"I know that it snows there," Inva said, cautiously.

"Yeah. The coldest place in the world, is the North. It ain't so bright there, either."

"I can't imagine it," said Inva.

"I couldn't have imagined this place, either," said Laela. "But I bet you'll like the North," she added encouragingly. "It's our place."

Inva blinked. "When I was younger, I wondered what it would be like. But I don't think it would be . . . the place for me even if I could go there."

"But yeh *are* gonna go there!" said Laela. "Don't yeh know?"

"I'm sorry, my lady?"

"Arenadd—the King's—here t'bring yeh home," said Laela. "You an' all of our people."

Inva said nothing. She looked completely bewildered.

"He's gonna take that off yeh," said Laela, pointing to the collar. "Yeh can grow yer hair out again, live free in Malvern— be in yer own land at last."

She didn't get any of the joy or excitement she'd expected. Instead, she got the same blank look as before.

"But where would I live?" Inva said eventually.

"I dunno," said Laela. "I'm sure there'd be somewhere. Don't yeh wanna be free?"

Inva blinked and shook her head slowly, as if trying to push away an idea that bothered her. "I . . . I don't know . . . my lady."

Laela didn't know what to say after that, but she felt inexplicably guilty as she finished her food, as if she'd somehow insulted her new friend.

A nother day passed. Laela spent it seeing more of the city with Oeka and a couple of other griffiners. Her fellow Northerners seemed far less excited by Amoran than she was. They grumbled over the heat, insisted on wearing their own clothes instead of adopting the local dress, and showed awkward dislike toward the local people. Laela heard them muttering among themselves in the dark tongue, and wondered what they were so upset about. Maybe they were homesick.

She didn't feel homesick herself. She missed Yorath, but she was happy enough in Amoran. Then again, she hadn't lived in the North long enough to be that attached to it. Not enough to remember every detail of it after the months she'd been away.

That evening, tired out from the heat and suffering from a sudden fit of wistfulness over Yorath, she curled up on her bed and idly played with the other keepsake she'd brought. It was the note that had been with the gem, and she ran her fingers over the crude, faded letters, trying yet again to decode them. She'd learnt more about reading and writing on the voyage, and knew quite a few Northern words by now, but somehow none of these looked familiar. She knew the letters but not the words they made.

She tried sounding some of them out instead, talking to herself in an undertone.

" 'D . . . deee'? 'Deeeeaah'? 'Efff'? 'Arr'? Oh, blow this for a game of soldiers." She put it down and sighed. Was she really so stupid that she still couldn't read? Yorath made it look so easy. She sighed again and wondered how he was. Did he miss her, too?

She moped for some time before she realised she was doing it, and dragged herself out of bed to make herself stop. She hadn't seen Arenadd since the night they'd arrived—it was probably time she went to see how he was doing.

Oeka came after her. "Where are you going?"

"To see Arenadd," said Laela. "Just makin' sure he's goin' all right. An' t'see if he wants any advice."

Oeka clicked her beak. "You never stop trying to fuss over him, do you?"

The griffish term she'd used translated literally as "act like a brooding mother." Laela scowled. "He's so immature some-times, he needs someone t'do it. Who else is gonna say no to him if it ain't me?"

"I should not argue," Oeka conceded. "You have a power over him I cannot understand."

"Yeah, it's called mutual respect," said Laela. "Yeh might've heard of it."

She ignored the guards outside Arenadd's chambers and strode in without bothering to announce herself.

Arenadd was there, alone. He was slumped on a couch with his head back, staring at the ceiling. When Laela called his name, he barely moved.

"Hey," she said, coming closer. "It's me. Wake up."

Very slowly, Arenadd dragged himself upright. His face was ghastly. Once his skin had been pale. Now it looked grey, and glistened with sweat. His eyes were dull, his expression slack and lifeless.

Laela felt her insides twist. "Ye gods, yeh look horrible! What's wrong? Are yeh sick?"

Arenadd coughed. "Oh, hello." His voice was low and weak.

Oeka nudged her human hard in the hip. "Laela, you should find a healer. He looks as if he is dying!"

"Arenadd, should I go and get someone?" said Laela. "Do yeh need . . . ?"

"Just get me some water," Arenadd croaked.

She found a jug on the table and filled a cup for him. He fumbled with it as if he barely had the strength to hold on to it. But once he'd drunk the contents, he looked slightly better.

"There," said Laela. "Better now?"

"A little," said Arenadd.

"So what's up?" said Laela. "I didn't know yeh could get sick."

Arenadd raised his eyebrows. "Neither did I."

"Have yeh seen a healer?"

"The Emperor suggested it, but I refused," said Arenadd. "I can't let them find out what I am." He shuddered. "And they wouldn't be able to help me anyway."

"Then what are yeh gonna do?" said Laela.

"I don't know."

Those simple three words sounded so unnatural coming out of Arenadd's mouth that Laela didn't know what to say.

Arenadd didn't seem to notice. He grimaced and pressed his hand into the scar in the middle of his chest, where Erian Rannagonson's sword had impaled him all those years ago. Sweat beaded on his forehead, and he groaned.

Laela stepped closer, reaching out. "Are yeh all right?"

"It hurts," Arenadd gasped. "It won't stop hurting . . . ever since we got here . . ." He slumped again, breathing rapidly.

Laela knelt beside him, casting a desperate glance at Oeka. "Do yeh have any idea why it's happening?"

Arenadd managed to pull himself up again. "It's Gryphus," he said. "He's here . . ."

Instinctively, Laela glanced over her shoulder. "What d'yeh mean?"

"He's here," Arenadd repeated, his voice riddled with pain. "This is his place. His land. The sun's so bright here. It's unbearable." He gasped again and made a noise that sounded almost like a strangled scream. "Oh, Night God help me, why did I come here? I'm surrounded by sun worshippers; they're all full of *his* light, I feel like I'm going to be sick whenever I go near them." His eyes darted wildly, as if expecting to see enemies in every corner. "He doesn't want me here. He wants me gone. He's protecting this land against me. He's taken—"

Laela grabbed his hands. "Stop it. Arenadd, stop it. Calm down. Just breathe. In an' out, slow like. C'mon. It's gonna be all right."

He breathed deeply and began to look calmer. "I've lost my powers, Laela."

Laela could feel how cold his skin was. "What? What d'yeh mean?"

"I feel stronger at night," said Arenadd. "Last night I tried to go into the darkness . . . where I'm strongest." He stared at the ceiling. "I couldn't do it. I couldn't get there. The way . . . just wasn't there any more. I don't know if I'm even immortal here."

Laela felt sick to her stomach. "What about Skandar? Is he . . . ?"

"Hah." The sound was half laugh, half cough. "Skandar doesn't even know I'm like this. He's been off this whole time, enjoying himself. He's had thirty-seven different females since we've arrived here." He coughed. "I counted."

Laela had to laugh. "At least he's keepin' his end of the agreement. Arenadd—" She lost her grin very quickly. "Are yeh serious? Do yeh really think yeh ain't immortal here?"

Arenadd nodded weakly.

"Well, for gods' sakes, we've got t'get out of here!" said Laela. "We've got t'get yeh home an' away from this damned place, before somethin' goes really wrong."

Arenadd pulled on her arm, using it to drag himself to his feet. "No," he rasped.

"Arenadd—"

"*No.* I'm not leaving." He breathed in shakily. "Not until my business here is done. I won't leave without my . . . without my brothers. My sisters."

"Screw them!" Laela yelled. "You're more important than them, damn it, an' if—"

"No." Arenadd waved her into silence. "No. If I leave now, this whole . . . thing will be for nothing."

"But what if you die?" said Laela, almost plaintively.

"I've survived worse," said Arenadd. He was trembling slightly as he stood there. But his voice sounded as confident as always when he said, "Thank you for helping me up. But please don't tell anyone about this. I trust you, Laela."

"Lips are sealed," said Laela. "Oeka, can yeh keep this to yerself, too?"

The small griffin had been looking on uncertainly. "You will know if I do tell anyone else," she said.

Laela supposed that would be the best she could get out of her. "How much longer are we gonna stay here?"

"I'm not sure," said Arenadd. "But I think"—he winced again—"the Emperor won't be suspicious if I want to hurry things along. He's a generous man. So, how are you enjoying yourself?"

Laela wasn't fooled. "I like it fine here."

"Good. Well . . . you can go now. Get some rest."

"Don't yeh need me to—"

"No, no. I'll be fine. Go on."

Laela gave him a nervous and unhappy look, and left the room with Oeka skittering along after her.

* * *

As Laela disappeared, Arenadd had a sudden, wild urge to call her back. He said nothing. Exhaustion and pain gripped him, and he turned to slump back onto his couch, but paused when he noticed something on the floor. It looked like a scrap of old cloth—Laela must have dropped it on her way out. Arenadd picked it up.

Every bone in his body screamed in protest when he sat down. He felt as if they could shatter at the slightest impact. His entire body felt hideously fragile.

He waited until the pain died down, telling himself again and again that the day was nearly over. Night would come soon—blessed, cool night. All he had to do was hold on until then.

When he felt a little better, he examined the piece of cloth, wondering vaguely why Laela had been carrying it.

There was writing on it. Arenadd squinted at it. It took him a few moments to realise why it looked so odd—it was written in Cymrian. He hadn't read anything that wasn't in his own language in a while. Parts of it were smudged out, but he managed to decipher the gist of it.

" 'How are you?' " he read. "Something, something 'not very' . . . 'come and see you' . . . 'I love you very much'?" Arenadd chuckled to himself. A note from Yorath, no doubt. Odd that he would write it with charcoal on a piece of cloth, though. And why would he have written it in Cymrian?

Uncertainty wormed its way inside him. He knew Yorath's handwriting, and this wasn't it. These words did look like they'd been written by someone educated, though, even though the crude materials made them look messier than they might have.

He examined the signature at the bottom. Someone had put a thumb print over it, but he thought he could guess at it . . .

The feeling of uncertainty twisted and became cold.

*I know this handwriting,* he thought. *I know it.*

He looked at the signature again, and felt the coldness spread over his entire body.

*Arren.*

The piece of cloth crumpled in Arenadd's hand. "I wrote this," he whispered.

But why? And to who?

# 24

# The Sun Temple

The next day came, and Laela's new necklace came with it. The jeweller was shown in just after she'd finished breakfast and presented his latest piece of work with a bow and a proud smile.

Laela took it eagerly and examined it with wonder. It was all in silver, as she'd asked. The stone had been set into a magnificent amulet in the shape of three snakes, their bodies all entwined and their heads pointing outward to form a rough triangle. Even the little loop that attached the whole thing to the chain was a small snake.

The stone glittered, seeming smaller but somehow more precious in its new home.

Laela took off the heavy golden creation Inva had brought her that morning, and replaced it with the amulet. It felt wonderfully cool against her skin, and she grinned and touched it. "It's beautiful."

The jeweller looked very pleased at that, and even more so after Inva had given him his payment, which Laela thought looked like a lot of money. She didn't care.

Even Oeka looked impressed when she came out and saw the snake amulet. "A very fine thing indeed," she remarked. "The human did fine work." She sat on her haunches and idly groomed her tail-feathers. "So tell me. It is our third day of doing what we please. What did you think we should do today?"

"Dunno," said Laela. "We've seen the marketplace an' the

palace"—she doubted she'd ever see that much gold again for the rest of her life—"I ain't sure what we'd want t'see next."

"We have not yet seen the great Sun Temple," said Oeka. "It is said to be a magnificent sight."

"Oh!" Laela fiddled with the amulet. "Of course! I'd forgotten. I've got t'see it before we go. What about you, then? Are yeh up for it?"

"I would be very interested to see it," said Oeka.

"Well then, that's where we'll go," said Laela. "Inva, we've decided we'd like t'go see the Sun Temple today. That okay?"

Inva smiled slightly and bowed. "I would be glad to show you the pride of this city, my lady. When would you like to go?"

"Now, of course," said Laela. "Before it's too hot out there. C'mon, let's get goin'!"

"Certainly, my lady."

Laela followed Oeka out of their lodgings, with Inva close behind. The slave looked cheerful today, and Laela had to ignore the urge to try to make conversation with her—it never worked. Even so, she'd decided that she rather liked her reserved attendant.

Outside, the city was bustling, as always. By now, Laela was used to people staring at her, and she ignored them.

Inva had brought a small portable shade-cloth with her, and as they left the shelter of the marketplace, she moved closer to Laela, holding it over her head. The long tassels that hung from it helped keep away the flies, and Laela made sure to keep pace with it, grateful for the shade.

The city was built on a hill, but while in the North important buildings were usually built on high ground, in Amoran, they were lower and closer to the river—where it was cooler. But the great Sun Temple of Instabahn was on the highest ground in the city—the closest to the sun. Laela saw it well before they reached it—a weird, irregular shape against the wide-open desert sky. It didn't look like a building at all. In fact, it looked like something else she knew.

She halted. "Is that . . . wait, that's a . . ." She rubbed her eyes. "That's a giant . . . *man*. What the . . . ?"

"It is a statue, my lady," said Inva. "Made in the likeness of the great god Xanathus. It's said to have taken a hundred years to build."

Laela only just heard her. As she walked on up the hill, the sheer size of what she was seeing slowly stripped away all sense of reality. There was no way it could be real. Human beings couldn't make something like this . . . no. It was impossible.

The statue wasn't really a full representation of the great sun god—only his chest, shoulders and head, thrusting upward out of the ground as if the rest of him were somewhere under the earth. The huge hands, shaped to include elegant, tapering fingers, were cupped outward, holding the entrance to the Temple between them like an offering. The arms were part of the front wall, and the shoulders made the roof. The colossal head reared into the sky, as high as the Council Tower at Malvern. It was bald, made from smooth, sand-yellow stone. The features were wide and benign; the lips set into a haunting smile. The eyes—too big for the face—were two enormous blue gems that glowed in the sunlight.

Laela, staring up at it, was struck by a sudden, irrational fear. Accepting that something this huge could exist was almost too much, and for a moment she fought the urge to run away, or to bow her head rather than look at it any more.

"This," said Inva, from somewhere far away, "is the great god Xanathus. The Lord and Father of Amoran and all its people."

Laela breathed deeply. "Xanathus . . ." *Gryphus.*

"He has another name in your land, my Lady," said Inva.

"Yes," Laela said, very quietly. "He does."

Beside her, Oeka had lain down on her belly. "By the sky," she breathed. "What magic is this?"

"Gryphus' magic," Laela told her, without thinking. But inside she believed it. She looked at the entrance, and then at Inva. "Can I go inside?"

Inva averted her eyes from the massive stone face. "You can, my lady, provided that your griffin goes with you. I will wait outside."

Laela paused. "What, you ain't comin' with us?"

"It is forbidden, my lady," said Inva. "Slaves may not go in."

Laela frowned. "Wait here, then."

There was no door on the arched entrance to the Temple. Instead, heavy yellow drapes had been tied back to reveal the dark space beyond. Laela hesitated for a moment, but Oeka had already gone in. Laela followed.

Beyond the drapes, a short passage led to the single chamber that made up the inside of the Temple. It was huge inside, made all in the same yellow stone as the outside. But it was full of gold as well. Gold discs, representing suns, had been placed at intervals along the walls, and more gold had been inlaid into the elaborate friezes that were carved everywhere. There were no seats; only brightly woven mats on the floor, and an altar at the far end. Light shone down in two beams from the ceiling and bathed the golden statue that stood there. It was a smaller version of the giant impossibility that made up the Temple—a slender, smiling man, holding a large copper dish in his outstretched hands, just above the altar. Pale flames flickered inside it.

Laela walked toward it as if in a dream, ignoring Oeka completely. The statue seemed to be waiting for her, its shining face locked in that distant, enigmatic smile.

A shape stepped in her way. "Welcome," it said.

Laela jerked to a stop. "What the . . . ?"

The stranger was a man—bald, wearing a yellow kilt. His skin had been covered in gold paint, so for a moment he looked like a living version of the statue behind him.

"Who are yeh?" Laela said unceremoniously, almost resenting the interruption.

The man smiled and folded his hands together. "I am Ocax," he said. "I am a priest of Xanathus."

He was speaking griffish, Laela realised. "I'm Lady Laela," she said. "Chief advisor to King Arenadd."

Ocax ignored her. He had seen Oeka, and now he stepped closer to her and knelt, laying his head on the ground.

Oeka looked bewildered for a moment, but quickly recovered. "Rise, human," she said.

Ocax rose, but kept his head bowed. "Mighty griffin," he said. "Herald of Xanathus. I am not worthy to speak to you."

"You may speak," said Oeka. "So, human—you are a priest of this Temple?"

"I am, Sacred One," said Ocax. "It is my task to bring oil to fuel the sacred flame, and to accept the offerings of those who come to worship."

Oeka glanced at Laela. "This is a mighty temple. Did your kind build it alone?"

"No, Sacred One," said Ocax. "The power of great Xanathus bound these stones together and blessed them with his grace."

"Then you have pleased him," said Oeka. She paused. "I am Oeka, of Tara. My human is Master of Wisdom."

Ocax finally looked at Laela. "A worthy human to have your favour, Sacred One."

"Thanks," said Laela, by now thoroughly uncomfortable. "I came t'see the Temple."

"It is a modest thing, compared to the great Temple in the capital," said Ocax.

"I've never seen a temple this big or magnificent," said Laela, and she meant it.

Ocax smiled. "Thank you, Lady Laela. Have you come here to pay homage to Xanathus?"

Laela glanced at Oeka. "Uh . . . yeah. Sure."

The priest looked keenly at her. "Do you know Xanathus?"

Laela thought of the dream where she'd talked to Gryphus. "I think so."

"Then come forward and know him better," said Ocax.

Laela went closer to the altar, as he gestured her to. "Xanathus is a sun god, isn't he?"

"*The* sun god," Ocax corrected. "The only sun god. He may have other names in other languages, but he is the sun, the day and the light. He is life, he is love. There is no other."

Laela thought of Arenadd's frightened ramblings. "Then he's Gryphus," she said confidently. "This is his place."

Ocax smiled. "Long ago, a strange people came to Amoran. They were pale-faced and spoke a strange language, but they revered the sun, and when our ancestors saw that they knew that they were a blessed people. They taught them the ways of Xanathus. Those people carried his teachings to their new home."

"Cymria!" said Laela. "So the Southerners learned about Gryphus here."

Ocax pointed at the altar. "See that symbol? Do you know it, Laela of Tara?"

It was a circle, with three curling lines that met in the middle and spread outward. Laela stared at it and laughed in disbelief. "I've seen that! It's carved on the door of the temple in Sturrick! That's Gryphus' . . ." She trailed off.

"Xanathus' symbol," Ocax said solemnly. "The sun's symbol. We have revered it for thousands of years."

Laela kept her eyes on the gold-inlaid sunwheel, and felt as if all she knew were unravelling. Arenadd had been right—this was Gryphus' place. All these people belonged to him. Amoran was a huge country—she'd been told that plenty of times. So much land, and so many souls, all Gryphus' own. No wonder Arenadd couldn't bear to be here.

She looked up at the eerily smiling statue, and thought of the crowned, bearded man from her dream. Could they possibly be the same person?

If they were, then what would they think of her?

Laela suddenly felt afraid. She was a Northerner. She had promised her soul to the Night God. And here she was, before the altar of Gryphus. Did he hate her? Did he want her gone from his lands, like Arenadd?

Ocax had been watching her. "Do not be afraid, Laela," he said, as if he were reading her mind. "You are one of his children."

Laela glanced at him. "I'm a Northerner."

"But you do not have Northern eyes," said Ocax. He smiled and touched her cheek. "I have never seen such eyes as yours. They are as blue as the sky. Like the eyes of Xanathus."

"My mother was a Southerner," said Laela.

"Then you are a child of Xanathus," said Ocax. "Women are sacred to him; they give life, as he does."

"But my father was a Northerner," said Laela. "I figured since I was halfway Southern an' halfway Northern, I could choose my own god."

"And which god have you chosen, Laela of Tara?"

Laela hesitated. She had been going to say the Night God, but something stopped her.

"If you spoke to Xanathus, you would know which god was yours," said Ocax.

Laela shook herself. "The gods ain't exactly known for bein' talkative."

"But Xanathus can speak to you," said Ocax. "Here, in this Temple. If you wish it."

"How?" Oeka interrupted.

Ocax bowed to her. "There is a ritual, Sacred One," he said.

"A rite which calls Xanathus to speak. If your human would like to, she can perform it. I will help."

"That is a matter for my human to decide," said Oeka.

"What 'ritual' is this?" said Laela. "How's it work?"

"It is simple enough," said Ocax. "All you need do is cast a certain herb into the sacred flame. I will perform the chant, and before long, Xanathus will appear to you."

*Stuff and nonsense,* thought Laela. But she couldn't help but be curious all the same. She looked at the golden statue, and then at the priest. He had an odd, twitchy look about him and his eyes were bloodshot, but she didn't believe that he would ever try to assassinate anyone. Vander had told her a few things about the priesthood in his home country, and nonviolence was supposedly one of their most important principles.

"All right," she said. "Let's do it."

The priest smiled. "Wait for me."

He went away through a door hidden behind the statue and returned a few moments later holding a small, woven bag. Laela stood close to the altar as he asked her to, her hand resting on Oeka's head.

"You should stand back, Sacred One," said Ocax. "A griffin does not need to breathe in the holy smoke."

Oeka huffed to herself and moved away.

"Now." Ocax gave the bag to Laela. "Take this, and cast it into the flame. Do not be afraid."

"Right." Laela opened the bag and peered inside. It was full of something dried and shredded—it looked vaguely like meat.

"Fungus," said Ocax. "Gathered from the rocks in the Valley of the Wind. It has magical properties."

Laela sniffed it and grimaced; it didn't have a very strong smell, but for some reason it made her head spin. "So I just throw it in the bowl there?"

"Yes. The smoke will open your mind and allow Xanathus to speak to you."

"It ain't dangerous?"

"No." He smiled. "I have done this many times. It was this ritual that first called me to become a priest."

"All right then." Laela reached over and tipped the entire contents of the bag into the flame. The dried fungus went up at once, but the oil soaked into it and made it burn slowly instead of vanishing. At once, smoke began to rise from the bowl—thick, yellowish smoke.

Ocax looked horrified. "You were only supposed to throw in a pinch!"

"Sorry—" Laela began, but in that instant the smoke hit her nostrils. It poured into her lungs, and in a heartbeat it had spread through her entire system. She turned to Ocax, asking for help, but she couldn't tell where he was. Her head began to spin. She turned around, wide-eyed. Her head felt as if it were growing larger and larger, floating toward the ceiling. Everything around her had turned yellow, full of tiny sparks like pollen. Oeka wasn't there any more, but that didn't matter; Laela had forgotten all about her. She'd forgotten about Arenadd, too, and Yorath, and home. Everything fled out of her mind in an instant, and she was flying, suspended in a delicious cloud of sweet yellow fog.

She grinned; her mouth seemed to be out of her control and wanted to do nothing else.

Humming inanely to herself, she turned to see if the altar was still there. It was, and the statue was still there, too. Only now, it was moving.

Laela squinted at it. "Here, why are you movin'?" She giggled. "Are yeh bored? Want t'come out an' get some air an' that?" She giggled again and couldn't make herself stop.

Very slowly, the statue straightened up. In its hands the bowl had become a ball of pure golden flame, so bright it hurt to look at.

Laela stopped giggling. She backed away. "What . . . ? No . . . stop . . . I don't like this . . ."

The statue came toward her, its golden feet clanging on the stone. The face had lost its distant smile. Now it was alive, moving and changing its expression.

Laela tried to back away further, but her feet suddenly refused to move. The light hit her face, burning straight through her eyes and into her skull. She threw up her hands, trying vainly to protect herself. "No! Stop! Stop it! Go away! *Help!*"

The statue halted. She could hear it breathing; deep, rumbling, metallic breaths. *Laela*, it said.

Laela turned her head away. She was trembling in fright. "Leave me alone."

*Laela,* the voice said again. *Look at me.*

It was impossible to disobey. Laela raised her head and saw those blank blue eyes, staring straight at her. "No . . ."

*Laela,* said the statue. *My child. Do you know me?*

"No," said Laela. "No, I don't know . . . I don't . . ."

The statue raised a golden hand, holding it out. It was glowing with heat. *Then perhaps you know them.*

Laela turned, and saw a point of light in the fog—three points of light, growing brighter. The fog moved around them, gathering inward as if the lights were drawing it in. Forming shapes.

Laela saw the first of them emerge, and her entire body went cold. "You . . ."

The ghostly shape of Bran smiled at her. "How's my little girl then, eh?"

Laela reached out to him. "But you're . . ."

". . . with Gryphus now," he said. "Laela . . ."

She looked at the fog beside him and saw another shape. A woman's shape. And on his other side, a man. The woman had long hair and a kind face, but there was no smile on it. Something had left a deep and terrible slash in her throat, and blood had soaked into the front of her gown.

The man who was with Bran looked more like a boy to Laela, but that was probably because of his eyes—they were round and bright blue, like a child's. His hair was blond and tousled, and his face peppered with freckles. But he, too, had a ghastly wound on his throat, and his face was as pale as death.

Bran came closer, reaching out with a pale but still big hand. "Laela," he said. "These two wanted t'come see yeh."

Laela cringed at the sight of them. "Why?"

Bran put a hand on the woman's shoulder. "This is your mother, Laela."

The woman smiled sadly. "Laela. My little Laela. How you've grown."

Laela stared at her, more frightened than anything else. "Mother . . . ?"

"Yes," said the woman.

"I never knew yer name," Laela mumbled.

"Flell," said the woman. "I am Flell. Flell of Eagleholm. *Lady* Flell."

*"Lady?"* Laela blinked. "Dad, yeh never said she was a . . ."

"I was a griffiner," said Flell. "At Eagleholm. Like my parents."

Laela looked at Bran. "Why didn't yeh tell me, Dad? Why . . . ?"

"It was too painful t'talk about," said Bran. "I didn't think . . . didn't see how it would help yeh t'know it."

"Laela," said Flell. She moved away from Bran and came closer, her feet making no sound on the floor. "Laela." Her hand reached out. It was soaked in blood. "Laela, my sweet daughter . . ."

Laela wanted to get away from her. "Why are yeh here, Mother? What d'yeh want?"

"I want to know why," Flell whispered.

"Why what?"

"Why you're here," said Bran.

"Why you're worshipping the Night God," said Flell.

"Why you're with *him*," said the boy.

"Arenadd is my King," Laela told them boldly. "An' he's my friend."

"Laela," said Bran. "He murdered your mother."

Laela faltered. "What . . . ?"

Flell put a hand to her throat. "He killed me in Malvern," she said softly. "As I tried to defend your cradle from him."

"No," said Laela. "Stop it."

The boy shoved his way forward. "Don't you understand?" he sneered. "The man you're living with killed your entire family. Your mother. Your grandparents. Your uncle." His expression twisted. "I'm your uncle, ashamed to admit it though I am." He touched his throat and added, half to himself, "He killed me in the Sun Temple."

Laela stared at him. "Who are yeh?"

He drew himself up. "I am Lord Erian Rannagonson."

"Erian . . . ?" Laela laughed weakly. "This is stupid. I ain't got no uncle, an' certainly not Erian Rannagonson."

"You miserable little traitor," Erian snarled. He turned on Flell, pointing accusingly at her face. "I told you! I told you when I first saw the squealing little brat in your arms. Told you to smother it before it grew up. But you didn't listen, and now it's grown up into the Dark Lord's lap-dog. A shame on our entire noble line!" He put his hands to his throat, squeezing until blood oozed over his fingers. "By Gryphus, I'm glad I died rather than see our father's blood defiled by being mixed with that *filth*." And he spat.

Each word felt like a stab to the heart. For a moment, all Laela could do was gape in horror, but the Northern ferocity that had come from her father rose up inside her, and she went hot with rage. "Now look here!" she yelled. "I never got no say in who my dad was, any more'n you did." She sneered. "An' them's fine words comin' from a bastard anyway, Erian."

Bran and Flell laughed uproariously at that. Erian gaped, and then scowled and turned away with a curse.

Flell became serious. "Laela," she said. "There's no shame in your heritage. I loved your father with all my heart, and I believe that he loved me. But listen to me now. We were allowed to come back to speak with you so that we could warn you."

"You're in danger, Laela," said Bran. "Terrible danger."

"What d'yeh mean?" said Laela. "What danger? Oeka can protect me if anythin' . . ."

Flell touched her shoulder, but she couldn't feel it. "Don't you understand? You, Laela, are the last of the line of Baragher the Blessed. The only descendant of Lord Rannagon, who the Dark Lord killed in Eagleholm. His mistress commanded him to destroy all his surviving relatives—and that included you."

"After Rannagon, he killed his son, Erian," said Bran. "Then his daughter. An' *her* daughter . . ."

"Me?" said Laela. "He was meant to kill me? But he didn't . . ."

"No." Bran looked away. "Not you. I saved yeh. Carried yeh away from Malvern before he could finish it."

"You've got to get away from him, Laela," said Flell. "Run away. Never let him find you! If he ever realises who you really are, he won't rest until he's killed you."

Laela's fists clenched. "No," she said. "I won't."

They stopped at that. "Laela, he'll do it," said Bran. "Yeh don't know him like we do. Yeh haven't seen what he can do."

"I have," said Laela. "I've seen it."

"Then get away!" said Flell. "For gods' sakes, save yourself!"

"No," said Laela. "I don't believe it. He wouldn't hurt me. Never. Not for anythin'. I know it."

Erian returned. "You don't know anything, half-breed. He's a murderer."

"He's—"

*My child. Listen.* Gryphus' voice rose above them all, deep and powerful. Light glowed all around, and the statue appeared again, standing with the three ghosts. *You do not understand,* he said. *You see the world with Southern eyes. Your nature is of the day. You are the Risen Sun, the last survivor of the sacred blood. My grace is on you, as it is on all your family. You alone can stop him.*

From somewhere far, far away, a voice came drifting. ". . . Laela . . . ?"

"I don't want t'stop him," said Laela. "All he wants t'do is protect his people."

*The Shadow That Walks must be punished!* said Gryphus. *He must perish for his crimes, before his mistress uses him again!*

The distant voice came again, calling plaintively. "Laela . . . ?"

Erian turned to look out at the temple interior, now beginning to show through the fog. "You're wasting your time, Master," he said. "She's her father's daughter."

"Laela . . . ?" The voice sounded louder now, calling out. A *living* voice.

Laela looked at the ghosts and realised they were beginning to fade. "What about my father?"

*Your father is dead,* said Gryphus. *A cruel death, at the end of a cruel life.*

"Laela . . . ?"

The vision was disappearing; the fog thinned, and Gryphus' light dimmed.

Flell was crying. "He'll kill you. He'll kill you if you don't get away."

*Laela!* Gryphus came close, urgent now. *You must not listen to the Night God's lies. If you do not accept your destiny, your soul will be cast into darkness forever. You must believe this! The Dark Lord has no heart; he cannot love, he cannot feel. He does not care for you, and he will destroy you.*

Laela opened her mouth to shout at him, to tell him to leave her alone, but in that moment, as he began to vanish at last, she looked past him and saw the dark, gaunt shape, slowly and

painfully lurching toward her. Calling her name. "Laela . . .
*Laela* . . ."

She looked into the eyes of Gryphus again, and said, "He
came for me. He came into your Temple, just for me. Even
though it hurts him. He cares."

Gryphus looked solemnly at her, and vanished. Beside him,
Flell disappeared, too, and Bran faded. Only Erian was left; a
vague shape in the air, outlined in fog.

Laela saw Arenadd clearly now. He walked like an old, old
man, shaking in every limb. His breath sounded like a death
rattle.

She reached out to him with the beginning of a smile, and
started to speak, to tell him she was safe, that she was going to
take him out of this place and get him home, where he could
rest, and she would look after him . . .

Erian had seen him, too. "You son of a bitch," he breathed.
"Come back to look for me, have you?" He charged, fading with
every step, his war-cry a distant howl of wind. He raised the
vague outline of a sword, and stabbed it into Arenadd's chest.

Arenadd jerked suddenly, lurching backward as if a real
sword had struck him. Laela saw him put his hands to his chest.

There was blood on his fingers.

Laela ran toward him. "ARENADD!"

The floor jerked under her and turned sideways to hit her in
the head, and the world slid out of her grasp.

# 25

## Half-Breed in Charge

Laela opened her eyes, and groaned. The first thing she noticed was the heat; her entire body felt as if it was in an oven. She was in bed, and the sheets were stuck to her with sweat. The instant she moved, sickening pain slammed through her head. The pain rose with every heartbeat, as if each thud were driving a spike into her forehead. Her vision flashed red.

She rolled onto her back, and the effort of doing just that nearly paralysed her. She lay there, gritting her teeth as the pain spread through her body. Her stomach felt as if it were on fire, and her lungs burned with every breath.

*Oh, gods,* she thought. *I'm dying.*

A few moments later, a harassed-looking Amorani woman appeared. She said nothing and helped Laela drink some water. The water felt like a blessed gift from the gods themselves; Laela gulped it down and sighed as it cooled her down from the inside out.

When the cup was empty, she managed to rasp out a few questions, but the woman only glanced briefly at her and said nothing. Most likely she didn't speak Cymrian, and Laela was too confused to try griffish. She accepted another cup of water and watched resignedly as the woman left.

The water had helped her to wake up, though, and she lay still and tried to think. The memory of what had happened in the Temple came back slowly, but it felt confused and unreal.

Laela put a hand to her forehead. It was slick with hot sweat. Maybe she'd been sick. A fever. She'd had fevers in the past, and they always made her have strange dreams.

*But I did go to the Temple, though,* she thought. That was the last clear memory she had. She didn't remember getting sick at all.

Something had happened in the Temple. There'd been some-one else there . . . She'd talked to them . . . A priest? And he'd . . . done something . . .

The pain rose sharply in her head, and she hastily shut her eyes and stopped thinking.

When the pain had faded again, she opened her eyes and yelled.

Oeka hissed in alarm and moved away from the bed. "Laela! What is wrong?"

Laela sat up. "Openin' my eyes an' finding a huge beak shoved in my face didn't do my heart no favours," she mumbled. "What's goin' on?"

"You are in the . . . place where the Amoranis bring the sick and wounded," said Oeka.

Laela lay down again, very carefully. "Did get sick, then."

"You were very bad," said Oeka. "They were afraid you would not recover."

"Had the weirdest dreams," said Laela. The pain in her head was fading now.

Oeka cocked her head. "I am not surprised. The fungus the priest burned is a very powerful drug, and you took many times the safe amount." She paused. "Many who burn as much as you did go insane and do not recover."

Laela shuddered. "Holy gods . . ."

"I am glad that you are well again," said Oeka. "Laela, ter-rible things have happened while you have been ill."

"What terrible things . . . ?" Laela began, and stopped, as a horrendous noise split the air. She cringed and put her hands over her ears. Even Oeka tried to hide in fright.

Someone was screaming.

Laela's heart pounded. "What the . . . ?"

Another awful cry drifted down the corridor into her room. Laela heard shouts and running feet, and glimpsed several people dashing past her doorway. She heard another scream after that, but this one was smothered into silence. That only made it worse.

Another memory came back to her, all too quickly. She dragged herself out of bed, swearing at the ache in her limbs but ignoring all her own discomfort now.

Oeka lifted her wings. "You must not—"

Laela turned on her. "Where's Arenadd? What happened to him? For gods' sakes, is he all right?"

"No," the griffin said shortly. "The King is gravely wounded."

"What d'yeh mean, wounded?" said Laela. In her head, she saw that terrible moment in the Temple . . . but surely that had just been an hallucination.

"The Amoranis tried to assassinate him," said Oeka. "The Emperor is denying that he had anything to do with it. Lord Duach thinks it must have been one of the priests, but they, too, are denying it . . ."

"But nobody tried t'kill him," Laela said blankly. "I never saw . . ."

"You were so full of fungus-smoke, you would not have known your own name," said Oeka.

"You were there," said Laela. "What did yeh see?" She looked around for her clothes, found them, and clumsily started to put them on.

"I was not there," said Oeka.

"What?"

"After you breathed in the smoke, you went mad," said Oeka. "You began talking to the walls, laughing, and wandering about . . . When I tried to bring you to your senses, you acted as if I were not there." She paused, her tail twitching rapidly. "The smoke . . . gathered itself around you. I could not go inside it. It was as if there were some force . . . keeping all others away. The priest tried as well, but he could not touch you, either."

Laela froze at that. "What d'yeh mean? How could smoke . . . ?"

"I do not know," said Oeka. "The priest said it was the power of his god, keeping your meeting with him from being disturbed. I did not know what to do . . . I was afraid for your life. So I left the Temple and flew as fast as I could to find help. I went to the Mighty Skandar himself, and begged him for his help."

"Yeh went to . . . ?" Laela could hardly believe it. She tried to imagine the proud little griffin ever begging anyone to do anything, and failed.

"Skandar did not want to help," said Oeka. "So he sent his human in his place."

"He sent Arenadd into the Sun Temple?" said Laela. Very quickly, her disbelief turned to anger. "That son of a . . ."

Without any warning, Oeka rose up, her feathers puffed out so that she appeared to double in size. "Do not speak that way about the Mighty Skandar!" she screeched.

Laela faltered and winced. "Arenadd got hurt in there," she said. "Somehow. But it wasn't no living man what did it."

"Few would believe you," said Oeka.

"It doesn't matter," said Laela. "I've got t'see him, an' fast."

"You have your own illness to concern yourself about," Oeka said stiffly. "And the King is in good hands. The Emperor has sent his finest healers."

"An' how d'yeh know they ain't gonna try an' hurt him, too?" said Laela. "He needs me."

She ignored anything else her partner said and left the room—unsteady on her feet but too determined to let it slow her down. Out in the corridor, there were dozens of people, all talking at once and getting in each other's way. There were Amoranis there, of course, but there were Northerners, too—Laela saw most of the griffiners who had come with them on the ship.

Lord Duach, the most senior of them, looked the most upset. He was shouting something at an Amorani man, who looked as if he were doing his best to calm the angry Northerner down, and failing.

Laela marched toward him, pushing people out of the way. "Oi!" she shouted, ignoring the flare-up of pain that caused. Duach didn't notice her, but she solved that by grabbing him by the arm. "Oi, I'm yellin' at you!"

Duach turned irritably. "What . . . ? Oh! Lady Laela, I didn't know ye were awake . . ."

"Well, yeh know now," said Laela. "What's goin' on? Where's Arenadd?"

"In there," said Duach, gesturing at the door next to the one that led into Laela's room. "I can't tell ye much else about what's going on," he added, glaring at the hapless Amorani he'd been yelling at.

Laela turned to the victim. "What's happening?" she said, using griffish.

The man only looked back helplessly and said something in his own language.

Laela snapped. "What the . . . ? He doesn't speak griffish, yeh thick-headed blackrobe! For gods' sakes, someone go an' find Lord Vander or someone else what can translate for us."

Duach went red. "How dare ye . . . ?"

Laela reached over and grabbed him by the ear-lobe. "Listen t'me," she hissed, "I dunno if yeh've noticed, but the King's out of commission, an' I'm the most senior official here. So I reckon if he's not givin' commands, then I'm the person yeh'll be listenin' to instead, got that? You"—she turned and pointed at Penllyn, one of the other Northerners who was there—"go an' find Lord Vander, an' make it snappy."

Penllyn glanced at Duach and hurried away.

"Good," said Laela. "Now, what's goin' on?"

It had gone very quiet in the hallway all of a sudden. Everyone was staring at her now. She ignored them.

Duach was clenching his teeth. "The Amoranis have betrayed us," he said. "They tried to kill the King, and now they're keeping him here and refusing to let any of us see him. And they tried to kill ye, too, while they were at it!" He tugged at his beard. "I told the King we shouldn't come here, an' now see what's happened! These filthy sun worshippers have us at their mercy. Without the King . . ."

Laela suddenly realised how frightened he looked. "Calm down," she said. "He's survived worse. What's happened with the negotiations?"

"Nothing's happened," said Duach. "They're saying that unless the King marries this princess of theirs, they won't send any of the slaves home."

A moment later, Vander arrived. Laela wanted to hug him when she saw him coming. "There yeh are," she said. "Now listen, we need some help here."

Vander watched her closely as she spoke, his dark eyes

gleaming. "I'm at your command, my lady," he said when she was done.

Part of Laela was screaming at her now, telling her this was impossible, that she couldn't possibly be doing this. "I need yeh to translate for us," she said, quite calmly. "We want t'find out what's happened to the King an' whether he's all right, but the healers here don't seem t'speak Cymrian. Can yeh do somethin'?"

Vander nodded. "Certainly, my lady." He turned to the healer and spoke rapidly to him in Amorani. They carried on an animated conversation while Laela and the other Northerners looked on impatiently.

Finally, Vander turned to Laela. "The King was not attacked," he said.

"So ye say—" Duach began.

"Shut up," said Laela. "Vander, what's this about? Why do they think he wasn't attacked?"

Vander gestured at the healer. "He says that the King's wound is not new, but an old one that re-opened suddenly. They have been trying to treat it, but it will not stop bleeding."

"I knew it," said Laela. She didn't even think before she said it, but the instant the words were out of her mouth, she believed they were true. "The Amoranis had nothin' t'do with this," she said, more loudly. "I was there. It was a ghost attacked the King, not a man."

"My lady, ye were under the influence of a powerful drug," said Duach. "Yer story can't be relied on."

"Maybe not, but I'm master of you now, an' I say that's what we believe," said Laela.

"I don't understand, though," Penllyn interrupted. "Why would an old wound suddenly re-open like that, unless someone . . . ?"

"He went into the Sun Temple, yeh idiot!" Laela yelled. "That's why! Don't yeh get it? Don't yeh understand why he's been so sick? This is Gryphus' land, Gryphus' place. He's not welcome here. But he came here anyway," she added more quietly. "T'set our brothers an' sisters free."

"He is a noble man, my lady," Vander said softly. "I have always thought so. I do not like to see him suffer this way."

Laela shook her head. "There's nothin' for it," she said. "We've got t'take him home. Now."

"The King is in a very serious condition, my Lady," said Vander. "It would do him no good to move him now."

But Laela knew in her heart that she was right. "We're takin' him home," she said. "If he stays here, he'll never get better. In Malvern, he'll heal."

"I agree," said Duach. "This journey was a mistake."

"But the slaves," said Penllyn. "And the Emperor. The negotiations aren't finished yet."

"Leave that t'me," said Laela. She saw the doubtful looks she was getting and drew herself up with all the pride a griffiner should have. "I am the Master of Wisdom. My word is final. Now, go. I have t'see the King, an' I'll do that alone."

That said, Laela turned her back on them all and strode into the room where Arenadd lay.

There wasn't much she could do there. Her friend lay on a stone slab, with a sheet covering his lower half. He was as pale as a corpse, and his scars looked red and raw. In the middle of his chest the old wound left by Erian's sword had indeed re-opened. It had been heavily bandaged, but Laela could see a thick line of blood soaking through them, following the length of the cut.

Arenadd was unconscious, breathing slowly. His face was lined with pain.

Laela touched his forehead and stiffened when she realised that his hair, once pure black, was now shot through with grey.

When she saw that, she knew her decision had been the right one.

"I'm sorry, Arenadd," she whispered. "We've done everythin' we could. Now it's time t'go home. The North'll miss those slaves, but it'll miss you worse."

Laela hurried out of the room and found the Northerners and Vander waiting, along with Oeka. They all looked at her expectantly.

"How is he, my lady?" Vander inquired.

"Comatose," said Laela. "Again. But this time he ain't gettin' up anytime soon." She thought quickly and pointed at Duach. "Right, here's what yer gonna do. We're takin' him outta here an' back onto the ship, an' I'm gonna need someone t'keep watch over him. Skandar's gotta be there, too—make sure he's somewhere Skandar can get to him, 'cause I reckon that'll help."

Duach nodded very readily. "At once."

"Good," said Laela. "Once he's on board, keep him out of the sun. Keep him cold—cold as yeh can. Use water, fan him—whatever yeh can think of. The heat's makin' it worse. An' . . ."

"Yes, milady?" said Duach, now very attentive.

"Pray," said Laela.

The Northerners there who knew her looked a little surprised. "Of course, milady," Duach said politely.

"Do it," Laela growled. "Trust me, if there's anything up there at all, it's watchin' over him. You're gonna make sure she doesn't get distracted."

"I will." Duach glanced at his fellows. "Penllyn, ye can come with me."

"Right." Penllyn nodded.

"As for the rest of yeh," Laela continued, "yer stayin' here."

"What do we do, then?" one of them asked.

"Same as what yeh were doin' before," said Laela. "Be guests. *Polite* ones." They muttered at that, and Laela raised her voice. "Yeh just insulted our hosts pretty damned badly, in case yeh didn't notice. Now go—make it up to 'em. Or else."

"Or else what?" one Northerner said in a sulky undertone.

Laela leaned in threateningly. "*Or else.* Got it?"

"We'll do as ye command, milady," Duach said, covering the moment. "In the meantime, what will ye be doing?"

"Finishing what we started," said Laela. "Vander?"

The diplomat straightened up. "Yes?"

"I gotta go talk to the Em—" Laela broke off, remembering herself. "I mean, I need t'go talk to the Emperor. Once I've been back t'my room an' cleaned myself up. Could yeh let him know what's happened an' say I need to talk to him?"

Vander smiled to himself. "Of course."

"Right." Laela waved at the Northerners, unceremoniously shooing them away. "Get to it, you lot. I got work t'do."

She walked off without waiting for a reply. For an instant, she thought she didn't know the way, but then she saw Oeka strutting ahead—silently showing her where to go. Laela fell in beside her and let her partner lead the way out of the hospital and through the palace, where she entered her guest room very gladly.

As always, a collared figure was waiting for her with infinite patience.

Laela couldn't help but smile. "Inva. By gods, I'm glad t'see . . ." She trailed off. The shaved head had confused her for a moment, but now she saw that this was not Inva but some other female slave.

The newcomer bowed low. "Inva is not here any more. I am here to serve my lady now, and must be a better attendant. The gracious Emperor apologises for my predecessor."

Laela gaped, and then shook herself. "What happened to Inva?"

The new slave stared politely at the floor. "Your previous attendant has been punished and will not be here to cause you trouble again, my lady."

"Punished?" Laela exclaimed. "For what?"

"My predecessor allowed you to be harmed, my lady," said the slave, still avoiding her eye. "This is punishable. She has been sent away and will not be allowed to serve fine nobles such as yourself again."

"I—" Laela stopped abruptly, and gave in. There was no point in yelling at this poor woman, who was only doing as she'd been told—just as Inva had. This wasn't the time or place to go on about it. Besides, there was work to do. "Right, then," she resumed as smoothly as she could. "What's your name? I'm Lady Laela."

"I am called Telise, my lady."

"Nice to meet yeh, Telise," said Laela. "Now then, if yeh don't mind, I've got a meetin' with the Emperor, an' I need some cleanin' up."

"At once, my lady."

Laela's mouth felt hideously dry from so much talking. Her headache had been growing steadily worse ever since she'd woken up as well, so now she submitted very gratefully to a cool bath with soothing oils, and the gentle attentions of Telise, who was at least as well trained as Inva had been.

Oeka stayed close by and groomed herself with the help of her own personal slave, who had apparently been allowed to stay. "You have done well," she said.

Laela, half-asleep in the cool water, didn't look up. "Can't go home till we've sorted this out. Gotta do my job."

"Your job was to advise the King," said Oeka.

"Still is. But he told me I'm his second-in-command here, an' that means I gotta take charge now. So that's what I'm doin'. Simple. Besides, I ain't leavin' Inva an' all her friends behind."

"I am sure they will be grateful," said Oeka through a yawn.

Laela mumbled something and dozed briefly while Telise massaged her head—which did a wonderful job of making the headache go away.

She woke up reluctantly and got out of the bath to accept yet another new outfit. Despite having spent so much time unconscious, she was dying for some more sleep, but she settled for a long drink of water and some exotic fruit while she waited for the Emperor to send for her.

It took longer than she had expected, and she nearly fell asleep again on her couch, but she came back to her senses when Telise answered the door, and then turned to say, "The Emperor sends for you and your sacred partner, my lady."

Laela stood up automatically and walked out, with Oeka padding along beside her.

Outside, Vander was waiting, with Ymazu and a pair of powerful-looking guards. Laela glanced nervously at them, but they said nothing, and only stood silently on either side of the diplomats.

Vander bowed his head briefly. "My lady, the Emperor would like to see you."

"Good," said Laela. "Will yeh come with us, Vander?"

"We shall," Vander said briefly. "Ymazu and I are expected to attend. Come, and we will show you the way."

Laela nodded to Oeka, and the pair of them followed Vander and Ymazu. The guards silently fell in behind, uncomfortably close to Laela and Oeka. Clearly, the Emperor was taking no chances.

Vander and Ymazu led the way toward the centre of the palace, an area Laela hadn't seen yet. At the end of their journey, the corridors, already open and airy with large glassless windows, opened out even further into a column-lined walkway. Beyond that was a large courtyard. The city outside had looked barren to Laela, but the courtyard was beautiful. It had been filled with plants, all lush and green. Vines covered the walls, festooned with bright red flowers. Water splashed into a shallow pool that was covered in lillies. Small, ornamental trees grew around the edges, filling the air with a pleasant, spicy aroma.

Despite the circumstances, Laela felt much calmer here. This, she decided, was the perfect place to negotiate. Peaceful, friendly, and elegant.

The Emperor was waiting by the pool, sitting cross-legged by the base of a tree. He was wearing the usual white kilt although this one was edged with bright red and decorated with gold beads. His bald head nearly shone in the sunlight.

He looked very relaxed, but despite that, there was another thing in the garden that added the faintest hint of a threat. This time, for the first time Laela had seen, the Emperor's partner was there.

She almost missed it at first—the griffin lay on her belly among some bushes, nearly unmoving. The slow flicking of her tail had given her away. Her feathers were magnificently patterned with browns and yellow-golds, and the splash of green on her wings had melded in with the plants around her. Even her beak and forelegs were brown. Her eyes were the colour of sand and stared unblinking at the newcomers.

Laela had learned a lot about how to behave around the Emperor and his partner. So had Oeka. The pair of them stood where they were and let Vander and Ymazu go first.

The two diplomats approached the Emperor and his partner. Vander stood with his head politely bowed, while Ymazu took a step toward the other griffin.

Laela, watching, frantically tried to remember her name. She couldn't come up with anything.

The Emperor's partner didn't stand up, and barely even turned her head when Ymazu lowered her own in submission. She opened her beak, and said something. Ymazu replied.

Finally, the two griffins looked toward Vander and the Emperor, neither of whom had moved.

Vander knelt, and spoke in Amorani. The Emperor answered him, and finally stood up to look at Laela and Oeka. Acting on some unspoken signal, Vander and Ymazu both stood aside, leaving Oeka to approach the Emperor's partner, who now stood to receive her. Standing, she was much taller than Oeka, but lighter and slimmer.

Oeka bent her forelegs and touched her head to the ground. "Great and powerful Zaerih, I am Oeka of Malvern. I come to you as an inferior in every way, and carry no plan to attack or insult you, who are dominant over me and my human."

Zaerih—*that* was her name, Laela remembered with relief—gave Oeka a long, slow look. Oeka said nothing and stayed exactly where she was, allowing the other griffin to scent her.

Zaerih gave her a rough shove with her beak, pushing her away. Oeka resisted for an instant, but quickly realised that she was being dismissed and loped back to Laela's side.

The formalities finally over with, the Emperor smiled and gestured at Laela to join him. "Sit with me," he said.

Laela obeyed, sitting cross-legged opposite him, by the pool. "Thank you for seein' me, Sacred Ruler."

"I am honoured to receive you, Lady Laela," the Emperor said gravely. "May I ask how your King is faring?"

"Not well," Laela said honestly. "Sacred Ruler . . . the King is very badly hurt. But—" She raised a hand, and her voice as well. "But there's no blame on you. The doctors yeh sent did a good job; yeh've been takin' good care of him, an' me as well. I know there's been some tension, bad things bein' said, but I'm here to tell yeh there's no problem. I was a witness. You had nothin' to do with this, an' neither did any of yer good people, Sacred Ruler. Yer our friend, our good friend, an' I know the King would say the same if he were here. But obviously he ain—isn't, so I've come in his place."

"You are his highest official here?" said the Emperor, unreadable.

"I am," said Laela. "My words are his. What I say, he says."

The Emperor smiled. "He told me this. That is why I granted you an audience."

Laela's heart beat faster. "Good. Then here's what I have to say."

"Speak," said the Emperor.

Laela took a deep breath. "The King needs t'be taken home, an' quickly. Only Malvern has the medicine he needs. But before we leave, I'm here t'finish the negotiations. So tell me what's left t'be done, an' I'll see it done."

The Emperor frowned. "You are certain that the King must be sent home?"

"I am," said Laela.

"But what medicine can your people have that mine do not? The doctors of my palace are the finest in the world."

"They are," said Laela. "An' they've done good work for him an' for me. But they don't have what he needs." She smiled slightly. "He needs snow. Only the North has that."

"Very well," said the Emperor. "Your people must treat him as they see fit, and if our help is not asked for, then so be it. I hope that he will return when he has recovered, so that we may complete our treaty."

"We can do that now," said Laela. "I'm empowered to do it."

But the Emperor shook his head. "Our treaty cannot be sealed without the King."

"Why?" said Laela. "What did yeh need from him that I can't give?"

"The marriage," said the Emperor. "The King must marry my daughter, or the treaty will be void."

"Can't she come back with us?" said Laela. "The ceremony could happen in Malvern once the King got better."

"That is not good enough," said the Emperor, not angry but firm. "The ceremony must happen on Amorani soil. There must be a wedding. We are prepared for one."

"Can't we seal the treaty some other way?" Laela asked in desperation.

"No. We complete every new alliance this way. There must be a meeting of two souls, a binding of two families. This is vital."

"I understand," said Laela. "But the King is unconscious, an' he's never gonna wake up unless he goes home. He can't get married this way."

"Then he must come back later," said the Emperor, unmoved. "Without the marriage, there is no treaty. Do not waste our time in arguing over this, Lady Laela."

Laela knew there was no chance of Arenadd ever setting foot on Amorani soil again. If he ever tried, she would stop him. But there was no way the Emperor was going to change his mind.

"Then maybe we can do this another way," she said at last. "Could someone else here maybe marry her instead?"

"Only a member of the King's family may make the marriage," said the Emperor. "It must be royal blood to royal blood, or the wedding would be meaningless."

Laela rubbed her eyes. She was quickly running out of options. At this point, it looked like she was going to have to accept the inevitable and go back home with the treaty half-finished. And when—if—Arenadd recovered, she would have to tell him that she had failed and that he would have to go through another six months of agony because she had been unable to finish what he had started.

She settled on a compromise. "I understand, Sacred Ruler. If yeh don't mind, I'd like some time t'think about this."

"Of course." The Emperor smiled. "You look very tired, and are more than welcome to rest. I will see you again tomorrow, when you are ready."

"Thank you, Sacred Ruler." Laela stood up, signalling the end of the meeting.

She left the garden with Oeka, feeling exhausted and angry with herself. There had to be some way to resolve this, *had* to be. But how could she ever persuade the Emperor to change his mind?

She was so worried that she didn't notice that Vander and Ymazu had followed her until she had nearly reached her own rooms. When they arrived, Vander took a step toward the door. "With your permission, my lady?"

Laela brightened up slightly, realising that he might be able to help. "Come in."

She and Oeka entered first, with both Vander and Ymazu. The two diplomats made themselves comfortable. Telise and Oeka's own servant were instantly on hand, offering refreshments.

The guards from before had come along as well, but to Laela's relief, they stayed outside, stationing themselves on either side of the door. She sat down on one of the odd cushion-chairs provided, and accepted a drink.

Vander, sitting with Ymazu directly behind him, folded his hands and looked frankly at Laela. "You did well with the Emperor. I was impressed."

"Thanks," said Laela. "Doesn't look like it worked, though." She put her head in her hands. "I dunno what I'm gonna do, Vander. I really don't."

Vander put his head on one side. "My lady . . . may I ask if you are married?"

"Eh?" Laela looked up. "No, I ain't."

Vander smiled in his mysterious way. "The Emperor will accept nothing but a marriage—one of his family to one of the King's. Any man or woman with the King's blood will do. Whether legitimate or not." With those words, he fixed Laela with a penetrating stare.

She frowned. "That's nice, but there's nobody here with his blood except him."

"If you say so, my lady." Vander smiled again. "Now, I will leave you to rest and consider your next discussion. I hope that my advice is . . . useful."

With that, he stood up and left the room with Ymazu.

Laela stared up at him. "Huh. I know what he's gettin' at."

"So do I," said Oeka. "He still believes you are the King's daughter."

"The Emperor does, too," said Laela, remembering. "When we first met him, he looked straight at me an' made some comment about Arenadd's family rising to power. An' I suppose I do look like him a bit . . ."

Impulsively, she snatched up a hand mirror and examined her reflection carefully. There was the hair, obviously, and maybe something a bit similar about the nose and the chin . . .

Not for the first time, she wondered whether it could be true. Could she really be *his* daughter?

No. She dismissed the notion, yet again. It was impossible. He couldn't father children; he'd told her so himself. And he'd never been with a Southerner. There was no way.

And yet . . .

"If I *was* his daughter," she said slowly, "then I could do the marriage. I could finish this thing myself."

"But you are not his daughter," said Oeka.

"I know, but . . . I dunno. Maybe I could . . . pretend, like."

Oeka's neck feathers rose. "You mean lie? To the Emperor?"

"Yeah. I mean, no. Of course not. Don't be daft. I couldn't do that."

Oeka slowly scratched her flank and made a low, soft, rasping sound. "Could you do this thing?" she asked eventually. "Are you willing to?"

"I couldn't," said Laela. "No way. Could yeh imagine the trouble I'd be in when the truth got out?"

"It depends," said Oeka.

"On what?"

"I have been listening, too," said the small griffin. "And I think I understand how this thing would work. This mating is not about power, only symbolism."

"So?" said Laela.

"So it does not matter that you are not his daughter and will never inherit his throne. The Emperor does not want a marriage between the current or future ruler of the North—he only wants a member of the King's family, any member. He said so himself today."

"So what does that mean?" said Laela.

"That it will not matter to him if you do not rule. As long as you are a Taranisäii in name, it will be enough."

Laela rubbed her chin. "What do yeh think I should do, then?"

"Tell the truth," said Oeka. "Or part of it. Say you are the King's daughter, but are not legitimate. You are a Taranisäii but will not inherit the throne. Tell him that, and tell him you are still willing as a Taranisäii to accept a mating with a member of the Emperor's own family. See if that will satisfy him."

Laela stared. She mumbled something, began a proper reply, and then trailed off into silence.

Oeka huffed. "I know I am not clever like one of your kind, but I have used my best judgment. I do not know if my advice should be followed . . . Decide for yourself. I am sure that your own reasoning will be better."

Laela found her voice. "Since when did *you* start soundin' humble? Dear gods, the world really has gone mad."

Oeka snapped her beak. "I have given all I have to offer. It is your decision."

"You've been happy t'make decisions for me before."

"Yes," Oeka admitted. "But no matter her species, every female must choose which male will fertilise her eggs. That is her decision and nobody else's."

Once, Laela might have laughed at her partner's awkward choice of words, but not now. Now they only served to sharply remind her of what was really at stake here. Not Arenadd's quest or the Emperor's anger if she was caught, or even the slaves whose freedom depended on her now. She was more than willing to help them, and to do her duty as Arenadd's aide.

The real question was how far was she willing to go for their sake? Was she willing to do what Oeka had suggested—that is, marry some Amorani man she had never met? Sleep with him, most likely? Was she willing to betray Yorath?

"I gotta think about this," she muttered.

"Think, then," said Oeka, looking quite relaxed. "Take the time you need."

"Right," said Laela, and that was more or less all she said for the rest of that afternoon.

She couldn't sleep that night. Telise brought her a beautifully refreshing dinner of fresh fruit and some very mild wine, all of which did a lot to make her feel better, and the doctors had sent over some thick, gritty medicine that tasted vile but finally got rid of the headache.

Afterward, she should have been more than ready to sleep and let herself recover, but she didn't. Her mind wouldn't let her.

Neither would her chest. Fear and worry were emotions that seemed to live inside her rib cage, and that long, awful night it felt ready to burst. Her heart fluttered periodically and made her feel ill.

She tried to relax, tried to make herself sleep, tried to tell herself that everything would be all right—but she couldn't. And the answer to her problems just seemed so simple. All she had to do was accept that this was beyond her. There was nothing she could do about it except go home and hope that Arenadd got better.

But she found herself thinking of Inva instead. She had come to like the older woman, and to sympathise with her. She was obviously very intelligent, and highly educated as well. She deserved a chance to live free. But where was she now? Punished, Telise had said. Sent away. And Laela had a horrible feeling about just where that might be. Inva had suffered, and was probably still suffering, and all because of Laela's own stupidity.

Laela rebelled at that. No, it wasn't *her* fault what had happened to Inva. It was the system that had done it—the system that forced people to live the way she did and treated them like so much rubbish by way of return. It was the system that had punished Inva when she hadn't done anything.

Right there and then, Laela vowed to herself that she would not go home until she had found Inva again and helped her in any way she could. Testified to her innocence, at the very least. But that wouldn't be good enough. No, Laela decided, she would *free* Inva instead. Buy her freedom and take her back to the North.

That decision made her feel better.

But after that, she got to thinking about the others. How many others like Inva were there? How many hundreds or thousands of other Northerners were out there, treated like property and probably killed as soon as they stopped being useful? How many were there who had it far worse than Inva ever had?

All of a sudden, she found herself thinking about Arenadd. She remembered the scars on his neck, and the lash marks on his back. She thought of the black robe he always wore. And the slow, chilling realisation came to her, the thought that she could guess what all those things meant. And there was the way he spoke, too—his passionate insistence that all men should be free, that slaves should be rescued, his utter hatred for the system that let them live that way at all.

*He was a slave,* she thought. *He must have been. That's why . . .*

No wonder, then, that he hated Southerners so much. No wonder he had spent his entire life killing them and driving them away. No wonder he was prepared to do anything and everything in his power for those here in Amoran.

"An' me?" she said aloud, to the dark ceiling high above. "What does that make me?"

Unexpectedly, she found herself feeling utterly ashamed of her Southern blood. Ashamed, too, that she had ever let herself hate Arenadd for setting his people free. For the first time, she felt as if she understood those people who hated her for being a half-breed, and in that moment she did feel ashamed of it. Inherited shame.

The feeling passed quickly. It wasn't her fault, and there was no such thing as a race that was better than any other. She should know.

But like it or not, she was a kind of Southerner, and she couldn't help but feel as if she had a responsibility to try to make amends. After all, it had been Southerners who had sold those slaves to Amoran in the first place. And as a Northerner, she had a duty as well. A duty to her people, and to her King.

Those were inspiring thoughts, but they still led her back to the one question that had put her in this state in the first place. Was she willing to go through with this? Lie to the Emperor? Marry a man she didn't know? Betray Yorath?

In the end, shortly before dawn, she settled on a compromise. She would speak to the Emperor again and find out more. She wouldn't lie, but she would ask questions, and at least find out if a half-breed bastard was an acceptable match. That should do to begin with.

As she drifted off to sleep, she forced herself not to think about what she had seen in the Temple. It was too soon to think of it. And besides that, she wasn't sure if she ever wanted to.

# 26

# Laela Paramount

By the time morning came, Laela was exhausted. Her eyes were dry, and her headache had come back with a vengeance.

She dragged herself out of bed regardless, and once her breakfast had been served, she sent Telise to pass on a message to the Emperor requesting another audience.

The slave returned just as Laela was finishing breakfast, bowing low. "My lady, the Emperor will see you this afternoon."

Laela rubbed her forehead. "Why not sooner?"

"The Emperor will see you when he chooses," said Telise, with an iciness that surprised her.

"Right then." Laela gulped down some water and tried to think. "In that case, while we're waitin' . . . I want t'know where Inva is."

Telise looked blank. "Your previous attendant?"

"Yes, her," said Laela. "Middle-aged woman, no hair. What have they done with her?"

"She has been punished—"

"I know," Laela growled. "Punished how?"

Telise looked nervous. "Punished fittingly, my lady."

"Where is she, then? You said she'd been sent away. Where to?"

"I don't know, my lady."

"Then who *would* know?"

"Master Zel, my lady. He is master of the slaves who serve here."

"Right." Laela stood up. "I want t'see him. Now."

"Yes, my lady."

Oeka appeared, bright-eyed, with her tail twitching. "Where are you going?"

"I'm gonna go find out what happened to Inva," said Laela.

"Why does it matter? Why are you not seeing the Emperor?"

"He ain't available right now," said Laela. "Anyway, I wanna find out what happened to Inva—see if I can help."

Oeka fell in beside her as she left the rooms. "Why would you want to help?"

"Because I'm the one who got her in trouble," said Laela. "They blamed her for what happened to me. She wasn't even *there*!"

"What do you care?" said Oeka.

Laela had expected something exactly like this. "Because I'm human, an' I don't just care about myself."

"You would be wiser if you did," said Oeka. "No-one else will care for you as much as you yourself."

"See, this is why griffins ain't ruling the world," said Laela. She grinned. "C'mon, yeh selfish goose. Let's go do some altruism."

"I do not know that word," Oeka said primly.

"Me neither," said Laela. "I just copied it off someone. Hurry up, Telise! We can walk faster than this, y'know."

"Apologies," Telise said smartly, and hurried off down the corridor.

They had to leave the neat quietness of the guest quarters and move on into a noisier, busier part of the palace that griffiners probably weren't meant to see. What Laela *did* see, along with that, were slaves—far more of them than she had seen before. Some Northerners, some Amorani, some from Maijan, some belonging to races she had never seen before, but all of them shaven and collared, and all of them hard at work. She passed a big long room where dozens of slaves were busy washing clothes and linen, and caught a glimpse of a massive kitchen where dozens more were preparing meals and washing pots and plates. To her surprise, aside from the occasional patrolling guard, she didn't see anyone who looked like a supervisor watching over them. But the slaves worked industriously anyway, as if they had nothing else to do but the jobs that earned them no pay, and no respect.

And that was exactly how it was, of course.

Eventually, Telise guided them through all this and into a slightly quieter area, where a smaller group of slaves were busy stripping the petals off flowers and putting them in bowls. Telise weaved her way through them and stopped by one man who didn't seem to be doing anything. He was Amorani, and the stubble on his head was grey, which was just about the only hint to his age.

As Laela and Oeka caught up with their guide, the man turned to them and bowed briefly. "Sacred griffin, I am blessed to see you and your human."

Oeka had been enjoying this sort of treatment long enough that she didn't react much to it now. "Why do you speak to me, slave?" she rasped.

The man bowed again, more respectfully this time. "I have just been told that your human wished to speak with me, Sacred One. Am I mistaken?"

"Not if you are Master Zel."

"I am," said the man, eyes flicking briefly toward Laela.

"Let her speak with you, then," Oeka said, bored, and settled down to groom.

Laela took her cue. "Master Zel, is it? I'm Lady Laela."

Zel inclined his head toward her. "I am honoured to meet you, Lady Laela," he said, in polished Cymrian. "How can I serve you?"

"I'm looking for someone," said Laela. "A slave called Inva. She was my attendant before Telise."

"I know that name," said Zel. "And I offer you my greatest apology and shame that I sent her to you. I hope that Telise is a better attendant for you."

Laela hadn't missed Telise's anxious looks toward her. "She's doin' a great job," she said kindly. "But I wanted to know where Inva's gone."

"She has been sent away," Zel said at once.

"I know," said Laela. "But to where?"

"To the slave market, to be sold to a new master. She will not be allowed to serve nobles again."

Laela groaned inwardly. "Look—Zel—that ai—isn't right. She shouldn't have been sent away."

"Why not?" Zel looked very politely disapproving. "She allowed her master to be placed in danger and was punished for her negligence."

"It wasn't her fault," said Laela. "She only did what I told her."

"That does not matter," said Zel. "She did not obey the command given to her to keep you from danger at all costs, and this lapse is punishable."

The sheer injustice of it infuriated Laela. She opened her mouth to retort but quickly shut it again as common sense caught up with her. She wasn't going to get anywhere arguing with this man, and besides, there was no reason why she should be arguing with him at all. He was her inferior, and she had learned that you didn't argue with inferiors. Instead, you just ordered them to agree with you.

"Bring her back," she said.

"I cannot do that," said Zel, but cautiously.

"Bring her back," Laela repeated.

"She cannot be brought back."

"All right, then," said Laela, changing tack. "How about I tell the Emperor that you ain't doin' your job? I'm his guest, an' it's your job t'keep me happy. If I say bringin' Inva back would make me happy, then you have t'do it. Otherwise, I'll be unhappy. An' when I get unhappy, I get nasty. An' when I get nasty, I make people's lives hard. Are yeh startin' to get what I mean, Zel?"

If the head slave was affronted by this not-so-subtle threat—the kind of threat Laela was best at—he didn't show it. "Very well then," he said in flat tones. "I will send out for her to be brought back at once. Shall I have her brought to you once she has returned?"

"Yes," said Laela. "An' make it fast," she added nastily. "I want her back by tonight."

"It shall be done," said Zel, and there was something about him and the way he said it that made Laela completely confident that he would and could do just that.

"I must be the worst guest this palace has ever had." She

smirked to herself as she left. But there was real satisfaction mixed in with her smugness. She only hoped her next meeting with the Emperor would go as well.

While she waited for the afternoon to arrive, she made several other visits. First she checked in with the other Northern griffiners, making sure they were all well and assuring them that she had placated the Emperor and was due to see him again soon.

She also visited the docks where the *Seabreath* was still moored, to see how Arenadd was doing. She found him unchanged, still comatose, but breathing steadily. Skandar was with him, patiently guarding his human. Evidently, he had finished enjoying Amoran's various pleasures. His partner was more important.

"Don't worry," Laela told him. "We're goin' home soon, an' he'll get well. Just look after him. I never saw a griffin who took better care of his human." She didn't say that last part just to flatter him, and he seemed pleased even if he didn't say anything.

"When *are* we going home?" asked Penllyn.

"Soon," said Laela. "I'm just about done talkin' to the Emperor. We'll be leavin' in a matter of days."

"We'd better," Duach muttered.

Laela took one last look at Arenadd's deathly pale face. "We will."

The meeting with the Emperor finally arrived. This time he received Laela in an elegant room that must have been his official audience chamber. Vander was there, with Ymazu, and Zaehri, the griffins sitting on velvet floor-pads obviously made just for them.

Once the formalities were over, Laela sat on a couch opposite the Emperor while Oeka chose a pad of her own and lay on it, with her front paws outstretched.

"Lady Laela," the Emperor began. "May I ask how your King is faring?" Off to the side and behind his ruler, Vander listened closely.

"Unchanged, Sacred Ruler," said Laela.

The Emperor looked a little sad. "That is not good. Have you made a decision yet, Lady Laela?"

"I'm in the process," said Laela. "But I wanted t'ask a question, if yeh don't mind, Sacred Ruler."

He smiled. "Ask."

Laela took a deep breath, and leaned forward. "This marriage that we need has t'be between a Taranisäii an' one of yer own family, yes?"

"Yes," the Emperor said firmly.

"Then I wanted t'ask," said Laela, choosing her words carefully, "can the Taranisäii be any Taranisäii?"

"As long as he or she is one of the King's family," said the Emperor.

Sheer nervousness made Laela dizzy. "Is . . . does . . . does the person have t'be . . . er . . . legitimate?"

The Emperor frowned. "I do not know that word, my Lady."

Laela hesitated, gave up, and plunged ahead. It was now or never. "Can the Taranisäii be a bastard?"

There was a pause.

Then the Emperor smiled, a big, white-toothed smile. "Ah. You wonder if you, beautiful lady, can take your father's place and marry one of my family."

Laela gaped. "Er—"

"Your loyalty to your father is impressive," the Emperor went on. "But it is not so surprising. He has been very kind, and taken good care of you. I suppose it is only natural if he has no legitimate children to call his own."

"Er, thanks," said Laela. This was just about the last thing she had expected.

"The King often spoke of you," said the Emperor, still smiling. "I could see how much pride he takes in you. And how much he loves you. It did my heart good."

Laela couldn't believe this. The Emperor was actually spinning her lie for her, deceiving himself without any help at all. She couldn't think of anything to say.

"But I must answer your question," said the Emperor, interrupting her thoughts. "The answer is yes. If no other Taranisäii is available, you will be suitable despite being born outside of marriage. We are lucky as well—my youngest son is here in

Instabahn, and he is very obedient to his father. He will be glad
to do his duty to his country."

"That's . . . good." Laela swallowed. "If . . . er . . . if I married him, would—would I have to stay here?"

"No, no," said the Emperor. "The marriage would be purely
ceremonial. Symbolic only. You will not have to live together
unless you choose to."

"Oh." At that, Laela relaxed completely.

"In fact, it is better if you live in your own countries," the
Emperor remarked. "That way you will link our two great
nations, as two ends of a chain hold a ship to a shore." He gave
her an intelligent, bright-eyed look. "This arrangement is satis-
factory to me. Does it satisfy you as well, Lady Laela Taranisäii?"

Laela glanced at Vander, and at Oeka. She was unreadable,
and he looked ever so slightly pleased. "Yeah," she said at last.
"I mean, yes. I'll do it."


Laela was committed to her dangerous game now, and she
prepared to play it all the way to the end. Once she and the
Emperor had made their agreement, she went to see the other
Northerners and bluntly told them that the alliance was settled
and she herself would be getting married in Arenadd's place.

Most of them looked surprised, and some, Duach in particular, were impressed.

"I don't believe it," he said. "How? How did ye talk him
into it?"

Laela shrugged. "It didn't have t'be the King. The Emperor
was willin' to accept an alternative."

"Why ye, though?" said Duach. "Why not one of us?"
Despite the objection, he didn't sound offended.

Laela fidgeted—now came the tough part. "Er . . . well, it's
'cause . . . I'm kind of a . . . in the right place."

Duach put his head on one side. "What place is that, then?"

"The Emperor wanted a Taranisäii," said Laela. "Any Taranisäii." That at least was true. "I asked what about me, an' . . .
well, he said yes." There. She hadn't lied.

Duach's expression cleared, and he cackled. "Hah! Knew it.
Yer a real chip off the old block, aren't ye?"

Laela smiled sadly. "Looks like it."

"He's happy with a bastard, then?" Duach asked, quite bluntly.

"So he says." Laela glared.

"Good!" said Duach. "That's perfect. When's the wedding?"

"Tomorrow at noon, but I want you an' Penllyn t'stay here. I ain't takin' a risk."

"Of course." Duach smiled knowingly at her. "None of us would, and especially not ye of all people." He looked serious. "I've been unkind to ye, but I know ye well enough to know that nobody's more loyal to the King than yerself."

Unexpected shame took hold of her. "Thanks," she mumbled, and left, unable to make herself stay any longer.

When she got back to her rooms, she found herself greeted by two people. One was Telise, and the other was none other than Inva. She looked tired and worn, and there were bruises showing on her face and arms, but when she saw Laela, she all but ran to her. All her former reserve gone, she just about threw herself down at Laela's feet and stayed there, pressing her forehead into the ground.

"Inva!" Laela gaped, and then grinned. "C'mon, get up. Nobody kneels to a half-breed!"

Inva got up at once, looking slightly embarrassed, but she still bowed her head. "Thank you," she said, hands clasped in front of her. "Thank you a hundred times. Xanathus bless you for what you have done."

"Hey." Laela reached out and touched her on the shoulder. "It's all right."

Telise gasped in horror. Laela ignored her.

Inva looked up, clearly bewildered. "You . . . you saved me. I don't understand. What did I do . . . ?"

"You were innocent," said Laela. "I got yeh into trouble, so don't thank me. I just made up for what I did wrong."

"But I allowed you to go into danger," said Inva, looking horrified. "You nearly died, and I did nothing to stop it."

"Are yeh daft?" Laela exclaimed. "What happened happened in the Temple, an' you weren't allowed in—yeh told me so yerself!"

"But it was my responsibility to guide you and make certain that you were well cared for," said Inva.

"An' yeh did a great job," said Laela. "Honestly. I ain't never been looked after so well. Now stop arguin'. You're safe again, an' we've got a weddin' to get ready for."

Inva hesitated, and then, for the first time since Laela had met her, she smiled. "Of course, my lady. I will be happy to help."

# 27

# Sun Wedding

On the night before her wedding, Laela went to visit Arenadd one last time.

He was still comatose, still pale and ghastly with sweat, and the bandage wrapped around his chest was still stained with blood. His breathing was so slight she could scarcely see it. He looked like a man on his death-bed. Worse, he looked like a man who was already dead. The grey in his hair looked even more pronounced than before.

Laela reached down to touch his forehead and pulled her hand away. He was burning hot. He'd never felt like that before. She had touched him plenty of times when he was well, and he had always been cold. For him, coldness was a sign of health . . . or strength, at least.

She sighed and sank into a chair by his bedside. "What am I gonna do with you?"

The question went far deeper than it seemed. What *was* she going to do?

Since the incident in the Temple, she had pushed the vision she had had out of her head. There had been too much to do, too many other things to worry about. But now she let herself think it over, reliving it in her head as well as she could.

Had it been real? Had she really seen what she had thought, or was it just a hallucination that had nearly killed her?

But she already knew the truth. The vision had been real; it had to be. With it and her dream, she had now seen Gryphus twice, and both times it had felt completely real. Both times he had told her things she couldn't possibly have known. And if the dream had been vivid, the vision in the Temple had been twice as real. She could have imagined Bran easily, but she couldn't have imagined her mother. Not like that, not so perfectly that the woman she saw looked like her.

And the other thing she couldn't ignore was that she had seen Gryphus at two different times and in two different ways, but that both times he had told her almost exactly the same thing: that she was the Risen Sun, and she had the power to . . . to . . .

"To kill you," she whispered, eyes turning to Arenadd, lying there helpless.

She stared at him, watching his chest rise and fall ever so slightly, and tried to make herself accept what she knew must be the truth: that he had killed her mother and all the rest of her family as well.

It was easy enough to believe. They had been Southerners, and who else was he most famous for killing? She had seen him kill now, and she had begun to understand what he was capable of.

She remembered the ghosts, and the wounds that had been on them. Their throats had been slit, cut clear across by something very sharp. Identical wounds to those she had seen on the pirates. Wounds that fitted the blade of Arenadd's cherished sickle—the same one he had used in all their lessons when he had taught her how to fight.

Laela felt sick. Arenadd Taranisäii, her best friend, the one she had trusted her whole life to, the one she was doing everything for, the one she had hugged and sympathised with . . . Arenadd Taranisäii had murdered her entire family. He had made her an orphan and stolen the life she could have had forever. He had nearly killed *her*, while she was in the cradle.

"That's what Gryphus wants," she said to herself, so quietly she barely heard it. "He wants me to take revenge. To—to kill him."

She stood up, moving to stand over Arenadd, and glanced quickly at the door. Nobody was around. Skandar was up on deck, enjoying some fresh air, and Duach and Penllyn were staying away to give her some time alone.

She looked back at Arenadd. She was unarmed, and there were no weapons in the room, but she could manage without one. He was so weak that she could probably suffocate him with a pillow or strangle him. Nobody would ever know it had been her; they would assume he had simply passed away in his sleep.

She didn't move.

Arenadd's face twitched, and he mumbled something inaudible.

All of a sudden, Laela wanted to laugh. Here she was, after everything he had done, pretending to be his daughter. And the thing was, the odd thing was, that in his own way he had almost been like a father to her. He had protected her, given her a home, given her everything she needed. He had been a friend, had watched over her, had taught her everything he knew. And when trouble came, that awful day in the Temple, he had willingly gone into danger in order to try to save her, and had nearly sacrificed his own life in the process.

Laela slumped back into her chair and put her hands over her face. This was impossible; it all was. She was no murderer, and Arenadd was . . .

. . . was all she had. If she killed him now, she would not just be killing her family's murderer but also the only one left in the world who cared about her as a father would. Without him, she would be alone in the world again.

And the South would lose the enemy who had become its greatest protector.

When she realised that, Laela knew there was no way she could kill him.

She got up and stalked out of the room.

Laela got married the next day, without having met her prospective husband beforehand, in the very same Temple where she had nearly died.

She spent the morning in her rooms with Telise and Inva, both of whom worked to prepare her for the ceremony. If she'd thought they had pampered her before, that was nothing compared to now. After a light breakfast, the two of them spent literally the entire morning up until noon bathing, massaging, painting, filing, combing, brushing, anointing, and decorating the bride-to-be, before they helped her climb into the most elaborate outfit she had ever seen in her life. It started with a skimpy two-piece thing not unlike what she had worn on the first day, but over the top of that went entire layers of veils, scarves, and bits of jewellery covered in tiny gold bells.

She was half-convinced that she wouldn't even be able to walk underneath all of it, but when she was finally allowed to stand up, she found that the outfit was surprisingly light.

As she prepared to leave, Oeka came to join her, having spent the morning with her own attendant plus a second, who had been called in especially. Her coat nearly shone, but it was barely noticeable under the jewel-encrusted headdress and the tassels that hung from her wings. Even her beak and talons had been coated in gold leaf.

She said nothing but walked by Laela's side as they set out into the palace with the four slaves forming a retinue around them. When they left the palace, they found themselves joining a procession, which moved off the moment they had taken a place halfway along, moving at a sedate pace along the sandy street, where dozens of people had gathered to watch.

Shaded by palm leaves, which Inva and Telise held over her head, Laela looked ahead. At least a hundred people were in the procession behind and in front of her. Guards, nobles, griffins—and servants to attend to most of them. Decorated poles swayed overhead.

At the very front, she could catch a glimpse of an entire phalanx of griffins swaggering along side by side, all headdressed and bursting with complete, arrogant self-confidence.

No sign of her future husband, though, as far as she could see. She walked along obediently, forced to keep a slow pace by the rest of the procession and the ridiculous sandals she had to wear.

It took a painfully long time to reach the Temple—not that she wanted to see it again in a hurry. When the entrance finally loomed above her, her stomach twisted. She didn't know what to expect when she entered, and was very relieved when it turned out to be nothing more terrifying than the same long, stone room, only now festooned in flowers. People and griffins lined the room, leaving a passage down the centre to the altar, where Laela's intended waited for her.

She walked forward, with Oeka. The rest of the procession had fallen away, and only Inva and one of Oeka's attendants were left, walking silently in the rear.

And there he was, waiting for her under the gaze of Xanathus' golden statue. The Amorani Empire's youngest Prince, whose name she didn't even know, but who would be her husband by the time she left the Temple.

Laela wasn't sure what she had expected him to be like, but she knew for certain it hadn't been this. Part of her had thought he would be bald, like his father, and she had definitely thought he would be much older than her. She was wrong.

The Prince didn't look more than a year away from her in age, and he had a full head of thick, dark hair. A diamond stud twinkled on one side of his nose, and the smile he greeted her with was nearly as brilliant. All in all, he was . . .

*The damned best-looking man I ever saw!* Laela thought, almost frantically.

The Prince held out a hand to her. "Welcome, my beautiful flower of Cymria."

Laela fought and lost a battle with a big goofy grin. "I'm honoured to meet you, Prince," she said, taking the hand.

His grip was delicate, but strong. "I welcome you in Xanathus' name." He spoke Cymrian, and his voice was rich and wonderful to listen to. "Come, stand beside me."

Laela joined him, oblivious as Oeka greeted the Prince's own partner. "I'm Laela," she said in an undertone.

"And I am Akhane," said the Prince, with another dazzling smile. "You are far more beautiful than I ever expected."

The two griffins parted, standing face-to-face in front of their partners but far enough back to make them easily visible to the onlookers. The Emperor was there, too, standing beside the statue of Xanathus with his eldest wife.

From where she stood, Laela could see that the other Northerners were there, too. They had been allowed to stand right at the front of the Temple, on her left-hand side. They wore their own ceremonial outfits, but their griffins must have insisted on receiving the same kind of pampering as Oeka. They blended in with the Amorani griffins quite well.

With everyone in place, Zaerhi let out a piercing screech from somewhere behind the statue.

Silence fell, and as everyone settled down, a priest appeared from behind the altar as if by magic. He was bald and gold-painted, like Ocax, but as Laela and Akhane turned to face him over the altar, she saw that he was a much older man—probably the head priest for this Temple.

The ceremony began.

It was in Amorani for the most part, and other parts were in griffish, but Laela quickly lost track of it anyway. At certain points, she was prompted to repeat something the priest had said, and she dutifully obeyed, but most of the time all she did was stand there in a kind of daze. She kept stealing glances at the Prince, and he returned every one of them, bright-eyed and smiling.

Laela's head spun. *This ain't right!* she thought, over and over. *Princes aren't this handsome outside of stories. Or this . . . sweet.*

She had agreed to get married for the sake of duty. She had never once expected that she would be getting the man of her—damn it, of *any* girl's dreams into the bargain. But here he was anyway, in the flesh, and she couldn't help but feel some regret that she wasn't going to live with him. Maybe he could come back with her to the North anyway, if she talked him into it . . .

She realised quickly enough how silly that idea was. If he came back with her, then sooner or later he would probably realise she had been lying about her parentage. And he wouldn't want to leave his homeland just for her sake.

But with that in mind, Laela dropped her former determination with regard to the wedding night. She wouldn't get to keep this spellbinding man, but damn it all, she was going to sleep with him come what may—even if that did mean spending the rest of her life disappointed by every other man she met.

She gave his hand a squeeze and thrilled when he squeezed back.

The ceremony ended when the Prince anointed Laela's forehead with oil, announced something in Amorani, and leaned in to kiss her. She returned the kiss eagerly, and the crowd cheered.

And that was it. She was married.

Another procession took Laela back to the palace, but this time she walked to the front by her new husband's side. Another feast had been laid out in the hall. A huge main table had been set up, and she sat at the head of it by the Prince's side,

where dish after exotic dish was laid out for her to try. She ate
plenty, even when she didn't recognise the food, which was
most of the time. Everything was delicious.

The Prince stayed by her, and so did every bit of the charm
he had showed in the Temple. He kept his attention on her,
pointed out the best foods, and talked almost only to her. Small
talk for the moment, nothing very serious, but Laela drank in
every word. She felt like she was in paradise.

Oeka, meanwhile, looked to have had good luck, too. The
Prince's partner was a big, dark brown male griffin, and he and
Oeka were eating the carcasses provided—in between making
playful darts and hops toward each other. Even Laela knew
enough by now to recognise griffish flirting when she saw it.

The feasting went on well into the afternoon, and featured
several performances by dancers and musicians, and even a pair
of entertainers, who juggled a handful of razor-sharp knives
between them. Laela enjoyed herself immensely.

When the celebrations finally began to quiet down, Prince
Akhane stood up—signalling that it was time for him and his
bride to leave. Laela went with him quite happily, and the two griffins followed at a relaxed distance. They went, not back to Laela's
rooms, but to another, much larger chamber that she quickly
realised must belong to the Prince. The vaulted ceiling was painted
with a beautiful mural of suns and clouds, and the walls were lined
with bookshelves recessed into the stone itself. The large, silk-
covered bed had netting draped over it to keep out mosquitoes, but
that only served to make it look more exotic and exciting.

The Prince courteously ushered her to a low table surrounded by cushions. "Please do sit with me. I hope my room is
to your liking."

"It's beautiful," Laela said honestly, accepting the seat. In
the background, Oeka wandered off into the adjoining nest
chamber with her new friend, and Inva and the other attendants
stationed themselves discreetly around the room, ready to leap
in the moment they were needed.

The Prince sat down close by Laela—close enough that they
were touching. "How did you enjoy the feasting, my lady?"

"It was great," said Laela. She smiled shyly at him. "Yeh can
call me Laela now, I think. I mean, now I'm yer wife an' all."

"Of course, Laela." He smiled back. "Call me Akhane, then. Forgive me if I am awkward, but this is my first . . . I mean, I have never . . ."

"What is it?" Laela wanted to touch his face.

He smiled again, but there was a hint of nervousness there now. "You are my first wife. I have never married before."

"Me neither," said Laela. She settled down, leaning against him. He put an arm around her, his hand resting on her lap. For a while the two of them stayed like that, warmth mingling, hearts beating in time.

"I hope I ain—I'm not too disappointing for yer first wife," Laela said eventually. "I mean, bein' what I am."

"What?" Akhane's arm tightened slightly on her. "No, not at all. I hope I did not make you think so; if I did, I did not mean it."

"I'm a half-breed, though," said Laela. "And a b—not legitimate."

"I don't mind." The Prince lifted her chin so he could look her in the face. "Your eyes are magnificent. Blue as the sky. I have never seen eyes like them."

Laela realised she was blushing. "Thanks . . ."

"You seem ashamed," he commented. "Is being a half-breed so shameful?"

"I dunno," said Laela. "I mean, it's . . . not easy sometimes."

"Tell me about it." He sounded as if he really was interested. "I have always wanted to know more about your homeland. Tell me about your life there. What it is like for you as a half-breed."

So Laela told him. She told him about the North and about the South, and about how both the races there lived. She told him about the Eyries, and the wars. And she told him about what it was like to be a half-breed in Cymria. He listened and almost never interrupted, only asking a few quiet questions here and there, and she found herself going on, telling him things she had forgotten she knew.

"You love this place," Akhane said when she had finally begun to run out of words. "This land you came from."

"Yeah." Laela smiled. "Yeah, I guess I do."

"I would dearly love to see it one day," Akhane mused. "Perhaps I will come and visit you there."

"Please do," Laela blurted. "I'm sure yeh'd be welcome. I could show yeh everything—the Eyrie, the Hatchery, the Temple . . ."

"I would like that."

Inva had put some wine on the table for them. Laela took some and drank to soothe her dry throat. "So that's about all there is from me," she said, feeling bolder now. "Why don't you tell me about *you* now?"

"Me?" Akhane sounded a little taken aback. "Oh . . . there is not much for me to tell."

"Tell just that, then," said Laela. "I wanna know more about my husband."

"As you wish." Akhane sipped from his own cup, and began. "I was born here in Instabahn, and the Emperor is my father as you know. But the Emperor has five sons, and I am the youngest, born from one of his minor wives. She came from the Maijan Islands, sent over as a gift by her father, who governs one of the islands. I am—was—the only one of the Emperor's sons to be unmarried, and since I am a lowly son, there was no hurry to find a first wife for me."

"What do you do, then?" asked Laela. "Does the Emperor ask yeh to do things for him? Do yeh have duties?"

"Few," said Akhane. "I have no prospect of ever taking the throne, and my duties are purely ceremonial. Most of my brothers are governing the outlying states or fighting in Erebus, but I am the scholarly member of the Imperial Family, and spend most of my time with my books. But I travel as well, to Maijan and even to Erebus. To learn."

"Learn what?" Laela nearly squirmed with excitement—she didn't think she'd even heard of Erebus, which lay even further east than Amoran.

"Everything there is to know," said Akhane. "But I have a great interest in magic and the mysteries of the gods." He drank more wine. "I chase legends, myths, rumours, always searching."

"For what?" Laela was loving every moment of this.

Akhane's brow furrowed slightly. "I am convinced that griffins are not the only living creatures that can use magic. Somewhere in this world, I believe, there are humans who have unnatural powers—perhaps magical, or something beyond even that."

Laela thought of Arenadd. "And what have yeh found?"

"Nothing. Nothing solid. But I will go on searching. Perhaps I should try your own homeland next, do you think?"

His tone was playful, but Laela nodded. "I think there are things in Cymria that might be like what you're lookin' for."

"You do?"

"Yeah, I do."

"Well then, I shall have to come by one day." Akhane stretched, and glanced at the window, where the light was beginning to turn gold and orange. "Now then, there is a more important matter to speak of."

"What's that?" Laela's heart beat faster in anticipation.

"As your new husband, it is traditional that I give you a gift," said Akhane. "On our wedding night, you may name any gift that I can give, and you will have it."

"Oh." The question caught Laela off guard. She looked speculatively around the room, taking in the decorations. "Anything?"

"For you, anything."

"All right, then." Laela pointed. "That's what I want."

Akhane followed her finger. "Her?"

Inva froze.

"Yeah, that's right," said Laela. "I want her. That slave right there."

"Are you certain . . . ?" Akhane looked nonplussed.

"That's all right, isn't it?" said Laela. "Slaves are property. So yeh can give one to me."

"Certainly, but it is a very odd gift to ask for," said Akhane. "She is only one house-slave, and I did not think your people kept slaves—especially not of your own kind."

"We don't," said Laela. "But I ain't keepin' her. I want you t'give her to me, so I can set her free."

Inva hadn't moved, or spoken in all this time. Her face had gone carefully blank.

"And then?" Akhane inquired.

"An' then she can decide what to do," said Laela, raising her voice for Inva's benefit. "But if she wants, I'll take her back home an' give her somewhere to live. That'll be up to her, though."

"Very well, then," said Akhane. "If you want her, she is yours. But one slave is a very modest gift, especially if you do not intend to keep her."

"Agreed," said Laela. "I'll take a hundred."

Akhane broke into a fit of coughing. "One hundred . . . ?"

Laela couldn't help it: She burst out laughing. "All right, I was just jokin'. We'll pay for them."

Akhane managed to stop coughing and laughed as well. "It is fine; I already knew that you and your father were here to bring your kind back to their homeland. We have many darkmen here, spread over the Empire—I doubt anyone knows just how many. It will take a long time and much trading to gather them all, and we will need to find new slaves to replace them before we let them go."

"I know." Laela sighed. "It's hard. But I did this for them, so they could come back to us eventually."

"I understand," said Akhane. "And you understand that I admire you very much for it. Without slaves, your nation will always be small, but you place loyalty to your people before power to your country. If only more countries in this world had that love for humankind. And I will give you one hundred slaves, as you have asked."

Now it was Laela's turn to choke. "What? I mean—*really*?"

"Yes. With my father's help, I will see it done. It will take time, but this one here will go back with you at least. The rest will follow."

Laela kissed him. "Thank you. Thank you so much." She kissed him again.

He looked surprised, but he was quick to kiss her back. "Shall we . . . ?" he said eventually.

Laela kissed him a third time by way of an answer. For the briefest moment, as she held him close, she thought of Yorath. But Yorath was at home, and she was going back to him. Akhane was here right now, and there was a good chance she would never see him again. And she owed him this much at least.

Not that she honestly wanted to do it just for his benefit. She was more than happy to do it for herself as well.

# 28

# The Dark Lady

After what had happened in the Temple, whatever insane will had been keeping Arenadd together disappeared. He woke a few times, briefly, but into a world full of such agony that his mind refused to bear it and no matter how hard he tried to stay awake, he slid back into a half-conscious state where there was no thought, no sight or hearing, and only the vaguest sensation of pain. His mind, set free from the bonds of his ruined body, lost itself in dark dreams and memories, and he drifted away—unable to sense night or day or the passing of time.

Somewhere in the remnants of what had been his thoughts, he knew that he was dying.

He was too far gone to be afraid any more.

The dreams were his world now. He saw Skade; sometimes human, sometimes griffin, but always with a smile in her eyes that was just for him. She flitted here and there through the shadows, holding out a hand—inviting him to join her. Skandar was there, too, screeching defiance at the great light of the relentless sun. And others, too. People he thought he'd forgotten long ago. His old warriors, dead during the war. Arddryn was with them, scowling to herself. Sometimes, she looked like Saeddryn.

And there was a white griffin. She said nothing and never looked at him. Arenadd saw her flying, always away from him, looking for something she had lost.

An egg hatched, and Laela came out of it, but she didn't have
a smile for him now. She wore a black robe, and her brow was
furrowed. She looked much older than he remembered.

Only the Night God was missing. Arenadd wandered alone
through a night without moon or stars, searching for her—
calling her name. But she never came, and no voice answered
his cries. He needed her now, but he knew she wouldn't come.
She knew he had betrayed her.

The dreams went on for a long time, but eventually the day
came when they grew confused. He began to wake up from
them more often, and every time he woke, the pain was a little
less. And the more he woke, the more he began to realise that
the dreams weren't real, that he had another place to belong to,
a *real* place. When he realised that, the part of him that wanted
to wake grew stronger, and he fought to hold on to it. He remembered what had happened, and knew other, far worse things
must be happening even now while he was helpless. Anxiety
worked at him, and only helped him to wake up once again.

His eyes opened at last, and he could see. Paralysed, he
peered at the ceiling above him. It was wooden. There was light,
so it must be day . . . but no, he thought . . . too dim. Coming
from somewhere. *Lantern,* his inner voice said after a fierce
struggle. *Lamp.*

Night, then. He sighed very faintly. Blessed night.

After that, he closed his eyes and slept again.

But he woke again several more times—always at night, and
each time he felt stronger and stayed awake longer.

Little by little, he pieced together that he was in a ship's
cabin—the same cabin he'd lived in on the journey to Amoran.

His mind was painfully sluggish now, but it didn't take him
long to realise that he must be on his way home.

His first feeling was relief. No more blazing sun. No more
strange, dark-skinned sun worshippers. No more Gryphus, glaring down from the sky with hatred.

But relief was quickly followed by guilt and despair. The
slaves. He hadn't freed them. He hadn't completed the alliance
negotiations with the Emperor.

His entire journey and all the suffering it had brought had
been for nothing.

Arenadd closed his eyes again, nursing his pain, and slept.

* * *

Two days later he woke again. The moment he opened his eyes, he felt new strength in his mind and body. He was recovering.

He breathed deeply and turned his head for the first time since his accident.

Laela was there, sitting beside his bed. She wore a light gown, and her expression was guarded.

Arenadd felt his lips twist into a weak smile. "Laela," he rasped.

Laela nodded curtly. "So yeh've come back to us at last, Sire."

"Going . . . home?" Arenadd managed.

"It's the best thing for yeh, Sire," said Laela.

He slumped onto his pillows. "But the slaves . . . the *agreement* . . . I never . . ."

"I took care of it, Sire," said Laela.

Arenadd stared stupidly at her. "What?"

"I said I took care of it," said Laela. She examined her fingernails. "I sealed the deal with the Emperor. The alliance is signed. There are a hundred slaves comin' home with us, an' the Emperor promised the rest would be ready once we'd sent payment."

"Payment?" said Arenadd. "What . . . payment?"

"Goods, mostly," said Laela. "Wool, silver, furs . . . that sort of thing. I bought most of the ones we've got with us now with the treasure from that pirate ship. The Emperor gave me the rest as a present."

Arenadd lay there, quite unable to grasp the magnitude of what she was saying. "But how . . . ?"

"I'm the Master of Wisdom," said Laela. "Second-most senior out of all the Northerners who were in Amoran. With you out of it, Oeka an' me took charge. I did what I thought was best."

"The marriage," Arenadd said eventually. "I didn't . . ."

"Sorted," said Laela. "I did that, too."

Arenadd struggled to raise his head, and gave up. "How?"

"The Emperor's got a son," said Laela. "I married him. It was a very nice wedding."

"You . . . *married* the Emperor's son?"

"Yeah," said Laela. "He ain't comin' North with us. It was more like a formality. The Princess gets t'stay home. But Vander's with us. Him an' Ymazu. They're gonna leave us when we get to Maijan. So that's it, then," she finished, as if it were nothing very important. "I've sorted it all out, an' we can go home. Job done."

Arenadd lay still, breathing rapidly. "You see now," he whispered. "You really are . . . like me." He coughed. "The better side of me."

Laela didn't smile. "I wanted t'ask yeh somethin'. I've been waitin' weeks t'ask it, an' I ain't waitin' any longer."

Arenadd tried to sit up. Instantly, pain crackled through his chest, and he fell back.

"I wouldn't do that if I were you," said Laela. "Yer chest's got a hole as long as my finger right through the middle. I gotta say, though, yer lookin' pretty good for a man who had *this* taken out of him." She took something from a table beside her and held it up.

It was a piece of sword blade, as wide as Arenadd's hand.

"Them Amorani healers are damn good," said Laela. "They couldn't figure out why the wound wouldn't stop bleedin', so they went in there an' had a look, an' sure enough they found this lodged right inside yer rib cage. Looked like it'd been in there a while." Her eyes narrowed. "Ever since the day Erian an' his sister Flell died, I'd guess."

Arenadd stared at the piece of metal. His expression did not change.

"Funny coincidence," Laela went on. "But it's that day I wanted t'ask yeh about." She paused, taking a deep breath. "Flell's child. The one yeh didn't kill."

Arenadd looked away. "I don't want to talk about it."

"I don't care whether yeh want to or not, because you're gonna talk about it now," Laela said coldly. "The child. Yeh said it was still alive somewhere. What'd yeh do with it?"

"Sent it away," Arenadd muttered.

"How? Who with?"

Arenadd closed his eyes. "There was some man there . . . a Southerner . . . had a griffin. He burst in after I . . . after Flell was dead. Saw me by the cradle. I don't know who he was. He pleaded with me not to kill the child. And I . . . I don't know why . . . I listened to him. I didn't know him, but . . . he stopped me. I gave him the child. Told him to take it away, far away, and never come back. I never saw him again."

Laela felt sick. "The man," she said. "Yeh don't know his name?"

"No."

"What did he look like?"

Arenadd's eyes opened. "Big man. About your age. Had a beard." He sighed and the eyes slid closed again. "Funny; I remember him so well . . . remember his voice, anyway. It was strange. He acted like he knew me. I remember how he called to me, and it felt like his voice . . . woke me up, somehow. 'Don't do it,' he said."

At that, Laela lurched forward in her seat. She nearly vomited. *Breathe,* she told herself furiously. *Breathe!*

She breathed deeply, and a strange giddiness came over her. "So yeh still think if yeh ever found the child, yeh'd kill it?"

The eyes opened once again. They were as black and cold as the gemstone around Laela's neck. "Yes."

There was no humour in Laela's smile. "I saw somethin', yeh know," she said. "In the Sun Temple that day. An' it was the same thing I saw once before, in a dream. The first time, I didn't believe it was real. The second time, I didn't believe it, either. But when I talked to Oeka about what happened, I started havin' second thoughts. Turns out while I had that vision, there was somethin' else goin' on—somethin' no-one else could explain. The priest who was there said the same thing. I'm a simple woman, Sire. I've always been that way. I ain't no fancy thinker; I see it, I hear it, I touch it: It's real. But after what happened, even somethin' so fantastic, I don't want to believe it is startin' t'feel a lot like somethin' real. Know what that is?"

Arenadd was watching her with a confused expression. "What are you talking about, Laela?"

"It's Gryphus," she said simply.

He recoiled. "What? No, that's not—"

"—Possible?" said Laela. "Hah. You seem t'believe the Night God's spoken to yeh. I've heard yeh callin' her name plenty of times since yeh've been unconscious. An' now I've seen Gryphus, twice, an' he's told me things I couldn't possibly have known." She looked at him, her blue eyes steady. "An' one of them things is that I'm the child."

Arenadd stared, winced, and laughed. "No. That's not possible."

"My foster dad's name was Bran," Laela said steadily. "Branton Redguard. He was a big man with a beard. He told me my mother was murdered. He said he caught the murderer standin' over my cradle, an' rescued me from him. An' now, thanks to Gryphus, I know that murderer was you."

"No," Arenadd said again. "Flell's child wasn't . . ."

"Flell's child had bright blue eyes," said Laela. "Like her mother. Like her uncle. Like her grandfather, Lord Rannagon. Flell's child came from the line of Baragher the Blessed. I couldn't understand it," she added, "when Gryphus came to me. He said I was blessed, called me his chosen one. He said I was the only one of my line left, the only one . . . with the power to stop you." She looked up, terrible in the firelight. "The only one who could punish the Dark Lord for his crimes."

Arenadd listened. All of a sudden, he looked quite calm. "And what did you tell him, Laela?"

"I said no," said Laela. "I said I didn't believe him. I said it was none of my business what you'd done. I said I didn't know how t'fight yeh, an' I didn't want to do it anyway. Because you were my friend."

"Am I?" said Arenadd, very softly.

Laela fixed him with a stare. "Are yeh?"

Silence—deep, foreboding silence.

"Yeh came into the Temple t'look for me," said Laela. "Into the place where Gryphus was the strongest. Even though yeh had to have known what it would do to yeh. Just t'help me. But tell me, Arenadd—are yeh my friend? Now yeh know who I am, do yeh want t'kill me? Would yeh?"

"No," said Arenadd. He reached out to her, his hand trembling. "No," he said again. "I would never hurt you. Never. Not even if the Night God herself told me to."

"But yeh killed my mother," said Laela. "An' my uncle, an' my grandparents. My entire family, gone. All of them murdered, by you. An' I know yeh loved every moment of it. I *know* yeh did. Don't lie about that, Arenadd. Not now. Not t'me."

"Yes," Arenadd whispered. "I did."

"It's nighttime now," Laela said in conversational tones. "No-one's about. Some sailors on watch, but they'll leave if I tell 'em to. If I tied yeh up an' put some weights in yeh pockets, yeh'd go right t'the bottom of the sea. An' no matter if it killed yeh or not, no-one'd have any chance of findin' yeh. I'd consider that enough punishment for my mother's sake."

"And are you going to do that, Laela?"

"No," said Laela. "I ain't. No matter about my family; I'm part of the North now an' the North needs yeh. The South needs yeh, too. If yeh weren't there t'stop it, yer cousin'd invade the South in a heartbeat. So I'm takin' yeh back there in one piece, an' when we get there, I'm gonna go on workin' for yeh. 'Cause if that's what it takes t'keep my mother's people safe, then I'll do it no matter what."

Arenadd smiled. "I always knew you were a special person, Laela. Now you know it, too."

"Don't think I've forgiven yeh, Arenadd," Laela said sharply. "I ain't ever gonna forgive yeh. I'm gonna stay your follower, an' I'll do my duties, but we ain't friends no more, an' next time yeh feel like pourin' yer heart out, talk to Skandar or the wall or somethin'. Because I ain't doin' it for yeh ever again." She stood up and bowed stiffly. "Get some rest now. I'm gonna go tell everyone yer feelin' better."

Then she left, leaving Arenadd feeling more alone than he could ever have imagined.

Even so, he looked at the door that had closed behind her, and his eyes still had some of their old sly glitter. His plan was working. She had become every bit as ruthless and manipulative as she would have to be. She had learnt far more from him than she could have realised, and one day it would be vital to her.

"You've come into your own now, Laela," he murmured. "I knew you would. You're the Dark Lady through and through."

# 29

# Home

Several more days passed, and the *Seabreath* followed the chain of islands back to Maijan. The further away from Amoran they sailed, the stronger Arenadd felt. His wound finally began to heal again—but at normal, mortal speed. It was enough.

He slept and ate as much as he could, and those mortal nourishments helped him recover. He wondered if his powers would return when he set foot on Northern soil again.

When the ship docked in Maijan, Vander came to see him for what they both knew would be the last time.

The diplomat was plainly dressed and had his messenger dragon perched on his shoulder. He looked as calm and collected as always, but there was a hint of tension in his voice when he said, "How are you feeling this morning, Sire?"

Arenadd could sit up in bed by now. He sipped some water and inclined his head politely toward him. "Much better thank you, my lord. How's your journey been so far?"

"I cannot complain," said Vander.

"And how's Ymazu? I heard she laid her eggs."

"Yes indeed, Sire. Five of them—an unusually large clutch. The Mighty Skandar is the father, of course."

Arenadd raised a sly eyebrow. "You'll have to carry them. I hope you're prepared for that."

"They are not the first clutch Ymazu has had, Sire," Vander said stiffly. "We have carried eggs with us before."

"Of course. But it must have been difficult for you not to have a clutch of your own, so to speak."

"A diplomat's life is often a lonely one, Sire," said Vander. "I have been longing to settle down for many years now."

"Every man needs a place to call home," said Arenadd. "And someone to share it with makes it feel like one."

"Yes." Vander scratched the dragon's ears, and finally smiled. "For what my advice is worth, Sire, I think you would do well to keep your Master of Wisdom close. You will not find a better advisor or a better friend if you live for a hundred years."

"I know." Arenadd smiled, too. "She's something very special."

Vander chuckled. "You are no ordinary man, either, Sire. You know," he added unexpectedly, "I pride myself on my ability to judge a person's nature, and my memory is superb. But even so, you still managed to surprise me, Sire."

"Oh, how?" said Arenadd.

"When I saw you again, after so many years, I was astonished by how much you had changed," said Vander. "I barely recognised the boy I met in Eagleholm once upon a time. But now I see I was wrong." He smiled and smoothed his moustache. "Underneath, you are still the same mischief-maker you were then. Oh yes, I knew your reputation in Eagleholm. Every man in the city said you were very thoughtful and quiet; not the sort of man who would make trouble. You did your duty and never challenged authority, you were very gifted at talking to commoners. You were not a fighter, you were good with books and numbers." He laughed softly. "But everybody knew how the mild-mannered Northern boy they looked down on was bedding Lord Rannagon's daughter."

Arenadd froze.

"It was a scandal, you know," said Vander. "Few could understand why Lord Rannagon had not moved to put a stop to it. But the Lady Flell would tell anyone who asked that she loved you. Now that was a fine way to irritate the Eyrie Council!"

"Yes," Arenadd managed. "I . . . I suppose. Now, I'm tired . . ."

"Of course, Sire," said Vander. "Forgive an old man his

reminiscences." He bowed low, murmuring, "Farewell, Arren Cardockson."

Then he was gone, and Arenadd never saw him again.

Weeks passed after Vander left, and the *Seabreath* and its new companion—the former pirate ship *Serene*—sailed back toward Tara with all speed. Gradually, week by week, the heat grew less and less. And with every week, Arenadd felt better. After a month he was strong enough to walk again. Another week after that he was up on deck, talking to the griffiners and sailors and training Laela in the art of the sickle.

But he spent most of his time with Skandar. The dark griffin had refused to live belowdecks any more, and instead slept in the open, by one of the masts. He'd made himself a nest there with straw and some stolen washing, and spent his time sleeping, eating, or idly flying overhead with the other griffins. He was more than happy to see Arenadd, though.

If their time in Amoran had weakened Arenadd, it looked to have had the opposite effect on Skandar. When Arenadd saw him again after emerging from his cabin for the first time, the giant griffin practically shone with lazy good health. His coat was glossy and his eyes bright, and his sides were thick with solid muscle and more than a little fat. He'd spent their entire visit to Amoran doing nothing but eating, fighting, and mating, and it showed.

Arenadd found he had almost nothing to say to him. Skandar, never talkative, seemed happy enough just to have him there, and the two sat silently together for long periods, neither speaking nor needing to speak.

Arenadd would stare out over the sea, his expression serene. When Laela was near, he would watch her. He never tried to speak to her, and she pretended he wasn't there.

Once, in the evening while the sailors were in a cheerful mood and had decided to play some music, Laela and Oeka were up on deck and began to play together. Oeka, who'd grown a lot since leaving the North, nipped at her human's hands and shoved at her—inviting her to play. Laela pushed back, and they wrestled and chased each other around the deck while the sailors laughed.

Arenadd sat with his back resting against Skandar's flank, and kept his eyes on Laela. She looked happier than he'd seen her in a long while. Her long hair fell around her face, black and glossy, and her angular features were alight with laughter.

*Gods, how could I not have seen it?*

It wasn't the first time he had thought that.

T he final weeks of their journey home passed peacefully enough, and Laela felt immensely relieved when she felt the air begin to grow steadily colder. Tara's shore was thick with snow when it came in sight, and chunks of ice floated in the sea.

"My first Northern winter," she remarked to Oeka.

The griffin sighed and wrapped her tail around her paws. "I hate snow."

Laela understood her almost perfectly by now, and only smiled.

Skandar had already flown on ahead and landed on the beach, and he was waiting for his human when he disembarked. Arenadd put a hand on his shoulder. He'd taken to using a walking stick again, and he pointed it at Duach. "The Mighty Skandar and I are going back to Malvern, and Lady Laela and Oeka are coming with us. I want you to stay here and organise transport for our new citizens. Feed them well, get clothes for them. Keep them warm."

Some of the slaves had already come off their ship. Arenadd had personally removed their collars, and their hair had begun to grow back, but they still looked strange. They huddled together, staring blankly at this new land they found themselves in.

"They ain't so different from how I was, once," Laela remarked to Arenadd.

"They're not so different from how I was, either," said Arenadd.

Laela smiled at him for the first time in months. "They'll find a way t'live. They're Northerners, after all, an' if we survived, so can they."

Skandar nudged her heavily in the back. "Come," he rumbled. "Come now. I carry."

Arenadd climbed onto his partner's back, and helped Laela up behind him.

Oeka watched resignedly. "I am nearly large enough to carry you."

Laela caught the hint of resentment, and smiled inwardly. "There's no hurry."

Oeka rasped noncommittally, and took off a few moments after Skandar.

Skandar flew over the vast snowy reaches of his kingdom, his wings beating powerfully. Below, everything was white, darkened by trees and the occasional brown cluster of houses. To Laela, it looked like a country she'd never seen before—as strange to her now as Amoran had been.

*But it's my country,* she thought. *I'll make my home here again.*

She and Arenadd spent the rest of the journey back to Malvern close together—flying on Skandar's back during the day, and sharing their quarters at night. But it was a joyless kind of closeness. They rarely spoke to each other unless it was necessary—Laela talked to Oeka, and Arenadd didn't speak at all. He seemed less upset than preoccupied; Laela often caught him fixing her with a penetrating stare, as if he were looking for something. She pretended not to notice.

And then, finally—Malvern.

Skandar saw its walls approaching first. He opened his beak and sent out a ferocious screech, sending his own name ahead of him. A little while later, he screeched again, and again, as Malvern drew closer. By the time he reached it, the griffins circling over the towers had long since heard him. They began to gather, flying out to meet their lord.

Skandar screeched again at the sight of them. It was a sound full of challenge, but none of the oncoming griffins answered it. They circled and flew behind him, riding on his slipstream back toward the Eyrie. He'd been away a long time, but they still recognised him as their master.

Skandar flew straight to the Council Tower and landed on its wide, flat top. The human inhabitants had had plenty of warning, and by the time his talons had touched stone, Saeddryn was already there, with Aenae, and Iorwerth and his partner Kaanee were with her. The other councillors were just arriving.

Arenadd slid off Skandar's back. He landed awkwardly and nearly fell, catching himself by grabbing his partner's wing.

Laela got down, too, and quickly handed him his walking stick. He took it and leant on it while Skandar went forward to meet his son and the other griffins there.

Kaanee bent his forelegs and put his head down, displaying the vulnerable back of his neck to Skandar in a sign of submission. The other griffins did likewise, and Skandar acknowledged it with a quick huff through his beak.

Aenae faced his father arrogantly, with his head held high. He was a head shorter than him, and not as powerfully built, but he was bigger than Kaanee.

Skandar's feathers puffed outward, making him look even larger. He opened his wings, holding them above his own head, and hissed.

Incredibly, Aenae didn't back down. He raised his own wings and hissed back, his tail twitching like an angry cat's.

Skandar's hiss swung around into a snarl. He rose up and hit his son hard across the face, throwing him to the ground. Aenae landed on his belly and stayed there. Blood glistened on his feathers. Skandar stood over him, huffing his aggression.

Very slowly, Aenae got up. He made no sound, and only bowed his head.

Skandar rasped in satisfaction, and turned his back on his son with a dismissive flick of his tail. "Am home. Am master."

Arenadd laughed rather unpleasantly. "Getting ideas above your station isn't a good idea when Skandar's about. Now." He limped toward Saeddryn, leaning on his stick. "Dear cousin, you look younger every day."

Saeddryn smiled and bowed to him. "Welcome home, Sire."

Iorwerth bowed, too. "It's good to see ye home, Sire. We've already begun preparing a feast in yer honour."

Arenadd inclined his head. "I'd love that. Thank you, Iorwerth."

The Master of War had obviously been expecting a refusal, and he looked pleased. "So tell us, Sire—how was Amoran, and the Emperor? An' how are ye?"

"The visit went well," said Arenadd. "We got everything we were hoping for. But we have Laela to thank for that."

Iorwerth smiled with genuine warmth at her. "Lady Laela, forgive me. Ye look well."

Laela nodded to him. "Iorwerth. Same thing to yeh."

"So the slaves have been freed?" Saeddryn interrupted.

"Yeah, they have," said Laela. "We both saw t'that. Arenadd an' me, I mean."

"There's no need to be so modest, Laela," said Arenadd. He turned to Saeddryn and Iorwerth. "I had . . . an accident, while we were in Amoran. It was none of the Emperor's fault—it was nobody's fault. But while I was unwell, Laela completed the treaty and bought our brothers and sisters their freedom. We've brought a hundred of them with us, and the rest will follow."

Iorwerth laughed aloud. "Ahah! I knew it, Sire! I knew we'd see them come back! An' Lady Laela was behind it, ye say?"

"Yeah, I was," said Laela. She shrugged. "I was only doin' my duty t'the King an' to our friends."

"The first group of them are on their way here now," said Arenadd. "But we'll discuss that later. For now, we all need rest."

"Then I shall see ye later," said Saeddryn.

Arenadd caught Iorwerth as he started to leave, and muttered something to him. Iorwerth nodded back, and a moment later they were both walking off as if nothing had happened.

Laela had seen it. She frowned, then shook her head and walked off after Oeka, deciding that she was too tired to wonder about it for the time being.

She didn't know whether to be surprised or disturbed to find that her room hadn't changed at all since she'd last seen it. Someone had obviously been in to clean it up and put fresh sheets on the bed, and there was a bath ready and a good fire in the grate, but this could have been her room at the end of an ordinary day—not after more than nine months away.

She yawned and stripped off her clothes before climbing into the tub, while Oeka went into her nest.

The hot water felt good. Laela sighed and relaxed into it, feeling it soothe her sore muscles. She actually fell asleep, and woke up to find the water cold. Shivering, she gave herself a cursory wash and got out. There was a new, warm woollen gown waiting for her on the bed. She put it on, her mind suddenly full of one person.

Yorath.

Laela realised that she hadn't thought about him in ages.

Guilt made her shiver. Poor old Yorath. Did he still miss her? Was he waiting now, expecting her to come and see him?

The guilt only lasted briefly, though, before she started thinking of the feast instead. The thought of food made her stomach gurgle, and she sighed to herself and pulled on her boots before going to fetch Oeka. The griffin was awake, and just as eager to go—though more to find out what had been happening while they'd been away.

Outside, a passing servant told them the feast was being held on top of the Council Tower, where celebrations usually were.

Sure enough, when Laela emerged into the open air, she found herself surrounded by the sounds of music and laughter. People and griffins were everywhere, mingling freely. Night had come by now, and long, metal stakes holding torches lit up the place. A group of musicians were playing, and tables had been set up and laden with food.

Some of the feasters were sitting down, but plenty were walking around freely. A few people were even dancing.

Oeka saw the carcasses that had been laid out for the griffins. "I will go and eat now, Laela," she said. "Go—find food for yourself. Enjoy yourself!" she added. "We are home, and all is well. This is our night."

Laela nodded vaguely and wandered off among the crowd. She stopped at the nearest table and helped herself to a slab of bread covered in hot venison, and some cheese, roasted carrots, and a toffee-coated apple to follow. The finest mead, all the way from Fruitsheart, had been brought out, and she gulped down a mugful. It warmed her up and made her feel better, so she had another one.

"Gods, I needed that." She sighed.

Without any warning, a man appeared to her right. He shouted something at her in the dark tongue, and clapped her hard on the shoulder.

Laela almost hit him before she realised he was being friendly. "Hullo," she said, using griffish.

The man grinned and held out a hand. "Sorry," he said. "Had a little too much t'drink."

Laela linked fingers with him and gave the traditional tug. "I understand that just fine," she said. "I'm plannin' t'have too much myself, in fact."

The man laughed loudly. "That's the spirit. Name's Dewitt. My dad's the Master of Building."

"Pleased t'meet yeh," Laela said politely.

"I'm more than pleased t'meet ye, my lady," said Dewitt. "I'm honoured."

Laela laughed awkwardly. "I ain't nobody special."

"Ye freed the slaves, my lady," said Dewitt, completely serious now. "I heard the whole story."

"I did my duty," said Laela.

Dewitt looked keenly at her. "Yer duty to who, though?"

"To the North," said Laela.

He grinned. "Thought ye'd say that. Well, I've got more drinkin' to do, so if ye'll excuse me . . ."

Laela let him go and refilled her own mug before wandering off through the crowd. To her surprise, more than one person stopped her to say similar things as Dewitt. They called her by her title now, all of them. Lady Laela. There were no suspicious looks or half-hidden sneers.

Laela, by now a little drunk, ran into Arenadd almost without realising it. He had been talking quietly to someone, and when he saw her, his expression faltered for an instant before he relaxed again. "Laela, there you are," he said. "We were just talking about you."

Laela nodded briefly to him. "Sire."

The person Arenadd had been talking to was a woman—and Laela was surprised when she recognised her. It was Aderyn—the priestess who had first begun to teach her about the Night God.

Tonight, Aderyn was wearing a fine silver gown, and she looked at Laela with open admiration. "So here ye are," she said. "Home triumphant, eh, my lady?"

Laela smiled at her. "Hullo. By the Night God, I'm surprised t'see yeh here. How've yeh been?"

"I've been well," said Aderyn. "But not as well as ye, by the sound of it. The King tells me ye did us all a great service in Amoran."

"My duty," Laela said automatically.

"A great service," said Aderyn. "To the King, to the North, to the darkmen—an' so to the Night God herself."

Laela grunted noncommittally. The idea of doing anything for a god didn't appeal to her much now.

"So Aderyn and I have decided," Arenadd cut in. "Tell her, Aderyn."

"Yes, Sire." Aderyn folded her hands over her stomach. "We've decided it's high time ye were welcomed into the Night God's arms, Laela."

Laela's insides lurched slightly. "What d'yeh mean by that?"

"That it's time for the womanhood ceremony," said Aderyn.

"Oh."

"We've decided the Crow tribe is right for ye," the priestess went on. "So yer own ceremony must happen on the night of the new moon—an' it'll be a while before that happens!" She chuckled and pointed at the sky. "See how bright the Night God's eye is tonight. I've never seen it so big. She must know great things are happening down here."

Laela followed her hand, and gasped. The moon was enormous. Tinged with gold, it sat on the horizon like a massive . . .

. . . eye.

Laela shivered. "Is it meant t'do that?"

"It's happened before," said Arenadd. "It's a sign that the Night God is watching very closely." He kept his eyes on the moon as he spoke, and Laela caught just a hint of unease in his voice. "Very closely," he said again, more quietly.

"Well," said Aderyn. "What do ye think, my lady? Are ye ready for it?"

"I suppose so," said Laela, without enthusiasm.

"Good. Then I'll take it up with the High Priestess. I'm sure she'll be happy t'ask the Crow priestess to conduct the ceremony."

"Yeah." Laela took another swallow from her mug and muttered a quick "Excuse me" before walking off.

She didn't want to think about the Night God now. She didn't want to think of Gryphus, either. Once upon a time, she'd been more or less indifferent to the whole idea of gods, but now they made her feel sick and frightened. She was tired of it all.

She distracted herself with another drink and some more food. It left her stomach feeling warm and wonderful, and she relaxed again.

Laughter rose from the crowd nearby, and Laela stopped and

watched as Penllyn staggered away, helping a visibly drunk
Saeddryn. She laughed, and only laughed again more loudly at
how Aenae primly ignored the jokes being thrown at him.

Saeddryn's gown was a mess, and the silver circlet with the
crescent moon she wore was askew. She muttered some half-
coherent curse, before Penllyn led her away through the trapdoor and down into the tower.

Laela took a swig of mead and snickered to herself. She
hoped Oeka hadn't missed it.

She turned, hoping to see her around, and froze when her eye
caught someone else. He had seen her, too, and now he was
coming toward her.

"Yorath."

Yorath had grown a beard. It made him look older, more
mature and reserved. "Laela."

They stood awkwardly, neither one willing to speak.

"How have yeh been?" Laela said eventually.

Yorath smiled, but it was a careful smile. "I've been . . . well,
my lady."

"Don't call me that, Yorath," said Laela.

"I have to," said Yorath. "Ye're a lady now."

There was another awkward silence.

"I heard about the Amorani prince," said Yorath. "I'm happy
for ye. Really."

"What?" Laela started. "No, Yorath—stop. It wasn't like
that."

"Really? How wasn't it? My lady."

"I never even slept with him, Yorath," Laela lied. "He didn't
come back with us. It was just a marriage of convenience. The
Emperor wouldn't let us seal the deal with him without it. It's
an Amorani custom."

"Oh." Yorath's face was blank.

"I had t'do it," said Laela, not sure whom she was trying to
convince. "Sometimes the realm comes before we do."

"Exactly," said Yorath.

Laela watched him unhappily. He wasn't angry with her, not
really. For her part, she didn't know what to say or how she felt.

"Well," said Yorath. "I'm . . . I think I'll go and get something to eat if that's all right with ye, my lady."

Laela searched desperately for something to say. Something,

anything. Something to reach out to him, to show him she still . . .

. . . still what?

Yorath took her silence as permission and walked away.

Laela, watching him go, tried to convince herself that she was upset.

But she wasn't. No matter how hard she tried, she felt nothing. It was as if Yorath were a stranger to her now. She'd enjoyed her time with him, but now it was over and there was nothing she could do.

The last of the enjoyment had gone out of the evening. Laela finished her drink, put the mug down on a table, and wandered off. She needed to get back to her room and sleep off the mead, and hopefully it would all look clearer in the morning.

She couldn't see Oeka anywhere, so she shrugged and went down through the trapdoor. It was warmer inside, and she stumped off down the sloped corridor and into the tower proper.

As she was passing a door, she heard the faint sound of a voice. She paused to listen, and grinned to herself. It was Saeddryn. No doubt the High Priestess was doing what Bran had always called "lettin' the drink do the talkin'."

Laela pressed herself against the door and listened.

That was when she realised there was more than one voice.

# 30

# Under the Watching Moon

The voices were speaking griffish. Even though Laela knew the language fairly well by now, here it was being spoken fast and fluently—and coming through a thick door—and she struggled to keep up.

". . . supposed to come back!" This was Saeddryn's voice.

"Did . . . could . . . try." A second voice. It was a man's, but Laela didn't think she recognised it.

". . . didn't try hard enough!" Saeddryn's higher voice carried more.

There was a sound of footsteps, as one of the speakers moved closer to the door. Laela started away instinctively, but returned when she heard the man's voice, more clearly this time. "He went right into the Sun Temple!" he said. "I did everythin' to goad him into it, and Seerae kept the Mighty Sk—"

"Shut up!" Saeddryn came closer, too. "Do ye want the whole Eyrie t'know?"

"Well, ye can forget tryin' again," the man snapped back. "It's impossible. The Night God is watchful and protective."

Silence.

"I know the Night God," Saeddryn said at last. "Don't ye dare question her will!"

"I'm sorry, Holy One," said the man. "But in all honesty, how d'ye expect us to ever succeed? With the Mighty Skandar there, nobody could ever—"

Something huge shifted its bulk on the other side of the door.

"I shall take care of my father," said another voice. A griffin's voice.

"There shall be no faltering," a fourth voice agreed. Another griffin. "I shall see my mother avenged."

"But how?" Saeddryn, a note of despair in her voice. *"How?"*

"Do not despair," said the first griffin. *Aenae,* Laela thought. "He has returned weakened. And he need not be killed at all. As long as the people believed it . . . how would they know he was not dead when he was put into his tomb?"

*They're gonna kill him,* Laela thought, quite calmly. *They want t'kill Arenadd. And Skandar, too.*

"Yes," Saeddryn muttered. "Of course! I've seen him rendered unconscious many times—put a dagger in his heart and leave it there, and he won't wake. If we could . . ."

"He saved our whole country," the man said coldly. "And ye're talkin' about burying him alive."

"But what else can we *do*?" said Saeddryn.

"If he could be persuaded to—"

"I already tried that! All of us tried it! He wouldn't listen! I know he did great things for us, but it's time this land moved on. Or would ye prefer to sit back and do nothing while we make treaties with *sun worshippers*?"

Laela moved away from the door. *I've stayed here way too long,* she thought.

She had. As she turned to leave as quietly as she could, the door opened. There was a shout, and before she could do anything someone had grabbed her by the shoulder. She didn't struggle as she was dragged into the room and hurled down.

Saeddryn stood over her. She looked furious, and a lot less drunk than she'd seemed. *"Half-breed!"* she snarled.

Laela stood up and brushed herself off as coolly as she could. "Lady Saeddryn." She looked toward the man who'd been with her, and nodded. "An' Lord Penllyn."

Aenae started up furiously, raising his talons. "You were listening!" he hissed. He looked very much like his father in that moment.

"Yeah, I was listenin'," said Laela. "Seems you lot've got somethin' t'learn about secrecy."

"What are we going t'do now?" said Penllyn.

"Kill her," said Aenae. "I will make sure that there are no remains."

"I think I got a better idea," Laela said hastily.

"And what is that?" demanded Seerae—Penllyn's griffin.

"Let me join yeh," said Laela. "Help yeh. I'm the one the King trusts most; I could be the answer to yer prayers."

"The King gave ye everything," said Saeddryn. "Why would ye want to betray him?"

Laela snarled at her. "Because he murdered my mother," she said. "That's why."

"What?" Penllyn's eyes widened. "When? How d'ye know?"

"I'm a half-breed," said Laela. "My mother was a Southerner, then, wasn't she? An' the King killed her, with his own hands. He killed my uncle, too, an' my grandparents. My whole family. Don't yeh think I want revenge for that?"

"Ye could have taken it this whole time," said Saeddryn. "An' if ye knew that, why did ye join with him in the first place? Why did ye save him from the river?"

"I was bidin' my time," said Laela. "Waitin' until I was as close to him as I could get. Doin' everythin' to make him trust me."

"But why rescue him?" said Saeddryn.

Laela thought of Gryphus. "I wanted him t'die on my terms," she said. "That's why."

Penllyn still looked nervous and suspicious, but Aenae had retracted his talons. "Perhaps we can make use of her," he said.

There was a glitter in Saeddryn's eyes that made her look very much like her cousin. "It seems we have a common goal, then, Lady Laela."

"Yeah, we do," said Laela. "But don't think I'm trustin' yeh until yeh let me out of here."

"Of course." Saeddryn stood aside, leaving the path to the door clear. "Go, then. I'll think on what ye've said, an' send a message when the time is right."

"Right." Laela nodded to her and strode away, aware of Aenae's stare on the back of her neck all the while.

When she was out of the room, it took a strong effort not to run. She did her best to look as calm as possible and walked rapidly away back up the corridor the way she'd come.

She reached the top of the tower again without any trouble.

By now, the feast was starting to wind down; most of the food was gone, and the guests along with it. Laela walked rapidly toward the other edge of the tower, looking for Arenadd.

But Skandar wasn't there, and she knew that Arenadd would be with him. Laela swung around and went back toward the trapdoor, her heart pattering frantically.

"*Laela!*" The cry came from above, and something big rushed straight at her.

Laela screamed.

"Laela! *Laela!* Do not do that!"

"Oeka!" Laela clutched at her chest. "Don't ever do that again!"

"Sorry." Oeka dipped her head briefly. "I was looking for you. Where have you been?"

"I went inside," said Laela. "Did yeh see where Arenadd went?"

"The Mighty Skandar has gone back to his nest, and his human with him," said Oeka.

"Then that's where we're goin'."

"Why?" Oeka complained. "I am tired, and I have eaten too much; I want to sleep."

"Later," said Laela. "This is important."

"What is it?" said Oeka.

Laela was already going inside. "I've got somethin' to tell Arenadd, an' I need you with me."

"Of course I will stay with you," said Oeka.

Arenadd's chambers were directly below the feast. Laela went into the audience chamber, noting the lack of any guards. At the far end of it, she knocked on Arenadd's door.

No-one answered.

She knocked again, harder. "Arenadd! Arenadd, it's me!"

The door opened, and there he was, still dressed and looking slightly surprised. "Laela. What's wrong?"

She pushed past him and into the bedchamber. "Are yeh alone?"

"Aside from Skandar. He's probably asleep right now. Laela, what's going on? You look frantic."

Laela pulled herself together. "Arenadd, it's yer cousin. I heard her, with Penllyn an' their griffins."

"What?" Oeka pushed in. "What is this, Laela?"

"Saeddryn's plottin' against yeh, Arenadd," said Laela. "Plannin' t'kill yeh! She's—"

"—not even slightly surprised," said a voice.

Laela turned. "You!"

Saeddryn stood in the doorway, her arms folded. "See, this is what I told ye from the start, Sire. Never trust a half-breed. They're half one way an' half another. Which half are ye going to trust?"

"Yeh followed me here!" Laela accused.

"Of course. Ye didn't think I was going t'trust ye that easily, did ye?"

"Well, it's too late," said Laela. "Arenadd knows now, an' you're dead." She glanced at Arenadd, to see how he was taking it.

Arenadd watched as Saeddryn stood aside and Aenae came in after her. Quickly, he crossed the room and took something from his desk. He stuffed it into his robe, and then turned to face his cousin. "Well," he said. "You *finally* decided to make your move, did you, Saeddryn?"

Saeddryn froze. "What's that supposed to mean?"

Arenadd sighed. "You really thought I didn't know what you were up to, didn't you? After all these years, you still underestimate me."

"I don't know what ye're talking about," said Saeddryn.

Arenadd stood very still in the firelight, seeming to grow taller every moment. "No-one can creep up on the Shadow That Walks. No-one can kill him. No-one can withstand him. Did you really think you could outmanouevre me, Saeddryn? Defeat me? You, a mortal?"

"I've seen ye defeated before, Sire," said Saeddryn.

"And you've seen me outlast and destroy everyone who ever did," said Arenadd. "Haven't you?"

Saeddryn drew herself up. "Tara needs a new ruler, Arenadd," she said. "It has done for years."

Arenadd paused. "I agree."

Penllyn appeared, coming to join Saeddryn. "Then ye'll step down?" he said.

"Yes."

"*No!*" Laela went to Arenadd, taking him by the arm. "Arenadd, no!"

Arenadd grinned horribly at Saeddryn. "If you want this Kingdom so badly, cousin, then have it. But listen to me and remember this forever: I will never leave this land again. One day you'll die. Every day your death comes closer. But I will be here until the end of time."

"I know," said Saeddryn. "An' that's why we have to do this. I'm sorry." She stood aside, and Aenae charged, straight at him.

Laela screamed.

But Arenadd only laughed. He put his arm around Laela, holding her tightly to his chest, and stepped sideways, into the shadows.

Aenae's charge came up short. He ran into the fireplace and stumbled backward, shaking his head and snorting. Saeddryn ran forward to the spot where Arenadd had been and thrust an arm into the shadows, trying to find him.

There was no sign of him anywhere.

Saeddryn screamed. "*Damn him!* Penllyn, get out of here! Alert everyone. I want him found. We have to finish this, *now*."

Aenae rubbed his head against his flank, cleaning off the ashes. "Do what you choose," he hissed, rising again and stepping toward the archway into Skandar's nest. "I will finish my own battle tonight."

A small brown shape stepped in front of him.

Aenae paused. "Move, little griffin, or die."

Oeka hissed softly. "You will not hurt my human, or her master."

Aenae said nothing. He lifted one huge forepaw, and brought it down on Oeka's head.

Oeka closed her eyes. An instant later, her entire body went rigid.

Laela was terrified. She didn't know where she was or what was happening. Everything around her had plunged into icy blackness, as if she'd gone blind. All she could feel was Arenadd's arms, holding her tightly to his chest. Laela struggled, but a terrible strength had filled the King's body. His chest felt as hard and cold as stone, and when she pushed against his arms, they didn't move even slightly. She was utterly helpless.

The darkness seemed to rush past them, full of cold wind

and howling voices. Laela didn't know where they were, but she knew they were travelling. Somewhere.

Then, as quickly as it had begun it was over. The darkness disappeared, fading into ordinary night. Arenadd let go of her, and she staggered away, gasping.

"What was that? What happened? Where is this?"

It took her a few moments to calm down enough to realise they were in a perfectly ordinary alleyway. It looked as if it was somewhere in the city.

Arenadd leaned against a wall and looked up at the sky. "Relax," he said. "We're safe."

The moon still felt unnaturally bright. Laela could see Arenadd perfectly. "Where's Oeka?"

"I don't know. But don't worry; she can look after herself."

"What *was* that?" said Laela. "That . . . darkness."

Arenadd shrugged. "I took you through the shadows," he said. "It was the best way to escape. We're in the city."

"The shadows? Is that yer power?" Laela was shaken.

"Yes," said Arenadd. "I've got it back now, it seems." He breathed deeply. "Gods, that felt good. No—stop!" Laela had started to walk toward the end of the alley.

"Don't go out there," said Arenadd. "Just stay here for a bit. We can't risk being seen."

"Why are we here?" said Laela. "Saeddryn's—why did we leave? Why ain't we goin' back? She's a traitor; she ought t'be in a cell by now!"

"We're waiting for Skandar," said Arenadd, ignoring her. "He'll find us soon enough."

After that, he refused to say anything and only kept his eyes on the sky.

Eventually, Skandar did indeed find them. Laela saw him flying overhead, and Arenadd sent out a call to him.

Moments later, the giant griffin landed. He was dishevelled and looked furious. "Why you here?" he demanded.

Arenadd went close to him, speaking rapidly in griffish.

Eventually, Skandar calmed down. "Go, then," he said.

Arenadd got onto his back and leant down, offering a hand. "Get on," he said. "Hurry."

Laela glanced back, toward where the Eyrie rose high

against the night sky. But she knew she couldn't go back there without him. She didn't trust anyone else there, not any more.

The moment she was on Skandar's back, the giant griffin took off with a lurch and a flick of his wings.

Laela had thought they were going back to the Eyrie. But they weren't. Skandar turned himself and flew away from it— away from the city. The walls passed beneath them, and they were flying over open country. And still they kept going.

Skandar flew over a river. Ahead, a second river gleamed silver in the moonlight; between them was nothing but forest. A little further southward the two rivers met, and that was where he landed, touching down in a small clearing where the moon- light made the snow look like crushed diamonds.

Laela landed and nearly slipped over. She clamped her hands under her arms and hugged herself tight; it was freezing. "What in the gods' names are we doin' here?"

Arenadd stood beside Skandar. His eyes were on the sky. "Laela, listen . . ."

"I ain't gonna listen to nothin' except the truth!" Laela blazed. "What's goin' on? Why've we come here? We've got t'go back, now, an' stop Saeddryn!"

Arenadd finally turned his gaze on her. "She has followers, Laela. Plenty of them. And supporters in the city."

"So?"

"The High Priestess is extremely powerful," said Arenadd. "I rule the body, but she rules the soul. People believe that the Night God speaks through her. If I moved against her now, it would mean civil war."

Laela couldn't believe what she was hearing. "She's a traitor! If people knew that . . . An' what's wrong with that, anyway? Since when were you scared of fightin'? I thought that's what yeh wanted."

"Human right!" Skandar interrupted. "Aenae enemy. Know it already. Fight enemy! Kill!"

*"Not against Northerners!"* said Arenadd. "No. Skandar, *no*. I will not fight my own people. I will not fight my own cousin."

"Then you fool!" said Skandar.

"Skandar's right," said Laela. "If yeh don't fight Saeddryn, yeh'll lose yer Kingdom. An' if she gets t'be in charge, she'll attack the South right away. I know it."

Arenadd looked upward again. "The moon's still bright," he muttered. "She's watching me. Watching me close now. She knows . . ."

"What're yeh talkin' about?" said Laela. "Who knows? Knows what?"

"I don't have much time." Arenadd came toward her. "Laela, I have to tell you something important."

"What tell?" Skandar rasped. "Not time talk, time fight!" He leant to the side, offering his shoulder. "Come. Come now. Come fly. We fight, like before."

"No." Arenadd backed away from him. "Skandar, no. I won't. My fighting days are done."

Skandar stood up straight, furious now. "Then *I* fight!" he said, and with that he ran away and hurled himself into the sky.

"Hey!" Laela took a few steps toward the edge of the clearing, staring helplessly skyward as the dark griffin disappeared.

"He'll be back," Arenadd said wearily, from behind her.

Laela turned. "What was that all about? Now we're stranded!"

"He'll come back," Arenadd repeated. "He always does. Laela, listen. *Please* listen."

"Fine," said Laela. "I'm listenin'. Why're yeh so jumpy?"

"We're being watched," said Arenadd. "Look."

Laela looked where he was pointing and saw the moon. It hung directly overhead now, and if it had looked huge before, it was massive now. It looked as if it could fall on them at any moment. "What the . . . ?"

"It's my master," said Arenadd. "She's watching. She knows."

"Knows what?" said Laela, not looking away from the moon.

"That I've betrayed her," Arenadd said softly.

"Betrayed her?" said Laela. "How?"

"In everything," said Arenadd. "I promised to invade the South, but I didn't. I made a treaty with sun worshippers. I found you at last, but I didn't kill you. And she knows."

Laela began to feel frightened then, more than she ever had before. "But she can't do anythin' to us, can she?"

Arenadd laughed bitterly. "She can do anything she likes with me. I belong to her. You'll see." He stopped suddenly. His good fist clenched, and a cold shiver went through him.

Laela moved closer. "Arenadd? What's wrong?"

He groped for her hand and held it. "I feel . . ."

The moonlight was wrong. It shone down on the snow, painfully bright at first, but then brighter and brighter, impossibly strong. The snow shone with it, like a million tiny mirrors, and before long, the entire clearing had turned pure white.

Laela looked upward, and horror filled her soul.

In the sky, the moon was fading. Its light dimmed as the clearing grew brighter, and it shrank, moving through all its phases in a heartbeat until it was gone altogether.

But it wasn't gone. All of its light was in the clearing now.

Laela couldn't see. She shut her eyes tightly, unable to look at the light, and held on to Arenadd's hand.

The light faded, just a little. When Laela opened her eyes again, the clearing was full of mist, and it gathered itself up like the fog in the Temple. And like that fog, it made a shape.

The shape of a tall woman. A Northern woman. Her features were hard and cold, and sharp. She wore nothing but a light silver mantle that left most of her body bare, but she showed no sign of feeling the cold at all.

In one hand she held a sickle. In the other was the full moon, somehow no larger than the blank hole in her face, where her eye should have been.

The Night God held the moon, cupping her hand around it so that its light shone through her fingers. But her single pitch-black eye was on Arenadd.

The King of Tara let go of Laela's hand, and fell to his knees. "Master," he breathed.

The Night God stepped forward, leaving no tracks in the snow. *Arenadd,* she said, and her voice wasn't so much loud as unbearable, so full of power it hurt to hear it.

Arenadd did not look up. "Master, I—"

The terrible eye turned toward Laela. She quailed and fell to her knees, unable to say anything.

*Arenadd, why have you betrayed me?*

He looked up now. "I did what was best for my people."

*What is best for my people is what I command,* said the
Night God. *Are you a fool, Arenadd? Has drink rotted your
mind so much?*

Arenadd stood up slowly. "No, Master," he said. "My mind
is clear. What I did was for the best."

The Night God's light brightened again, searingly. *You dare
place yourself above me, little shadow?*

"I did what my heart told me." Arenadd sneered at the irony.

*You knew what the consequences were,* said the Night God.
*You knew that you faced your doom if you did not obey.*

"Yes, I knew."

*Yet you disobeyed me all the same.*

"Yes."

The Night God sighed. *Do you still wish to serve me?*

"I serve my people," said Arenadd.

*Then serve them now,* said the Night God. The sickle rose,
pointing straight at Laela. *Kill her.*

Laela got up and tried to run, but the mist still filled the
clearing, and she couldn't escape from it. She was trapped. "*No!*
Let me go!"

Arenadd turned to look at her. "Master . . ."

*Do it,* said the Night God. *You know what she is. She must
be killed.*

Arenadd didn't move. "But I—"

*Kill her!* the Night God repeated. *Kill her, and your sins will
be forgiven. Kill her, and you shall have your Kingdom back.
Kill her, and all will be well.*

Laela didn't dare go closer, but she held out a hand to Arenadd. "Please," she said. "Don't kill me. Please, Arenadd."

*Do it,* said the Night God. *I command it.*

Arenadd turned and looked her in the face. "I refuse."

The Night God's hand lashed out, hurling him across the
clearing like a doll. He landed at Laela's feet.

Laela knelt and helped him. "Arenadd! Please no—"

The Night God lifted the full moon and put it into the hole
in her face, making a new and terrible eye. *You know the price
for your failure,* she said, very calmly.

Arenadd raised his head. "Yes. I know it."

*Then obey me!* The Night God pointed at Laela. *She is the
last of those I commanded you to kill. The last of the line of*

*Baragher the Blessed. Her blue eyes are an insult and a blasphemy to me. She must die!*

Arenadd struggled to get up. "Master, she's only a child. She's been a great help to me, and to my people. Without her—"

*I warn you one last time, Arenadd,* said the Night God. *If she lives, she will take all you have. She will cost you everything, and you will be made nothing.*

Arenadd got up and faced his master, one last time. "I don't care what the cost is. I won't kill her. Not now, not for anything."

*She is of the blood of Rannagon, who murdered you! She is—*

"No!" Arenadd stood tall, facing her with the last of his strength. "I know who she is now. You knew, and you never told me. You lied to me."

*Kill her!*

"She's Arren Cardockson's daughter," said Arenadd. He put a hand on Laela's shoulder and gave it a gentle squeeze. "She's his daughter," he said again, more quietly. "She looks just like him. Poor Arren."

Laela's shock was too much to make her stay silent. "My father? You knew my—"

The Night God's anger faded, and a terrible calm came over her. *If you will not obey me, then I do not need you any more.*

Arenadd pushed Laela aside and darted away from her. "Laela, get away—"

The Night God caught him, lifting him in one hand as if he weighed nothing, and plunged the point of her sickle into his chest. A deep hole opened over his heart, but no blood came out.

Instead, black mist poured out into the night. The Night God gathered it up in her hand and swallowed it, dropping Arenadd to the ground as if he were nothing but rubbish to be thrown away.

And then she was gone.

Laela rubbed her eyes, blinking in confusion. The clearing was full of nothing but snow and rocks—no mist, no light. It was as if nothing had happened. But she knew it had when she found Arenadd lying in the snow. There wasn't a mark on him.

Laela touched his face. "Arenadd. Arenadd, wake up!"

His eyes opened slowly, and he peered at her. "Laela."

She almost sobbed in relief. "Yer all right! I thought . . ."

"Laela." His good hand reached into his robe, and dragged out a small scroll. He thrust it into her hand.

Laela took it. "What's this?"

Arenadd's hand dropped onto the snow. "Give . . . Saeddryn," he whispered, and his eyes slid closed.

Laela stuffed the scroll into her clothes and shook him gently by the shoulder. "Arenadd. Arenadd! Wake up! Open yer eyes, damn it!"

He didn't move. Laela ran her hands over him, searching for any sign of injuries.

There was a wet patch on the front of his robe. She pulled it open, and took her hands away at once. "What . . . ?"

The old wound left by Erian Rannagonson's sword had opened once more and begun to bleed. And as Laela watched, it happened before her eyes: Slowly, one by one, every one of Arenadd's old scars re-opened. Blood trickled down his arms and onto the snow, turning it red.

Laela pulled at the edge of her gown, trying to use it to stop the flow, but she may as well have tried to dam a river. The blood soaked into the cloth and kept on coming, more and more of it. Arenadd's skin turned grey, and then as white as the snow that had begun to drift down from the sky.

A sickening crack broke the silence. And then another, and another. Arenadd jerked slightly and gasped. His eyes opened.

Laela touched his face. "Arenadd. Arenadd, can yeh hear me?"

His eyes rolled back into his head, and he jerked again as more awful cracks rifled through his body.

And then it was over.

Sobbing, Laela put a hand on his chest.

She screamed.

Arenadd's eyes opened slightly. "Bran," he whispered.

"Arenadd." Laela sobbed harder. "Arenadd, I felt a heartbeat. I felt a—"

Arenadd stirred, but he could not move. His arms and legs were bent at horrible, unnatural angles. Barely audibly, he said, "Arren."

Laela lifted him as gently as she could, cradling his head in her lap. "What is it? Arenadd, what is it? What should I do?"

Blood gurgled in his chest, and trickled out of his mouth. "I . . . am . . . Arren."

It was the last thing he ever said.

Quietly, watched over by the moon and mourned by his daughter, Arren Cardockson died.

# 31

## The Shadow Walks

Nearly a month after Saeddryn's cousin disappeared, when the people had finally accepted that he was not going to return, the day of Saeddryn's coronation as Queen of Tara had finally arrived.

Few people protested. Arenadd had lost a lot of popularity after his refusal to invade the South, and even more after he'd gone away to Amoran, "abandoning" his Kingdom in the process. Saeddryn was what they wanted now, and she was happy to oblige.

A platform had been built, just outside the gates of the Eyrie, for the ceremony. Everyone in the city could come. Saeddryn had thought of that; she wanted her coronation to be for everyone, great or small.

She sat on the carved chair that had been brought out for her and felt just a hint of apprehension as she watched the excited crowd below.

She didn't feel any guilt over Arenadd. The idea of killing him—or trying to—had been revolting to her. She'd wrestled with herself for years before she'd even begun to contemplate it.

And then Arenadd had solved her problem for her. He'd vanished, and that was far better than death. His story would become legend, and the name of Taranisäii would keep that grandeur for a long, long time. If he *did* return, and found her, Saeddryn, wearing the crown . . . well, what could he do? She was only doing her duty. The North *needed* her.

Aenae, standing beside her, stirred and sighed. With the Mighty Skandar gone, he was the strongest griffin in Malvern. Saeddryn knew he didn't care about the Kingdom or its people. All he'd ever wanted was to prove that he was stronger than his father and take his status.

Iorwerth and Kaanee stood on her other side. Saeddryn had been afraid that they wouldn't support her, but they had. Iorwerth was very unhappy about the King's disappearance, but he'd agreed that if he wasn't coming back, then Saeddryn was the logical choice to succeed him.

Saeddryn was pleased about that. Iorwerth was a useful man, and having him on her side was a great help.

The people had gathered. Lynedd, a senior member of the priesthood, had been chosen to perform the ceremony. They hadn't been able to find the crown, so a replica had been made. Saeddryn kept her eyes on it as the ceremony began.

Finally, the moment came for the crowning. Saeddryn bowed her head, waiting for the crown to be lowered onto it.

That was when she heard the voice.

"I am the shadow that comes in the night . . ."

It came from somewhere behind her, where a false wall at the back of the platform supported long, black drapes.

Saeddryn froze.

". . . I am the fear that lurks in your heart . . ."

Lynedd had heard the voice, too. She stopped and turned, glancing uncertainly at the guards.

Saeddryn stood up. "Who's that? Who's there?"

"I am the Shadow That Walks," the voice whispered.

Saeddryn paused, uncertainly. "Arenadd?" She faltered. "Is that ye?"

A low laugh came from somewhere nearby, and a figure slipped out and onto the platform. A tall, thin shape, clad in a black robe. Long, curly black hair fell over its shoulders like a mane.

"Arenadd," Saeddryn breathed.

The figure turned, and she saw the bright blue eyes, staring straight at her.

"Close."

Laela stepped toward the High Priestess and held something

out. "A gift for yeh," she said. "From yer cousin. He told me to give it to yeh."

Saeddryn took the scroll and unrolled it. She quickly scanned what was written on it, and her face went white. "What . . . ?"

"That's right," said Laela.

The crowd had reacted with great excitement when she'd appeared. More than a few of them started chanting Arenadd's name.

"Read it," said Laela. "Read it to them."

The scroll had begun to tear in Saeddryn's fingers. "It's fake," she whispered. "A forgery."

"It isn't," said Iorwerth.

Laela nodded to him. "He left a copy for yeh, didn't he?"

"He did," said Iorwerth. "I didn't know if ye were coming back, my lady. But now ye have, his orders must be carried out."

Laela nodded at Saeddryn. "Read it, then. Let them know."

Saeddryn looked up at her. "Where is he? What happened to him?"

Laela's expression hardened. "He ain't comin' back. Read it."

Saeddryn had no choice. She went to the front of the platform, where every one of the gathered people could see her.

" 'By royal decree,' " she read, " 'I, King Arenadd Taranisäii the First, name my daughter, Laela Taranisäii, as heir to my throne and all my property. I hereby command every griffin and griffiner in the Eyrie to serve her loyally through all the days of her reign.' "

Laela came forward, to stand by Saeddryn's side. "There, that wasn't so hard, was it?" she murmured. Without waiting for an answer, she raised her voice. "I am King Arenadd's daughter!" she yelled, for all the crowd to hear. "I am his heir!"

The people went mad. Some shouted Saeddryn's name, some Arenadd's—and some Laela's.

"I brought the slaves home!" Laela yelled. "I served the King. I was his friend. I am his heir. He decided it long ago." She paused. "I am the rightful Queen."

The crowd roared.

Laela turned to Saeddryn. "So what's it t'be?" she asked quietly.

At that moment, a small brown griffin came flying down

from a rooftop and landed by Laela's side. Laela stroked her head, but kept her eyes on Saeddryn.

Saeddryn looked at the crowd.

Then she stepped aside. "If that's what the King wanted," she said softly, "then so be it." She knelt and bowed her head. Iorwerth knelt, too. Aenae and Seerae started forward angrily, but Oeka hissed warningly at them, and they faltered and backed away.

Saeddryn looked up. "The realm is yours," she said, through gritted teeth. "Queen Laela."

Laela reached into her robe and brought out Arenadd's crown.

It fitted perfectly.


Far away from Malvern, the Mighty Skandar lay silently in a clearing beside the cold body of his human. He had nearly gone home, nearly gone back alone, as he'd said he would.

But he had turned back well before he got there. He wanted to fight, wanted it more than anything else. But not like this. Not without his human.

So he'd turned around. Maybe if he talked to him again, he could make him come. Or if he said no again, he could force him to come. Arenadd couldn't argue if Skandar just picked him up and carried him away.

So Skandar returned to the clearing and found him there, lying in the snow.

Arenadd's body had already gone stiff. Dozens of wounds had opened on his chest and body, and from these wounds, blood had flowed and dried. The snow around him was red with it.

Skandar tried to wake him, but he wouldn't get up, wouldn't open his eyes. But Skandar had seen him like this before. He would wake again. He would come back. He was a magic human, after all.

So Skandar lay down beside him and waited.

He would wait for a long time.

# About the Author

K. J. Taylor was born in Australia in 1986 and plans to stay alive for as long as possible. She went to Radford College and achieved a bachelor's degree in communications at the University of Canberra before going on to complete a master's in information studies. She currently hopes to pursue a second career as an archivist.

She published her first work, *The Land of Bad Fantasy*, through Scholastic when she was just eighteen, and went on to publish *The Dark Griffin* in Australia and New Zealand five years later. *The Griffin's Flight* and *The Griffin's War* followed in the same year and were released in America and Canada in 2011.

K. J. Taylor's real first name is Katie, but not many people know what the *J* stands for. She collects movie sound tracks and keeps pet rats and isn't quite as angst-ridden as her books might suggest.

Visit her website at www.kjtaylor.com.

**Don't miss
the first book in the Fallen Moon series**

## K. J. TAYLOR

# The Dark Griffin

**THE FALLEN MOON, BOOK ONE**

Despite his Northerner slave origins, Arren Cardockson
has managed to become a griffiner. With his griffin,
Eluna, he oversees trade in the city of Eagleholm, but
he knows his Northern appearance means he will never
be fully respected. When Arren and Eluna are sent to
capture a rogue griffin, Arren sees a chance to earn
some money and some respect, but his meeting with
the mysterious black griffin begins a dangerous chain
of events . . .

*Available now from Ace Books*

penguin.com